A TRIAL BY BLOOD

SHERILEE GRAY

Play List

- BLACK OUT DAYS – Phantogram
- CHANGE – Deftones
- THE NIGHT WE MET – Lord Huron
- YELLOW LEDBETTER - Pearl Jam
- THE PASSENGER - Iggy Pop
- OCEAN EYES - Billie Eilish
- GRAVEYARD - Our Last Night
- QUIETLY YOURS - Birdy

These are the songs I listened to on repeat while writing and plotting A Trial by Blood!

For Bella,
Watching you grow into the awesome human you are has been one of
the biggest joys of my life.
Love you forever and always.
And yes, no matter how old you get, you will always be my baby xoxo

Prologue

Ronan

Sir's hands were too hot against my cool flesh, but starved, I ignored his grasping and clawing, his nails digging into my biceps and chest, and drank deeply, even as his blood burned a path to my stomach.

Dhampir had been trading their bodies for sustenance for as long as our kind had walked this Earth. Sir had told me repeatedly that this was the price that must be paid to feed—the vampire half of our DNA was diluted with human blood, making us lesser in every way, tainted, unworthy—I was lucky to have someone willing to feed me at all.

Sir fell back on the bed, but I kept my fangs buried in his wrist, my hunger nowhere near abated.

He ran his hand down my side. "That's it, Ronan. Very good. Take your reward. You did the right thing bringing Luna back. She was confused for a while, but you're her brother, we're a family, she belongs with us. We'll find a new home, and you'll make sure that knight won't find her again. Things can go back to the way they were."

Luna had escaped Sir, with the help of one of the knights of Hell, and I'd used my powers to get my sister back from the demon hunter.

But the confusing things Luna had been saying the last few days kept echoing through my mind. For some reason, one I didn't understand, I had kept her here for days without telling Sir she was back. My sister said a lot of things that puzzled me, and I found for the first time since we became Azel's wards, I doubted him.

He'd kept Luna and me apart for years, since we were children. She said she believed me dead. Could she be lying? But why would she? Maybe so I would return her to her mate? She seemed determined to return to him.

But she'd also reminded me of things I'd long forgotten, and those memories were confusing me even more.

"Ronan?"

I ignored him and took another pull on his vein, my hunger still fierce, even as I fought not to throw his blood back up.

A memory of Luna, still small, running through our childhood home, smiling, pushed forward. She'd smiled. Which meant, she'd felt. It was a logical conclusion. I remembered she'd taken my toy and broken it. I'd then taken her doll and hidden it. Why would I do that? She said we'd both had the ability to feel then, to experience and express emotion, that it was because of Azel that I'd lost that ability.

An image flashed through my mind.

Blood.

Luna screaming.

My mother falling to the ground.

"Ronan?" Azel shoved me away. "Did you hear me?"

"Yes." I quickly licked his wrist, sealing my bite.

He stood, walked naked to his clothes draped over the chair, and dressed. I did the same. I wanted to shower first, but Sir was impatient to see Luna.

I followed him down the hall, and he motioned me ahead, grinning as I unlocked the door to Luna's room. We walked in, and Luna stumbled back, throwing up her hands, trying to use her powers to lift her block, but my own powers were too strong, and I easily suppressed hers, especially now that I'd fed.

Spencer, one of Sir's servants, ran to her, putting himself between us and my sister. Was he attempting to protect her? Why would he do that? Did he think I was going to harm her?

Luna recoiled, tugging Spencer back as Azel stepped forward. "I'll die before I go anywhere with you," she said.

Azel moved in close to me and gripped the back of my neck. A strange feeling coiled in my stomach and every one of my muscles tensed. The urge to shove him away came to me unbidden.

"Don't be like that. I've missed you," Sir said to her.

"You've missed my power. You missed the power I gave you, *Azel,*" she fired at him.

He huffed a low laugh even as his eyes narrowed. "You call me Sir, and I don't *need* you, little girl." He squeezed the back of my neck. "You are lucky I showed an interest in you and your brother at all."

Luna laughed. "You're delusional."

Sir went still, his gaze moving over her. "You've changed."

"You have no idea, asshole."

"You dare speak to me like that?"

"I'm sure you're more powerful than me, a lot more, but not as powerful as you pretend to be. How much did the angels take from you when they threw you from Heaven?"

Sir's eyes flared.

I frowned, looking between Luna and Sir. "Is it true? Are you an angel fallen?"

"No," he bit out. "The knights have done something to her mind. She's confused."

"You've seen the scars, Ronan, just like I have. He had wings once, but they tore them from his back," Luna said.

The small cross necklace Luna wore glinted under the light. It had been our mother's. A memory flashed through my mind. The last time I'd seen our mother wear it, it had been covered in blood. Luna had opened the floodgates with everything she'd been telling me, and the memories kept coming, like they'd been locked in a strong box, and all this time, my sister had held the key.

The sound of Luna screaming for her assaulted me once more. A vision of Azel carrying her away, gripping my hand, and pulling me after him. I'd turned back before we walked through the door.

Our mother lay on the floor. He'd removed her head. Her body in a pool of her own blood.

I'd called for her, crying and fighting. I remembered that now.

Luna said when a dhampir was taken from their human mother too early, their bond was broken, and they lost the ability to feel. Luna's emotions had returned. She'd said it was because she'd found her mate.

I didn't know for sure if that was true, but I'd felt emotions too once, before Azel had taken us; I knew that now to be true.

I turned to Azel. His face was red, the expression one I recognized as anger. He was about to hurt my sister.

Sir threw up a hand, firing his power at her.

Luna braced for the hit—

I threw up a block in front of her. Sir's power didn't reach her, didn't even brush past her.

He spun to me. "What the fuck are you doing?"

I stepped away from him. He'd controlled me since I was a child, and I hadn't considered there might be another way because he made sure I believed the things he'd said. But he'd lied about so many things. "You're a fallen angel."

Sir said nothing, his anger growing. I could tell by the look in his eyes.

"You lied," I said. "Our mother. You killed her."

Sir's jaw worked. "It was necessary."

Power vibrated through me, my protective block thickening and growing until it was so dense Sir had no hope of breaking through.

Hurting Luna was wrong. I didn't want that. I didn't want him to hurt her. "Go. Take Spencer and the other demi with you," I said to her. We were holding another of the knight's people here. He'd been loyal to my sister. He should be released as well.

"No," Sir roared, again trying to use his powers and failing.

I shook as I fought against his power. I was stronger, but I hadn't fed for long enough. Sir always left me hungry, never fully satisfied. I couldn't hold him off indefinitely.

"Go," I said to Luna again.

She hesitated. "Come with us."

I shook my head as Spencer grabbed her hand and tugged her from the room. I used my powers to shut the door behind them and lock it.

"Don't do this, Ronan," Sir roared.

I shook harder as Sir's powers relentlessly hammered into mine, but I had to wait until Luna was passed the block I'd created over this building, until I felt her lift her own shield, hiding herself from Sir.

He screamed with fury. "Don't let her leave us!"

"Us?" I shook my head. "She left *you*."

Then I felt it, the hum of her power, the vibration of the barrier she'd lifted to conceal herself and the males with her, brushing against mine.

I was all but drained, and Sir could see it. His eyes grew bright, and he laughed as soon as my power collapsed, striding toward me. I didn't understand why it was so important to me or what this sensation in my chest meant, but I fought him. My dhampir instincts roared forward, taking hold, and I fought with everything in me.

I couldn't be here, not anymore. I couldn't be here with him.

The sounds of smashing furniture, of tearing fabric, and shattering glass filled the apartment as Sir fought to dominate me, to force me to submit.

I'd die first.

The words filled my head, coming from somewhere deep inside me, a part of me I didn't recognize.

He threw me across the room, and I hit the wall, crashing to the carpeted floor. There was blood everywhere. Mine. Sir stalked toward me, a sneer on his lips.

I lay still, gathering what little strength I had left.

Sir kneeled beside me. "Are you done, Ronan? Is this tantrum over with?"

I'd given my loyalty to the wrong person. Sir wouldn't have that from me, not anymore. He'd bested me, but only because I was weakened. He needed me more than I needed him. I knew that for certain.

I didn't show or give affection, because I didn't feel it or understand it. But I knew what it looked like. I'd seen other people express it. I'd seen Luna with her knight.

I lifted my arms, beckoning Sir closer. He was taken aback, momentarily confused. He smiled. "I knew you'd see things my way." He cupped the side of my face. "You're confused. Luna confused you, lied to you. We'll get her back, yes?"

I nodded, lying, and remained still as he leaned in and pressed his mouth to mine, kissing me. I didn't like the way it felt. I never had. But I let him do it until I felt him relax.

Sliding my hands up his shoulders, higher, I cupped his face like I'd seen on television shows. My fangs tingled, extended—then I jerked his head to the side and buried them in his throat.

I drew deeply, once.

His surprise made him pause.

I sucked on his vein a second time.

He shoved me away, face red with fury. It wasn't much, but it was enough to give me the strength I needed.

I threw up another block. I could use my power in different ways to create different kinds of barriers. This was the kind I'd loved as a child. I could vanish. I could make entire buildings vanish with me, entire streets, if I chose to. The world around me was still there, but they walked by me, through me, and had no idea I was there.

Still weak, I struggled to my feet and stepped through Sir as if he were a mere shadow. He spun this way and that, screaming my name, demanding I come back, then pleading.

I walked out the door without looking back.

A month later

I stumbled down the street, not knowing where I was or how I got there. I'd been wandering for weeks. I was weak, starved for blood, for Azel's blood. My mind screamed at me to find him, telling me that he was the only one who could quench this constant thirst. His blood was poison to me, but I was addicted to it like it was a drug.

I had to fight the need, but I wasn't sure how much longer I could last. My survival instincts were driving me at this point. Logic, the only thing I understood, was being smothered by my predator's nature, by the vampire blood that made up half of me.

I spotted a sign up ahead.

Hell Fire.

The sounds of people and music drifted out. A bar.

My hand was on the door, shoving it open before I knew what I was doing. Red covered my vision as I searched the room. The sounds of at least thirty heartbeats were a chaotic pounding in my head, along with the rush of blood pumping through veins.

A female stood across the room. She was smaller than me, intoxicated by the looks. Easy prey. Hers wasn't the blood I wanted, but I'd take anything at this point.

My fangs tingled and elongated. I took an unsteady step toward her, then another—

Someone moved in front of me. I tried to go around them, but they grabbed my shoulder, and I was too weak to pull away.

I looked up through the red haze at the male who stood between me and my prey. Shifter. But not animal, not of this world at least.

Hellhound.

The big male scented me. "What do you want, dhampir?"

I opened my mouth, but nothing came out, my throat too dry to form words.

He growled. "I know you weren't gonna try and fucking feed in my bar, motherfucker."

I swayed and he righted me. Then his eyes narrowed, and he scented me again. He cursed. "I know you. Your scent's similar to your sister's. She's looking for you."

I shook my head, or tried to.

"You don't want to be found?" he muttered.

I shook my head again, then my legs collapsed from under me, and I hit the floor.

I was jostled, then I was moving. Consciousness came and went. I had no idea how much time had passed, but when I opened my eyes again, another hound was holding a glass to my lips. I tried to pull away, then the scent hit me.

Blood.

I grabbed it and gulped it down. It was still warm. I'd only ever drank Sir's blood. My whole life, only his. This was good, but it wasn't enough. My thirst could only be quenched by him. I finished the glass and threw it across the room, jumping to my feet. A hound tackled me to the floor before I could take another step.

"Release me. I need his blood. I need Azel's blood," I rasped, my throat still raw.

The big hound's brows snapped together. "You don't know?"

I fought, trying to dislodge him, but I wasn't yet at full strength, and it was impossible.

The hound shook me. "Azel's dead. Your sister killed him."

I stilled. I felt nothing. I was incapable of it. But I knew if I was released now, I would kill, then I would keep on killing, trying to quench a thirst that could never be sated. "Have you told anyone I'm here?"

"No."

"I would like it to stay that way." I may not understand emotions, but I had faint memories of them and understood the concept. Luna suffered when she was near me, and though I didn't feel any emotional tie to her, I did feel a connection. She deserved my loyalty. I had unknowingly caused her pain, and I found I didn't like the idea of repeating that, not in any way.

I was mostly numb to physical contact, to pain and pleasure. But what rose in me now, slicing through me, causing me to grit my teeth as my thirst grew again, was as bad as it got. "Do you have a strong cage or a cell? I need something that will bind my powers and stop me from escaping."

"We have a cage made from Hell-forged steel. No being, not even Lucifer himself could break free from it," the other male said.

"Lock me in it. Now."

Chapter One

Ronan

Three years later

The sun was only just rising when I got out of my car and headed down the street. No one would see it there, it was as simple as a thought for me to use my power to conceal it and myself. No one would know I was here because that's the way I wanted it.

Winter had set in, and frost floated past my lips as I looked up to the window on the second floor of the Thornheart family home. Rose's room. I strode toward my destination; something inside me, on a demon level, drew me to this house, to Rose again and again. I didn't understand it; coming here every day wasn't logical, and I wanted to understand it.

But the only thing I was certain of was this was where I had to be.

Using my powers and lifting my block, essentially turning me into the invisible man, I could move anywhere I wanted undetected. Doors and walls were no barrier to me. When I'd been Azel's servant, I'd concealed our home, an entire mansion.

The hair on the back of my neck lifted, and a strange feeling, as if my stomach was suddenly hollow, came over me. It happened a lot when I thought of my time with Azel. Something else I didn't understand. I quickly shut down the memory and walked right through the front door as if it weren't there and into the Thornheart residence.

It was quiet, the curtains still drawn, the family still asleep in their beds. I took the stairs to Rose's door. It was slightly ajar, as always. I walked in and searched out her frail figure in the shadows, so small under the covers.

Magnolia was asleep in the chair beside the bed, and Nia, Iris's familiar, lay on the bed with Rose, pressed to her side. The dog's big brown eyes were trained on Rose. Nia was here a lot, even without Iris. Lately, she helped the family watch Rose at night. Rose tended to have her episodes then, times when she would occasionally stop breathing altogether. So while Magnolia slept, Nia would watch her.

There was another chair on the other side of the bed, and I took it. I didn't understand why I couldn't stay here all night and watch her myself. It seemed logical to me. They could rest, and I would keep her safe. But when I mentioned it to Relic, the hellhound said I shouldn't do that. That it would seem odd to the family. I couldn't say one way or the other if that was true, which was why I deferred to the hounds when I had a question about such things. They'd spent more time with humans, or at least beings who understood emotions, and had a good grasp on what was expected as far as social etiquette went.

He didn't understand that I needed to keep Rose safe, which was why I came anyway. I just didn't tell anyone.

My gaze moved over her face. When I was in the same room as her, I struggled to look anywhere else, and when I was away from her, I was clock-watching until whatever took me from her was over so I could return.

Again, I didn't understand it, but as an emotionless being, the only thing I could rely on was instinct. I'd ignored it most of my life, had denied that part of myself, even when it screamed at me to leave, to run, to hide. I'd been conditioned to ignore it. The day I left Azel was the first time I'd truly listened. And the hounds, who also struggled with emotions, had helped me to understand why I should keep on doing it.

Rose whimpered in her sleep, her arms coming out of the covers, her head shifting on the pillow. I stood and leaned over her, my instincts telling me to touch her, to try to soothe her. Again, something I didn't know anything about, but I'd watched Rose's sisters with her, and with their mates. Touch seemed to be the key to soothing someone in distress. That, and softening your voice when you spoke.

I expanded my block, so Rose was with me, and lay my hand against her cool skin. Touch. "You are safe, Rose," I said, pitching my voice low. I wasn't sure of the correct words, but safety seemed appropriate and something everyone desired.

She whimpered again, and the sound caused a tightening in my chest that grew wider. It wasn't a pleasant sensation. Why were my hands trembling? I'd have to ask Relic what the physical response meant. "Be at ease, Rose."

Her hand suddenly gripped mine. I stilled and looked down at the way she clung to me. I found I didn't want her to let go, but finally, she stopped her thrashing and drifted back into a deep sleep. Her hand slipped from mine.

I pulled my power back, so it only surrounded me, and took

my seat again, but for some reason, left my hand close to hers even though she wasn't touching me anymore.

I continued to watch her as she slept.

As always, I lost time when I was with this female, and I jolted in surprise when Daisy, Rose's mother, walked into the room. Magnolia had woken, and Nia was no longer on the bed. Somehow, I hadn't noticed any of it.

Daisy gently woke her daughter, and my muscles locked like they always did when her eyes opened and her blue gaze moved around the room, like she was searching for something. Daisy sat beside her, taking her daughter's hand, and I did what I always did at this time; I walked back down the stairs and through the front door, then back to my car. After making sure no one was watching, I dropped the block concealing it and me, then took the paper bag holding the fresh apricot danish I'd picked up for Rose's breakfast on my way here and headed back to the house.

I knocked this time, and a sleepy-eyed Else, Rose's seventy-two-year-old great aunt, opened the door. Her lips curled up. "Morning, sunshine," she said and looked down at the paper bag in my hand. "What's on the menu this morning?"

"Good morning, Else. An apricot danish." We did this every morning. I understood this to be a normal social exchange, what was expected, so I engaged for Else's benefit.

She chuckled. "Go on up then. I'm sure Rose is expecting you."

I didn't know why she was smiling or chuckling, and I didn't understand the look in her eyes. They were always sharp but softened somewhat whenever she opened the door to me. "Yes, as I come by every morning, I expect she is."

She chuckled again. "Exactly." She patted my arm, then limped off toward the kitchen.

I took the stairs two at a time. The murmur of voices reached me before I got to the top. Daisy was still there, and I paused at the door and knocked this time, something else Relic had told me to do. Walking into a female's bedroom without knocking was not something you should do, apparently.

"Come in, Ronan," Daisy called.

"Good morning, Daisy," I said, showing Rose's mother the proper respect before I turned to Rose. I'd been gone only a matter of minutes, but again, my muscles tightened. Her blue eyes were huge in her face. She still looked tired, but her lips curled in greeting, like her aunt's had when she saw me. "Good morning, Rose."

"Good morning, Ronan," she said. Her soft voice was weaker this morning.

"How are you feeling today? You look tired."

Her smile changed but remained, and her eyes seemed to sparkle. "You just answered your own question."

"Yes, I suppose I did," I said and moved to the seat I'd sat in a short time ago, placing the paper bag with her danish on the bedside table.

"You, on the other hand, look well rested." She tried to shift but failed.

I instantly moved to her, knowing what she wanted to do, because we did this every morning. I drew back the covers and carefully scooped her into my arms. Daisy rushed forward and put several pillows against the headboard, and I eased Rose back into position, then covered her again. "I feel well rested." Whenever I was with Rose, I felt energized, again the reason was a mystery.

Daisy patted my shoulder. "I'll head down and get breakfast ready. Do you want anything?" she asked, like she always did.

"No, thank you." I could eat food but didn't need it.

Daisy walked out, leaving Rose and me alone. I took in her sunken cheeks. "Are you hungry?"

"Nope, but that's not going to stop you from trying to feed me, now is it?" She looked to the paper bag on her bedside table. "What did you bring me this morning?"

"A danish." I tore the bag open and tore off a small portion. "Apricot, because I know you like them."

"I do." She tried to lift her hand, but it shook so badly she couldn't do it.

My body reacted to the sight in several ways. My muscles tightened, and a spot in the center of my chest grew warm, which should be impossible. It also felt as if I had a rock in the pit of my gut. "Let me," I said and held the morsel to her lips.

Her cheeks colored, a sight Relic told me meant embarrassment. I had to search out the meaning online when he struggled to explain it, not ever feeling it himself. I still didn't fully understand. But I knew it meant she was not feeling completely comfortable. I slipped it past her lips and didn't bring up the color of her cheeks, because Relic told me I shouldn't. That it was impolite. It was all very confusing, honestly.

She chewed and swallowed, and I helped her sip water to wash it down. "Another piece?"

"Okay."

I slipped another small piece into her mouth and watched her chew and swallow it. Only then did the rock in my gut ease.

"So, are you going to talk to me today, or just watch me eat?" she asked, the smile again curling her lips.

"I'm going to do both," I said. "What would you like to talk about?"

"What do you have planned after your visit with me?"

I didn't want to go anywhere, but I did have somewhere I needed to go later. "It's Luna's birthday today. I've been invited to the knight's compound to share a meal."

"That sounds nice. Will you say hello to everyone for me?"

"Of course."

My hand was near hers and she inched hers over, her fingers covering mine. I stilled completely because I didn't want her to take her hand away. I didn't really understand what pleasure or pain was, physical sensations were muted for me. I'd been numb to them the majority of my life. But when Rose touched me...something happened I couldn't explain. The only thing I could compare it to was feeding, that first pull on a vein, the way my nerve endings would kind of zing and wake up as the first drop of blood hit my tongue.

"Tell me what you did last night, while I was here cooped up in this room?" She stared up at me expectantly.

The way she looked at me now managed the same feeling, a kind of awakening. I might not feel both physical and emotional pleasure, but as a child, I had. I struggled to remember the sensations and wondered if this was similar to it? That...awakening that came over me when she touched me or when her eyes met mine, or when we talked, or I watched her eat and sleep?

Was that why I returned every day, that sensation? Perhaps her touch activated the pleasure receptors in my brain's cerebral cortex —like a kind of muscle memory from my childhood? But if that was the case, why now? And why did it only happen with Rose?

"Well?" she said, one of her fingers sliding over my skin. "Spill the beans. Let me live vicariously through you."

I opened my mouth to talk and had to clear my throat to loosen my oddly tight vocal cords. "I trained with Relic. Then went to the fighting pit and fought one of the hounds. He said inappropriate things. Relic said I should beat his ass, so I did. Afterward, the hounds went to the bar for females and alcohol, and I went to my room to wash off the blood and sweat," I said. "I also slept." I didn't tell her I only slept for a few hours, then came here and sat at her bedside in the early hours of the morning.

She blinked up at me several times. "Okay...we need to back up a few steps here. You fought one of the hounds?"

"Yes."

"He said inappropriate things?"

"Yes." I didn't like the things he said and neither had Relic. The hound suggested the fighting pit, and I'd agreed.

"What did he say?"

I broke off another piece of pastry. "He called me a dirty blood sucker, and a few other things as well." The hound had also said some things about Rose after learning about the time I spent here. I didn't know why it mattered to him. But he'd said I was here fucking a walking corpse. He was being derogatory about her physical condition. His words had caused a physical reaction; I'd felt hot, and my head had a throbbing sensation. I tried to explain this to Relic, who had been visibly angry, and that's when he suggested the fighting pit. I knew better now than to tell Rose that part of the story, though.

"What an asshole. You won?"

"Yes." I held the pastry to her mouth, and she accepted it. My nerve endings sparked again.

"Were you hurt?"

"I was injured, but I barely register pain and I heal fast."

Rose blinked at me again, and she seemed to shiver. "And what about the hound? How injured was he?"

"Very. But they heal fast as well. He'll be fine in a few days."

"A few days? W-what did you do?"

"I beat him, then tore out his tongue." The blood in my veins had felt thick, and that rock in my gut had become a boulder. One moment I'd been hitting him, and the next, I'd wrenched his mouth open and taken hold of his tongue. Relic had been pleased. He'd said the other male had "deserved it for talking shit about my female." Rose wasn't mine and I'd tried to tell him that many times but had given up. Hounds were territorial, and it was the only way he could understand why I spent so much time here. I certainly couldn't explain it.

I had enjoyed the sensations I'd felt afterward though, after I'd hurt the hound, when I'd looked down at him on the ground soaked in his own blood. My nerve endings had sparked and fired like they did when Rose touched me.

I broke off more of the danish and held it out to her. She was staring at me, her mouth slightly open. I tried to slide the pastry between her lips, but she brushed my hand away.

"You tore his *tongue out*?"

"Yes."

"Holy shit. Which hound?" Her heart was beating faster; I could see the pulse in her throat fluttering wildly.

My mouth went dry, and I quickly looked away. "Tyson."

Her eyes grew rounder. "Oh my god, Ronan. That male is huge."

"He is also slow."

She laughed softly. "Okay, well, your night tops mine by a mile." Her smile was back, but she was breathing faster.

"Are you okay? You're breathing heavily." I pressed my hand to her chest. I could feel her heart pounding hard. "Rose?"

"I'm fine. Your story, it's exciting. My heart's pounding because I'm imagining you fighting in that pit," she said. Her voice had grown husky.

"And that affects you physically?"

"Yes," she said. "Do you think yours would pound if I told you I'd fought someone?"

I shook my head. "My heart no longer beats, remember?"

"I'd forgotten." The look on her face changed, then she whimpered. "I'm going to be sick."

I snatched up the bowl by the bed. They kept one there for this purpose, and I helped her to sit forward, holding it below her chin. She shuddered, her entire body quaking as she threw up the tiny amount of food I'd managed to get her to eat. Then she continued to dry heave, but there was nothing left in her stomach to come up.

The rock in my gut grew again, becoming a boulder like it had last night. Then it kept on growing, and the center of my chest became hot and achy. I held her to me, supporting her slight weight until she was done, then eased her back to the pillows.

"I'll be right back." I took the bowl to the bathroom to empty and clean and rinsed a washcloth in warm water. When I walked back out, I thought she was asleep. I moved to her side and gently wiped around her mouth.

"R-Ronan?"

"Do you need the bowl again?"

"No." Her eyes opened, but they were heavy. She'd be asleep again soon. "Can you...can you come back after your visit with Luna? I have something to ask you."

"Of course." I'd planned to return anyway. "Why don't you ask me now?"

She shook her head, the movement barely noticeable, but I noticed everything she did. "Later."

Then she closed her eyes and drifted off to sleep.

And I took my seat by the bed once more.

Chapter Two

Rose

"You wanna watch a movie later?" Magnolia asked as she held a glass of water to my lips.

I dutifully took a sip, even as my stomach protested. "I'd love that."

I swallowed several times. The water wasn't going to stay down long. Fierce hunger hacked and sliced at my stomach. My mouth so dry, it felt raw. The feeling was my constant, never satisfied, never easing. Up until the last week or so, I was able to take small amounts of food and liquids. I wasn't sure that was the case anymore. The pastry Ronan had given me had rebelled as soon as it hit my stomach. I'd hoped to hold it down until he left, but nope. My dignity was well and truly out the window.

Now I couldn't even hold down water. I didn't think I had much longer left, but another day of this, another hour, god, every minute was torture.

This needed to be over, for all our sakes.

I coughed and wretched, and Mags grabbed the bowl and held it below my chin as the tiny sip of water I'd had came back up.

Mags had not long ago turned twenty-one. She was three years younger than me, but my baby sister was the one looking after me. I hated that she had to do it and loved her for it at the same time.

"It's okay," she said, rubbing my back with a shaky hand. "It's going to be okay."

It wasn't, and we all knew it. Magnolia and my entire family were suffering. They were suffering more than me, and I needed their pain to stop. I couldn't be the cause of it anymore. But that wasn't the only reason, and I hoped Ronan agreed to help me. Time had run out, and tonight I'd ask him what I'd been building up the courage to ask for a while now.

She rushed to the bathroom with the bowl and came back with a cloth. She wiped my mouth and chin, a forced smile on her face that looked as agonized as I knew she was feeling.

I collapsed back against the pillows, and Mags started messaging someone on her phone. Mom, no doubt. Updating her on her daughter's decline.

"How's the h-harvest going?" I forced past my raw throat.

Since a witch's magic never fully left them—not even when we died—our bones continued to pump magic into the earth, which meant our family cemetery was a place of immense power and plentiful resources. Every blade of grass, pebble, and plant held magic absorbed from the bones decaying beneath them.

The uses of the resources there were limitless. Mom and Arthur spent hours every day in our cemetery, making sure every-thing was thriving and that Else and Mags had what they needed to make the elixirs, potions, and medicinals they sold in Willow's store, The Cauldron.

If a coven had an old cemetery like ours, they were considered powerful and not to be messed with. No other coven had a burial ground more impressive than ours. Which was why it was heavily warded. Only people we wanted to pass through the cemetery gates could.

"Yeah, good. We should be set for the winter. And Art planted new bulbs before the first snowfall, so we're set for spring."

Art was Mom's familiar, an owl shifter who preferred his human form. He was middle-aged with dark brown skin, neatly cropped hair, and the kindest brown eyes I'd ever seen. And a year ago, he and Mom had finally admitted their feelings for each other. Seeing them so happy together, seeing Mom so happy, was all we'd ever wanted for her.

"That's good, right?"

She nodded, but the worry in her eyes had not diminished.

"How's Bram?" I asked. "I haven't seen him in a few days." I needed my sister to focus on anything but me.

Her amber eyes lifted, and the pain didn't lessen. Bram was her best friend and familiar. The crow shifter usually never left her side. He was extremely protective of her. He was also completely and utterly in love with her. Mags either wasn't aware of this or chose to pretend she wasn't. She'd been through some things that had altered her in ways even we didn't know the full extent of, though, and Bram had been taking the brunt of it. Her mood swings had been extreme and often fell to him to manage. The highest of highs, and some serious lows. Through it all, Bram had been there. Steadfast. But I'd noticed his absence lately, even from up here in my bedroom.

If Mags didn't want to talk about something, she didn't. And I kind of expected her to tell me she didn't want to go there. Instead, she pulled up her knees, lifted her feet to the chair, and rested her chin on her arms. "He's busy a lot with his new job," she said, her voice filled with something that hurt me to hear it.

"What's going on?"

She shook her head, her thick, wavy black hair falling over her shoulder. "Honestly, I don't know. He's...he's pulling away from me, Roe."

"Why would he do that? You're his best friend. He loves you."

"He keeps saying he's with his brothers, but I think he's seeing someone." Mags looked to the window and unconsciously zipped her jacket to her throat and tugged down her sleeves, covering her scars. "Why else would he be acting so secretive? He disappears for hours, sometimes a day or two. Then he comes back and lies about where he's been and acts like nothing happened. I *know* him, Rose. Better than I know myself. I know when he's lying." She let out a shaky breath. "I fucking hate this."

"You need to talk to him. Really talk to him. He's too important to let something or someone else get in between you."

Her lips curled up again, in an imitation of a smile. "Maybe he's met someone who can give him something I can't?"

Did she mean? Was she finally admitting that she knew how Bram felt? We all tiptoed around the subject. It was up to them to figure out, and any interference from us would only make it harder. So, as much as I wanted to ask about his feelings for her being more than just friends, I erred on the side of caution. "Like what?"

She shrugged and chewed her lip, not meeting my eyes. "I haven't been a good friend to him lately. I know that. I've been leaning on him constantly. He's put up with my moods. My rages. I've been so lost in my own head, in my own problems, I haven't been checking on him." She looked up, and that false smile was back. "Basically, Bram is over my shit, and I don't blame him. He's put up with more than anyone should have to."

Okay, so no. She wasn't referring to a romantic relationship. But she was also wrong. Completely. "You could do anything, say anything, nothing will change how Bram feels about you."

"Yep," Mags said. "The poor guy is stuck with me. He's my familiar. He'll always feel obliged to look after me, whether he wants to or not."

I squeezed her hand. "I don't believe that."

"You don't have a familiar, Roe. You don't know." She said it as gently as she could, but I still had to fight not to flinch.

"No, you're right, I don't know. I'm sorry." Not having a

familiar had caused me a lot of pain growing up. I'd waited, but no one had ever come.

Mags flew out of her chair suddenly and wrapped her arms around me. "I can't believe I said that. I'm sorry, Roe. God, I'm such an asshole."

A great weariness came over me. The kind that meant it was only a matter of minutes before I was pulled into a deep sleep. "It's the truth. You don't need to be sorry." My limbs felt impossibly weak, and I patted her back as best I could. "I-I'm going to rest now."

"Okay," she whispered.

"Love you."

"Love you too."

She tucked the covers around me and sat back on the chair.

I closed my eyes, unable to do anything else.

Darkness closed in, heavy and cold, sucking me under. Taking me closer to the other side than I'd ever been before. Taking me closer to Death.

So close, I could feel his breath against my cheek.

Ronan

The knight's compound was an old warehouse several stories high. Willow, Rose's oldest sister, had warded it and still did regularly. It made it almost impossible to find, and anyone who came close felt compelled to get away as fast as possible. The Thornhearts were friends to the knights and had been for many years.

I stood in the common room on the sixth floor. The knights, their mates, and offspring were all gathered around my sister. There was a lot of talking and laughter. They'd sung "Happy Birthday" to her before Eve had carried in a giant chocolate cake with "Happy Birthday Luna" written in purple frosting on the top.

I wasn't sure why Luna wanted me here. My sister said she liked having me close. I may not understand why, but if she needed that, I would give it to her. After years of suffering because of the way I'd blindly followed Azel, I owed her that much.

I wished I could say it was because I felt affection for her, but that wasn't something I was capable of. I did, however, remember what it was like to care for her, to feel protective over her. Childhood memories, yes, but it was something, and I found myself thinking of it often and clinging to.

I watched Gunner smile at my sister, a warmth in his eyes that was unmistakable. I curled up my lips, attempting to imitate the action for some unknown reason. It felt foreign, strange. I lifted my fingers to my lips and felt them. My mouth had changed position, but I knew there would be no warmth in my eyes, not like Gunner's.

Luna turned, and I stopped what I was doing, quickly dropping my hand. She walked over, rested her hands on my chest, and smiled up at me. There it was again, warmth. The first time she touched my chest after I came back, she'd pulled away quickly. She said it upset her that my heart didn't beat anymore. My sister's had stopped as well for a while, but after she met Gunner, it had somehow come back to life.

"You have love for me, don't you?" I asked, even though I knew the answer. She'd said many times that she held affection for me.

Her smile slipped and her head tilted to the side. "Yes, Ronan, I love you. You're my big brother."

"How does it feel?" The words were out of my mouth before I knew they were coming. But I left them there, hanging between us, because I was curious. I saw the way Rose and her siblings were with each other. How Daisy and Else were with the girls, and I found myself watching them often, trying to imagine how it felt.

"You want me to describe love?" she asked.

"Yes, if you don't mind."

She chewed her lip, her gaze sliding around the room to all the people gathered there and back to me. "It's not really something that's easy to describe. When I see you after being separated from you for a while, I feel excited. I get a feeling in my belly, an urgency, I guess, and a warmth in my chest. I feel like smiling. I know I'd do anything for you. Whatever you asked of me. All I want is to see you happy."

"Even though you know that's impossible?" I asked, trying to imagine what she'd described and failing.

She shook her head. "Not impossible. Look at me. I was like you are now before I met Gunner."

My sister still held hope that I would be like her, that my emotions would return. I wasn't sure if I wanted that or not. "The love you feel for Gunner, is it the same as what you feel for me?"

"No," she said. "It's very different."

Intellectually, I knew this, but it was impossible to imagine love at all, let alone different kinds of the emotion. "Because there is sex involved?"

"Yes," she said. "Though..." She chewed her lip again, and something shifted behind her eyes. "You know sex doesn't always involve love, yes?"

I nodded as my stomach gripped in an unpleasant way. The act wasn't something I enjoyed. The way Luna described love, I couldn't imagine the emotion and sex going together very well at all. "And you still love Gunner, even after you give him your body?"

"What Gunner and I share is completely different from what we shared with Azel," she said.

"But you give him your body, so you can feed, yes?" That's how dhampir had lived since the beginning of their existence. Our kind bartered their bodies for blood.

"No. He gives me his blood without expectation. He feeds me

because he loves me and wants me to be healthy and happy. We have sex because we enjoy giving each other pleasure. We give freely to each other, Ronan. That's what love is."

She wanted me to understand what she was saying, I could see that, at least. But it was impossible, and we both knew it. "Sex is pleasurable?" Again, the words came from me before I knew they were coming. I'd seen others enjoy sex at the feeding club I went to, but I still struggled to comprehend that it was possible.

She blinked, and a bloody tear suddenly streaked down her cheek. "Yes, Ronan. Sex should always be pleasurable and consensual."

I frowned. "But you're a dhampir." I touched her cheek, swiping away the tear. "Why are you crying?"

She shook her head and another tear fell. "Dhampir can feel pleasure during sex, Ronan. Even without emotions. What Azel did to you, and to me, was so incredibly wrong. That wasn't sex, that was abuse. When you're with someone you love, or someone you choose to give yourself to, it's nothing like...like what he did to us."

I had wondered. "Is sex similar to the feeling we get during feeding?"

"Yes, but far more heightened." She swiped the tears from her face. "It's so much better."

I nodded, not because I understood, but because she was trying so hard to get me to understand. "Thank you for explaining it to me."

"Do you ever think about him? Azel?" she asked, her voice now husky and her eyes red.

I'd caused her distress, and I hadn't meant to. "Sometimes I dream about him. Memories of my time with him, or that I'm still with him."

Her hand pressed against my chest again. "Do you want to dream about him?"

"No." The word came from me, and it was louder than I

expected. "No, I don't want to dream about him. I don't want to think about that male at all."

"What's wrong?" Gunner said, suddenly at my sister's side. His gaze sliced to me, and he looked angry. "What's going on?"

"He didn't do anything," Luna said. "We were talking and Azel came up, and…"

"Fuck." Gunner pulled Luna into his side, wrapping his arms around her. His mouth went to the top of her head, and he kissed her hair, then he bent low, pressing his mouth to her ear, saying something only my sister could hear.

The others in the room turned our way. I didn't know what I'd done, but I'd caused this. I'd made my sister cry on her birthday, and I had no idea how or why?

"I think it's time I leave. Thank you for inviting me," I said to Gunner.

He didn't look up.

I strode from the room and out the door, taking the elevator to the ground floor where my car was parked. I needed to get to Rose, anyway. She'd asked me to return, so she could ask me something.

Whatever it was she wanted, I would give it to her.

I didn't know why, but since meeting her, my instincts wouldn't allow anything else.

Chapter Three

Rose

I stared out the window. It was breezy this evening. The light outside the front door below made the swaying trees glow, and as they moved, the lightly falling snow danced around their bare branches. It was pretty. I wanted to be out there. I wanted to feel the wind and snow on my face and soaking through my clothes.

I wanted a lot of things.

Nia was with me again, while my family bustled around downstairs. I could hear them on the wooden floor, their chatter, the clink of dishes as someone loaded the dishwasher, and the TV going in the distance. They'd left me to rest. It was all I did, all I could do.

Mags had brought up her laptop earlier, and we'd watched a movie. I'd stared at the screen blindly. My mind on the dream I'd had. No, not a dream. Something else.

Death had come to me again while I'd slept, and he was growing impatient. At first, I thought they were dreams, had hoped it was only a nightmare, but I quickly realized it was so much worse.

Last year, my family had removed the souls of two evil witches from Limbo and sent them to Hell where they belonged, and in doing so, unknowingly pissed off Death. Now he wanted my soul as repayment. He wasn't taking no for an answer and was using his brother, Somnus, the personification of sleep, to reach me.

I could only assume he'd zeroed in on me because my time was almost up, but I hadn't told anyone about his visits, that he often came to me, or what he wanted because it would only make my death so much harder on everyone.

"The debt must be paid." His words rang through my mind, and the threat in his horrifying voice sent cold dread down my spine. I was terrified that if I didn't let him take me, he'd come after someone else in our coven, someone I loved, and I wouldn't let that happen.

But Death was only one of the reasons I needed to die. Soon, the mother, also known as Mother Nature—the Great Goddess, the Creatress of all life—would call for me. It could happen at any time, and if I didn't go when she did, and I was still alive, my family would lose everything.

Both Willow and Iris had completed their tasks and passed their trials when the mother had called—and it was during Iris's task that we'd gotten Death's attention. The mother put witches through tasks and trials as a way of testing their skill. If they passed, we got to keep the magical gifts the mother had given our coven over the centuries. If the witch failed, the coven lost them all, making us weak and vulnerable. And if she called on me, that's exactly what would happen.

I couldn't even stand, let alone fight my way through a demon-infested forest, which was expected when she called you. I wouldn't even make it through the meet and greet with the giant serpent she possessed for the occasion—let alone when she *bit* you, leaving you with permanent tattoo-like markings made by her magical venom.

There was no way I'd survive that.

Willow was the oldest and now Keeper of our coven, a role that was never meant for our branch of the family. It was a long and twisted story, but here we were, and after Willow passed, the mother decreed that since the position of Keeper had moved to a new branch of the family, each of us—Iris, me, and Mags—had to pass a task and trial of our own to prove our line was worthy of keeping the magical gifts she'd bestowed on our coven. To lose those gifts would be devastating to not only our family but to our entire coven.

It had been two years since Willow passed, a year for Iris. The mother had given us all time to prepare, but it didn't matter how much time I'd had, I physically couldn't do it. I honestly thought I'd be dead by the time my turn rolled around.

But I wasn't, and time was running out.

"I'll stay with Roe," Mags said outside my room. Her voice was hushed, but I heard her. I was frail and dying, but my hearing was just fine. My family forgot that sometimes. Probably because I was usually asleep.

"Rowena really wanted everyone from the family there tomorrow," Willow said. My sister arrived a short time ago, conveniently in time for dessert.

"Rowena will understand." That was Mom. There was a pause. "I understand why she wants to meet with us, I'm just...I'm not ready..."

"I know," Wills said.

Mom sobbed, the sound muffled. Willow or Mags were hugging her.

This meeting with Rowena had something to do with me. She was the head of our coven and Mom's second cousin. If she was in town, it had to be important—like what happened to the coven when the mother stripped us of her gifts because I was too weak to answer her call and do what was needed.

There was no way I'd let them suffer because of me.

The sound of a car door closing echoed outside, and I knew who it was instantly. I'd asked Ronan to come back, and he had. Anything I asked, he obliged. I didn't know why, but I was thankful for it. For him.

I loved my family with everything in me. But Ronan was the reason I'd put this off as long as I had. It didn't matter that he didn't feel the way I did. I'd wanted to squeeze in every second with the male I was madly in love with before I died. But I couldn't wait anymore, and the conversation I just overheard made that all the more clear.

His knock came downstairs, the low murmur of his deep voice, then nothing. His steps were always soundless as he climbed the stairs. Then he was there, standing in the doorway, tall and lean and handsome. He was wearing black trousers and a white shirt under a long black jacket. His dark hair was combed back, and his square jaw, freshly shaven. His violet eyes came straight to me, like they always did when he entered the room.

"Rose, how are you this evening?"

"A lot better now you're here," I said, because I'd given up pretending. He may not understand the things I said and why, but I did. I wasn't going to hold back. I told him when I was happy to see him because I wanted him to know he was important to me. What did I have to lose?

With Ronan, I didn't need to wonder if he loved me, too, because I knew he didn't. He couldn't.

He studied me for long seconds, like he often did when I said things like that. "I make you feel better?" he finally asked as he walked to my bedside.

"Yes. You make me happy, Ronan." Yes, I was being brave, saying everything I felt, but it still wasn't easy. And my face heated as soon as the words left me.

"Why?" he asked, surprising me.

That impassive violet stare hadn't left me, and my heart beat faster. "You always take such good care of me," I said. "You bring me food and read to me...and listen to me talk and vent. But mostly, you don't treat me like I'm different." I swallowed hard, my face stupidly getting hotter. "And you don't look at me with pity or disgust."

His head tilted to the side, studying me with laser-sharp focus, in a move that showed that under it all, he was still a predator. "Why would I look at you in disgust?"

Out of all the things I'd said, that was the one he chose to ask me about. "The way I look, Ronan. I know you don't feel, but you have two eyes in your head. I'm ugly."

His brows snapped together. "Ugly?"

I thought I actually heard surprise in his voice. Was he serious? Of course, he was. Ronan didn't know how to be anything but himself. There was no pretense, no game playing, all of that was beyond him. I wasn't about to list everything off. My hair, so thin I was now bald in patches, my body, nothing but bones covered in skin so thin you could see every vein through it. My face, drawn and narrow. And the thing that upset me the most, the hump on my back that had continued to grow, making me hunched and disfigured in a way that was not only humiliating but scared the hell out of me. Instead, I said, "You don't find me ugly?"

I lay completely still as his gaze flicked over my face, then down my body, buried under the covers. "No," he said.

"No?" He had to be lying, but Ronan didn't lie. He never lied. It seemed there was a first time for everything.

He shook his head.

Pain sliced through me. Why was he lying to me? I didn't want lies from him, not him. Irrational anger welled inside me. "Look at me, Ronan. I'm hideous."

He frowned. "It's but a shell, Rose. Even your illness can't conceal the true nature of your soul."

I blinked up at him. "My soul?"

He removed his jacket and draped it carefully over the back of the chair, then sat. "Yes."

"And what is the nature of my soul?"

His violet gaze lifted from my mouth. "I may not understand emotions, but I recognize beauty, in many forms. I also know good from evil. Your goodness shines through." He was looking deep into my eyes. "Your soul, Rose, is bright. It's beautiful."

I opened my mouth, then closed it. I didn't know what to say, what to do. I'd never heard Ronan speak like that, not once.

"Would you like me to read to you for a while?" he asked, breaking the silence as if he hadn't just rocked my world on its foundation. "Or would you like to talk further? You said you had something you wanted to ask me?"

"Hey, guys," Iris said, poking her head around the door. Her chestnut hair was pulled back in a ponytail today, and her deep brown eyes softened when they landed on me. I loved that she didn't try to hide the black mark on her cheek anymore. What had once caused her pain, she now wore with pride.

"Iris," Ronan said, that deep voice sliding through me.

"I'm heading out. I need to get back to the keep."

Iris lived in an old keep in the middle of the forest with her mate, Draven, and his wolf pack, but like Willow, she was here often.

"What's happening tomorrow night?" I asked. "I heard Willow and Mags talking. Rowena's here?" I didn't want anyone to miss out because of me.

"Oh...yeah, I'm not sure what it's all about. You know Rowena. I'm sure it's nothing Earth-shattering." She wouldn't meet my eyes.

Yes, it was definitely about me. They were planning for the worst. They knew as well as I did that the mother would be calling soon and what that would mean for the coven. "You should all go."

"It's fine, Roe. Mags and Bram will be here with you—"

"No. Whatever this is, it sounds important." I turned to Ronan. "Will you stay with me tomorrow night? That way, Mags and Bram can go as well." And it was also kind of perfect for another reason.

"Of course," he said, then turned to my sister. "I'll take care of Rose."

"Thanks, Ronan. That's very kind of you," she said.

He inclined his head but said nothing more.

Iris came to me and kissed my cheek. Her eyes dipped to my dry, cracked lips, and she took a piece of melting ice in a cotton ball and gently ran it over my lips. "I'll tell Mom Ronan will be with you tomorrow night." She wouldn't meet my gaze, but I could see hers growing glossy with unshed tears. "Right, I better get going. Love you," she said.

"Love you too."

Then she left and it was just Ronan and me once again.

"So, would you like me to read to you?" he asked again.

"Yes, please. I'd like that." Once everyone was settled for the night—Mags with Bram, if he was here, Mom and Arthur in front of the TV, Else in her workroom, and Iris and Willow at their homes with their mates—then I'd tell Ronan why I'd asked him to come here tonight.

I waited an hour.

The TV went up, which meant Else had decided to watch TV instead and commandeered the remote, and I could hear music in the distance, coming from Bram's treehouse, which meant he was home, thank goodness, and Mags was with him.

I waited until Ronan finished the chapter of the fantasy he was reading to me. I preferred romance novels, but I hadn't had the courage to get him to read some of my steamier ones. I kind of regretted that now.

"Ronan?" I said when he turned the page.

His beautiful, emotionless eyes lifted to me. "Yes?"

"We've read enough for tonight. I think it's time we talked." My nerves shot through the roof. But nothing would deter me. This couldn't wait any longer.

He closed the book and placed it on the bedside table, and waited.

"I have something I need to ask you."

"Yes."

"I'm going to explain how I'm feeling, my reasons for my request, and then I'm...going to ask you, and I'd appreciate it if you'd...wait until I f-finish before you answer," I said, weakness making my speech break and stumble. Ronan didn't usually interrupt, but if he suddenly decided to now, I didn't think I'd find the courage to ask again. "Will you do that for me?"

He sat back in the chair, his penetrating stare not leaving me. "Of course."

"I'm going to die, Ronan," I said, licking my dry lips.

His brows lowered, but he said nothing.

I quickly pushed on. "I know t-this, you know it, my family knows it." I swallowed, trying to get some moisture in my mouth and failing. "Right now, I'm in pain...all the time," I rasped past my dry throat. "Else came to talk to me today...about trying IV fluids again since I c-can't hold even water down anymore." I swallowed reflexively again. "The last time she tried it, I had a seizure. It w-won't work, nothing will work. I'm slowly starving to death, Ronan. And my slow drawn-out death is hurting everyone around me. I can't take it anymore."

I paused, and Ronan said nothing. His violet eyes were steady on me, waiting for me to continue.

"B-but there's another reason...for the request I'm about to ask you. The mother will be calling for me soon. There is no chance of me passing her task, and definitely not the magical trial that follows. She won't care that I'm sick, it would still be seen as a fail, and my family, my coven, will suffer for it. They'll...they'll lose so much." I reached out, using the last of my strength to cover his cool hand with mine. He didn't need comfort, but I did, because what I was about to ask was huge.

Ronan waited for me to say what I wanted, and I met his steady gaze. "Will you help me die, Ronan?" It wasn't hard, the words came easy, the relief at finally speaking them immeasurable.

He didn't move, not a millimeter. He didn't blink. He just stared at me. If I thought he was capable of it, I'd think he was in shock. "Ronan?"

He blinked. "You want to die?"

"Yes."

"And you want me to aid in your death?"

I tried to swallow again. "Y-yes."

"How?"

I felt my face heat. I hadn't expected him to ask that, not yet, anyway. "I want you to drink from me...until my heart s-stops beating."

Ronan blinked again. "You want me to feed from you? Drain you?"

"Yes."

Ronan

Her logic was sound. The reasons she gave me for wanting to die made perfect sense. It would be better for Rose if her suffering were to end. But when I thought about her gone, about her lying still and cold in this bed, the boulder in my gut returned, but worse, it was as if it were covered in pointed spikes. "Your family won't want this, Rose."

She licked her lips. They were dry and cracked, and I remembered what her sister had done earlier and reached for the wet cotton pad.

"Can you do it in a way that they won't know? So they assume I died in my sleep?" she said before I dabbed it gently across her lips, as Iris had done.

Something came over me, a sensation I'd never experienced before, one that was unpleasant. Like the spiked boulder in the pit of my stomach was battering my insides. The pain was physical, but also not. How was that possible? It shouldn't be. Rose watched me, waiting for my answer. "Possibly. My saliva has powerful healing properties. If I drain you, then lick the wound before your last breath, it will heal over and no one will know." The boulder grew. It grew so big that I felt it in the center of my chest and almost drew in an unnecessary breath.

"If you agree to this, no one can ever know you helped me. They'll be angry at you, Ronan, and I don't want that."

Her eyes were huge as she watched me, waiting for my answer. "Your sisters, Rose, they love you as mine loves me. I may not understand it, but the way Luna explains it, if I were to no longer be here, she would suffer greatly. Your sisters, your mother, your aunt..." *Me.* The word exploded through my head out of nowhere. I frowned. *Me?* The thought was illogical. Why would it affect me? "They wouldn't want you to be taken from them."

Her hand still covered mine. "Ronan," she said, her voice soft, "I will be t-taken from them, anyway. And soon. I'm in pain. Seeing me like this is hurting my family. At least when I'm gone it'll be over. I'll be at peace, and so will they, knowing my pain has stopped."

How could I deny her? Why would I even think to? What she said made sense. I didn't need to understand or feel pain to know I didn't like the idea of her suffering. Ignoring the boulder in my gut, I met her faded blue eyes. "Yes, Rose, I'll help you."

Her lids drifted shut and a shaky breath passed her lips. When they opened again, they glistened. "Thank you, Ronan. Th-thank you." She squeezed my hand and her lips trembled. "We can do it tomorrow night."

The house would be empty. It would be just her and me here.

There would be no better time.

Chapter Four

Ronan

I didn't like crowds.

The club was full, people pushing and shoving. I didn't want to be touched by these strangers. They were drinking, dancing, singing, and laughing too loud. I quickly headed for the door on the other side of The Bank's main room.

I hadn't planned to come here, not yet. I'd fed only a week ago. I'd trained myself to last at least a couple weeks before the need became too much and the physical effects of depriving myself showed. But tonight, I was to feed from Rose. I would drain her until her mortal heart stopped beating. If I was to do that without losing myself to a frenzy, to blood lust, I needed to prepare. I would not cause Rose more pain by biting too deeply or accidentally tearing her fragile skin when thirst overtook me. I would take every measure to ensure she felt nothing but pleasure, like everyone did when a dhampir drank from them.

Yes, tonight, Rose would die.

At my hand.

The boulder didn't return at the thought because it hadn't

left, not since the night before when Rose made her request. I didn't understand the feeling, and no matter how long I lay awake trying to identify it, I found no answers.

The vampire at the door inclined his head when he saw me and opened it so I could pass. The Vault was another club, below the main one, a place where blood drinkers could come and feed freely from beings who were eager to be fed from. Killing donors was forbidden here. This was a place of pleasure. Pleasure of the flesh for the gift of blood. It was a tradeoff I understood, even if it were something I actively tried to avoid.

I opened the massive iron circle in the side of a brick wall. The door had once led to an actual vault; the building above had been a bank at another time, hence the name.

Despite the night being early, the scent of sex and blood filled my senses as I entered. There were always people here willing to offer themselves to the beings who frequented this place. I stood by the door and waited. As always, I didn't have to wait for long. A male and two females came to me, the scent of their arousal already strong. I had to fight the instinct to step back when one of the females reached out and touched my arm.

"Let me feed you," she said and pressed her body into mine. She had dark hair and eyes, as did the male with her. My hunger was not induced by either of them. I turned to the other female. She was lean, with blond hair, eager, but she held herself back.

"You," I said to her. "Come with me." Without checking that she followed, I walked to the couch I preferred and sat. She moved closer and attempted to mount me. I shook my head, holding her back. "Lay on the couch, please. On your back. Rest your head in my lap and give me your hand." She obeyed, her eyes wide, her body trembling with desire. Her other hand went to my chest, and I brushed it away. "You will not touch me, and I will not touch you. You may, however, pleasure yourself."

She nodded, watching as I brought her wrist to my mouth and

then bit into her flesh. She arched, moaning immediately, her legs falling open.

"Please," she cried. "Touch me."

I ignored her and let her blood fill my mouth, swallowing it down.

"Oh god. Fuck me, fuck me while you feed from me, please." She shoved her hand between her legs. "Please."

She whimpered and sobbed, then thrust her fingers in and out of her body. I looked away and closed my eyes. I didn't want to watch her. I didn't like the way it made me feel. Tonight, I'd be feeding from Rose like this. Rose who was too weak to move. She wouldn't be able to do what the female I was feeding from now was doing. She wouldn't be able to ease the ache between her thighs that would come when I fed from her.

Would it cause her more pain?

For reasons unknown, I would do anything for that female, including end her life. Could I ease her desire as well? Would she want me to? Suddenly, a pair of pale blue eyes filled my mind. Rose's eyes. Often when I fed, it was Azel who invaded my mind, which was why I tried to avoid it. I didn't want that male in my head or the memory of his grasping hands and acid blood on my tongue.

Rose's blood wouldn't taste like that. It would taste more like the female I was drinking from now. Would Rose's be sweet, like the female lying across my lap, or rich like spiced wine? The female's wrist in my hand was slight, fragile, and as I drank more deeply, lost in the frenzy, the high of her blood nourishing me, sating me, it was suddenly Rose's hand in mine. It was her wrist I'd buried my fangs into.

It was wrong to think about her that way, it had to be, but I couldn't get the image out of my mind. My hunger grew, yawning wider. I was ravenous, as if I hadn't fed for months, not a week. My stomach ached, heated, swirled. It wasn't unpleasant, no, it was the opposite. My fangs ached, tingled, and I wanted to release her wrist, then drive my fangs back into her flesh, then again and again.

I groaned, instinct taking over, finding it hard to resist doing what my mind was showing me. Lifting Rose in my arms and taking her throat, not her wrist. Holding her close, her cheek against mine, her breathy whimpers brushing my ear, her fingers grasping me to her tightly.

Rose.

Oh god, Rose.

The flesh between my thighs stiffened, becoming an iron rod in my trousers.

Hissing, I pulled my fangs from the female lying across my thighs, forced myself to lick the bite to seal it, and stood. She almost fell to the floor, and I quickly stopped her from hitting the ground. "Apologies," I said, then strode from the room, out the door, and through the main club.

Confused.

Aroused.

I woke like that sometimes, but I ignored it. I didn't want sex. Didn't think about it. What Azel and I had done wasn't something I ever wanted to repeat. I gave him my body in exchange for his blood. I didn't want *him*. I didn't enjoy it. I tried not to think about it.

Yes, on occasion, my cock grew stiff when I fed, but not like this. Never like this.

I rushed out the door and onto the street, letting the sounds around me fill my head, drowning out the ones my mind had conjured, letting the sights push away the images of Rose that had filled my mind while I fed.

I shouldn't be thinking about her like that.

If I told Relic, he'd tell me it was wrong. I knew it was wrong.

The boulder grew claws and teeth, and I rubbed at my chest, the pain becoming almost unbearable. Not muted, not numb like it should be, like it always had been. What was happening to me?

I needed to gather my control, because in a few short hours I would be with Rose.

For the very last time.

Rose

I walked quickly through the forest, but the dark figure stayed behind me.

"When are you coming to me?" he said, his voice utterly horrifying. "I grow impatient, witch."

A clearing was just ahead, and I turned to Death before I reached it. He stood there, shrouded in his black cloak, his twisted wooden staff planted against the forest floor. I couldn't see his face. I'd never seen his face. "What will you do when you have me here? Will you hurt me?" I asked. "Will you make me suffer?"

"No, not at my hand. That's what Hell's for, witch. Any suffering you endure here will be of your own making."

I didn't know what he meant by that.

"Your soul is mine. Let go. Or should I take someone else from your coven?"

"No, please. I'm coming."

He took a step closer. "When?"

"Tonight."

His hand gripped my wrist, his flesh burning mine, and I cried out. "I'll be waiting."

My eyes flew open.

I was back in my room, in my bed, unable to walk or move. I rubbed my wrist, looking down at it. There was a red mark on my skin. I shivered.

"Rose?" My mother's voice sounded panicked.

I turned my head on the pillow and blinked up at her, trying to fight the grogginess I still felt.

She was shaking. "You were dreaming, sweetheart. That's all. Just having a bad dream."

I'd stopped breathing by the look on her face. They didn't think I knew, but again, I'd heard them talking. It was the reason I always had someone with me. Sometimes when I slept, I stopped breathing for a while, and it scared the hell out of whoever was with me.

My sisters had all stopped by today to spend time with me, Else and Art as well, and now Mom. They knew the end was near, there was no way they couldn't. Else had tried the IV this morning, and I'd seized like I knew I would. I'd passed out for a while, and when I woke, Mom, Else, and Mags had been around me crying.

Maybe I only had a day or two left, but I couldn't endure another night of this, and neither could they. What happened after I died was out of my control, but my death would be on my terms.

And it would be tonight.

At least my turn for the worst had given me the chance to say goodbye to everyone in my own way. Mom was the last.

She gripped my hand, and I held hers back. "I'm so glad you're my mom," I said, trying to keep my voice strong.

"It's a privilege to be your mom, Roe." She blinked rapidly.

Yes, she knew, and she was fighting to hold it together for me. I could say a lot of things, but talking wasn't easy right now. From last night to now, I'd gotten a lot worse. The thirst, the hunger had become unbearable, breathing so difficult. So I said the words that said it all, words that she already knew, but I was determined to share with her anyway. "I love you."

"I love you too," she whispered and brushed her knuckles down my cheek. "We're not going anywhere tonight, my sweet girl. Rowena can wait. We'll all be right here."

No. That wasn't the plan. "No," I rasped.

"It's not that...we're just...there was just a change of plans, that's all," she rushed out, trying to cover for the real reason, her fear that I would die while they were gone. As if I didn't know what state I was in. And I would, but not because my body had given up on its own. I wasn't going out like that. I was dying the way I wanted.

The only way to get that was to give her the truth, or at least some of it. "Ronan," I whispered. "I want...to be alone with him, Mom. I-I have to tell him...t-tell him..."

"Shh, it's okay," she said, tears filling her eyes. "I know. I know. It's okay, sweetheart. We'll leave for a while, okay?"

They knew, they all knew how I felt about Ronan. Neither of us was saying what was coming, but she was going to give me that time with him. She'd give me the world if she could.

Mags sat with me until it was time for them to go. Magnolia talked, I didn't, couldn't. I took in my beautiful baby sister, knowing this was the last time we'd ever see each other.

"You're the strongest person I...I know," I forced out when Mom called her to come down, which meant Ronan had arrived.

Mags moved to the bed and cupped the side of my face, shaking her head. "Nah, that's you, Roe. It's always been you." She pressed a kiss to my hair. "See you later, okay?"

I swallowed thickly and nodded, then watched as she walked out the door, my heart in my throat.

Ronan didn't come up right away, and I thought I knew why. Mom had cornered him. When he finally walked in, and those gorgeous eyes came to me, he gave away nothing. He never did.

"What did she...say to you?" I asked.

His brow lifted.

"Mom, when you came in."

"She told me to have a care with you." His expression didn't change. "I didn't understand what she was saying. I'm always careful with you."

I smiled at him, and his gaze on my mouth became intense. "Yes, you are. A-always."

Mom poked her head around the door. "We're heading out

now, sweetheart. We'll only be a few hours at most." Her eyes were soft, and I could see her reluctance to leave.

I nodded.

"Love you, sweet girl," she said, then she bustled off, calling everyone to hurry up.

There was a flurry of sound, of movement, then the door was slammed shut. A minute later, cars started, and everyone left. And the house was engulfed in silence.

Ronan walked to the side of the bed. "Are you sure you want to go through with this, Rose?"

I nodded as I looked into his violet eyes. I loved them. They were cold but exquisitely beautiful, and despite how emotionless that gaze was, they were reassuring. He had no idea that those eyes falling on me the second he walked in the room, waiting for it, reveling in it, was one of the things that had kept me going this long. I was positive of it.

He sat. And this time, it was he who took my hand, offering me physical comfort. His eyes were still emotionless, but he was going to give me what he thought I needed, even if he didn't understand it, even if he didn't want or need it himself.

"How would you like me to do it?" he asked, his voice impossibly deep.

For once, my face didn't heat; there was no shame or embarrassment. My emotions felt raw. This was the last time I'd be with him, and I was going to ask for what I wanted. "Will you h-hold me when you do it?"

"Yes," he said instantly.

He kicked off his shoes, drew back the covers, scooped me up, then he got onto the bed with me in his arms. He carefully pulled the covers over my legs, bringing them up to my chest. "Is this okay?"

"It's...perfect."

His expression was solemn as he stared down at me. "Where would you like me to feed from, Rose?"

I lifted my hand to the side of my throat. "Here."

His Adam's apple slid up and down, and he nodded.

It was a struggle, but I lifted my hand to his jaw. I'd wanted to touch it for a long time. It was strange to touch him this way, and wonderful. He'd obviously shaved that morning, but I could feel the stubble already there. He said nothing, just sat there and let me touch him. "I'm so g-glad you came...into my life, Ronan."

"I'm glad as well, Rose," he said.

I wasn't sure if he truly knew what that felt like, but he'd come back every day for over a year. Something brought him here to me, and whatever it was, whatever he felt when he came here, I was grateful for.

Now was not the time to hold anything back, and I couldn't die without saying what was in my heart. "I know you don't understand l-love, romantic...or otherwise—"

"Luna tried to explain it," he said. "It's a good feeling. It gives pleasure beyond the physical, yes?"

"Yes," I whispered and brushed my thumb over his firm lips. I mustered all my remaining strength, I needed to get this out, all of it. "I n-need you to know that...I'm in love with you, Ronan. N-not as a sister loves a brother...but as a female loves a male." I took a ragged breath. "You are the only male...I have ever loved, the only one I will ever love...and the months we've spent together have made the u-unbearable...bearable." I held his violet gaze. "If I could have l-lived a full life...I'd want to live it with you."

Chapter Five

Ronan

Rose's words moved through me. The sincerity of them was stark in her eyes. She loved me, was in love with me. It seemed impossible. How could she have those feelings for someone like me? Someone cold and unable to return the sentiment.

For the first time since I could remember, I wished I had the ability to give that back. That I could feel as she did. That I could truly know how it felt, what it meant, and that I could offer it to her in return. "You honor me, Rose. I may not fully understand what you gave me, but I do know it's a precious gift, and I assure you, I will hold it with me always. I promise you that." And I meant it.

What would I do tomorrow or the next day and the day after that? Coming here, and visiting with the tiny female in my arms, was what drove me from my bed every morning. Rose gave me focus. She had become my purpose.

I didn't know why, but she had.

There were things that filled my mind time and again when it came to Rose, and it was only fair that I shared them with her after her declaration. It was all I had to give her in return. "When I'm with you, when I walk into this room and see you, when you smile at me, the sound of your voice, your laugh, your scent, I feel this... warmth, here." I pressed my hand to my chest. "I don't know what it is, Rose, but it's yours. Only you give that to me. And I fear that when you're gone, I'll never feel it again, that warmth. That I'll be cold again for the rest of my life."

She blinked her big eyes up at me. They glistened, and her lips trembled. "Thank you...for giving me that."

I inclined my head. "It's the truth."

Her chest rose and fell shakily. "Can I ask one more thing of you before we do this?"

"Anything."

"I want you to be the first and last, the only male I ever kiss." Her throat worked. "Will you kiss me?"

"Yes." There was no hesitation, the word coming from me without thought.

She blinked. "Are you sure...you told me once you d-didn't like it?"

I thought about it. I hadn't wanted Azel to kiss me, but he had. Not often. But enough for me to know I didn't like it. I thought perhaps with Rose, it might be different, and I realized I wanted to do it for her and for me. Kissing her, the memory of it, I wanted that. "I didn't like it because I didn't want to kiss the person who kissed me."

"And you want to k-kiss me?" she whispered.

"Yes...I find I do."

I'd watched television. I'd seen my sister, and Rose's sisters, with their mates. The hounds with various females. There were many ways to kiss. Rose was frail, delicate. She would need to be kissed gently and slowly. I lifted my hand and cupped her pale cheek, like I'd seen Warrick do with Willow. Why did my hand feel strange against her skin, and why were my vocal cords so tight?

She stared up at me, and I did what she had. I gently ran my thumb over her lower lip. I'd liked the feeling and assumed she would also. Her tongue darted out to swipe over it and touched the tip of my thumb. I enjoyed that as well. My gaze dropped to her mouth.

Her breath shuddered in and out, her slight frame trembling in my arms. I lowered my head and gently, so very gently, pressed my lips to hers. A wave of warmth pulsed through me, and my lips tingled in a similar way to my fangs when I was about to feed.

I lifted my head a fraction, then touched lips with her again, and again, the sensations fired through me, like every nerve ending in my body had laid dormant and only now were brought to life. I held my lips to hers for several seconds more, then lifted my head again.

She stared up at me as a tear slid down her cheek. "T-thank you, Ronan."

The boulder in my gut exploded, sending shrapnel through my body. It was pain—pain that wasn't entirely physical but hurt all the same and had me holding her closer to me. Somehow, I wasn't numb to it, not with Rose. Could I really do this? Could I take her life while I held her to me? Could I wake up tomorrow and carry on as normal, knowing that she no longer existed in this world?

"Rose." My voice was rougher than it had ever been in my life.

"Please, please, don't change your mind. Please...I can't live like this anymore."

Her suffering was visceral. It lined her face and changed her voice. How could I say no?

"It's okay. Be at ease," I said and ran my hand over her thin hair like I'd seen her mother do so many times, not knowing how but attempting to comfort her.

She slumped in my arms, then gripping my hand in hers, turned her head to the side, offering me her throat. The vein was dark through her paper-thin skin, pulsing.

Trembling for some reason I couldn't explain, I leaned in and pressed my lips to her skin just above that vein.

"Are you ready, Rose?" I said as invisible sparks licked across my skin when I got a taste of hers.

She didn't answer.

"Rose?"

She jolted in my arms, her entire body going stiff before a cry exploded past her lips.

I cupped her face. "Rose? Rose? What's happening?"

Chapter Six

Rose

*C**ome to me, child. Now.*
A female voice rang through my mind.

"Rose?" Ronan said gruffly, taking hold of my chin and turning me to look at him.

"She's c-calling, Ronan."

"Who? What are you talking about?"

"The mother. It is too l-late. Oh god, it's too late." This couldn't be happening. I wanted to pull Ronan down, beg him to feed, to end this now. But I didn't know what would happen if Ronan went ahead and ended my life, not now that the mother had called. I couldn't risk it.

"What can I do?" he said. As always, he wanted to help, to make it better for me, even though I was sure he didn't understand it or know that's what he was doing. It was always his first instinct to protect me.

But there was nothing else I could do. In a split second, everything had changed. "Keep me a-alive...at least until I talk to her?"

"Why would you do that?"

I gripped his hand tighter. Ronan knew what my sisters had been through before me, why the mother was calling, and why it was so important to our coven. What he didn't understand, was why I couldn't ignore her call now. Not only would it infuriate her —and losing her favor wasn't something any coven wanted. But the main reason? "I have to at least try to explain my situation to her. To a-ask her to spare my family. To beg her not to take away their gifts because of me."

He nodded slowly. "Where do you need to go?"

Thank god. "Oldwood Forest. But it's dangerous. There are... d-demon's everywhere. I'm so sorry to ask this of you—"

"You won't be in any danger with me, Rose." He lifted me and lay me back on the bed. "We need to dress you. It's cold outside."

I couldn't believe this was happening. I'd been prepared to die tonight, not this. Ronan was opening and closing drawers, pulling things out. I hadn't worn actual clothes in months. Nothing I owned fit me anymore. Everything hung from my body now.

He slipped thick socks on my feet, then a second pair over the top of those. Then he worked a pair of sweats up my legs, carefully lifting my hips to pull them up to my waist under my nightgown. I blushed but fought back my embarrassment. There was no one else here to help. And thank the goddess for that. My family would never have let me go. They would have resigned themselves to losing our gifts or, worse, one of them would have gone in my place and risked the mother's wrath.

"Lift your arms," Ronan said.

My face grew hotter still as I did as he asked. He lifted the nightgown over my head, and I did my best to cover myself as he pulled a thermal over my head and helped me put my arms through the sleeves like a toddler. I hated this so damned much I wanted to scream.

The timing of this, of her calling to me. Could that really be a coincidence? She was everywhere, saw everything. The mother had engineered this, she had to have, and I hated her for it. Ronan put a shirt on me next, then a sweater.

"Jacket? Hat?" he asked.

"Downstairs."

Ronan scooped me into his strong arms and carried me downstairs. Sitting me in the armchair by the door, he propped me against the back, then found a woolen hat and pulled it down low before searching through the jackets hanging by the door. He grabbed Mom's long quilted one and helped me into it, pulled on his own, then I was back in his arms, and he was carrying me outside into the snowy night.

Despite all my layers, the cold bit into me instantly. Ronan strode quickly to his car and carefully sat me in the passenger seat, buckling me in, then around to the driver's side, got in, and started the engine.

The snow grew heavier as we drove, but it didn't take long for us to reach Oldwood. The forest was just beyond the city itself, at the southernmost end of the larger Roxburgh State Forest.

He lifted me out and strode toward a gap in the trees.

"What about the demons?"

"They won't know we're here."

"What? H-how?"

"They won't see us," he said.

Then I felt it, his power, the buzz of it surrounding us. "What kind of...power do you have?"

"It's similar to my sister's," he said. "But also different."

Luna could block herself and others. She was incredibly strong. "What can you do, Ronan?"

"I have concealed houses, entire streets and the beings on it. Concealing us both is no effort on my part." Then he strode into the wood and headed toward the clearing where the mother would be waiting for me.

The cold had settled deep in my bones despite the layers of clothing Ronan had put on me, and it was only going to get worse.

The sounds of wind whistled through the trees, while the strange calls and roars of demons and other creatures exploded into the night every now and then. Ronan didn't pause or flinch, he strode quickly toward our destination.

All too soon, we reached the clearing, and Ronan strode right out to the middle. "What should I do now?" he asked.

There was a circle of rocks near us. "I need to light a fire there." I pointed to the rocks. "And I need to...undress."

His brows snapped down. "You can't. It's freezing out here."

"It's part of the ritual, and I'll need something sharp. Do you have a knife?" We'd been in such a rush, and it'd been so long since I'd been strong enough to practice magic, I hadn't even thought to bring my own.

"This doesn't seem like a good idea."

I touched his arm. "It's how it has to be."

Ronan held me against him with one strong arm and slipped his jacket off, then tossed it on the snowy ground before he carefully sat me down. "I have nothing to start a fire."

I wasn't sure I could do it. "It's okay. Can you help me undress?"

His jaw worked before he kneeled down beside me and helped me remove my clothes. Once my sweater, shirt, and thermal were off, he dropped the coat over me, then slid off my pants, socks, and underwear. He placed a small pocketknife in my hand. Humiliated, I couldn't meet his eyes.

All that was left was starting the fire. I stared into the circle and drew on the tiny embers of magic I still felt inside me. They were faint, barely there, but it stirred as I called on it, as I willed the fire to ignite.

A spark flashed in the center, then small flames licked up, racing around the edge. I collapsed back, the effort of performing such a simple spell too much for me. I looked up at Ronan. "You need to go. As soon as I say the words, she'll come to me."

He shook his head. "I'm not going anywhere. I'll be right here beside you. She won't see me."

The look on his face brooked no argument. I felt his power leave me, and as soon as it did, Ronan was no longer there, though I knew he was, just blocked from my sight.

Gripping the knife in a shaky hand, I pressed it to my arm and sliced, unable to hold in my hiss of pain. "Guide me...old ones. I am your s-servant, the Keeper's sister chosen to...f-fulfill the rite of Coven Thornheart." The wind immediately picked up speed, frigid air flying around me so fast it hurt. "I'm here to accept...m-my task. Whatever you ask, I...I will undertake." The coat was ripped from me, and shards of fine ice and snowflakes battered my naked, emaciated body. The icy wind stole my breath, and I hugged myself, my hair plastered to my face, my teeth clenched against the agonizing cold.

Then it came, the rattle both Willow and Iris had talked about. The mother was coming.

I searched the shadows, then slammed my eyes closed, remembering that I wasn't to look at her until I was told I could, but I felt her presence. It was heavy, suffocating, dark and light, violent and joyous all at once. I'd never experienced anything like it in my life.

There was a hiss and a tickle against my arm. The serpent tasting my blood, making sure I was the witch she'd summoned.

Open your eyes, witch.

I did as she asked and gasped at the awesome sight of her. Nothing my sisters had told me could have ever prepared me for this. Her shiny, obsidian eyes were on me, moving over my nakedness.

You didn't come alone. Her voice was hard, full of fury.

She knew Ronan was there. "I'm sorry, Mother. But I am unwell. I couldn't journey here on my own."

One moment Ronan was hidden behind his block, and the next, he stood there. His face was blank, but his fingers were curled into fists at his sides.

Begone. The mother hissed in my mind.

Ronan was thrown from the clearing. I watched as he jumped to his feet and tried to charge back in, to get to me, but he slammed up against an invisible barrier. The mother had locked him out.

The serpent's massive head swung back to me. *Explain yourself, witch.*

I hugged myself tighter. I was going to be hypothermic soon. At least I would get my wish. I would die tonight, not the way I'd wanted, but there was no way I would live through this. First, though, I had to try to make the mother understand. "Mother, I have been s-sick...my whole life. An unexplainable illness...that my family has tirelessly tried to find a cure for. There isn't one. I'm going to die. There is no stopping it... I am too w-weak to pass your task or fight in a magical battle. I have come here tonight to beg your mercy. To ask you not to punish my coven for something that is out of their control."

Is your heart still beating, witch?

"Yes." Though I didn't think she expected an answer.

"Then save your excuses. I expected more from the sister of Willow and Iris Thornheart. I see before me a coward, ready to give up when there is much to fight for. Not all tasks require the witch to have physical strength, but all require mental strength, stubbornness, and an iron will. Your sisters did not pass their tasks alone." Her head swiveled to Ronan standing at the edge of the clearing, his eyes locked on me. *And neither will you.*

Oh god, she won't listen. She doesn't understand. "Mother, please. Look at me, at my body. I'm close to death."

Are you willing to use the time left to fight for your family? Your coven? Her steely gaze locked on mine. *There is only one answer I will accept, witch.*

I did want to fight for my family. That's why I needed to die. If I tried to do this, I would fail. I would fail without a doubt, but she wouldn't take no for an answer. So I gave her the truth, what was in my heart, even though it was impossible. Because I would do anything for my family, even try to live for a little while longer. "Y-yes," I choked out.

Then you must complete the task I give you by the time the vines meet. If you fail, you will be unworthy of trial, and gifts past will be returned to the mother. If you complete your task yet fail to win your trial, again, your coven's gifts will be returned to the mother.

She spoke the words into my mind, referring to herself in the third person as she hissed and slithered closer. I knew what was coming, and I wasn't prepared for it.

She struck fast. Her long, razor-sharp fangs sank into my left shoulder. The pain was excruciating. Then she opened her mouth, released me, spun, and slithered off.

I lay there gasping for breath as wave after wave of pain radiated through me. Demons. I could hear them in the distance. Calling to each other, coming closer. Suddenly, the cold wasn't so bad anymore, and I closed my eyes as darkness crawled closer. I thought about Ronan, about our kiss. The darkness crowded in, closer still.

I was going to die.

This was it.

Chapter Seven

Rose

I blinked. Then blinked again.

I was still in the field. Snow drifted all around me. No, not snow. Something gray. Ash. There was a growl and a hiss, then a thud. I turned my head.

Ronan.

He stood only a few feet from me. His shirt was gone, and he was covered in blood, and piles of ash and mutilated demons, unable to move but still alive, surrounded me. Ronan turned, scanning the clearing. His fangs were extended, and his eyes were wild, feral. Not cold, not emotionless.

I'd never seen him like that in my life.

"Ronan?" I choked.

His gaze slid to me, and he strode forward. Then, without a word, he covered me with the coat and scooped me up. "We need to get out of this clearing. My powers won't work here anymore," he said. Tucking me close, he ran for the edge of the clearing.

"What h-happened?"

He didn't stop, he kept running. *Fast.* So fast, the forest was a blur around us. When he looked down at me, the rage I'd seen on his face was gone. The flat coldness was back in his eyes. "The demons got a head start. The block around the clearing didn't drop until the mother was long gone. They almost reached you before I could."

"So you...k-killed them all."

"Yes."

He held me tight. My hand rested on his chest, and it was slick with demon blood. God, how many had he fought on his own? He could have been killed.

We reached the car in record time, and he had me buckled up in seconds. He jumped in behind the wheel and sped for home.

No one was there when we got to the house. I'd never been more thankful. They wouldn't take this news well. I wasn't sure how I'd tell them. Ronan rushed me inside and headed straight for the bathroom. He turned on the shower.

"What are you doing?"

"We need to warm you. Your skin is ice cold." He tested the water, pulled away the coat covering my nakedness, then stepped in, still in his clothes.

I tried to cover myself as we stood there, humiliation burning my cheeks. His stare sliced to my shoulder. "She bit you. I tried to get to you, but I couldn't. I thought she was killing you."

His voice was different, deeper, rougher, but I couldn't see any trace of emotion on his face.

"It's part of the r-ritual," I said.

"These markings are part of it as well?" He brushed his thumb over my arm, then high on my shoulder.

I looked down. The tattoo-like markings the mother had given me were already showing, snaking across my skin. The intricate vine pattern covered my upper arm, and judging by the slight tingle along my shoulder and the side of my throat, they were there as well.

I knew without looking, there'd be a section of unmarred skin between the places Ronan had touched. "W-when the vines on my arm grow and touch the ones on my shoulder...the time I have to p-pass my task is up, and I fail." My family would see it as soon as they got home.

He nodded but didn't say anything. We stood there in silence for several more minutes.

"Are you warm?" he finally asked.

"Yes."

He turned off the water and stepped out, grabbing a towel and wrapping me in it. There was nothing I could do but allow him to dry and dress me. Ronan had seen every bit of my hideous body and now was running the towel over the revolting hump on my back, his hands over my thin hair as he dried it.

I'd be even more humiliated if I wasn't so exhausted. I didn't know how I'd stayed awake as long as I had. Adrenaline most likely. But every bit of energy drained from me now. I couldn't think or move, I could barely draw breath.

The darkness crawled back, surrounding me, taking me under.

Ronan

She was still breathing, but judging by how shallow each inhale was, I wasn't sure for how much longer.

I looked down at my hands; a vision of those demons, so many of them running for Rose, filled my head. I couldn't get to her. If I hadn't been as fast as I was, I wouldn't have made it to her in time, they would have torn her to shreds.

What happened afterward was a blur. I killed and killed until there were no demons left. Until there was no more danger to Rose. I tried to recall the finer details, but my vision had turned red. And when I'd finally returned to myself, Rose had been awake and as close to death as I'd seen her.

I looked at her again. So pale, her skin was almost the same color as her white-blond hair.

A door banged downstairs. The sound of voices, of shoes on the hardwood floor, then taking the stairs.

I stood when Daisy filled the doorway, Magnolia and Bram behind her. Daisy looked at me, her gaze dropping to my bare chest, to the scratches and bite marks marring my skin, then shot back up.

"Ronan?" She looked at her daughter and a cry escaped before she ran to her. "Rose? Sweetheart? Please, wake up, baby." She looked up at me. "What the hell happened?"

Magnolia rushed in. "Oh god, her neck."

Daisy's hand flew to her mouth. "Tell me that isn't what I think it is. Tell me you didn't take her to Oldwood Forest," she cried.

I frowned, confused. "I did as Rose asked. She wanted to speak with the mother, to explain her situation."

Magnolia screamed in rage and ran at me, punching me in the chest. Bram rushed forward, hauling her off her feet and into his arms.

"I don't understand?" I rubbed at my temples. Pain, again unmuted, exploded behind my eyes this time. "I thought—"

"She could've been killed. What the hell were you thinking!" Magnolia cried, swiping a tear from her cheek.

I shook my head. "I was there. I protected her from the demons. I did what she asked. Her request made sense. It was logical. She's dying. She wanted to help. She didn't want the mother to punish your coven. It was the right thing to do. She—"

"Logic?" Magnolia spat.

Daisy wasn't looking at me. She was weeping, clinging to Rose. "She's so cold," she whispered.

"You don't get it, Ronan, and you never will because you're made of fucking stone. Rose means more to us than magic, than power. I don't care about any of it. I'd give it all up to prevent her from feeling one more moment of pain. And you...you took her out into the freezing night. You let her lay there naked, afraid, alone. You let the mother *bite* her when there's barely anything of her, and now she'll blame herself even more when the mother takes our gifts away from us."

I looked down at Rose. I had done that, hadn't I? All the things that Magnolia said. I rubbed my temples again, the pain behind my eyes worsening. I'd hurt her. I'd hurt Rose. "I never meant to cause her pain."

"She won't survive this," Daisy said, tears streaming down her face. "I thought I had a little more time. A few more days, at least." She sobbed.

"Just...leave, Ronan," Magnolia said, and turned her back on me, climbing up onto the bed beside her sister.

Bram moved in. I inclined my head before he reached for me and strode out, down the stairs, and out into the snow. Bram shut the door behind me.

I should do as they asked. I should leave, stay away. But I couldn't do it. I didn't know how to describe it. It was as if she were the sun and I was a planet, ever moving around her, trying to get closer but not knowing how. Even when I was right beside her, it never felt close enough. I wasn't sure why, only that I felt a pull toward her. I lifted my block and walked back in, following Bram up the stairs and into Rose's room.

Then I stood across from her bed, because I couldn't leave her. Every instinct told me this was where I needed to be.

The rest of the family arrived within the hour. Iris and her mate, Draven. Willow and Warrick, Ren, her familiar, with them. Arthur, Daisy's familiar and boyfriend, was there comforting her. Magnolia and Bram hadn't left the room once. And Else was limping in and out of the room with all manner of lotions and potions, trying to feed Rose elixirs and covering her in foul smelling poultices.

Several hours had passed and Rose still hadn't woken up. I was tuned into Rose in a way I never had been before. When I walked into a room, I could hear every breath and every heartbeat of the people around me, but it was different with Rose. My heart no longer beat, it had stopped a long time ago, but I felt Rose's heart inside me, as if it were part of me, and it had been growing weaker by the hour.

She was dying.

This wasn't what Rose wanted, how she wanted it to happen.

Taking her out in the cold, what the mother had done to her, it was going to kill her.

And Magnolia was right. I had caused this.

Chapter Eight

Ronan

Morning arrived, Rose's room filled with sunlight, and still, she didn't wake.

Else and Magnolia were rushing between Else's work room and Rose's bedside, still trying different concoctions. But nothing was working. Daisy had stayed at Rose's side, holding her hand, talking to her unresponsive daughter and weeping. Willow paced, and Iris sat on the floor with a pile of spell and history books, searching for anything that could help her sister. Books that I knew she'd looked through many times before, searching for something that didn't exist.

Willow wasn't the only one who paced. I couldn't sit still. I could do nothing, and with every second that ticked by, I grew more and more restless.

"Has Warrick had any luck finding Vesa? Any sign of him at all?" Daisy asked.

Willow turned to her mother. "Nothing. And if anyone can find Rose's father it's him. But we don't have anything with Vesa's scent, and Rose's is obviously too different because it's not working."

"I know it's a long shot. But we've exhausted everything else. I didn't go looking for him when he left because I was glad to see the back of the man, but now..." She swallowed. "What if he could've helped? What if there was something in his family history that caused this?"

"What could a human have that could do this? We've tried human medicine, none of it worked. It's not your fault, Mom." Willow closed the space between her and Daisy and crouched down beside her. "Don't go there. We've tried for years to find Vesa. You did all you could, and honestly, I don't think he could help even if we had found him. He's just a human."

I looked at Rose. Warrick needed a scent to hunt. I needed blood. Her father's DNA flowed through her veins. I could track him, I just needed a taste. One taste of her blood, and maybe I could find the human who'd fathered Rose. Willow was right, it was a long shot, but there was still a chance he could help.

I needed to be alone with Rose, and it needed to happen now.

Striding from the room, I rushed down the stairs, walked outside, picked up a rock, and fired it through the living room window, then several more at the side of the house before striding back inside. If they thought they were under some kind of attack, it was logical that they'd all come down to protect the house.

"Stay with Rose," Iris ordered Nia before the entire family ran down the stairs, right through me as I took them, two at a time, back to Rose's room.

Iris and her familiar could communicate, and I couldn't risk Nia seeing me. I moved closer. Rose's hand rested on the covers, and I slid it to me, into my block. Nia was utterly focused on Rose's chest, on its rise and fall, and didn't notice.

I leaned down, my mouth close to her ear. "Rose?" My powers brushed against her in the hopes that she might hear me. "I need a sample of your blood. It won't hurt." I didn't like the idea of her not understanding what was happening or thinking I was preying on her, taking from her while she slept like I was some...some parasite. The word filled my head. Azel had called me as much often. I shook off the thought, lifted Rose's hand, and nicked the tip of her finger with my fang. Blood bubbled to the surface, and I sucked it into my mouth.

Her blood coated my tongue, and something wild and hot, something bright and vibrant pulsed through me. My nerve endings sparked, electricity shooting through my limbs. I sucked on her delicate finger again, wanting more. Nothing, no one had ever tasted as good as Rose.

I wanted to get closer to her; everything in me wanted me to get closer. I wanted to climb up onto the bed beside her, feel the warmth of her body, sip at her blood, feed from her, protect her, and care for her. My gaze sliced to her mouth. I wanted to feed her as well. What was this I was feeling? What was happening to me?

I froze at the sound of footsteps on the stairs and forced myself to lick her wound, to heal the cut, then placed her hand carefully beside her. Pulling my powers back, I rushed from the room as Daisy walked back in. I ran past the rest of Rose's family, who stood in the living room looking puzzled, while Arthur boarded up the broken window and strode outside.

The frigid air hit my face, and I used it to clear my head, to push down my confusion, and focus on Rose's blood, letting it move through me and become one with me. Blood had its own scent, something most blood drinkers were aware of, but not something Rose's family would know. It wasn't a "scent" as witches and shifters would interpret the word. It was indescribable, a knowing, a calling. For some of us, when you drank from a person, you knew where they were and sensed them for a time afterward. Those who were as powerful as me, anyway.

All my instincts were focusing on Rose, telling me to go back into the house to her. I forced myself to resist and focus outward.

To search for that part of Rose that didn't come from her mother, the part of her "scent" that was foreign to her, that wasn't witch.

What remained was most definitely not human.

Sprinting to my car, I started the engine, planted my foot on the gas, and headed for the city.

A short time later, I found myself at a place I'd been to before. I'd come when I was desperate to feed after Warrick and his brothers had helped me and before I knew of The Vault. Parking my car, I climbed out and headed for the bar across the street.

The place was packed with humans, their scent cloying in the confined space. They blocked my way, several females touching me as I shoved past, and I barely stopped myself from baring my teeth at them.

I didn't like people touching me—except Rose.

Rose.

I thought about her in that bed, so pale and still, and a strange feeling built in my chest, that same foreign feeling I had around her often, an awakening of some kind, but bigger.

A male stood behind the bar, and I pushed my way through the sweaty humans to get to him. "Are you the proprietor of this establishment?"

The human screwed up his face. "What the fuck did you just say?"

"Is this your bar?"

His fingers curled into a fist. "Who wants to know?"

I didn't have time for this; Rose didn't have time. I could sense her father here, or at least he had been here very recently. I didn't have his full name, but his first name was obscure enough that someone might have heard it. "Is Vesa here tonight?"

"Fuck off," the male fired back.

I grabbed the front of his shirt, yanked him forward, and slammed his head against the bar's wooden surface, then pinned it there. "Is Vesa here tonight?"

The human groaned and pointed to the fire exit. "Out there."

Releasing him, I pushed back through the crowd and shoved the door open. Someone yelped. It was dark, but I had no trouble seeing.

A male, tall and dark-haired, stood against the wall. His pants were down, and a human female had his cock in her mouth.

The male turned to me and scowled. "Get the fuck out of here."

I strode toward them, lifted the female to her feet, and turned her toward the door. "Inside, now."

She was unsteady on her feet—

Blood.

It was fresh.

She walked back into the bar, and I knocked the blade out of Vesa's hand as I turned back. Grabbing him by the throat, I shoved him against the wall.

No, definitely not human.

Shifter.

"What are you?"

"Get the fuck off me!" he yelled and yanked at my hand, still wrapped around his scrawny throat.

There was blood on his chin. "You fathered a child, a daughter with Daisy Thornheart, yes?"

His eyes widened then narrowed. "Who the fuck are you? Did Daisy send you to find me? If she wants money—"

That was answer enough. "What are you?" I asked again.

He scowled, pressing his lips together, refusing to speak.

He wasn't going to tell me, but I had the right male. My blood felt hot in my veins, and my gut gripped tight. I had to focus hard to sense what breed this male was—then it hit me.

My phone rang, and without releasing him, I checked the screen.

Magnolia.

"Yes?"

"Rose is asking for you," she said.

"She's awake?"

"She's in and out of consciousness, but she's struggling for every breath and her heart rate's dropped. I don't know how she's still hanging on." Her voice hitched. "Rose wants you here," she said, her voice cracked. "You need to hurry."

Rose was about to die.

"I'm on my way." I shoved my phone in my pocket.

The male squirmed in my fist, but I no longer needed him, and neither did Rose. I knew exactly what he was, and there was nothing he could give her that would help her now. Tossing him aside, I sprinted from the alley. My blood burned hotter in my veins. Maybe I was dying as well? There was pain in my chest. I needed to get to Rose.

I reached my car and yanked the door open. It tore off the hinges with a groan. Tossing it aside, I got in, started the car, and planted my foot on the gas.

I never lost control of my strength like that. Something was definitely wrong with me. My core temperature had increased even more, and sweat coated my skin despite the missing door. My gut felt as if it were full of spiked boulders, not just one, and my muscles were constricted so tight they were close to cramping.

I checked the clock, then the speedometer.

Four minutes and thirty-seven seconds had passed since I received the call from Magnolia. At my current speed, Rose needed to stay alive another five minutes and twenty-three seconds.

I stomped harder on the gas, pushing the car to its limits.

Make that another four minutes and fifty-one seconds.

The time ticked down in my head, until I finally saw the house ahead of me. I slammed on the brakes, stones spitting out from the tires as I skidded to a stop.

I jumped out and ran for the house, through the door, sprinting full speed up the stairs and into Rose's room. Her family stood around her. Her mother was kneeling by the bed, Rose's hand in hers. Everyone was sobbing.

Iris turned to me. "I'm sorry," she said. "It's too late. She's gone."

No. That couldn't be.

I strode to the other side of the bed, my body, my organs in some kind of distress. I was surprised I hadn't collapsed from all that was going on inside me. I wasn't sure what was happening, but I didn't care, the sun was calling me closer.

I looked down at her lying there, so small, so frail. I listened for her heartbeat. Nothing. My head dipped before I knew what I was doing, pressing my ear to Rose's still chest.

Nothing.

Something hot trickled down my face, and I brushed it away. Blood. I'd seen my sister weep before. These were tears. Why was I weeping? I looked down at Rose's face, and fire burned hotter in my chest. My hand lifted all on its own to touch her cool cheek. Another hot tear slid down my face and fell, landing on Rose's pale lower lip.

I reached out to brush it away, but it slipped into her mouth. I stared down at her, trying to understand what was happening. Trying to resist the urge to grab her from that bed and hold her to me—

Thump.

I stilled. Several seconds passed.

Thump.

I shut everyone out around me and zeroed in on that sound.

Thump.

I pressed my head to Rose's chest once more.

Warrick gripped my shoulder, and I turned to him. Willow was pressed to his side, weeping. Ren, behind her. He and Warrick watched me with a look I couldn't interpret. "Brother, she's gone," Warrick said.

"No." Blood. Rose needed blood. I knew what Rose was, what her father was. I knew what she needed.

My fangs extended, and I bit into my wrist.

Someone gasped.

I ignored them and took Rose's chin, opening her mouth, and pressed my wrist there. My blood slid past her lips to her tongue. I was yanked back.

"What the fuck are you doing?" Warrick barked at me.

I spun, throwing my arm wide, and punched him in the throat. He automatically released me, and I spun back to Rose and pressed my wrist to her mouth again.

Everyone was yelling and crying. Warrick came at me again, Ren joining him.

I spun and snarled, the sound coming from somewhere deep inside me, somewhere I didn't know existed. No one was going to stop me.

"Ronan, please stop," Daisy cried. "She's gone. Don't do this."

I forced myself to find the words. "She isn't dead. Almost, but not quite."

"What?" Willow whispered behind me.

"I found her father," I said. "He's a shifter."

Daisy blinked up at me. "No...he was...he's human."

Rose's lips trembled against my wrist, and I looked down at her, unable to look away. "He's a bat shifter. As Rose grew older, her need for human food would have become less, while her need for blood steadily increased." I looked up again. "Rose wasn't sick, she's been slowly starving to death. She needs blood."

Rose whimpered.

Daisy cried out. "Rose! *Oh goddess.* Rose!"

Rose's tongue slid over the bite mark I'd made, her instincts automatically kicking in, knowing somehow that if she did that she could encourage the blood to flow faster. Is that why I'd brought food to her each morning? Why I always had a driving need to feed her, nourish her. Somewhere deep inside, had I known this was what she needed?

"Roe?" Willow said, rushing closer.

Rose's hands exploded from the covers, and she grabbed my wrist with the last of her strength, her grip weak, her fingers cold.

"Drink," I said to her. "Take your fill." With each pull, I felt her heartbeat deep inside me, growing stronger, as if it were my own.

Her eyes snapped open. Glossy obsidian eyes stared back. Eyes of a bat. And the most beautiful thing I had ever seen.

Beautiful.

That word again. I'd never recognized it or understood it before Rose. I did now. Somehow, I knew exactly what it meant.

The room had exploded around me. Rose's family cried and hugged. But as I looked into Rose's black eyes, everyone else disappeared into the background.

They didn't exist.

There was only Rose.

Her eyes held mine as she drank from me, as she allowed me to feed her.

This was my purpose on this earth.

To sustain her.

It was a strange thought, but I knew it to be true with an absoluteness I had never experienced before.

Each pull she took on my vein sent shock waves through my body. I felt hot, and my limbs trembled as sensations I was not familiar with pounded through me. A stimulus overload. Too much. More than I knew how to process. The urge to pull away hit me, but I resisted easily, because the urge to feed Rose, to give everything to her, was so very much stronger.

And with each swallow of my blood she took, with those black eyes locked on me, something chipped away inside me. Like I was surrounded by an exoskeleton, and with every deep pull on my vein that she took, a piece of it fell away, exposing the vulnerable flesh beneath.

Rose tried to move closer to me, and I gave her what she wanted, scooping her out of bed. As soon as I lifted her from the mattress, wings exploded through her skin from high on her back. Bat wings, only they were white, fine, pearlescent wings that shimmered like something from a fairy book.

The room went silent. I felt their stares, on her, on me, but I couldn't tear my eyes from Rose as she drank greedily from my vein, getting her first taste of blood, finally experiencing what it was like to be satisfied in probably her entire life.

Exhaustion eventually got the better of her, and she slumped in my arms. Unconscious, but breathing strong and steady.

As soon as she shut her eyes, her wings snapped back, then vanished as if they'd never been there. Her back was smooth, uninjured. The hump gone, as if it'd never been there. Both bat and witch, her wings were magic.

Daisy closed the space between us and looked up at me. "You saved her, Ronan."

I couldn't speak, my throat so tight words were impossible—

Something tore inside me, the last of the exoskeleton falling away. It was like being crushed by a boulder, like I was being smashed to pieces. What was happening to me? But I knew, didn't I? Because I'd felt this before, as a child, before Azel killed my mother, then abducted my sister and me, before he tore us apart, then used and abused us for his own sick and twisted ends.

It was too much.

Daisy's eyes widened. "Ronan?"

I stumbled back a step.

"Brother?" Warrick moved closer. "Put Rose on the bed so her family can tend her."

I shook my head, a snarl ripped from me. Still, no words would come, but I couldn't put her down, I couldn't let her go.

Red covered my vision. I couldn't think as emotion washed over me, through me. I knew that's what it was, even if I'd forgotten how to identify it. I stumbled back another step, holding Rose to me.

No one was taking her from me.

~

"Ronan?"

I blinked. Blinked again.

The voice called my name again, momentarily pulling me from the quicksand.

I didn't know how much time passed, but Luna now stood in front of me.

"Ronan?" My sister rested her hand on my arm and squeezed. "You have to put Rose down. She's still not well. Let her family take care of her."

My sight cleared, and I looked around the room. Rose's family was there, all wide-eyed, watching me. Luna's mate, Gunner, stood beside her, along with Rocco, one of his brothers, watching me as well. I looked down at Rose. Luna was right, but I couldn't do it.

I met Gunner's worried gaze. "You need to take her from me. I can't...let her go," I forced out and turned to Rocco. "And you'll need to force me out of here or I'll try and take her back."

Rocco inclined his head. They moved as one. Gunner scooped Rose from me and handed her to Arthur. As soon as she was gone from my arms, the monster in me exploded. I went after her, but Rocco hooked me around the gut, Gunner, Warrick, and Ren, grabbed at me, Draven and Bram as well when I fought harder as they were forced to physically subdue and remove me from the room.

I roared and lashed out. I needed to stop, but I couldn't. Red covered my vision again. I was losing my mind as emotions slammed into me, one after the other. I wasn't sure how I would survive this.

Not without shattering into a million pieces.

Chapter Nine

Rose

A roar of agony reached into my subconscious and dragged me back to the surface. I opened my eyes. The room was in chaos. My family was here. And Ronan's sister, Luna, and so were some of the knights, and they were dragging Ronan across the room.

His violet eyes locked on mine, and he roared again as he tried to pull free but was towed to the door.

"Ronan!" My voice burst from me, loud, stronger than it had ever been.

Then he was gone, dragged through the door. His snarls and roars could be heard all the way down the stairs and only stopped when the knights had taken him away.

What little energy I'd had, I'd used up calling for him. I struggled to stay awake, to find out what was happening, but I couldn't keep my eyes open.

~

I ran through the forest, tripping over branches, stumbling through a creek, and scrambling up a bank on the other side. I glanced over my shoulder. Death was gaining on me fast, and he was furious.

"Witch," he said, low, deadly. "We had a deal."

"No, please. I'm not ready." I dug my fingers into soft soil and dragged myself up the bank.

He stopped where he was and slammed his staff down, making the earth shake. "This isn't over."

My eyes flew open with a gasp.

"Rose?" Mom filled my vision. "She's awake! Oh, thank the goddess, she's back." She cupped my face. "My sweet girl," she said and smiled as tears ran down her face. "You're back."

Magnolia ran into the room as I shifted under the covers, trying to gather the strength to move. I waited for the pain to hit, the weakness to overtake me, but there was none.

I sat up easily. "What the..." I looked down at myself and blinked. Then blinked again. I was looking down at someone else, I had to be. My gaze shot up to Mags, to my mother. "What?" Nope, I still couldn't find the words.

Mags grinned wide, and Mom's smile was soft, her eyes bright with joy. "You've been asleep for a full week. Your body needed time to heal."

Could this be real?

I shoved back the covers and carefully lowered my feet to the floor, still expecting my legs to collapse beneath me, but they felt as strong as the rest of me.

Still, I cautiously crossed the room and opened the bathroom door. I stood in front of the mirror, and my gasp echoed around the tiled room.

That wasn't me.

I was looking at someone else.

Mags moved up beside me, wrapping her arm around my waist. I looked at her smiling face, then back at my own. We looked like sisters. We were different, but for once, I could see the similarities too. My face had filled out, my cheeks were pink, and my lips were deep red. My pale blond hair was no longer thin or balding in places, it was thick and had a slight wave, falling halfway down my back. And my body...

I ran my hands over my hips. God, my thighs actually touched. I had a waist, because I had a butt, and my boobs, okay, they weren't huge, but I had them. I wasn't ultra-curvy like Mags. My sister was shorter and rounder. I was tall and willowy, but I most definitely had curves.

"How?" I whispered. "How did this happen?"

Mom followed us into the bathroom. "Ronan. He figured out what you were. What you needed. He saved your life."

"What I am?" I had a memory of Ronan standing over me, or me holding on to him. He was feeding me something. "What do you mean? He found a cure?"

"You could say that," Mags said with a grin.

"He found your father, Rose," Mom said. "Somehow, he found your father when no one else could." Her throat worked. "It turns out he's not...human."

I spun to face her. "What?"

"He's a bat shifter."

My heart thumped in my chest. "He's what?" Something heavy hit me in the back, or at least that's how it felt. I was thrown off balance, and I grabbed for the wall as Mom and Mags stumbled away. It felt as if I were carrying something heavy. I glanced over my shoulder, where something white and translucent and glittering rose behind me. "What the..."

"Wings," Mags said. "You've got freaking wings, Roe."

I struggled to keep my balance and gripped the edge of the vanity so I could turn and look at them over my shoulder. I couldn't believe what I was seeing. Bat wings, but white. They sprouted from high on my back where the hump had been. The wings weren't overly big, but they were heavy.

"I have wings," I rasped, stunned. "But how? Where do they go?"

"Your shifter side has somehow blended with your magic. They vanish completely, then just...reappear." Mom closed the space between us. "And there's something else you need to know."

I turned to her and almost lost my balance again. "There's more?"

"Yes, sweetheart, there's more." She swallowed thickly and tears filled her eyes. "All this time, you weren't sick, Roe, you were...goddess, you were starving. Ronan worked out that you needed blood." She took my hand. "That you needed to feed."

I jolted. "On blood? I needed to feed on blood?"

"Yes," Mom said, dashing her tears away and watching me carefully.

"And Ronan...what? He got me some?"

She shook her head. "He opened a vein and fed you himself, fighting off Warrick and Ren when we didn't understand what he was doing. He saved you."

I turned back to the mirror and stared at myself in shock all over again.

"Are you okay?" she said.

Was I? You'd think the idea of drinking blood would be disgusting. It wasn't. A flash of memory hit me. I'd held on to Ronan, clinging to him, drinking from his wrist.

Drink, he'd said in a deep, rough voice. *Take your fill.*

And I had, until I'd passed out. I spun back and nearly toppled over again. "They dragged him from the room. Why? Where is he?"

Mom chewed her lip. "He asked them to. He was having some trouble letting you go. In the end, he asked the knights to get him out of the room. I'm not sure what's going on with him. Luna's been with him, and we haven't been able to talk to her. One of the knights makes the deliveries and they're not telling us anything either."

"Deliveries?"

Mags leaned on the vanity. "We tried to give you blood while you slept. Everyone donated—the wolves, the hounds, the coven— but you wouldn't take it, you'd fight us. In the end, we had to call the knights. Ronan has been sending his blood over for you. His is the only blood you'd drink."

My heart thumped hard behind my ribs. He was sending over his blood? "I want to see him."

Mom shook her head. "I'm not sure that's what he wants, sweetheart. For whatever reason, he's been staying away. And the way he lost control in here with you." She chewed her lip again. "I think that maybe it's best he doesn't, for now at least."

Lost control? The sound of his roars and growls as they'd dragged him away and the look on his face filled my head. He had. He'd completely lost control. "But Ronan doesn't have emotions, how is that possible?"

"I don't know."

I needed to see Ronan. Somehow, I had to get to him. I had to.

Mom brushed my hair away from my face, staring up at me for several long seconds, then tears slipped over again, streaking down her cheeks. Then she grinned and pulled me in for a tight hug, her body shaking against me. "You're going to be okay, Rose. Oh goddess, you're really going to be okay."

Two days had passed since I woke, and the house was currently full of people. My family, hellhounds, wolf shifters, most of our coven, and a couple knights as well.

Mom had insisted on a celebration, and you would think after all the years of missing out, of sitting on the sidelines, not being able to join in, I'd be loving every minute of this, but I couldn't enjoy myself, not when I didn't know how Ronan was. Where he was.

At least I'd worked out how to vanish my wings, thanks to Bram. Though his wings were completely different in every way to mine, he'd helped me identify the muscles that controlled the motion of folding them back in, and we'd learned that when I did that, my magic kicked in, and they vanished. Folding them in wasn't easy, though, and they kept popping out and reappearing at inopportune moments. I'd taken to wearing tube tops under my shirts. My wings had sharp edges, and I'd shredded several T-shirts already. With my wings coming from high on my back the tube tops stayed intact at least and stopped me from flashing everyone.

Rocco and his mate, Kyler, stood across the room, talking to Willow and Warrick, and I made my way over to them. All of us sisters had different coloring, and Willow stood out in a crowd with her fiery red hair and bright green eyes. She immediately pulled me into her side, her face filled with happiness.

Warrick, my huge, close to seven-foot-tall brother-in-law, patted me on the shoulder with one of his giant mitts, his fingers adorned by several silver rings, most with skulls engraved into them, and grinned as well. "Fucking good to see you walking round." That was as sappy as the male got with anyone that wasn't my sister.

"Thanks, War, it feels pretty damn good too," I said.

I turned to Rocco. "So, you need to tell me where Ronan is."

He blinked down at me, and I could see the wheels turning, trying to think of what to say. The male wasn't going to tell me.

Kyler gave him a nudge. "Tell her."

I could have kissed her. I smiled at her instead. But then Roc shook his head, his navy-blue eyes leaving his mate and coming to me. "Disappointing my mate is my very least favorite thing to do. But it's for Ronan to share, not me."

Grrrr. "Why hasn't he come to see me? He came every day for months, now he's vanished. Something's not right, Roc. Please, you have to tell me."

He offered me an apologetic smile but shook his head again.

"There's a good reason he can't be here, Roe, but I promise you, he wants to be here with you more than anything. Now that's as much as I'll say."

I wasn't sure what to believe. What to think. What had happened in my room a week ago after he'd fed me, and why had they dragged him away? No one seemed to know. My family didn't understand, and I'd made Mags go over what happened that day with me at least twenty times.

I took in the massive warrior and scowled. It wasn't like I could force him to tell me. The male took in my expression and grinned. I grumbled under my breath and turned back to Willow.

My sister was watching me, eyes wide and glossy, and her lips curled up on one side.

"What?"

She shook her head. "Nothing, just...seeing you like this." She swallowed thickly and pulled me into her side. "I never thought I would."

I hooked my arm around her waist. "I guess there's no getting out of my trial now, huh?" Mags and Iris joined our huddle.

Willow looked up at me, her gaze fierce. "I don't give a fuck about that, about any of it right now, Roe. You're going to be okay, and nothing else is more important than that."

"*You-know-who* can go fuck herself," Mags said and winked at me, obviously meaning the mother, but thankfully she had the good sense not to say it out loud. "We're not thinking about that tonight. Tonight, we're celebrating having you here with us and knowing we always will."

Iris put her arm around Mags, and we moved together, wrapping our arms around each other in a group hug. "The four of us, standing here like this, I never thought it would happen," Iris said. "But you're here, Roe. You're strong and healthy, and goddess, so incredibly beautiful. I feel as if—"

"As if we could take on the motherfucking world and kick its ass," Mags finished.

"Yeah, as if we could take on the motherfucking world," Iris said, chuckling.

Willow grinned as tears ran down her face, as tears ran down all our faces. "Look out world, Rose has arrived and she's going to blow your motherfucking mind!"

"That's right, motherfuckers!" I choked out through tears and laughter.

We all hugged and cried and laughed.

Then we danced. We danced together like we never had before.

Chapter Ten

Rose

I woke with a start and blinked up at the ceiling. It was morning, and for once, I hadn't dreamed. There'd been nothing. No visit from Death. No nightmares. Nothing.

I didn't get my hopes up, it was a respite. Death wasn't going to just let it go—let me go. I forced the thought from my mind. I'd have to deal with that sooner or later, but I also had a task to complete. When I found out what it was, anyway.

I yawned and stretched. I'd been up late, studying spell books in the library. I had so much to catch up on. My stomach growled loudly—I also needed to feed.

I hadn't done that yet, at least not while conscious. How would it taste? At the thought, my mouth watered. This was so freaking weird. I was thinking about drinking blood, and again, I wasn't disgusted by the idea.

A shiver slid through me.

Not any old blood, Ronan's blood.

This whole thing was kind of...no, not kind of, it was totally insane. I wasn't only a witch; I was a blood-drinking, bat-shifting witch. And I had freaking wings that I didn't know yet if they actually worked, like would I be able to fly? Or were they just there? Like some bizarre decoration? I didn't know any other bat shifters to ask.

My hands rested on my stomach, and I let them slide up to my chest. Over my curves, curves I'd never had before. I'd never carried enough weight to have them. I moved my hands down over my hips to my thighs. My body felt foreign, but also right. This was how I was always meant to be.

My stomach rumbled again. The hunger yawning wider. I didn't like the feeling. I'd lived with hunger for so long, and now that I knew what it was to be satisfied, the empty feeling in my belly was almost unbearable.

How would I even drink Ronan's blood? Out of a cup? In a bowl with a spoon like soup?

What would it be like to drink from Ronan, from *him*, directly from his vein? I wished I could remember.

My body warmed at the thought, and there was a tingling along my gums. I tried to run my tongue along my top teeth—

Shit.

Mags said I had fangs. This was the first time I'd felt them. Hunger, thinking about feeding, and they'd slid from my gums. I ran my tongue over them again. They weren't like Warrick's or Draven's, and they didn't feel as if they were like Ronan's either. They were long and extremely thin, the point at the end incredibly sharp.

There was a knock on the door downstairs, and I tilted my head as someone answered it. Else, I could tell by her limping gait.

I couldn't hear what they were saying, but every bump and thump seemed to travel right to me—my hearing had grown stronger as well. A scent hit me, rich and dark and spicy. My mouth watered more, and I shoved the covers off, rushed across the room, and pulled the door open.

Luna stood there, her fist raised, ready to knock. It was the first time she'd come here since everything happened.

She looked up at me and her eyes widened. "Holy shit, Rose. Look at you. You're beautiful."

Her praise made my face heat, but I struggled to think of what to say, my attention immediately drawn to the bag she was carrying. The scent grew, and my stomach growled again, louder this time. My face got even hotter.

She grinned. "I brought this for you. I've kept it warm." She held out the bag.

I looked down at it. "This is...it's... This is Ronan's blood?"

She nodded, her expression unreadable. "Unless you don't need it? Is there someone else you're planning to drink from?"

I recoiled before I knew I was going to do it. "No," the word exploded from me. "I mean...no, I um, I don't want to do that."

Luna's smile brightened, and she held the bag out to me. "Feed, Rose. You must be really hungry by now."

I took it, then looked back up at her. "How? I haven't done this yet. Every other time, I was unconscious."

"It's in a thermos. Just use the cup on top." She took a step back. "I'll head downstairs and chat with Else. Come down when you're ready." Then she walked away.

I shut the door and walked to my bed, sitting on the edge. My hands trembled as I opened the bag and pulled out the thermos. The thermos with Ronan's blood was inside.

Ronan's *blood* was *inside*.

This was so bizarre. I took off the cup and unscrewed the lid, and the rich, spicy scent hit an all-new level. My mouth watered as it filled my senses. I wanted it, badly.

This was my life now. I was a witch who drank blood. This was insane. Like full-on bonkers. How was this my life now? But it was, and right then, my stomach twisted with hunger as the scent of Ronan's blood called to me.

Carefully, I filled the small plastic cup and placed the thermos on my bedside table. I looked down at it. It was deep red, and yeah, to me, it looked...goddess, freaking delicious. I lifted it to my nose and sniffed again, and moaned, that's how good it smelled.

Pressing the cup to my lips, I finally took a tentative sip. The taste, Ronan's taste, exploded in my mouth, igniting my taste buds. I downed the cup and refilled it, a kind of frenzy taking over me. Then I downed that too. My body was warm, and my limbs were deliciously languid. But my mind, my mind, was crystal clear, and Ronan filled it. I felt him, it was like he was there with me, and I wondered if he somehow felt me as well. If his blood connected us in some way. I had no way of knowing. No one to ask.

I tried to drink the next cup slower, but it was hard, and when I took another sip, my nipples tightened, and a deep pulse started between my thighs. Arousal. That was what I was feeling. I'd never felt it in my life, not like this.

This...this was something else. And my magic, it grew, strengthening inside. I finished the thermos, and my face was hot, my belly full, and my skin was all tingly. I walked to the bathroom and took in my reflection. My cheeks were pink, and my lips were a deep crimson. And my eyes were...they were black. Mags had warned me, but it was still a shock to see myself this way.

Ronan might not be here, but he'd given me this. This gift. He was going through something, and still, he was taking care of me.

Goddess, I missed him. I wanted to see him. I wanted to know if he was okay.

I quickly showered and changed, then grabbed the empty thermos and headed downstairs to talk with Luna. She was at the kitchen table, drinking coffee and talking to Else and Mom when I walked in.

"Morning, sweetheart," Mom said and held her hand out for the thermos. "Better?"

I glanced at Luna. "Yeah."

"You look healthier every time you feed." Mom cupped my

cheek. "I still can't believe it's true. If Ronan hadn't..." Her lips trembled. "If he hadn't—"

"But he did, Mom. And I'm going to be just fine. You don't have to worry anymore."

She smiled softly. "A mother never stops worrying, sweet girl." Then she carried the thermos to the sink to clean it for Luna.

Else stood, came around the table, took my hands, and kissed them. "I need to get to work." Then she limped off.

Mom put the clean and dry thermos in front of Luna. "I'll leave you two to talk. Thank you for doing this," Mom said to Luna. "You'll thank Ronan for me, won't you?"

"Of course," Luna said.

"How is he?" I asked as soon as Mom left.

Pain filled her eyes. "He's going to be okay."

Which meant he wasn't okay now. "Can I see him?"

Luna looked unsure. "Look, Rose..."

"Please. I need to know he's okay."

Her gaze softened. "I know you've spent a lot of time with my brother, and I know that you care about him, a lot." She glanced away. "You've definitely spent more time with him than I have."

I frowned. How could that be?

"Has Ronan shared any of his past with you?" she asked.

I shook my head. "Whenever I'd ask him anything about himself, he'd clam up."

"I'm sure you know at least some of my past?"

I did. A monster named Azel had held her prisoner since she was a child. He'd abused her, used her for her powers, and forced her to beg for blood. He'd tortured her, and if it wasn't so hard to kill a dhampir, she'd be dead. Luna managed to kill the evil male, and he went to Hell. Then two years ago, during Willow's trial, he'd tried to come back. Everyone had kept it from Luna and Ronan at the time, but Azel almost succeeded. "Yes."

The pain in her eyes returned. "Rose, when Azel killed our

mother and abducted me, he took Ronan as well. We were separated for most of our lives, but what I endured, he did as well."

Oh goddess. How had I not known that? Imagining what he'd been through, I grabbed the edge of the table. "I had no idea."

"I wouldn't normally share that, it's Ronan's story to tell, but when he comes to you, and he will, he's going to be...different. He'll be struggling, and he'll need your understanding. I'm hoping now that I've shared with you, you'll be able to cut him some slack if he behaves oddly. Or struggles with his impulse control. If he's out of line, you'll need to call him on it, correct him if he behaves in a way that's unacceptable, and explain why."

"I don't understand?"

Her head tilted to the side. "You saw Ronan being dragged from your room, yes?"

"Yes, but no one seems to know what happened."

She smiled softly, but there was still concern in her eyes. "He's regained his emotions, Rose. But not like me, not gradually. They hit him all at once. Ronan was old enough when we were taken that he has some memory of his life before, when he still had emotion. Those memories had been locked away for most of his life, but a part of his brain obviously recognized what emotion was, because it had processed them when he was little. So when they came back, they came back all at once, overwhelming him. He's struggling to cope with it, to understand all that he's feeling. It doesn't matter that he understood them as a child, they're foreign to him now." That pain filled her eyes again. "He's been through a lot in his life, Rose, and it's all hitting him now, all of it. So as much as I want to take you to him, he's in no condition to see anyone, not yet."

I gripped the edge of the table tighter, my heart breaking for him. Everything in me told me to go to him, that he needed me. Every instinct screamed at me to ignore Luna and fight my way to him. But I couldn't do that. The last thing I'd ever want to do is to hurt him. "Will you thank him for everything? And tell him I miss him, that I want to see him?"

Luna covered my hand with hers. "Of course."

"Do you really think he'll come to me when he can?" Hope filled me.

She grinned. "Oh, yes." Then she tilted her head to the side, and her expression grew serious again, her eyes sharpening. "And I pity anyone who tries to get in his way."

I didn't know what she meant by that. I opened my mouth to ask, but she stood.

"I need to go. I'll see you in a couple of days."

Then she walked out, leaving me with even more questions.

Chapter Eleven

Ronan

My body was an inferno, my mind a tangle of unwanted thoughts.

And every single one of those thoughts...or memories, came with emotions and a visceral response. It was too much.

Too much.

An image of Azel, of him touching me, of the way he had used me, filled my head once more, and I crawled to the toilet and vomited. Then collapsed on the ground in a shivering heap.

And all the while, Rose was right there with me. I could feel her, as if she'd become a part of me. She'd drunk a lot of my blood this past week, and now I could feel her. That knowledge was the only thing keeping me sane. I needed that; I needed to know she was safe while I was trying, and failing, to get the fuck off the floor.

I curled my fingers into a fist. I had to beat this.

The sound of the door opening in the main room and then shutting reached me.

"It's just me," Luna called.

The knights had brought me here to their compound, but I

hadn't let anyone see me since, not even my sister. They'd even brought me blood, but I couldn't bring myself to feed.

"Ronan, please."

The pain in her voice hit me hard in the chest. I'd heard it many times in the last couple of years, but I hadn't recognized it. I'd been numb, blind to it. Now I felt it deeply. I'd let her down, time and again. I'd stood by, believing the lies Azel spilled. I'd believed him when he said Luna was safe, when all the while he was using her as he had me, for her power, her body, poisoning us with his blood. I'd believed his lies, and my sister had paid for it over and over again.

I didn't know how to...to process it, how to continue functioning with that knowledge in my head. I smashed my fist into the tiled floor, desperate to release the feeling inside me.

My sister had suffered because of me, because I had been too weak of mind, too gullible to see the truth.

"Ronan, please let me see you," she said outside the bathroom door.

I shook my head, but the words wouldn't come out. The door handle turned, and I groaned, lifting my block, hiding from her when she pushed the door open and walked in. "Please, Ronan," she said again.

Pain wasn't only in her lavender eyes, it was etched on her face.

She was worried, afraid for me. I couldn't let her suffer like that, not for another moment.

So I did the only thing I could do, I let my block drop. And as soon as I did, her gaze fell to me. She cried out and dropped to her knees beside me. "Ronan, please, talk to me."

Humiliation burned through me, an emotion I had quickly become reacquainted with. I was still in the trousers I'd worn the day they'd carried me from Rose's bedroom. I'd lost my shirt, and I stunk of vomit and sweat. I hadn't even managed a shower in the last nine days.

Luna wrapped her arms around me, and I lay there frozen, like a fucking lump of ice, not sure what to do, how to react, how to respond.

"It's going to be okay. I promise you, it'll get better," she whispered.

I unclenched my jaw. "I'm being torn apart."

She rubbed my back. "You'll get through this; you have to, for Rose's sake. She needs you."

I shook my head. "I'm the last person she needs." The way I felt about her, the drive to be close to her was confusing, terrifying. The way I wanted her scared me so much I was paralyzed by it. Because I didn't just want to be near her—I wanted to touch her, hold her. I wanted to feed her from my vein again, not from a thermos. I wanted to feel her tiny fangs deep in my skin.

But what scared me most of all was how badly I wanted to drink from her.

"You're wrong. She wants to see you. It hurts her being away from you, just like you're hurting being separated from her."

I shook my head, my teeth chattering in my head. "I want to... to feed from her, Luna," I said, and shame filled me. Yes, it was another I'd recognized quickly. It was one of the first I'd worked out while I'd vomited into the toilet the first time. "I would never taint her that way."

"Taint her? I know you don't understand this, but Rose would give you anything, anything you wanted. She wants you to be happy, she wants to be with you and take care of you, like I know you want to care and protect her."

"How do you know that?" I gritted out.

Luna brushed my hair back from my forehead. "You haven't worked it out yet?"

I didn't know what she was talking about. Gritting my teeth, I shook my head.

"These feelings you're having for Rose, the reason you couldn't stay away from her even before you regained your emotions…" She took my hand. "The reason you regained them when she drank from you."

"Why?"

Luna smiled gently. "Because Rose is your mate, Ronan. Rose is made for you and you for her."

I shook my head harder. "No," I said, even when the realization filled me. Could it really be true? Something deep down inside roared, shaking me to the foundation. Yes. Of course, it was true. And on some level, I'd known, hadn't I? But I'd never allowed myself to even consider it a possibility.

"Yes, and she needs you to get better. She needs her mate by her side, and you need her just as much."

My eyes drifted closed, because I couldn't look Luna in the eyes when I said this. "I'll hurt her. I want…I want to feed from her, so badly. I want to bite her and touch her…and…"

"She's your mate, that's only natural. Feeling that way is how you're supposed to feel, Ronan."

My eyes snapped open. "She's too fragile, too delicate. The way I feel, so out of control…I wouldn't be able to stop. I'd…I'd hurt her."

"No, you won't. I know what you're feeling, and I know how strong your hunger for her is, but believe me, your need to protect and care for her is so much stronger. Because of that, you would never, couldn't ever, hurt her." She squeezed my fingers. "I promise."

"But these fangs, they've…they've been in Azel's vein." I shuddered. "I could never sully her that way, I could never—"

Luna gripped my chin, stopping me. "No. *He* doesn't get that, Ronan. Don't you dare let him take this from you. Don't you dare give him that. You are not tainted, or marked, or dirty. *He* is the monster, not you. We did nothing to deserve his abuse. Not one fucking thing, do you hear me? He's rotting in Hell for what he did. He's not here, don't you be the one to bring him back by giving him that kind of power."

The emotions grew so big I felt as if I was tearing down the middle. It was more than I could cope with, and I felt myself shutting down. I froze in my sister's arms.

"Ronan?"

I couldn't speak or I'd fall apart in a way I wasn't sure I'd ever recover from.

She held me tighter, weeping silently. "It's not your fault," she whispered, answering the question that lived in my heart. "None of it is your fault. He killed our mother, he took us from our home, and he manipulated us. We were only children, just trying to survive."

I couldn't speak, but at her words, something in me cracked open—it wasn't a bad thing. It was something else, something I couldn't name yet.

I lifted my arms and wrapped them around her in return, holding her just as tightly.

Chapter Twelve

Rose

I smoothed my hands over my new shirt. I'd gone for a quick shopping trip with Mags and Iris the day before, since nothing I owned fit anymore. I'd needed everything. I didn't even own a bra, I'd never needed one. Now that I had options, I was trying to work out what my style was. Willow and Mags were similar, favoring jeans and dark colors, some leather thrown in. Iris was more eclectic. Yes, she was a jeans girl, but she loved color and more often went for comfort, though everything looked awesome on her. I realized yesterday that I liked things that were flowy, soft colors, but I also kind of wanted to show off my new curves a little. Nothing too out there, but nothing that felt like a sack.

I looked at myself in the mirror again. My blue jeans hugged my long legs. Over my tube top, I wore a white thermal and a pale pink sweater. It was soft and fitted, coming down to my butt, and not skintight, but it had a deep V that showed the tiniest bit of cleavage. I was warm and comfortable and felt feminine. Some-thing I hadn't ever felt in my life. I really hoped I didn't have another of my random wing-unfurling incidents and destroy my new look.

I also had on some silver earrings, a couple bangles, and a fine silver chain with a small heart on it. The necklace was mine, but Mom had eagerly let me raid her jewelry box this morning for the rest. The vine markings on the side of my throat were also visible, but I was okay with that, it's not like they were going anywhere, and I guess they were kind of pretty really. I tugged my sweater down at my shoulder. They hadn't changed or gotten any closer, thank the goddess. I had no idea how much time I had, but so far, I seemed to have had a reprieve.

I picked up my new lip gloss and smoothed it on. I'd also gotten a little makeup, and I'd put some on this morning. I'd had trouble sleeping last night, so I should look tired, but somehow I didn't. I'd had this restless feeling inside me, telling me to leave the house, to go into the city. I'd fought it, afraid it was a bat thing—a blood thing.

What if I went into the city and drained a bunch of unsuspecting humans? I mean, I didn't feel murderously hungry, but what did I know? What I'd been feeling had definitely felt instinctual, though. So I'd resisted, too scared to move. I'd tried to take my mind off it by studying. There were books on spells, incantations, and potions piled all over my bedroom. When I'd finally gone to sleep, I dreamed, well, it'd been a nightmare, not Death. I still hadn't heard from him, thank the goddess. No, I'd dreamed of a demon. Everything had been dark except for firelight and a twisted hideous, horned demon that had stared at me with terrifying red eyes.

I shook it off. It was just a stupid dream. I had enough visits from Death to know the difference between a nightmare and something he'd created to torment me. I'd take the former every single time.

I fixed my hair, brushing my now-thick locks. It was glossy and healthy. So different than how it had looked only a short time ago.

What would Ronan think of the way I looked now?

Would he care?

I'd been trying to imagine him, not as the stoic, emotionless male who'd visited me every day for months but as some new version of himself. Luna said he'd regained his emotions. What would that look like? Would he be completely altered?

I had no clue, but I was seriously impatient to see him and nervous as hell.

Luna was due back today with more blood. She'd been once more since our talk. We hadn't spoken about Ronan the last time, and she hadn't been able to stay. Anticipation filled me because, even though I knew it wouldn't happen, I secretly hoped it would be Ronan coming to see me today. That instead of sending Luna, he'd come and offer to feed me himself.

My body heated and my cheeks burned.

Being as starved as I was for so long, puberty hadn't ever really kicked in, but it had now. I was a hormonal mess, and I didn't know what to do about it.

The sound of a car reached me from the street, and I walked to the window. Warrick and Willow pulled up, Relic behind them. They usually rode their bikes, but the snow had forced them to park them for the winter. I spun away, rushed down the stairs, and yanked the door open. I hadn't seen my sister in a couple of days.

She grinned and strode over, giving me a hug. "Love the new threads."

"Thanks."

Warrick joined us, and the massive hound hooked me around the back of the neck and shoved me against his chest, patting my back awkwardly.

I looked up at him while Willow chuckled.

He shrugged a colossal shoulder. "Still shocks the shit out of me every time I see you. So you gonna have to put up with me acting fucking weird for a bit longer."

I laughed and squeezed him back. "I'm cool with that."

Relic sauntered over. The male was close to seven feet, and like most of the hounds, was heavily muscled and covered in tattoos. His long, dark hair was tied back, and his jaw was clean-shaven. He gave me a head to toe, as only the cocky hound could. "Damn, female."

"Hello to you, too, Relic."

He offered me a sexy smirk, flashing his dimples, then Warrick released me from his bear hug, and we all headed inside. We gathered in the kitchen, where Mom, Else, and Mags were already sitting around the table. Art was making tea, and Bram stood behind Mags, looking kind of antsy for reasons unknown.

"Have you seen Ren?" I asked Willow. I hadn't seen him since he was here with Willow, the day everyone thought I'd died.

Willow leaned on the counter. "Yeah, I spent some time with him last night. Watched some TV, hung out."

My sister's familiar had been through something that had broken him, something that he survived when the odds of him coming out the other end weren't good. Ren was a fox shifter, and for nearly two years, he'd been living in the forest, choosing his animal form over his human. Recently, that'd changed. He was still quiet, unlike the old sociable Ren, and he didn't like being around a lot of people. But he was sleeping at his old place, a small apartment in the basement of his family's funeral home, instead of the forest, and working again. Which meant Ren spent most of his day with the dead. We weren't sure this was a good idea after what he'd been through, but he told Willow the dead were all he could handle right now.

There was no missing how happy Willow was that Ren was letting her back into his life. Their time apart had been incredibly hard on both of them.

Not that I'd know first-hand, since I didn't have a familiar— and considering how old I was, I'd resigned myself to the fact that I never would. That he was now able to actually sit and just spend time with Wills? "That's huge."

"I know," she said, pouring herself a cup of tea, then joining us at the table. "So, I have some gossip," she said, changing the subject. "This isn't common knowledge, but the demonology research and artifact department of the museum was robbed two nights ago, then the next night, one of the guards went missing."

"Really?" Mom said. "What was taken? How did you find out?"

Something twisted in my belly.

"I had a call from Trotman. The council is concerned, and they asked me to look into it. He didn't go into details, except that several priceless—and dangerous, in the wrong hands—demon artifacts were swiped."

Goose bumps lifted all over me. I rubbed my arms. Nathan Trotman was one of the only councilors we trusted. He'd been a friend to us in the past, and if he was worried, there was definitely something to be worried about.

"But that's not all, apparently, a private collection was also hit and at least one piece was taken. You know, that old mansion on Davenport Road, the one that'd been empty for a long time? Well, someone from the family moved back in, and they reported it to the council in case what was taken was found during the investigation."

"So you don't know what kind of demon artifacts were taken?" Else asked.

"Nope," Wills said and then sipped her coffee. "But I'm not liking where this is going, honestly."

Mags leaned forward. "Are you going to help?"

Willow glanced at Warrick, who was scowling. "No, and I feel kind of guilty about it, honestly. But besides Trotman, this coven doesn't really have any friends on the council. I'm not prepared to stick my neck out for them only for them to shit on us later. And it's one thing to search for stolen items, it's another when people start going missing."

"Fuck feeling guilty. You don't owe those pricks a fucking thing, dove," Warrick rumbled.

Relic pulled out the chair beside me, sat, then turned to me and raised a brow. "So what about you?"

"What about me?" I asked.

"You were called by the mother, yes?"

It wasn't that I'd forgotten about it, but the way I understood it, you'd *know* when your task was starting, like a calling…

Shit.

Like the urge to go into the city in the middle of the night, like dreaming about a hideous demon when you ignored that urge. *Shit. Shit. Shit.* "I was, but I don't know what my task is yet." The grip in my gut sank deeper and twisted. And for once, it wasn't hunger.

Everyone went quiet.

I looked around the room, taking in their concerned faces. "What?"

Else took my hand. "We're just worried, that's all, pumpkin. You've been through so much already."

And I'd been so ill all my life that I wasn't half the witch my sisters were. I didn't have a specialty. I was barely proficient with the basics. I wasn't much better off now than I was when I was lying in that bed as weak as a kitten.

Relic draped his arm across the back of my chair. "You want someone to help, babe? I'm there. You need someone to bust some heads or break down a wall…" He winked. "Whatever you need, I'm your hound."

My belly chose that moment to growl. Two days was as long as I could hold out between feeds, and Luna was due with Ronan's blood any time. Embarrassingly, at the thought, my fangs extended. Unlike my wings, which I'd been practicing folding in and out every day, I still didn't have any kind of control over them.

Relic's eyes dipped to my mouth, not missing the sharp points before I lifted a hand to cover them. His eyes darkened before he shifted in his seat. "You need someone to feed on, babe? I'll happily offer up my vein as well."

Relic was a flirt, but he was a good guy. It was a kind offer, but talking about it felt way too intimate. Still, even as my face heated, my gaze darted to the thick vein at his throat before I could stop it. I quickly looked away. Nope.

Yes, Relic was hot, without a doubt, but I didn't want anyone else but Ronan.

"That won't be necessary," Luna said from the kitchen door.

I hadn't heard her arrive, but it looked as if Art had let her in.

She held up her bag containing the flask. "Special delivery."

I smiled. "Hey, Luna."

She smiled back.

I stood, but Relic grabbed my wrist. "The offer's still on the table, babe, yeah? Both."

I inclined my head. "Thanks. I have no idea what my task will be, but I do know I'll need help. I might take you up on that."

"Cool." His gaze cut to Warrick and he winked. "Getting closer every day to having a feisty witch of my own, brother."

Warrick shook his head. "I wouldn't bet on that." Something moved between the males, a knowing look I couldn't read.

Relic chuckled, then turned to my baby sister. "There's still hope," he said, and the flirt gave Mags a look that could melt every pair of panties in a twelve-mile radius.

Mags rolled her eyes, then blushed, because she was a female, and not blushing right then would go against the laws of nature. Bram, who was standing behind her, didn't move, didn't flinch. He did, however, bare his teeth, looking utterly feral, and slowly shook his head. Relic didn't miss this, but instead of concern, he grinned wider. "Or maybe not."

Mags frowned at Relic and turned to look up at her familiar, but Bram's expression was back to stoic, like the exchange hadn't happened.

I tried to act casual and not too desperate as I walked over to

Luna and she handed me Ronan's blood, but I was pretty sure I failed. "How is he?"

She looked over my shoulder at the massive hound sitting there, still flirting with my entire family, then back to me. "He's uh...getting there."

She didn't sound overly confident.

I looked at my feet, not wanting her to see my disappointment.

She took my hand and led me into the hallway and away from the others. "Is everything okay?"

"It's nothing."

"Please, Roe, you can talk to me."

I chewed my lip and met her lavender stare, which was so much like Ronan's. "I'm pretty sure I had the call, you know, for my task last night. I was just...I was hoping that I'd have Ronan with me. Things can get dangerous, but it's fine. I know he's not ready, and Relic's happy to help."

Luna's expression was unreadable. "The main thing is you staying safe. Whatever you need to make sure of that, you do it." Her gaze slid to the kitchen doorway, then back. "Even if that means you have to rely on that flirty hound."

"He really is a terrible flirt."

Luna chuckled. "I've honestly never seen anything like it." She sobered. "When will you start?"

"Tonight. And I haven't told my family yet. Because as much as they want to protect me from this, I have to do it. And I can't delay any longer."

She pressed the thermos into my hand.

Goddess, I missed Ronan.

"Hey," Luna said and looked a little uneasy. "Can I ask you a favor? It's a big one, and if you say no, I'll totally understand."

After what Luna and Ronan had done for me, no favor was too big. "Whatever it is, it's yours."

Chapter Thirteen

Ronan

I sat on the edge of the bed and shoved my fingers through my wet hair. I'd managed a shower, my second one. I stood and paced across the room and back. Feeling restless, like a caged animal.

And it wasn't because I'd been in this room for close to two weeks. No, I felt trapped by all the emotions still swirling around inside me. At least I had enough control over them now that I wasn't throwing up and shaking. I'd crawled off the floor two days ago; now, I needed to get it together enough to feed.

The problem was the idea of feeding made me sick to my stomach, unless I thought about feeding from Rose. I shoved my fingers back in my hair and strode across the room again, then back once more.

There was a light knock at the door.

"Come in," I called and turned as it opened. My sister walked in, and the scent that hit me had me staggering and grabbing for the wall. The thermos I filled for Rose was gripped in Luna's hand, and it wasn't empty. "What have you done?"

Luna shut the door behind her and walked in, and I hung on to the wall tighter, close to falling flat on the floor all over again.

"I didn't do anything, Rose did. I told her you needed to feed, and she offered." She sat on the edge of the bed and placed the thermos on the bedside table. "She wanted to do this for you because she cares about you."

I n-need you to know that…I'm in love with you, Ronan. N-not as a sister loves a brother…but as a female loves a male.

Her words had been echoing through my mind, they hadn't left. If she knew the truth of my past, would she still feel that way? Would she be disgusted by me? I disgusted myself.

"She needs you," Luna said when I hadn't replied.

I trembled, and my mouth watered as the scent of her blood filled my room now. "I can't go to her like this." Luna stood and moved to stand in front of me, and my gaze slid to the thermos again, then back to her. "I can't let her see me this way."

She took me in, and the softness bled from her eyes as she planted her hands on her hips. "Believe me, I know how hard this is, and I know this has been a whole lot harder for you, having it happen the way it did, but, brother, your mate needs you."

I rocked back at her words. *My mate.* "I'll only hurt her."

"She felt the call, Ronan. Her task has begun. She'll be out there facing all kinds of danger. You know she can't do that alone. Are you okay with another male taking your place? Doing your job as her mate? Another male at her side night and day?"

My muscles bunched tight, and my lips peeled back.

"Relic offered to help her, and Rose will have no choice but to accept. He even offered her his vein—"

A snarl exploded from me and I spun, my fist smashing into the wall, punching a hole right through it.

Rose was mine.

Mine.

"That's what I thought," Luna said and closed the space between us. She took my snarling face in her hands. "You can do this. I know you can. You're one of the strongest males I know. And *you* are exactly what Rose needs." Her eyes locked on mine. "Feed, then go to her. Go to your mate."

~

It was snowing lightly when I pulled up to Rose's family home. My gut was in knots, and if my heart could beat, I had a feeling it would be pounding in my chest. It wasn't a feeling I liked. Rose's blood had helped a lot. I couldn't even put it into words how I'd felt drinking it. A shiver moved through me.

I gripped the wheel, trying to focus, taking a moment to gather my control...

A familiar scent reached me.

Hound.

Relic. He was already here.

Luna had loaned me the car, since I'd torn the door off mine, and it took everything I had not to do it again. I got out, and any misgivings I had about coming here so soon vanished when Relic's scent grew stronger—followed by Rose's, unique and delicate. I growled as I strode to the door. I'd always used logic to navigate situations, and I tried to draw on that now, but logic was nowhere to be found.

I didn't knock, ignoring social etiquette completely, and opened the door, striding into the house. Rose's voice traveled from the kitchen, but even if it hadn't, I would have found her easily. She called to me. I was sure she didn't know she was doing it, but her scent, her voice—everything about her—called to something inside me.

I hadn't laid eyes on her in two weeks, and it felt as if an eternity had passed. Now, with her sweet scent surrounding me and the taste of her blood still on my tongue, I would have decimated anything that had gotten between us, and that included the hellhound with her.

My lips peeled back, the physical response involuntary, as was the snarl crawling up my throat as I rounded the corner.

And then I saw her.

My legs felt weak all over again.

I locked my knees as I took her in from head to toe.

Then she turned to me, her blue eyes hitting and locking on mine. They glowed with health. Her cheeks were pink, and her lips were fuller and deep red instead of bloodless. Rose shone with vitality.

I'd done that.

I'd fed her.

I'd nourished and restored her.

Emotions rioted inside me, and I took a step toward her before stopping myself, afraid of what I might do when I reached her. Things I'd never imagined before filled my head, raw and primal things.

I curled my fingers into a fist to stop from reaching for her. Rose, on the other hand, jolted out of her surprise and raced across the kitchen. I didn't know what she was going to do until she collided with me, pressing in tight, resting her head against my chest, and throwing her arms around my waist.

"You're here," she said.

After feeling nothing, being numb to touch for so long, this was a complete and total overload. All of it. The way her body, now soft and rounded, pressed against mine, her warmth. The affection she poured into me, I felt that too. My emotions were a volatile mix inside me, so potent and hot, I trembled from it. I wanted to pull away and greedily receive more of her affection at the same time.

"Ronan, brother, good to see you," Relic said, breaking through to me.

Somehow, I'd forgotten he was there. My arm banded around Rose, still clinging to me. My instincts raged inside me. I wanted to roar at him, to attack. But I fought for logic. Relic was a good male. He'd helped me, like his brothers had when I'd stumbled into their bar. So I fought my territorial instincts, because that's what they were, I recognized that much, and forced myself to say his name in greeting.

He studied me. "I was going to help Rose—"

"That won't be necessary. I'm here now." *Rose is mine, she is my female, and no one goes near her but me.* The voice in my head was utterly foreign, but also, without a doubt, part of me. A part not fully realized but growing stronger by the day. Luna was right —Rose was my mate. The bond I felt for her so strong, it had cut through the numbness, my cold, emotionless shell, and drawn me to her, even when I hadn't known how to interpret what I was feeling.

My instincts had brought me back to her time and again.

Relic grinned for some unknown reason and crossed his arms. "Yeah, brother, you are. And I'm fucking pleased to see it." He strode to me and gave me a chin lift. "You need help with anything, I'm here." Then he walked out.

Rose still held me, and she was looking up. Our eyes met, and I was held in place, instantly drawn so deep I wasn't sure how I'd ever surface or if I wanted to. My gaze dipped to her red lips and mine tingled. A strong urge filled me, roaring at me to lower my mouth to hers and touch, like I had while I'd held her in my arms —the night I was supposed to take her life.

"You're here," she said again, voice soft, so soft, my skin tingled from the sound of it.

"Yes." I quickly released her. It was the only way to gather my control, to lock down the wild emotions clamoring for dominance inside me. The feel of her pressed against me was too much, too soon—not muted, not numb. "You look..." There were no words to articulate what I was feeling at that moment, at seeing her like this. It was impossible.

I was having enough trouble thinking clearly as it was. I couldn't think if she was touching me.

"I've been so worried about you," she said, lifting her hands as if she were going to touch me again, then quickly lowered them.

I stuffed my hands in my pockets so I didn't reach for her and pull her back against me. "Luna said you might know what your task entails?" I didn't want to talk about the last two weeks, I couldn't, not with Rose, not with anyone.

Her eyes were wide and hadn't left me. I wish I understood what I saw in her eyes, but I didn't. I felt all these things, but that didn't mean I could name them or fully understand them yet.

She chewed her lip and straightened. "Well, not really. I know where I need to go, but not what any of it means. Not yet."

Her voice had a slight huskiness to it that sent an indescribable sensation shooting up my spine.

"That's why Relic was here. He helped Iris at the beginning of her task, and I wasn't sure if you'd be able to..." Her voice trailed off. "If you'd even want to—"

"Whatever this task brings, Rose, I'll be the one to help you, not Relic." My voice was calm, but inside I was roaring and snarling. I wanted to go after Relic and make sure he understood that Rose was mine, whether it was logical or not, and the only reason I hadn't was my need to be near Rose. Just the thought of her with him, with any male, had the ability to drive me to insanity. Which was why I couldn't stop the next words that spilled from my mouth. "And you will turn down any other male that offers, because no one can protect you the way I can." My voice sounded rough, harsh to my own ears, but there was no holding it back. "No one."

Rose

My heart pounded at the fierceness in his violet eyes. Did he understand what he was feeling? Did he have any idea how much of it radiated from him now? The violence I felt when he walked into the kitchen and saw Relic beside me, the possessiveness, then and now; it saturated the room.

I was glad my family wasn't here right now. Neither of us needed an audience.

"I won't ask anyone else," I said, because that fierceness was still there, so bright and wild. I could literally feel him clinging to the edges of his control. His gaze kept darting to the door Relic had walked through, like he wanted to charge after the hound. "I only need you with me, Ronan," I said, and my voice shook. Not from fear. Never that. But because I felt what he was feeling, or at least I thought that's what was happening. This was Ronan, the male who had been there for me for months. He was that same male but also irrevocably changed.

I remembered what Luna said, how Ronan would be struggling, that he could behave in ways that were extreme or unpredictable. That his impulse control wouldn't be so great. So as much as I wanted to be close to him, I forced myself to keep some distance. The last thing I wanted was to make this harder for him. And being in the same room with him now, there was no doubt in my mind he was struggling.

His gaze moved over me, and I fought back a shiver when his eyes came back to mine, because that once emotionless stare was communicating a whole lot of emotion now.

"Where are we going tonight?" he finally asked, strain in every word.

"An old mansion on Davenport Road." After Willow told us about demon artifacts being stolen and my reaction to it, I knew where I needed to go. The first location that was hit, the private residence. "There have been two robberies in the last few weeks, both times demon artifacts were taken. And from what I understand, powerful ones. I'm almost certain my task has something to do with those robberies. I don't know what kind of artifacts they are or what they can do, but I think that's a good place to start."

"So you'll need undetected access to both of these places?" he said.

Goddess, that stare, the way it made me feel. My belly swirled. Would I ever get used to it, how different it was now? Hot, not cold. Full of fire. "Ideally, yes."

He cocked his head. "That won't be a problem."

This whole thing was so weird. He was being weird. I was being weird. Neither of us knew how to be around the other all of a sudden. "Excellent. Shall we go?"

I sounded like I was talking to a stranger. Not the person I was most comfortable in the world with. I hated this.

We headed for the door. I was so glad no one had come home. Mom would worry, and Mags would get pissed at the mother all over again, and Else would try to feed me a bunch of immune-boosting elixirs that tasted horrible, because I was *still recovering*. I was stronger and healthier than I'd been in my entire life. But after so many years of being sick, it was hard for my family to believe I was okay, to let go, and finally stop worrying.

I reached for the front door handle, and Ronan stopped me. "You're not dressed warmly enough. You need a coat and hat, some gloves."

"Oh, right." I was in such a hurry to leave, I'd momentarily forgotten it was cold as hell outside.

I pulled a woolen hat on and grabbed one of Mag's coats, shoving that on as well. I didn't own any myself, I'd stopped going outside in winter several years ago, I'd always been too frail, so I grabbed an old pair of Iris's gloves she'd left here as well. I smiled and turned for the door once more.

Again, Ronan stopped me.

This time he turned me to him, grabbed the lapels of my jacket, and pulled them around me before he proceeded to do up the buttons. I stood there in shock. When he finished, he looked down at me, and my knees wobbled at the expression on his face.

"Better," he said gruffly.

"Thank you.

He dipped his chin, opened the door, and led me outside into the light snow.

Chapter Fourteen

Rose

The house was on the edge of town. A huge two-story place painted a deep gray, and some of the paint was chipping. The garden was overgrown, but it was easy to see it would've been beautiful at one time. One of the tall iron gates was open, the other side swinging drunkenly in the chill breeze.

Ronan tilted his head back and scented the air. "Not witch."

"I think he's a shifter of some kind. I'm not entirely sure. I did some research earlier today. This house has been in the same family for one hundred and fifty years. They're wealthy. The original owner was an opera singer. She sang all over the country, made a lot of money, and married a wealthy male. A happy marriage by all accounts. It was empty for a long time, but from what I understand, someone in the family recently moved back."

"That explains why the house is so rundown."

I glanced up at the massive house and hugged myself. "Whoever lives there now has to be lonely living in that big house all on their own."

Ronan looked from me to the house and back. "Yes."

Could the conversation be more stilted? I rubbed my hands together and smiled, pretending we weren't acting like total freaking strangers. "So how do we do this?"

"Do you remember me carrying you through the forest the night the mother called you?"

"It's a little hazy to be honest."

His features shifted into an expression I'd never seen on him. I wasn't sure what emotion I was looking at right then. "If I use my powers, no one will see us. It'll be as if we're not there."

A memory of Ronan covered in blood filled my head, the rage in his eyes. That was when the walls began to crack, wasn't it? In that field. I'd never seen him look like that before. He'd said his powers couldn't work in that field, and he'd killed the demons coming for me, a lot of them. "You were holding me, and you ran through the forest to get me back to the car."

"Yes." His fingers curled into a tight fist, but his expression remained the same. "And on the way in, I used my powers to conceal us."

That's right. He'd dressed me and carried me through the snowy forest. "Everything looked kind of like it was underwater."

He nodded, his gaze burning hot, so hot I wasn't sure how he hadn't burned himself out from all I saw in his eyes. "You remember?"

"Some of it."

"So you know I'll keep you safe?"

That was the second time he'd said something like that. "Yes, of course. I trust you, Ronan. I know you won't let anything bad happen to me."

His eyes darkened. "Never." He took my hand and headed toward the gates.

The air around us changed before we got there, becoming a little distorted. He'd lifted a block of some kind to conceal us. I could feel it hovering around us, tingling over my skin.

It was dark and shadowy, and I shivered as we reached the door. "This place gives me the creeps." I looked around. "So how do we get in?" Ronan didn't slow, he carried on walking, towing me along behind him—and walked *right through the door*. I drew back, pulling on his hand, looking down at his as he gripped mine tighter.

The rest of him was already gone, on the other side of that massive wooden door.

Holy shit.

Sucking in a sharp breath, I kept walking, following him through it to the other side. He turned to me, and I stared at him in shock. "We just walked through that door," I whispered. "*Through it*, Ronan."

"Yes, we did," he said, taking in our surroundings. "And you don't have to whisper. No one will hear us."

"This is insane. Are all dhampir as powerful as you?"

Ronan tilted his head to the side, the move somehow demonic, pure predator. *That's because he's half vampire.* Before he regained his emotions, Ronan had coldly explained how he'd beaten and brutally ripped out a hellhound's tongue, and I was in no doubt, with emotion in the mix, he'd just become far more dangerous.

"The only other dhampir I know is my sister, and yes, she is very powerful, though not as strong as me." He glanced around the room again. "Where shall we begin?"

A shuffling sound came from above us. A male walked onto the landing, then made his way down the stairs. My instincts told me to hide, but Ronan stood unmoving as the male took each step.

"Reptile," Ronan said, not even trying to lower his voice. "And possibly something else as well."

I edged in behind him, feeling exposed and so freaking wrong. Two weeks ago, I'd barely left my house, my bed, and now I was out at night with Ronan, breaking into some guy's house to investigate a robbery.

"Maybe he's an older relative? You know, this kind of feels like a scene from one of the books you read me," I whispered, gripping his hand tight and peering around his arm.

Ronan turned from the grizzled-looking male as he continued to make slow progress down the stairs. His lips twitched. Not a smile, not even close, but his eyes brightened. "You're still whispering."

Was he actually amused? I forced myself to step out from behind him and straightened. "I forgot."

"Shall we start upstairs?"

"Okay," I whispered.

His lips twitched again as he gripped my hand tighter and headed for the staircase. The elderly male passed by us without batting an eyelid. God, so weird. Ronan led me to the top floor, and we stared down a long hall. It had dark wood wall panels and a long red, black, and gold carpet that ran the length of it. Portraits had been hung between each of the many closed doors.

I didn't know what it was, but the creepiness factor rose like ten notches. "Do you feel that?" I said.

"What?"

"Like someone walked over your grave. Something up here gives me goose bumps and not the good kind."

"There's a good kind?"

I looked up at him in surprise. "You've never had goose bumps?"

"I'm not sure."

"It's when your skin gets all tingly and tiny bumps lift all over your skin. It can feel kind of nice, depending on the circumstances."

"Then yes, I have experienced it." His stare stayed intense.

I wanted to ask when, but the way he was looking at me, I was having trouble thinking.

"We'll start here," he said, tearing his gaze from mine and moving to the first door.

"Should we split up?"

"No," he said, in a way that said it wasn't open for discussion.

We walked in and Ronan turned on the light.

"Won't he see that if he comes up here?"

"No."

Okay, Ronan was *seriously* powerful. All the time he'd been visiting me, he'd barely ever talked about himself. I'd asked questions and he'd given me short answers and changed the subject, and after talking to Luna, I knew why. My heart clenched, and I gripped his hand tighter at the thought of what he must have been through.

"There's nothing in here." He led me to the closet and opened the door.

It was empty. A creaking sound came from downstairs, like hinges that needed oiling. I listened, but the current owner of the house stayed downstairs.

We made our way along the hall, searching the rooms until there were only two left. Ronan pushed one of the doors open and we stepped in. This bedroom was being used. There were two large dressers and a massive bed, a desk, and a huge freestanding wooden wardrobe. The sheets were thrown back, the bed unmade. There was a large mirror on the other side of the room, and I walked over to check it out. It was the perfect size to hide something behind. Like a safe or whatever? I felt around, but it was secured to the wall firmly. "Ouch." There was a sharp piece on the edge, and I'd cut my finger. I sucked on it...

The glass rippled.

I turned back and blinked several times. But it kept rippling. My ears felt blocked and there was pressure behind my eyes.

A face appeared in front of me. I jumped and spun around, but no one stood behind me. I turned back to the mirror.

Ronan rushed over. "What is it?"

"The old man, the one from downstairs, he's right there..." My voice trailed off when his face flashed from old and wrinkled to young and handsome. It flickered back and forth between the two faces.

"Rose?"

"You can't see that?"

"See what?" Ronan's voice turned urgent.

"I think...I think I'm having some kind of vision." The faces kept flickering. "Two faces, one young and one old, the man downstairs," I started. "Blood. There's blood covering them, both of them. Coating their skin, their hair." Then it was gone.

I stumbled back, and Ronan grabbed me, steadying me. He turned me to him, a look of concern covering his face. Something I'd never seen from Ronan before.

"Are you okay? Rose? Look at me."

I looked up at him, my heart pounding. "Y-yes...I'm fine. I'm not sure what happened, but I'm okay."

Ronan's nostrils flared, and he took my hand. "You're bleeding."

"I cut myself on the edge of the mirror." I lifted my finger, and Ronan's gaze locked on it. His nostrils flared again, and he quickly looked down, but not before I saw the point of one of his fangs extend past his upper lip. My blood, it was affecting him.

I quickly sucked it again, and his head shot up, that stare locking on my mouth. He made a strange rough sound that vibrated through his chest before he cleared his throat. "What do you think it meant? What you saw? Has anything like that ever happened before?"

My skin felt tight and tingly, and I forced my eyes to stay on his and not look at his mouth again. "I have no idea what that was. Nothing like that's ever happened to me before."

"Are you feeling steady enough to walk?" he asked, looking as if he were about to pick me up.

"I'm absolutely fine. All better."

He gave me a stiff nod and we got back to searching the room.

We poked around a bit more, but there was nothing of interest here. This obviously wasn't where he kept his collection. Ronan kept that firm grip on my hand and led me to the final door. Like the other rooms, there was nothing of interest.

We made our way back downstairs. The elderly male was in the living room now, the TV on. He had a tray in front of him, eating his dinner, by the looks of it. It was sloppy looking, pale, like uncooked sausage links but without the links. "What the hell is he eating?"

"Intestines," Ronan said and moved closer to the other male. He scented the air. "Demon."

"What?" It was a struggle, but I managed not to gag.

Ronan walked from the room, pulling me along with him. He paused, looked around the big room, then headed for the door under the stairs. The hinges creaked loudly when he opened it.

"Why didn't you just walk through?"

"Because I wanted to see if this door was the one we'd heard him opening when we were upstairs."

"Good thinking." A disgusting smell hit me instantly: decay. Most definitely decay. I threw a hand over my mouth. "Oh god."

Ronan clicked on the light, and it revealed steep stairs to the basement. "Stay behind me," he said, and we made our way down. The smell grew stronger with every step, and it was so much harder not to gag. We reached the bottom and Ronan turned on another light.

And thank the goddess for Ronan's power because there was no holding in my shriek of alarm. The room was opulent. Dark wooden shelves lined the walls, displaying a collection of demon artifacts and other things. Skulls that were obviously demon. Jars with disgusting *things* floating in them. There was an expensive-looking rug on the floor, an antique lead lamp that had to be worth a lot, and a worn leather chair to one side with a drinks tray beside it.

Someone had obviously been sitting there earlier because there was a glass with a little bit of amber liquid still in it, the ice not completely melted. There was only one way in or out that I could see, the door we'd walked through.

Then we both turned back to the horror in the middle of the room. I'd been trying to avoid looking at it again.

A male demon was strung up in the center of the room, his head hanging to the side, a gag across his mouth. His skin was gray, and his stomach was sliced down the middle, his innards spilling out of his body.

"I assume this is where the intestines came from?" I'd never seen anything so horrific in my life.

"Yes," Ronan said.

"He's eating demons?"

"It appears that way."

I glanced at Ronan. His face and voice were emotionless, like the old Ronan, like nothing had changed. I wasn't sure what to make of it. "Why would he do this?" I searched the room for clues, something. But there was nothing else. "This has to be some kind of ritual, right? But for what? And why hasn't this demon turned to ash?"

Ronan clenched his jaw, then his grip on my hand grew tighter. And just like that, the new Ronan was back. "I have no idea. I've never seen a demon being held in this way before. And he hasn't turned to ash yet because he's still alive."

"What?" I spun back, and the demon's eyes were wide open, watching us. "How can he still be alive after that?"

"Unless you remove their heads, they don't die."

I knew this, but still, seeing it with my own eyes was something else. "We should help him. This is cruel."

"This is a venious demon." He motioned to its hands. "They poison their victims with their venomous claws, causing paralysis, so they can then eat their victims alive. It's a slow, agonizing, and horrific way to die. The venious are sadistic, demented, pure evil."

I swallowed loudly in the quiet room. "I think we'll just leave him there then."

"That would be wise."

I took in the room again. "So is the guy upstairs a monster as well, just a different kind?"

"It appears that way."

Wonderful.

I forced myself to take pictures of the room with my phone, not easy when Ronan was still holding my hand. But he obviously needed to have some kind of physical contact with me for his power to work on both of us. Somehow, I managed it, snapping all the pictures I needed.

Ronan led me back upstairs, and we did a quick search of the rest of the house. We didn't find anything else, thank god. I didn't think I could handle much more after the gruesome sight in the basement.

We were about to leave when a shout came from the living room. Ronan changed directions, leading us back toward the demon-eating old male who had been enjoying some intestines while he watched his favorite show.

But when we rounded the corner, there was a whole other kind of show taking place. A full-on horror show.

"What...what is that?" My stomach churned.

"He's shedding."

"Shedding?" Then I watched as the elderly male literally peeled his skin and flesh from his naked body. "Oh, goddess. That is..." I wretched. "Disgusting. Why is he doing that?"

"I assume because his outer skin has aged more than he'd like."

There was a wet thud as the old skin hit the hardwood floor, then the bloody, slimy body that it had encased straightened. Using his hands to sluice all that muck from his face, then shoving back wet hair, he looked down at the mess on the floor. "Fuck," he muttered as he stepped out of the pile of skin.

A male now stood there, taller than before, muscled, and definitely younger, a lot younger. I could tell even with all the blood and gore on his fresh new skin. "My vision. That's it. Him, like that. Old, then young."

"You're sure?" Ronan asked, taking in the other male.

"Yes, I'm positive of it. Why would I have a vision of this?"

"I don't know."

This was incredibly frustrating. "Do you think he needs to eat demon organs to bring on this...shedding?" I asked, eyeing the naked guy across the room.

"It would seem so."

I'd never seen one before, a naked male, that is. This guy was attractive, despite the blood, which felt weird to notice after what I'd just seen him do, but there you go. The male cursed again, then strode from the room.

A low kind of growling sound came from Ronan, and I spun back. He was watching the male walk away as well, and he didn't look happy. The shower came on in a different part of the house.

"I think we need to come back and talk to him," I said. "We need to know what was stolen. I'm not sure how else we can find out."

Ronan's jaw clenched. "We'll come back in the morning and talk to him then."

Ronan led us back across the room and *through the door*. He strode across the yard and out the iron gates and didn't let my hand go until we were back at the car.

I frowned and looked around us. "Everything still looks all wavy. Your power didn't drop."

Ronan unlocked the car and walked back to the passenger side. "No. I haven't dropped it yet."

"But you let go of my hand. How is your power still surrounding me?"

He opened the door and motioned for me to get in. "I don't need to make physical contact for my power to work on others," he said.

"Oh." *Oh.* I quickly got in. Ronan had held my hand the entire time, refusing to let me go for even a moment.

My belly grew warm, and I bit my lip to hide my smile as he climbed in beside me and started the car.

Chapter Fifteen

Ronan

The car was engulfed in silence when I pulled up outside Rose's house and turned off the engine. She turned to me, cheeks pink, eyes bright. She looked so different, but she was still the same female, and looking at her now, every instinct inside me roared for me to get closer to her.

I'd been fighting myself since I walked into the house earlier, and it hadn't gotten any easier. No, the gnawing, gripping pull toward her had only increased. I'd almost succumbed in that house. The scent of her blood had pushed me closer to the edge.

"So...here we are," she said.

I could hear her heart beating faster, her blood rushing through her veins, and her breath bursting past her lips as she looked over at me.

"Yes," I said. "We are."

Her hands were twisted together in her lap. "Thanks for tonight, Ronan. For coming with me to that house."

For some reason, when she said my name now, my gut

clenched, and my skin heated all over. "You don't need to thank me. I wanted to." She licked her lips, and my groin grew heavy.

"You did?"

"If anyone else had gone with you, I would have hurt them," I said, the truth falling from my mouth. My gaze dropped to hers. "Why are your lips so shiny?" I couldn't stop looking at them.

She blinked, then again. "I'm wearing lip gloss." She licked them again, and I got another wash of heat across my skin. "Are you telling me you would've tried to hurt Relic?"

"Yes." Lip gloss. I liked the way it looked. I also liked her lips without it.

Her eyes widened. Was that the wrong thing to say? I had all these conflicting thoughts and emotions inside me, but I didn't know which I should allow to take the lead, which I should resist, and which ones I should allow to guide my actions and the things I said.

"But it's Relic."

"Yes," I said, dragging my gaze back to hers, not sure why she was telling me something I already knew.

Concern transformed her features; I was more than familiar with that emotion. I'd seen it in my sister's eyes many times over the last couple of weeks. "He's our friend, Ronan. I'd hate if you two fought, or if you got hurt."

She was worried for me, and she also thought I was too weak to fight the hound. I didn't like the feeling that accompanied that thought, not at all. "You don't think I'm strong enough to protect you?" I asked, and my voice had changed, a grittiness to it now.

"Yes, of course I do. I just, I don't like the thought of you getting hurt—"

"I have bested him in the pit, Rose, more than once." The need to tell her of my conquests in the clubhouse's fighting pit seemed extremely important. I had to make her understand how strong I was. That Relic wasn't a better choice. A growl tried to crawl up my throat. "We are evenly matched. I assure you, I wouldn't let him hurt me. I've been in many battles, Rose. I've killed a lot of demons, and I've fought and bested other creatures. I'm strong and muscled. I'm a skilled fighter..." I stopped, my words trailing off at the look on Rose's face. I couldn't decipher it.

"I believe you, Ronan. I do."

I realized I sounded like one of the hounds at the bar when they were working at charming females into their beds. My face heated and I was having trouble meeting her eyes. "I'm...I'm not sure why I said that."

Her hand covered mine and tiny zaps fired through my veins. My gaze sliced to hers.

"You want to protect me," she said softly, and the feeling she'd described as goose bumps, I felt them. At the back of my neck, over my scalp.

"Yes, I do. And I will." The blue of her eyes had me transfixed. She licked her lips for the third time, and every muscle in my body tightened.

"I know how strong you are, Ronan. I promise you that." She shifted in her seat. "And I think it bears repeating, but I want you with me during this task. I don't want anyone else."

The heavy weight between my legs throbbed, now painfully tight against the zipper of my trousers. Her lips were so dark and plump and shiny. Kissing, when I thought about doing it with Rose, didn't make me want to recoil. No, it made my mouth water and my palms itch to reach for her. What would her lip gloss taste like?

The car was silent again as we stared at each other. My skin prickled again. "Do you feel that?" I asked.

"What?"

"My skin feels tingly, and there's this...this electricity in the air around us," I said. "I've never felt anything like it."

"I feel it too," she said and bit her lower lip. "And I've never felt anything like it before either."

I turned, searching the car, looking into the back seat, out the windows. "What is it?"

"It's you and me. It's chemistry," she said, her cheeks growing pinker.

"I don't understand."

"You like being with me, yes?"

"Yes."

"And I like being with you." She licked her lips a fourth time, and a low groan slipped out before I could stop it. Her throat worked, and she lowered her eyes before they came back to mine. "That's what you can feel."

"Is it?"

She nodded, but I still didn't understand. Usually, I would keep questioning her until I did, but this time I didn't. I couldn't explain it, but my gut was telling me to stop. So I did.

She opened the car door, and I managed to stop myself from reaching for her.

"I'll see you in the morning?" she said and climbed out.

"You will."

"Bye, Ronan." Then she shut the door and walked into the house.

I turned on the engine and backed out, but then I pulled over on the side of the street, shoved my door open, and using my power to conceal the car and me, I walked in after her.

I couldn't leave. Luna said Rose was my mate. Mates should be together. I'd seen enough of them to know that. Did Rose know we were mates? Did she feel this awful sensation in the pit of her stomach when we were apart?

The house was quiet when I walked in.

Everyone was in bed. All except Rose's mother. Rose was bidding her good night. She jogged up the stairs and I followed her. Should I let her know I was there? But if she didn't feel the same pull as me, to be together all the time, would she send me away? I didn't want to leave.

She walked into her room and shut the door. I followed.

Rose disappeared into the bathroom, and I walked in after her. She gripped the edge of the basin and smiled wide. I couldn't look away from her. Why was she smiling like that? Was it something her mother said? Or something else?

With a little huff of breath, she straightened and pulled her sweater over her head, then her shirt, followed by a tight band of fabric she wore under it. I froze in place. My eyes locked on her pale skin. She shoved down her jeans, and I curled my fingers into fists at my side.

She reached back and undid the scrap of fabric that covered her breasts and tossed it aside, before hooking her thumbs in her underwear and shoving them down.

Rose stood naked in front of the mirror.

This was wrong.

I shouldn't be here.

But I couldn't make myself move. The heavy weight behind my zipper became a steel rod in my trousers and pulsed hard. I squeezed it without thought and shuddered. I didn't usually touch it, not like this. But it ached, and the drive to ease it was impossible to ignore. I sucked in an involuntary breath, even though I didn't need to breathe.

High on her back, between her shoulder blades, her wings unfurled, pearlescent, and shimmery, delicate and gossamer fine. Beautiful. Rose, her wings, her sleek body, her curved hips, her breasts, and her ass, as Relic and the hounds would call it, every part of her was beautiful.

I recognized beauty now. Easily, when it came to Rose. It was impossible to look away. I didn't want to.

My balls throbbed and my shaft pulsed hard. I squeezed harder and groaned—

Rose turned, and my gaze dipped. Her nipples were tight and pointed. Her stomach soft and creamy. I looked lower. Between her thighs was smooth and delicate looking. I hissed.

Wrong. This was wrong.

I shouldn't be here. I hissed again, releasing the grip I had on my stiff flesh.

Stumbling back, I rushed from the bathroom and strode from her room, down the stairs, and back to my car.

~

I parked outside the clubhouse. Most of the bikes were put away for the winter, but to the outside world, the hellhounds looked like a human motorcycle club.

Shaking, I got out of my car and strode inside. I couldn't bring myself to go back to the knight's compound. The last two weeks had been hell. I couldn't spend another minute in that room, and I didn't want my sister to see me like this. At least here, the hounds could lock me away if necessary. Because the driving need inside me kept growing, and I wasn't sure I could stop myself from going back to Rose, from walking into her room again when it was wrong.

I thrust my fingers through my hair.

"Yo, Ronan," Relic called.

I turned as he strode toward me but kept walking. The door down to the den was always locked, and I keyed in the combination and opened the door. The cavern they'd dug down here was lit by wall sconces, and I headed for the room they'd given me to use when I was here.

"Ronan, brother," Relic called, jogging up behind me. "What's going on?"

I pulled the door to my room open and walked in and Relic followed. I paced across the room and back. "You need to lock me down," I gritted through clenched teeth. My fangs had extended and my gut was in knots. That boulder was back and bigger than ever.

"Why don't you tell me what's going on, then we'll decide if you need to be locked down?" He crossed his arms and watched me pace the room.

I wasn't sure he could help me. Hounds were almost as emotionless as I'd been, though Relic was somewhat different. He seemed more evolved than a lot of his brothers. I didn't know if that were true or if he was just better at mimicking the emotions of others. Something a lot of the hounds had learned to do while on Earth to fit in. I turned to him. I needed help, now, before I got in my car and drove back to Rose's house.

"When I saw you with Rose, I wanted to hurt you," I said.

"I'm aware."

"You need to stay away from her." There was an unmistakable snarl to my voice.

"She's yours, brother. I'm not gonna touch your female." He frowned. "What's going on, Ronan?"

I believed him. He wouldn't touch her, but that didn't calm the wildfire raging inside me. I shoved my fingers through my hair. "Something's...wrong with me," I bit out. I had no idea where to start. These males talked freely about such things, I'd heard them numerous times. Until I came here, I hadn't had the words. Why would I? I hadn't felt the things they'd described. I did now, though, so for Relic to help me, I needed to use their words.

"Okay," Relic said. "But I'm gonna need you to be more specific."

I planted my hands on my hips, and visions of Rose, her body, naked, beautiful, flashed through my head. Her image had been burned into my brain. Every time I closed my eyes from here on out, I'd see her. "I saw Rose naked."

Relic didn't move a muscle. "I'm not seeing your problem."

I shoved my fingers through my hair again. "It was wrong. She didn't know I was there. I saw her and I knew it was wrong to do that, to look at her while she was like that, but I...I liked it. I wanted to keep looking at her." I couldn't meet Relic's stare. "I want to go back and look at her again."

"That's normal, brother. She's your female. Of course you want to want to look at her like that."

He didn't understand. "Not only look. I got this feeling in my stomach, and my skin grew hot, and I...I wanted to...touch her as well. I've never felt anything like it."

His brows snapped together. "You've never felt it before?"

"No."

"You've had sex before, though, right?"

"Yes, but not with a female." Though, I'd barely registered what was happening when I was with Azel. I was numb, switched off, and usually starving, trying to feed as fast as I could before he stopped me.

"Did you get off?"

"Get off?" I had no idea what he was talking about.

"Did you come?"

"Where?"

His brows dropped lower. "Did you ejaculate?"

I flinched. I knew what that was, but I had never experienced it myself. "No."

His brows lowered. "Have you ever done it?"

"No."

Relic's chin jerked back. "Fuck." He scratched his jaw. "Right, well, what you're feeling, my brother, is lust. Rose is your female. You saw her naked and your dick got hard, yes?"

I swallowed, the sound seeming loud in the room. "Yes."

"You've had a hard dick before, though?"

"Yes."

"The reason it happened with Rose is because you want inside your female, Ronan. It's only natural for you to want her like that. It's not anything to freak out about. It's not dirty or wrong. Okay, yeah, maybe watching her when she doesn't know you're there, isn't so cool. Just don't do it again, at least not unless she's into it." He grinned. "The good thing is, I know how you can get your shit back under control."

My palms grew sweaty. "How?"

"You need to get yourself off, brother. Which is something else that's totally normal. We all do it. Stroke your dick until you come. It feels fucking good, and it'll take the edge off until you and your female work out your situation."

I wasn't sure what there was to work out. Yes, Luna said Rose was my mate, but that didn't mean Rose would want that. And just because I felt this connection to her didn't mean she felt it as well.

Relic opened the door. "I'm gonna leave you to it. But if you're really worried, come get me and I'll lock you down."

I inclined my head because my throat felt too tight to speak, and Relic left.

Could I do what he suggested? I'd never tried. Without my emotions, I'd never felt this way. It had been muted like everything else physical. I occasionally got hard while feeding and woke that way some mornings, yes, but from what I understood, that was something most males experienced. I ignored it and it went away.

It wasn't going away now, and this felt different from those times. I strode to the bathroom and splashed cold water on my face, then gripped the edge of the countertop, squeezing my eyes closed. Rose. Her beautiful eyes, her laugh, her lips. Her breasts and those cherry-colored nipples—the place between her thighs.

My cock throbbed harder. So hard, I winced.

I shoved my hand inside my pants, desperate to ease the growing pain.

It wasn't enough. My pants were too tight, they made it hurt more. I yanked off my jacket, then tore off my shirt and tossed it aside. My skin had always been cool, but not anymore, and right now, it was hot and damp with sweat. Hissing, I undid my pants and slid down the zipper. My briefs were tented, a damp patch on the fabric over the head of my erection.

I didn't think I could do what Relic said, but I needed to get my clothes off because they were making it worse. I kicked off my shoes and socks and pants, then hissed again as I pulled the elastic of my briefs over my stiff length and shoved them down as well. It jutted straight out. I'd never been like this. I'd seen myself hard. But not like this. I was longer and thicker than I'd ever been. The skin was darker, the veins more prominent, the head, wide and blunt and slick with a fluid that was leaking out.

Maybe the shower would help?

I switched it on, leaving it cold, and stepped in. It did nothing. The cold didn't really affect me, but I hoped this time it might with how heated my skin felt. I was about to get back out, go to Relic and tell him to lock me down, but as I turned, my stiff flesh bobbed and slapped into my stomach. My hand automatically reached down to grip it, and as soon as my fist curled around it, I groaned. Then I squeezed, needing more of that pressure.

It helped the ache a little, so I did it again, and my knees nearly buckled. I had the sudden urge to thrust my hips, and it was so strong I couldn't resist. I needed friction. *I needed it.* I gripped my shaft and slid my fist along it from root to tip, and then I did it again. It did feel good. Really good. So I kept on doing it.

The water eased my strokes, but not enough, so I lathered my hand with soap and stroked again. Images of Rose filled my head once more, and my hips thrust forward, forcing my cock through my fist faster.

The hounds talked about the place between a female's thighs, her pussy, they called it. How good it felt to slide their...*cocks* inside and...and fuck. Those were the words they liked to use. I was fucking my fist, wasn't I? That's what I was doing. What would Rose's pussy feel like around my cock instead of my fist? My balls tightened at the thought, making me moan low.

Then an image of her naked body filled my head again, of her lying back on the bed, of her spreading her thighs wide and beckoning me to lie between them.

"Oh, fuck." My cock pulsed in my fist, sensation shooting down my spine, down my shaft. I growled and groaned as I ejaculated against the shower tile, fucking my fist until I had nothing left, gasping for breath, for oxygen I didn't even need.

And the whole time, Rose was with me, her beautiful face filling my head.

Mine, roared through me.

She was mine.

Chapter Sixteen

Rose

Iris plonked down on the couch beside me as Willow walked in from the kitchen, carrying a mug of coffee. Magnolia sat in the chair opposite us, and she was staring out the window toward Bram's treehouse.

"Where's Bram today?" Iris asked, not missing the look on our baby sister's face.

"He had to work." She turned back to us. "He left last night and will probably be gone a couple days."

Wills tucked her legs up on the couch. "So what does he actually do? I don't think I've ever gotten a straight answer out of him about it."

Mags sat back in her chair. "Security of some kind, but he won't even go into details with me." It was obvious that this was a sore point between them. "Whatever he's doing, I think it's dangerous, even though he says it's not. He comes back with bruises and cuts sometimes. And he's all quiet and broody for a couple days. He said he isn't allowed to talk about it. I don't know

137

who he's working for, but I assume it's someone important." She chewed her thumbnail and looked back out the window.

This was hurting her. Mags and Bram told each other everything. Being left out of such a big part of his life wasn't sitting well with my baby sister, and I didn't blame her.

"I'm sure he'd tell you if he could," I said.

She shrugged. "I'm not so sure. He's been...different ever since Willow's trial, since the battle in the cemetery. Things between us have been...strained."

It probably had something to do with the way Bram felt about Mags, and that, as far as we could tell, she had only ever seen him as her best friend. Mags was still working through that awful day in the cemetery and what led up to it. We'd almost lost her during that time, and as a result, she'd changed irrevocably. She was still struggling with it all. I'd tried to get her to open up to me, but she refused, keeping it all bottled up inside.

Magnolia was full of rage and didn't know what to do with it, which meant she often directed it at the wrong people.

"I'm sure you two can figure it out. You and Bram have always been inseparable. If you tell him how you're feeling—"

"I have." Her gaze flicked back to us, but she didn't elaborate. "How's Ren?" she asked Wills, changing the subject. "He's answered a couple of my texts, but he's still keeping me and Bram at arm's length." Ren, Bram, and Mags were all close in age. They'd always hung out together. Yes, he was Willow's familiar, but he was also one of their best friends.

Wills sipped her coffee. "I spent time with him last night. He came by the clubhouse, we made dinner together and he hung out with Warrick and some of the other hounds." She smiled, but there was pain there. "He's struggling, but at least now he's letting me be there for him. He won't talk about what happened, but he's trying."

"That's a massive improvement," Iris said.

"It is," Wills said. "Hopefully, we'll be able to get him back with all of us soon. Hanging with the family again."

We all wanted that.

"How about you, Roe?" Wills asked. "Relic mentioned what happened yesterday. So you know what your task is?"

"I think so." We weren't allowed help from our families or coven, but we could talk about it. "The robberies, the missing demon artifacts? I'm almost positive it has something to do with that."

Willow sat forward. "Really? Well, shit. Have you told Mom?"

"No, and I'm not going to. Well, for as long as I can get away with it, anyway. She's still so worried about me, but honestly, I've never felt so strong. Nothing I say will convince her otherwise, though."

She sipped her coffee. "You know, I haven't turned Trotman's offer down yet, to investigate those robberies...what if I don't?"

"Wills, you can't help me."

"I know, and I won't, but the last thing you need, is whoever the council has investigating the case now, in your way while you're figuring this all out. If I agree, Trotman will call them off, and it won't be an issue."

That's exactly what he'd do if he thought Willow was on the case. The council might not exactly love coven Thornheart, but they knew what a valuable asset Willow could be to them. They'd been trying to get her on their payroll since her trial two years ago. She was the best, and they all knew it as well. "Won't the mother see that as you helping me?"

"Trotman called me before I knew anything about your task. I can accept, I just won't do anything about it." She gave my hand a squeeze. "Leave it with me."

I wasn't going to turn her down. She was right, the council would be dogging my every step otherwise, following the same leads, and things could get messy. "If you think it'll be okay, I won't say no."

"Excellent. All I want you focused on is staying safe," Wills said.

"I will, I've got Ronan helping me..." I shook my head. "I never knew he was so powerful."

Wills sat back. "Yeah, I've seen him in action more than once. I also know the male can fight. You couldn't be in better hands."

"You never mentioned his powers. I had no idea."

She sat back. "He's a private male. It wasn't for me to share."

"Has he worked out he's utterly and completely in love with you yet?" Mags asked, smirking.

My face heated. "I don't know about that..."

"You can stop that right now," Iris said. "We all know it, we're just waiting for Ronan to get a handle on those new emotions of his and figure it out."

"Do you know how Luna got her emotions back?" Wills asked.

"Because of Gunner, right? The whole mate thing?" I'd heard Willow talk about it before.

They all stared at me with stupid expressions on their faces.

I looked down at myself, then back up. "What?"

Willow gave me a shove and a look that said *duh*. "He's your mate, Rose."

Mates? "No...that can't be..." I was in love with Ronan, but mates? I'd spent so much of my life thinking I'd never get those things, the thought had literally never occurred to me. My heart skipped around in my chest. "Are you sure?"

"Ronan was a male without emotion, and yet he came back to you, day after day. He spent it caring for you, trying to feed you. He couldn't stay away from you. Warrick had limited emotions, remember? He didn't feel love before we mated. You're the reason Ronan regained his, Roe. And right now, I'd take a wild guess and say he's struggling big time with how he's feeling about you."

My heart raced faster, and my insides warmed. Ronan was my mate. "Luna said something similar. That he might be volatile or unpredictable while he works through everything."

Willow chuckled. "Girl, you're in for one hell of a ride."

My face flushed hotter, and they all cackled.

"That male is *intense*," Mags said, smirking. "I wonder what it'll be like to have all that focused on making his girl feel *gooood*."

My face was in flames now, because I had thought the same thing myself, many times.

"I'm not sure our Rose will ever share that with us," Wills said, then grabbed my hand and pressed a kiss to it, like she often did when I was sick. "I'm pretty freaking happy that right now he has that same intensity focused on keeping you safe."

"Hell yes," Iris said. "And leave Mom to us. We can run interference, and when she does find out what you're doing, we'll do our best to ease her fears."

"Thanks," I said, and my stupid eyes stung. This was all I'd wanted for so long, for my sisters to treat me as if I were like them, to not feel like they had to tiptoe around me, and I finally had it. "You guys are awesome, you know that, right?"

"That we do," Mags said. "So, have you taken those wings out for a test fly yet?"

I'd thought about it a lot. "Honestly, they don't feel strong enough yet. They feel heavy, and they throw me off balance when I extend them. At least they're not popping out randomly anymore. But I still need to build muscle."

"I'm sure Bram can help when you're ready to give flying a try," she said.

"I'll be sure to ask him when I feel ready."

There was another reason I was pleased when Wills had called to organize some sister time this morning. "Hey, so there's something I wanted to ask you." I instantly had their full attention. "So, while I was sick, my magic was as well. Thankfully, it's grown in strength with me. Then last night, while Ronan and I were out, I saw something...I *was* looking in a mirror and..." I tried to think of the best way to describe it. "I saw something that hadn't happened yet. A kind of vision that played out in the mirror, and only I could see it."

"Has the vision come to be?" Iris asked, all humor gone from her face.

"Yeah, it happened a short time later."

Iris looked to Wills. "Scrying?"

Wills nodded slowly, deep in thought. "That's what I was thinking." She looked at me. "Have you had any other visions like this?"

"No." I'd heard of scrying, of course, but I didn't know much about it, honestly. There'd been no need for me to study and practice magic, not when I'd been too weak to use it.

"Scrying nearly always comes from looking into a shiny object. If you have the gift, you can get messages or visions, and not only of the future. We've had a few seers in coven Thornheart, but not for a very long time," Wills said.

"It's obviously been sitting dormant, unable to grow to its full potential while you were sick." Iris smiled. "That's awesome, Roe."

Hope filled me. "You really think it's here to stay?"

"I do, but I guess we'll know for sure if it happens again."

"Good morning, Rose," a deep voice said behind me.

I spun around, and Ronan stood in the doorway. My heart immediately exploded to life in my chest. He was dressed in his usual dark trousers, but instead of a white shirt, he wore a black one. It was undone at the throat, and my mouth instantly watered. I was due to feed, and as soon as I saw him, my belly gripped tight, and not just with hunger for his blood. It was another kind of hunger altogether.

"Hey, Ronan." Could he hear the way my heart pounded?

"Christ," Mags muttered under her breath. "I need a knife to hack my way through all this tension."

I ignored her and stood, and his gaze slid over me from head to toe, then that square jaw tightened. I was wearing jeans again, they hugged my legs, and I'd pulled on a pair of black leather boots. This time, my sweater was a deep blue. I thought it brought out my eyes. My hair was down, and it had a bit more wave to it this morning.

"Are you ready to go?"

"Um, yeah, sure." I'd been hoping he'd have some blood for me. But he didn't have anything with him. Was he not going to feed me anymore? Did he think I could handle that side of things myself now? He didn't mention it, so I grabbed my bag and slung it over my head, said goodbye to my sisters, who were watching our exchange avidly, then strode out, Ronan right behind me.

He pulled on his long black woolen coat hanging by the door and I did the same.

"So I thought we'd go visit Mr. Reptile Shifter this morning," I said, since Ronan wasn't saying anything at all. "But this time we'll knock and see what information we can get from him."

We walked out, and he opened the car door for me. "All right." He shut me in and strode around to the driver's side.

When he got in, tension filled the car instantly. Did he feel it as well, like I had last night? Or was it only me? He pulled out onto the street, and we headed toward the outskirts of town and the house we'd broken into last night.

"So, how was your evening?" I asked, to fill the silence. I glanced at him again, and his jaw was doing that thing where it got all tight.

He looked at me, then away. "I stayed at the clubhouse."

"You're not going back to the knight's compound?"

He shook his head. "I prefer the clubhouse."

"Did you hang out at the bar...or...?" I wasn't sure what to ask, but I wanted to keep him talking.

His hands gripped the wheel tighter. "I spoke with Relic, then showered."

An image of him naked filled my head like a total perv. Jesus,

I'd gone from feeling nothing even close to desire ever to being a total horndog, and I had no idea what to do about it. "Me too," I said. "The shower part, I mean." Why the hell were we talking about showering? This was ridiculous. We'd talked more when I was sick, before Ronan regained his emotions, and I missed it.

"Then I went to the pits and fought."

I glanced his way, at those roughly spoken words. "You were in the pit again."

"Yes."

"Why?"

He glanced my way, and his eyes seemed to darken. "My emotions are volatile right now. I'm feeling a lot of things I can't name. I remember some from when I was a child. At least, I think I'm identifying them correctly. Some are new. Relic helped me identify some of the things I was feeling last night. But the one I don't need help identifying is anger. I'm angry, Rose, about a lot of things, and fighting helps me release some of it. So I fought for a while, then ate. Then I showered again and slept." He looked away, and I was positive some color darkened his cheeks.

"You know you can talk to me, right?" I reached over and wrapped my fingers around his wrist. "You were there for me, for months you were there when I needed you. I want to be there for you as well."

He seemed to freeze in place, then he lifted his hand, dislodging mine, but before I could pull it away, he grabbed it and held it in his, then rested it on his thigh. "Thank you," he said roughly.

We drove the rest of the way like that, with him holding my hand, and he didn't let go unless he absolutely had to.

When we pulled up outside the house, Ronan turned to me. "Reptile shifters are cold, and not just cold blooded. He'll look to me as the dominant one between us, and I'll have to let him believe that is the case. He'll also make advances toward you if I don't make it clear you belong to me."

My back straightened. Did he actually feel that way? That I belonged to him? Goddess, I wanted that.

"Don't mistake my behavior when we're in there as me thinking you're weaker. But I've seen this breed with their females, and he won't give us the answers we want if he thinks I'm not in control."

"In control of me?"

"Yes. He could attempt to take you from me if he thinks you're unprotected."

"Really?"

"Yes."

"What a pig."

Ronan watched me closely. "They're protective and dominant. They can be outwardly jealous and hostile to anyone who gets close to their females. But they don't mistreat their mates. They like to be in control, that's all. They're similar to hounds in that respect."

I screwed up my face, but yeah, he'd pretty much described Warrick, and Draven as well. Though, Warrick and Draven would never try to control my sisters. That wouldn't go over well at all. "What do you mean, try to take me?"

"If they see a female they want, they can be relentless at winning her."

I frowned. "Why do you assume he'd want me?"

"Because you're incredibly beautiful, Rose. Any male with two working eyes would want you."

He thought I was beautiful. *Do you want me?* My face heated. "I'm not so sure about that—"

"I am," he said. "Are you okay with me taking the lead?"

"Of course. If it'll get us the answers we need."

We got out of the car and headed up the driveway. Before we reached the door, Ronan took my hand again. "Stay close to me." He knocked.

It opened a few minutes later. The male I'd seen naked and

covered in blood and gore the night before stood before us, clean and dressed in a suit that hugged his well-built frame perfectly. His gaze went from Ronan to me and lingered. Interest lit his vibrant green eyes in an extremely overt way.

Ronan hooked his arm around my shoulders, a low growl rolling from him as he pulled me closer. The male watched this, studying us. "The female's yours?" he asked.

What? Had he seriously asked that question?

"Yes," Ronan said.

The other male took in Ronan again, like he was sizing him up. Was this actually happening right now? They hadn't even exchanged names; the other male hadn't even asked what we were doing there. This was utterly insane.

Finally, the male inclined his head. "What do you want?"

I opened my mouth, but Ronan tightened his hold on me, and I slammed my mouth closed again. "We'd like to ask you some questions about what was stolen from your collection."

"What business is it of yours?"

"You aren't the only one who's been robbed. We've been hired to investigate and hoped you'd be willing to share what you know?" he lied.

The man studied Ronan again, then finally stepped back and opened the door wider for us to come in. He turned his back on us, another obvious power play, letting Ronan know he saw him as no threat. I felt the muscles in Ronan's arm tighten. He hadn't missed this, and he didn't like it.

The male turned back and held out his hand. "Clay St. James."

Ronan took it. "Ronan."

"I'm not sure what I can tell you," the other male said. "I was away at the time. Someone broke in and took one of my effigies. It belonged to my grandfather..." He grinned, his eyes bright as they slid back to me, and winked. "The collection was his thing, not mine. So there's nothing I can really tell you about it."

"Do you have a picture of it?" Ronan asked.

"Yes, my grandfather cataloged all the pieces of his collection." He moved to a bookshelf and ran his fingers along several leather spines before pulling one of the volumes out. He leafed through it. "Here." He showed us the picture. It was ugly. A carving of a demon similar to the one we'd seen in his basement. This one had its tongue poking out.

"It was made of wood?" Ronan asked.

The male nodded. "Yes, carved from the branch of an ancient tree."

"Do you know what it was used for?"

"No clue. He collected what he liked but knew little of what they did."

Ronan turned to me. "Take a picture of it, Rose."

I pulled my phone from my back pocket and snapped a couple of pictures.

"Rose," Clay said. "A beautiful name for a beautiful female."

I shoved my phone back in my pocket. "Thank you."

Ronan tensed, his lips peeling back, his fangs extending. "Do not address my female. In fact, I'd prefer it if you didn't look at her."

I turned to him in shock. Okay, wow. He looked *pissed*. He wasn't acting. He felt territorial over me for real. I wanted to ask him about it, but I wasn't sure I should. He already seemed to be struggling with his emotions, and I didn't want to confuse him even more.

The other male's nostrils flared, and he turned to Ronan. "I meant no offense. You're a lucky male, but you obviously know that."

"I do. We'll be leaving now." Ronan's arm was tight around me as he turned and led me to the door.

"You'll let me know if you find my missing piece?" Clay said, following us to the door.

Ronan nodded and strode out of the house and down the path.

He didn't let go of me, not even when we reached the car.

"Are you okay?" I asked, because we were standing there, and Ronan was holding me tight, and I could feel every muscle in his body was tense.

No, this definitely didn't feel like an act anymore.

Chapter Seventeen

Rose

Ronan shook his head. "I didn't like the way he looked at you." His lips peeled back again, and his eyes darkened as he curled his fingers into a fist. "Fucking reptiles. I should have taken his fucking eyes out." He yanked the car door open for me.

Ronan never cursed. Not once. And for obvious reasons, besides that night in the forest, I'd never seen him angry. He was angry now. No, he was furious. "Ronan?"

"We need to leave. Now." He glanced back at the house and his fist clenched tighter. "Or I'll go back through that door and I'll tear his throat out."

Oh hell. "Ronan—"

"Car, Rose. Now."

I scrambled in quickly. I couldn't look away from him as he got in and started the car, jerked the wheel, and sped onto the street.

"Are you all right?" I asked a few minutes later.

The muscle in his jaw ticked once, twice. "Apologies for my behavior. I'm still navigating everything I'm feeling and..." He gritted his teeth and squeezed the steering wheel so tight it groaned. "I'm feeling...a lot of things. New things and...*fuck*." He slammed his hands against the wheel, then sucked in a breath and blew it out. Something I'd also never seen since Ronan didn't actually need to breathe. "Sorry," he said again. "Just...I need a minute."

I tried not to stare at him, but my gaze kept sliding his way. Ronan was different today, even more than he was the night before. The way he talked, not to mention the way he was looking at me.

Several more minutes passed as he growled and cursed under his breath and continued to squeeze the steering wheel, then finally, he said, "Where would you like to go next?"

This was so freaking bizarre. I decided not to address what had just happened. I wasn't sure that was a good idea with how long it took him to regain his control. "We need to check out the museum's demonology department, but first I think we need to speak to a demonology expert."

"I can get us a demon if you want? I'm sure I could make one talk."

Visions of Ronan striding into the woods and plucking out a demon, then *making him talk* filled my head. "Ah, no, I don't think that'll be necessary. I'm pretty sure the council has one on payroll. We need to find out who they use and track them down."

"Right," he said, his shoulders shifting under his jacket. "I've never been to the witch's council. Anything I need to know? Is it dangerous? If anyone tries to hurt you—"

"Nope, not dangerous," I said quickly. Looking at him now, so volatile and dark, you'd almost think he was looking for a reason to fight someone. "No one will give us any trouble."

"Good," he said, and his eyes darkened again. "Because if anyone tries anything, I'll kill them."

My god, who was this guy? He may be different in a lot of

ways, but he was still very literal. So when he said he'd kill them, he meant it. "There won't be any reason to kill anyone, I promise."

He dipped his chin, and without my say-so, my gaze slid to his throat. The tendons and veins there were bulging. My belly clenched in hunger. I quickly looked away. What should I do? Ask him if he'd give me blood when he dropped me home tonight? I didn't know how this worked. Did he expect me to go out and find my own blood now? I didn't know the etiquette for drinking blood. I'd heard there were clubs people could go to for the purposes of feeding. Is that where Ronan usually went? Should I ask him about them?

I shut down those thoughts because the very idea of someone else feeding him did not sit well with me at all. Did Ronan feel that way about me? He was my mate, after all, at least that's what my sisters thought. Did he feel it as well? I knew I didn't want to feed from anyone else. I hated the idea.

I slammed on the mental brakes.

This was definitely not the time or place for my mind to be in a spin about all of this. And if I kept thinking about his blood, the way it tasted and smelled, I'd jump him and latch on to his throat like a freaking starved mosquito. I quickly looked out the window, anything to take my mind off it. It didn't help, though, and I inwardly sighed in relief when we pulled into the council parking lot.

Grabbing my bag, I got out and dragged in the cool air.

"Rose?" Ronan said as he got out. "Are you unwell?"

Nope, just starving for your blood, and if you'd like to get naked while I feed, that would be awesome as well. "I'm fine," I said as heat crawled up my throat, and I forced myself to smile. His gaze dipped to my mouth and his eyes darkened again. I quickly looked away. "Okay, let's do this."

All witches had an ID that allowed access to the building, identifying the witch and their coven. But there'd been some changes recently, a tightening of security after Iris's task and a whole lot of not great things that went down here, which was why I was required to sign Ronan in as my guest. We were scanned as well, the magical kind that checked for spells or incantations a witch could use on themselves or others to cause harm.

My family didn't have many friends here. We'd ruffled a lot of feathers, especially the last couple of years, but there was one person who had always been kind. I just hoped Councilor Trotman had the information we needed and would be willing to share it.

"I don't like this," Ronan said as we drove down the bumpy, pothole-riddled road that took us deeper into the Roxburgh State Forest.

"Councilor Trotman wouldn't send us into some kind of ambush." I told him I was helping Willow with her investigation, and he'd given me what I wanted, a name. Though, I got the feeling he knew something was up. I left before he could question me further.

I grabbed the door handle as we bounced over more potholes. I'd never been to this part of the forest before, but I could already feel the powerful witch who lived out here, her magic reaching out to us. According to Trotman, Agatheena Burnside had lived in this part of the forest for over fifty years. She was unpredictable and kind of terrifying—his words. He'd advised me not to come out here. Unfortunately, I didn't have much choice. I needed a demon expert, and that was Agatheena, even if the council had stopped utilizing her expertise a while ago, for reasons Trotman didn't go into.

"Maybe we should call Bentley again. I'm sure he could get the information we need if we give him more time," Ronan said.

Bentley was the council's current demonology expert, and Trotman had given me his name as well. Bentley was a pompous ass and hadn't been interested in helping us. I was sure it had more to do with his lack of knowledge than anything else. "He was rude and arrogant and didn't know what he was talking about. And we don't have time for him to do the research." I pulled on my collar, tugging my sweater and shirt down over my shoulder so I could show him the tattoo-like vines left by the mother. "They've gotten closer, I'm sure of it."

Ronan glanced over and jolted. "I should have torn her throat out for that." He gripped the steering wheel tight again. "She almost killed you."

Fury rolled off him, filling the car. It was still hard for me to believe. Being with Ronan had always been—quiet. Still. Not anymore. Now he was this wild storm, emotions flowing from him, whipping around us. And sometimes, like now, it was strong enough to steal my breath.

It wasn't the first time he'd said something like that, and I knew he meant every word. Usually, what he said was logical, to him at least. This most certainly wasn't. "You can't kill her, Ronan. She's immortal, you know that. She's also incredibly powerful."

"Yes, but I...maybe I could have..." His brows snapped together, and his jaw tightened again.

He had no answer. No logical response. He was being ruled by emotion not logic, not anymore. Not now, at least.

"I'm angry," he finally said. "And other things. I don't like it. I have this sense of spinning, of being...out of control." He glanced at me again. "How can you stand it? How do you live with it? I feel as if I'm losing my mind."

"You can't hold on to the anger. It's not good to keep that bottled up inside you. If you keep holding on to those feelings, you won't have room for all the other wonderful emotions you have the ability to feel, the ones that make you feel good."

He looked at me, and his violet eyes were so bright, so beautiful, his face so stunningly handsome in his anger, I wanted to lean over and kiss him.

"What will I feel?" he asked.

His voice was impossibly deep, gravelly, not Ronan's voice, not entirely, because now it held notes of what he was feeling, even if he didn't fully understand what that was. "Happiness, humor, affection." *Don't say it.* "Desire—love."

His Adam's apple slid up and down as he drove, drawing my attention to it, and my hunger intensified. I told myself I wasn't going to push for anything from him, and yet I just couldn't help myself, could I? I had to go and remind him of the things I'd said the night he almost took my life.

"I understand some of the emotions I'm feeling. Anger, of course. When I was young, I had emotions, and I've regained a kind of visceral memory of some of them. Happiness, I know how that feels as well. Luna and I would play and laugh, and I remember the way it felt. Affection and love. I'd felt that for both my mother and sister, I know that, and I think I feel that way again. But I also understand there is more than one form of love, one I've never had the opportunity to experience."

That hurt when it shouldn't. Of course, he hadn't regained his emotions and fallen instantly in love with me. That would be ridiculous. Still, it stung more than it should.

"As for desire..."

My gaze shot to him. His gorgeous eyes came to me and the color deepened before he looked back to the road. "Yes?"

"I've experienced it."

"You have?" My heart was suddenly thundering in my chest. Could he hear it? Of course he could.

"Yes."

"Is it new to you, or something you felt before you regained your emotions?" *Shut up, Rose!*

"I never felt it before now." He glanced at me again, his stare dipping to my lips before he looked away. "And it seems to be one of the most difficult emotions to gain control over. I'm not sure I like the way it makes me feel."

"You don't like it?" My heart sank a little. Okay, a lot.

"I don't like the out-of-control feeling it gives me." He flexed his fingers around the wheel. "Base, like an animal. It's all-consuming and makes it hard to focus on anything else."

"It'll get easier," I said, and goddess, my voice was all breathy. "Desire can be something wonderful. I never really experienced it either. I was too sick—"

"And now?" His eyes sharpened when they came back to me. "You feel it?"

"Yes," the word came out a whisper.

"And you can control it?" he asked.

My face heated. Control, yes. Ease? No. "Um…yes, I can control myself." *Barely.*

He was quiet for several seconds. "Relic told me how to ease the intensity of the feeling. But it didn't last long."

"He did?" Hang on, did he mean…No, he couldn't mean what I thought he meant.

"Yes." His movements grew jerkier.

Don't. Don't ask. "A physical…um, easing?"

"Yes." He frowned, and color tinged his cheeks.

He was blushing. I'd never seen him blush, not ever. Ronan had never had a filter, had no concept of what was appropriate or not, and he obviously still didn't, but that blush told me he was starting to learn.

Jealousy fired through me, hard and fast. "With someone else? Sex?" What the hell was wrong with me? I had no filter either, apparently. But then, that was how Ronan and I had always talked to each other. He'd had no filter, so I'd spoken to him in kind.

The thought of him with someone else physically hurt. Fucking Relic. I was going to knee him in the nuts when I saw him next.

"No," he said roughly, then swallowed thickly. "Alone."

Relief filled me as an image of Ronan with one of those large hands wrapped around his hard length, his beautiful body bare and straining. Heat pulsed through me, and my mouth went dry. What did you say to that? *Yeah, me too.* Not that I'd been very successful. I'd been sick and sheltered my whole life. I mean, I saw movies with sex scenes and read books, but I'd never experienced any of it myself. I'd tried to touch myself but had only ended up even more frustrated.

"Oh, okay," I said, because I couldn't stand the deafening silence. I didn't want him to think there was something wrong with doing that.

Goddess, thinking about Ronan exploring his body for the first time—I shivered and quickly shut those thoughts down.

"This is as far as we can go," he said, dragging me from my dirty thoughts.

I looked around us. The "road" had thinned out even more, too narrow for a car. The path led deeper into the dense forest. "We'll have to go on foot the rest of the way."

He growled under his breath. "It appears that way. Put your jacket on, and your hat. Do you have gloves?"

"Yep, I'm ready for a hike in the Arctic." I chuckled at the stern look on his face.

"Hypothermia is no laughing matter, Rose."

"No, it most definitely isn't." My grin grew wider.

"Are you...teasing me?"

"Yes."

He stilled. "Your eyes, they grow brighter when you smile."

"Do they?" The male knew how to verbally knock me off my feet and had no clue.

"Yes."

He reached out and tucked my hair behind my ear and my breath caught.

"Your face, it's...I like to look at it. I never understood how people could risk everything, could give up or take a life for beauty, for a chance to gaze upon it, to be close to it. I think I do now."

Then he dropped his hand and opened his door. "Put on your jacket," he repeated, then got out of the car.

I sat there stunned while I watched him look around, searching the shadowy forest for danger. Had he really just said that? He strode to my door and opened it. "Ready?"

Chapter Eighteen

Rose

I yanked on my coat and shoved on my hat. "Yep, ready." I strode toward the path, but he grabbed my arm, stopping me.

"Gloves, Rose." He frowned, completely unaware that what he'd just said about me and beauty had completely thrown me.

"Right." I tugged them on, and immediately the buzz of Ronan's power filled the air around us. "You're using your power, yes? Are we invisible?"

"We are." He took me in from head to toe, I assume, making sure I was sufficiently covered up. "But I still want you to stay close."

"Will do." I took a step, and he grabbed my hand, and without looking at me again, headed along the path. He seemed to like holding my hand. Should I ask? We'd just talked about Ronan getting himself off, so I couldn't see why not. "You don't need to hold my hand to protect me with your power, right?"

"Right."

"Are you worried I'll run off and do something reckless?" I

asked, and held up our joined hands. I wanted to hear his reasoning for it.

He frowned again and looked at his hand wrapped around mine. "No." He thought about it for another few seconds. "I like the way it feels. It's a good feeling."

"Yeah, it is," I said, and he nodded, a look close to relief covering his face, as if my answer confirmed that he'd got it right. That what he was feeling was right. God, this whole thing was torture.

We walked deeper, and it grew darker the farther we went. And damp. The earthy scent was heavy, and there wasn't much in the way of wildlife, that I saw anyway, which didn't surprise me. The foliage was so dense the winter sun couldn't break through.

A strange growling sound came from somewhere in the trees, but Ronan didn't seem concerned, probably because we were completely invisible. Nothing, and no one would know we were there. We carried on, the sound growing louder. Then I spotted them, a group of demons. They were eating something, devouring it.

The demons that lived in the forest were different, in looks, anyway, than the demons who lived in the city. The demons who chose to live out here were the kind that couldn't pass as human no matter what they did, and these ones were perfect examples of that.

Tall and skinny, they were gray with a greenish tinge at their joints. They had pointed ears like elves and only holes where their noses should be. Their teeth were sharp and pointed and currently coated in a thick black fluid. We got closer, and then I saw what they were tearing into.

One of their own.

The demon lay motionless, its stomach torn open, insides spilled out.

"Goddess, I hope it was dead before they started eating it."

Ronan glanced at me. "Probably not. Their kind eat their

weakest. This one had obviously grown too old to keep up or perhaps it was injured."

"That's disgusting."

He led me around them, his grip a little tighter as we carried on past. "They don't understand loyalty. Many demons who live out here care only about their own survival. They're more like animals in that respect."

Well, that was horrific. We continued on, and the deeper we went, the more thankful I was for Ronan and his power. I saw demons and other creatures that I'd never seen or heard of before. Obviously, my knowledge was limited, but my sisters had shared what they'd seen, and they'd never described some I'd seen today.

I felt Agatheena's power stronger now. Her home had to be heavily warded. Not surprising, considering where she lived. There would be no getting to her unless she allowed it. The smell of wood smoke reached us next.

"She has to be close," I said, and then I saw it. "Oh, wow."

The cottage looked as if it were from a Grimm's fairy tale, but over the years had become part of the forest—trees grew close to its moss-covered stone walls, and a couple had even burst right through the thatched roof. Two thick pines stood on either side of a worn dirt path that weaved its way to the cottage's front door, their branches arching over the top. There were things hanging from those branches, thick twine tied around items, then secured to twigs and branches.

I strode up to take a closer look. "Shit."

Ronan growled beside me.

There were bones, some clean, some still covered in gore. Several skulls of different breeds of demon, by the looks. There were bits of fabric and several jars. One had an eyeball floating in it, another was filled with what looked like fingernails, another was half-filled with matted hair of various colors, and yet another had something, well, I wasn't sure what it was, an organ of some kind.

"There has to be another way," Ronan said. "Whoever lives here, I don't want you anywhere near them or that cottage."

"She's a witch, Ronan. I'm a witch. I'll be fine," I said, even though I knew that might not be the truth. I had to speak with her, regardless, I had no choice. I needed to know what the stolen demon effigy was for so I knew what my next move was.

His hand gripped mine tighter. "I don't trust this female."

"You haven't met her." I turned to him. "It's going to be okay. Let's just get this over with, then we can go home."

"I'd really rather you didn't go in there," he said, even as we moved to the entrance of the path.

I lifted my hand and the magic I felt zapped down my arms, burning like fire along my veins. I hissed and shook out my hand. A warning: Don't come close or you're toast. "She won't let me in unless I prove I'm a witch." I searched the thick trunks of the two "decorated" trees.

"What are you looking for?"

"A smooth patch, darker in color." Iris had told me about the magic door in the basement of the council building. The ancient wood knew who you were and could tell if you should be allowed entrance by your blood.

If this witch was as powerful as Councilor Trotman said, I wasn't getting near her without some kind of proof of who I was.

"Something like this?" Ronan asked.

I took a closer look, and on the side of one of the trunks was a knot. It was indented in the middle and a deep mahogany color, while the rest of the tree was a lighter wood.

"That's it, I'm sure of it." I took my knife from my pocket and pressed it to my finger—

Ronan grabbed my wrist, stopping me. "What are you doing?"

"I need to prove to this witch that I'm like her, that I'm not here to harm her, witches do that with blood."

"You're going to cut yourself again?" he said, and his voice sounded strange.

"Yes." He'd seen me do it when I was in Oldwood Forest. I saw a flash of his fangs. "Is that going to be a problem?"

He shook his head. "I don't like...I don't like you hurting yourself."

"This is part of who I am. It's what we do. You have nothing to worry about." I lifted the blade to my finger again.

"Rose..."

I made a slice in the tip, and blood immediately bubbled to the surface. I pressed it to the dark patch in the trunk. I'd tried to hide my wince but knew I didn't succeed when Ronan growled.

"Rose," he said again, his voice even more distorted.

His eyes were wild and his fangs were so long they'd extended past his upper lip. *Holy shit.*

"Fuck," he said and grabbed my hand when I lowered it from the tree. He looked down at my sliced finger. "It's deep."

"It's not that deep. Else has a balm that'll heal it quickly—"

He lifted my hand and sucked my finger into his mouth, his tongue gently sliding over the wound. I blinked up at him in shock. His eyes drifted shut, and he made a sound of pure pleasure. My nipples hardened, and I squeezed my thighs together instantly. Watching Ronan taste my blood, the look on his face, the sounds he was making, was the most erotic thing I'd ever seen in my life.

Finally, he slid my finger free and looked down at it again. "There," he said, his eyes literally glowing in the shadowy darkness of the forest.

I tore my eyes from him and looked down. The cut was gone —completely. "Oh."

"My saliva has healing properties." He licked his lips as if he'd been sucking on something mouthwatering.

Ronan tasted amazing to me when I drank his blood. It was everything I wanted, all I wanted, always. It fulfilled my cravings like nothing else ever had. Did my blood fulfill him in the same way? "How do I taste?" I asked before I could stop myself.

His nostrils flared, and his gaze dropped to my mouth again.

The creak of a door opening echoed around us.

I spun around as a very old, hunched-over female walked out of the cottage.

"What do you want?" she asked, making her way down the path, her familiar, a raven, perched on her shoulder.

I took a step forward, but Ronan grabbed my hand, holding me back. "We've come to speak with you, Agatheena, if you'll spare us a moment of your time."

She reached the end of the path, her ward still between her and us, and I barely held my ground when her piercing green eyes locked on mine. Her skin was wrinkled and saggy, her hair wiry and gray. I wasn't sure I'd ever seen another being as old as her. The raven's black stare followed me as it made a throaty caw.

"What would a daughter of coven Thornheart want to ask me?" she said, eyeing me with suspicion.

As I suspected, she'd gotten everything she needed from the drop of blood I'd given to the tree beside us. "I've been given a task by the mother, and I'd very much like to pass. I need information that I believe only you can give me, it's about a missing demon artifact."

Her eyes narrowed, and she took me in more closely. "Are you still welcome by your coven, child?"

"Yes."

"They know you have shifter blood?"

I paused. "Yes, they know."

"Not all covens are so tolerant," she said, her eyes flashing red, then back to blue.

Again, I forced myself to hold my ground when my immediate reaction was to jerk back. I'd never seen a witch with eyes like that. "Will you help me?"

"For a price," she said, studying me.

"What price?"

"A favor, at a date and time of my choosing."

"Rose," Ronan said, curling his fingers around my wrist.

"What kind of favor?" I asked.

"No," Ronan bit out. "Do not bargain with this female."

Agatheena didn't spare Ronan a glance. "Something simple, collecting something for me."

"Collecting what?"

She scowled. "Well, I don't know yet, do I? When I need something, I'll know, then you'll know." She turned away. "If you want my help, you will agree to my price, otherwise—"

"I agree."

She turned back and grinned, flashing yellow pointed teeth. "Excellent." She waved a gnarled hand toward one of the jars hanging on her tree. "The tree needs a lock of your hair before you can pass. And be quick about it." Then she headed back up the path and into her cottage, waiting for me to join her.

I pulled the knife from my coat again, but Ronan took it from my fingers before I could reach for my hair.

"You won't listen to me, will you?" he said.

"I need to do this, Ronan." He slid my hair over my shoulder and pulled a lock from underneath forward, his expression hard. I was positive I could hear him grinding his teeth. "You're angry."

"Yes," he said. "But not at you, at this whole situation. That you've been forced to put yourself at risk this way. I don't like it, Rose." He made a loop in a small section of hair and sliced it with my knife. "I fucking hate it."

It shocked me every time he cursed. Even the way he spoke was changing. He slipped in and out of the old Ronan and the new. From speaking in full precise sentences to cursing and talking far more casually. He was changing every day, becoming the male he would have been, or at least a variation of himself, if Azel had never come into their lives and torn it apart.

I slid the hair from his fingers and touched his arm. "I'm not scared because I have you to protect me."

He flashed his teeth, not in a smile. He still hadn't blessed me with one of those. No, this was a baring of teeth and fangs. "If anyone hurts you, Rose, I'll tear their throats out and drain their lifeblood until their hearts stop beating."

What did you say to that? A vow to murder anyone who hurt me? And I was in no doubt he meant every word. "Um...thanks."

He didn't respond, just unscrewed the jar hanging on one of the branches and held it toward me. I twisted the hair, curling it up so I could get it in, and he did up the lid, letting the jar hang once more.

"Let's get this over with," he said.

I took his hand and strode between the trees at the entrance to the path, Ronan right behind me—

He barked out a curse—and was thrown back, tossed across the forest floor. He sprang back to his feet immediately and charged the entrance again. And again, he was thrown back. He barely hit the ground before he was back on his feet.

His eyes were bright, wild, his fangs sharp. Fury rolled off him. "Come back!" he roared. "Now, Rose."

I turned to him, but before I could take a step in his direction, magic coiled around me and dragged me right up to the cottage. I called on my own magic. It sparked inside me, filling my chest, shooting down my arms, as I yelled out a spell, one to counter a magical attack, something Mom had taught us all as children, but Agatheena's hold on me didn't lessen. She was far too strong. The cottage door opened, and I was propelled inside, the door slamming behind me. "Let me go!" I struggled and shrieked, but couldn't break free.

Agatheena sat by her fire, and she turned to me as she sucked on the pipe she was holding. She blew out blue smoke right into my face...I instantly calmed.

She smiled, pleased with herself, and flashed those pointed yellow teeth again. "Stop your caterwauling. I'm not going to eat you, girl."

I saw it now. Agatheena wasn't only a witch. Those red eyes and her pointed teeth gave her away. "You're a demon, aren't you?"

"I'm a witch as well. Same as you, my blood is mixed. Got as much demon in my blood as you have shifter in yours." She shuffled to one of the cupboards in the small kitchen area and pulled down two mugs, then went about making tea. Her familiar followed, flying to perch on the back of one of the chairs at the table, staring at me again.

The panic I'd felt while being dragged in here was now completely gone. Whatever was in that blue smoke was extremely powerful. I looked around. There were...things hanging from the walls and ceiling, *things* I didn't want to look at too closely. There were also more jars in here filled with all kinds of stomach-churning items.

"What's your familiar's name?" I asked. The raven was all animal, not shifter.

"Dolores."

The bird shook out her inky feathers. "She's beautiful." Agatheena placed a mug in front of me. "So, are you going to hurt me?"

She filled it with tea. "No. How will you repay me if your innards are hanging from my ceiling?" She cackled at the look on my face.

A roar came from outside. Ronan.

"He's a feisty one. But slamming himself against my ward like that isn't going to get him anywhere."

"Will you let him in?"

"No," she said. "I have no interest in your mate storming in here and throwing a tantrum. I'd have to hurt him, and I don't think you'd like that."

"My mate?"

She sipped her tea. "You didn't know?"

"I was told he was, but I was too scared to believe it in case it wasn't true." Okay, that blue smoke hadn't just calmed me, it'd made me way more comfortable in this cottage of horrors than I should be. So much so, I was telling her all kinds of things, apparently.

She studied me. "He has his work cut out for him, protecting you."

Her words should scare me, but it seemed physically impossible right then. "Why is that?"

"There's darkness around you. It's powerful and relentless." She sat across from me. "I see two paths ahead of you, and both will bring you and your coven great pain."

Death, she had to be talking about Death and his demand for me to join him in Limbo. "Is there any way to avoid it? Is there another path?"

She took my hand and closed her eyes. Her eyes moved behind her lids for several seconds. When they opened, they were red demon eyes. "No. Two paths and both suck."

Again, I should have been freaking out, but nothing. "You asked if my coven had exiled me. Did yours?"

"When I grew older, and it became apparent what my father was, they threw me out. I was stronger than them; they were threatened. I've lived alone ever since. I prefer it that way." She leaned forward. "So, girlie, what do you want to know?"

I slid my phone from my pocket and clicked on the pictures of the stolen demon effigy. "We know this is of demon origin. Do you know what it's used for?"

"Why do you want to know?" she asked, a strange look in her eyes.

"I told you, it's part of my task."

"No other reason?"

I shook my head, the look in her eyes making me feel uneasy.

Her hands shot out, and she grabbed my wrist in a hold that would leave a bruise. Dolores cawed. Agatheena was old, but she had demon strength. There would be no getting away from her if she refused to let me go.

She closed her eyes again, as if she were looking inside me for the truth. Her lids snapped open, and she nodded once. "Good thing you're not lying to me, child," she said. Her voice was light, but the threat in her eyes sent ice through my veins. The smoke was obviously wearing off.

Ronan roared again outside.

I wanted out of this cottage—now. "What can you tell me, Agatheena?"

"The piece in your photo could be extremely dangerous in the wrong hands. It's used to summon Hayseous, a bargaining demon."

That didn't seem good, not at all. "What kind of bargain?"

She shrugged a rounded shoulder. "I don't know his specialty. It could be a lot of things. Fertility, beauty, love, immortality. The list goes on."

"And it's definitely real?"

She sat back with a groan and rubbed her knee. "I believe so, it appears to be marked."

"What kind of mark?" Ronan snarled and roared my name. He was losing his mind outside. I needed to get back to him.

"There are several different ones in existence, some real, some fake, created from fairy stories. The real ones are marked with a cross, in the bargaining demon's blood, somewhere on the item." She sat forward again. "That's all I have for you, girlie. So I'll let you leave, but when I call on you for my favor, you best get to it quick smart, understand?"

"I understand." Fear prickled across my skin as I stood and turned to leave—

She grabbed my arm, and I spun back. How the hell had she moved that fast?

"You need to be careful, daughter of coven Thornheart. That darkness is closing in fast," she said, then released me.

I nodded and rushed to the door. I almost expected it to be locked, but it opened first try and I ran out.

Ronan was at the end of the path, fists clenched, veins bulging in his throat, those fangs long and glinting. I ran faster as soon as I saw him, racing down the path to get to him.

I reached the ward, and again, I almost expected it to stop me from leaving, but I ran right through.

Ronan snarled, grabbed my hand, and yanked me through to him, then snatched me up in his arms and held me to him so tight I couldn't breathe.

I didn't care. I didn't need to breathe. I just needed him.

He lifted me in his arms and strode away from the cottage. "Did she hurt you?"

"No, she didn't hurt me. I can walk, Ronan. I'm okay."

"But I'm not okay, Rose." He bared his teeth. "I'm not fucking okay."

Chapter Nineteen

Ronan

I couldn't let her go. I held her tighter to me and broke into a jog. I needed to get her away from here, from that evil crone and this forest full of demons.

I needed Rose somewhere safe, somewhere no one could reach her or hurt her.

Emotions were all twisted up inside me. I recognized anger. Anger was always there, and fear. I thought I'd lost her. I thought I'd never be able to get to her. That she was being hurt and there was nothing I could do to stop it. But there was something else, that urge I'd felt even before my emotions returned, the one that had me taking her food every day, trying to feed her, it roared through me now.

Rose was my mate. I didn't doubt that now, and the need to care for her was pounding through me. I needed that more than I needed anything else, but twisted up in all of that was relentless desire.

I wanted to be close to her. I wanted my body pressed against hers. I wanted to feel the heat of her skin, hear the beat of her heart, the rush of her blood moving through her veins.

I sprinted through the forest, past monsters, creatures I'd never seen before, and so many demons. Danger, so much of it around my female, my Rose. I picked up the pace, until the trees were nothing but a blur as we sped past. Rose said nothing, she just held on.

Light broke through the trees ahead.

We were almost out.

Almost to the car.

Relief. I recognized it as it poured over me as we burst from the thickest part of the forest and I spotted the car. I hadn't dropped my power once, and I kept it in place as I carried Rose to the passenger side, yanked the door open, and carefully placed her on the seat, then dragged the seat belt around her, securing it.

I got in, started the engine, and got out of there, driving faster than I should over the pitted dirt road in a car that wasn't equipped for this type of terrain. Rose hung on, glancing at me every so often.

When I finally gained some semblance of control, I looked over at her. "Are you sure she didn't hurt you?"

"I promise. She told me what I needed to know and let me leave." Rose's stomach rumbled, and her cheeks turned a deep pink.

"You're hungry?" I asked, but I knew. I felt it now, now that I wasn't drowning in emotion. Fury filled me, with myself. My female was hungry. She was supposed to feed this morning. How could I have forgotten that? I'd been so desperate to get to her, to see her, I'd neglected to bring her blood.

"I'm fine, I'm used to—"

"Don't say it, Rose. Not now. Don't remind me that you were starving almost your entire life." I glanced over at her. "After today, I promise, you'll never be hungry again."

She watched me with wide blue eyes, then they dipped to my throat, and she swallowed. "I'll be all right," she said, always trying to make everyone else feel better. Never putting herself first. From now on, she would always come first. Always.

We reached the end of the track, finally, and I planted my foot. Her stomach rumbled again, and I had to bite back my snarl. I was so close to pulling over to the side of the road and feeding her there. But my instincts roaring to get her to safety were just as loud.

We reached the crossroads, the turn that would take us to her house, but I carried on straight ahead. I wasn't clear on a lot when it came to emotion or what was the right or wrong thing to say. But I was sure that for what I had planned, Rose would prefer privacy. Especially for her first time feeding from my vein, or at least the first time she was conscious for it.

"Where are we going?"

"The clubhouse," I said as we turned the next corner, then another.

"Why?"

Her voice was husky and made my skin tingle, lifting what I now knew were goose bumps all over me. "Because you need to feed." We drove up to the clubhouse gates. They were open, and I drove in, keeping my block in place when I saw Warrick and Willow were here, her truck in the parking lot as well as the hearse Ren sometimes drove.

I hit the brakes harder than I intended, and Rose jerked forward, her belt locking her in place. I cursed under my breath and shoved my door open.

Rose got out of the car, and I took her hand in mine and strode across the parking lot and into the clubhouse.

"You're still blocking us?" she asked.

"Yes." I glanced over at her. "I don't want any interruptions."

Her cheeks were pink again. "Oh, okay." She licked her lips. "Thank you...for this."

She didn't need to thank me. Feeding her was my honor, my privilege. And I knew now, something I was born to do. All this time, the answer had been right there. How had it never occurred to me? She'd been starving, dying, and all I'd needed to do was feed her. That rage grew hotter inside me.

I'd never forgive myself for not seeing that, for allowing Rose to suffer for even one second longer than she'd needed to.

We made our way down the stairs that led to the den below-ground. The hall was empty, and I let my block drop, pulling back my powers, and opened the door to my room. Rose followed me in, and I locked the door behind us.

She looked around my sparsely furnished room, then back to me. "Thank you for doing this. I promise I'll work something else out for next time. There are clubs, right? Maybe you could tell me the best ones? I have no idea—"

One moment I was across the room, and the next, I'd hooked my arm around her waist and backed her against the wall. "You want to feed from someone else?" The very thought made me want to punch a hole in the wall.

She stared up at me, her mouth opening, then closing. "No," she whispered. "But I thought that maybe you didn't—"

"No one but me will feed you. Only me, Rose."

She licked her lips. "Okay." Her pretty eyes slid down to my throat again, then back up. "Where do you want me to wait?"

"Wait?"

"While you do whatever it is you do, when you...the thermos—"

I shook my head. I wasn't strong enough to stop this, not after what happened in that forest, not after thinking I might have lost her. My need to be close to her was overpowering everything else. I was afraid for my sanity if I didn't give in to this need inside me. "From now on, you will feed from my vein." Just saying it, thinking it, had desire pumping through me, hotter than ever before.

"You want me to...I'm going to..." She swallowed thickly. "Ronan, are you sure?"

"Yes." I sounded demonic, my need coming through clear in my voice.

I was afraid I'd scare her, but she didn't step back or run. No, her sharp little fangs slid down over her full lower lip, showing me that she wanted it too.

"What do I do?" She sounded almost desperate, and when her stomach rumbled with hunger again, I snapped.

"Bed." I grabbed her hand and led her to it. Then, without delay, I lay on it. It would be easier for her this way. She stared down at me wide-eyed, her gaze trailing over me. "Come here, Rose."

"Right..." She climbed up beside me. Her scent filled my head, and I felt dizzy and desperate for what was about to happen.

"Where should I..." She licked her lips. "Where would you like me to feed from?"

My gut was in knots, but this was a good feeling, not an awful one. This was anticipation. My abdominal muscles tightened. "Where would you like to bite me?" My voice was back to demonic, so impossibly deep. Her face darkened, and my need for her to bite me, feed from me, increased.

"Is there anywhere you don't like to be bitten?" she whispered.

"I don't know. The day I learned you needed blood was the first time I'd let anyone feed from me." It had always been me, starved and waiting for Azel to allow me to feed from him. Making me addicted to his poisonous blood, using it to control me, manipulate me. The thought of Rose being hungry all day, that she'd needed to feed and hadn't felt as though she could ask me for it, made me sick to my stomach. Her belly rumbled again, and a snarl was torn from me. "I can't bear that you're hungry, Rose. Please bite me. Anywhere. You can bite me anywhere you want."

Her gaze darted to my throat once more, and her eyes changed, now obsidian. Her bat eyes. I sucked in another of those unnecessary breaths. "The vein in your throat seems…" She licked one of her fangs, and my cock stiffened even more. "Um…thicker. An easier target for a first attempt. Would that be a good place to start?"

"Yes," I bit out, close to grabbing her and putting those little fangs right there, where I desperately wanted them.

She nodded and shuffled closer on her knees, then, tucking her hair behind her ears, leaned in.

I stilled, watching, waiting. Ready to jump out of my skin.

"So I just bite and…and suck?" she asked.

"Yes." I reached up, unable to wait, and cupped the back of her head, drawing her closer. "I promise, instinct will kick in. You'll know exactly what to do."

She was hovering over me, and when her black eyes locked with mine, the impact was like a physical blow, but in a way that felt so incredibly good. More than good. It was pleasure and pain, desire. A wild storm inside me. A storm that only Rose could create and one that only she could calm. Then her eyes dipped down, her hunger driving her gaze to the vein in my throat.

She moved closer, and at the first touch of her soft, warm lips to my cool skin, I jolted in surprise.

"Are y-you okay?" she asked.

"Yes, don't stop."

Her tongue darted out, touching my skin again, sending zaps of sensation through me, and she moaned softly. What was she doing to me? I thought I knew what desire was, but what I did in the shower thinking about Rose the night before was nothing compared to this. Rose, so close, I felt the heat of her body, her mouth on my skin, her scent filling my senses. When she did finally bite me, I was afraid I'd lose control completely. I almost pulled her back, afraid of what would happen, but then her fangs grazed my throat.

"Rose," I choked out, not sure if it was a plea for more or a warning for her to stop.

She struck.

I jerked under her, but this time she didn't pull back. No, she slid her fangs free, making my entire body shudder from the pleasurable tingles dancing through me, over me, then opened her mouth over my vein and sucked.

Desire rocked through me, like nothing I'd ever experienced. Heat flooded my body. The urge to thrust my hips almost too much to resist. The need to touch her, to pull her closer, had me fisting the covers beneath me to stop myself.

Rose's tongue slid over my skin, encouraging my blood to flow faster, and I felt every deep pull on my vein through my entire body and down the length of my throbbing erection, as though Rose's mouth and hands were all over me.

She pressed closer, her smaller body pressing down on mine, our legs tangling together as her hands moved to hold each side of my head before her fingers delved into my hair.

Her legs moved restlessly, then spread over one of my thighs, and she moaned as she pressed down harder. I felt the heat of her there, between her legs, against my thigh, and I grew harder, so much so, it hurt. I squeezed my eyes closed, fighting desperately for control.

One of her hands slid down my chest, lower, over my belly, bumping against the waistband of my trousers and brushing the head of my cock. I hissed and grabbed her wrist, pulling it away. I didn't want her to touch me, not like this. Feeding her was my privilege, as her male—if she one day consented to be my mate.

I would never, ever expect anything from her in return for feeding her. Azel made me pay for it with my body every time, and after the frenzy of feeding, I'd realize what happened. I hadn't enjoyed it or wanted it. I wasn't able to experience the emotions of what happened to me then, but I could now, and I would never subject anyone to that. Not ever. I would never use her that way. I'd do anything to prevent her from feeling humiliated and used, violated. I'd die first.

"Touch m-me," she said softly against my skin.

I ground my teeth. "I can't."

Her fingers dug into my shoulders. "Please."

She rolled her hips against my thigh. I knew from the hounds that a female became wet when she was aroused, and Rose was highly aroused. The fabric of my trousers, below her splayed thighs, was damp from her need, and her scent was heavy—I breathed deeply—and so intoxicating. Her plea cracked me down the middle. "You don't want that, Rose. It's just the feeding."

I'd never experienced desire while I fed, not until I'd been delivered a thermos of Rose's blood—but then I wanted her all the time, feeding or not, didn't change that.

Rose sucked deeply one final time, then dragged her tongue over the puncture marks, knowing instinctively that's what she needed to do, then she lifted her head and looked down at me.

"It's not just the feeding." She pressed her forehead to mine, the black bleeding from her eyes until they were blue once more. "It's not."

She might think that now, but this was all new to her. My hands lifted on their own, and I gripped her hips, not sure if I wanted to hold her back or pull her down on me harder. "You said you started feeling desire once you were well."

Some of my blood smeared her lower lip, and she licked it up. I fought back my shiver of need. "Yes."

Ever since she'd told me that, it'd been making me insane, wondering who had caused that feeling inside her. It could be one of the hounds. Relic was frequently at the Thornheart residence. One of the wolves? They'd all been there for her, while I'd been at the compound, lying in my own filth, utterly useless.

"Who?" The word came out a growl, and my fingers dug into

her flesh, holding her tighter, desperate and afraid of her answer at the same time.

Her beautiful blue eyes, heavy with lust, searched mine. "Who?"

"Who made you feel that way, Rose? I need you to tell me who caused that need inside you?" She'd said she loved me that night. Did she still feel that way? She'd said she loved me as a female loves a male? But I'd changed, had her love for me changed as well?

"You don't know?" Her hair fell around us like a silken curtain.

Every muscle in me tensed. If it wasn't me, if she said someone else, I didn't think I'd be able to stop myself from tearing them to shreds. "Tell me." My voice was back to rough and demonic, and there was no controlling it.

One of her hands slid up from my shoulder to the side of my throat, her thumb brushing over my jaw, my chin, my lower lip. "You, Ronan. You're the only male who makes me feel that way. You are the only male I want."

Possessive, animal need flared bright inside me, even as I struggled to believe it could be true, that this beautiful female could want a male like me. I pulled her closer, afraid she'd take the words back and leave me. "Why?" I needed to know.

A small smile curled her perfect, crimson lips. "Because you never treated me like there was something wrong with me. Because you protected me, cared for me, and never pitied me. You read to me and tried to feed me, and you were always there. Every day, you were there." She brushed her thumb over my lips again, and the ache in my groin grew to more than I could bear. "You're also extremely handsome, and the freaking hottest male I have ever laid eyes on. I want to be close to you all the time, and even when we're together, it's not close enough."

Every word she said dug deeper and deeper, until the monster in me roared to the surface, wanting to keep her and never let her go. "Are you saying you're mine, Rose?"

"Yes, Ronan," she said, dipping her mouth closer to mine. "I'm most definitely yours."

My stomach clenched. Her words filled me with pleasure, but I didn't know how to be the male she needed. The male she thought I was. "I'm not sure I can give you what you need."

"You're exactly what I need," she said and rolled her hips against me, so hot and damp and perfect.

Shame burned my face. She deserved the truth. "I don't know what to do."

"Neither do I, but maybe we can learn together?" She bit down on her lower lip and waited for my reply.

I held her gorgeous eyes. I wanted to be her male. I wanted to be everything she needed, and I hated that I didn't know how. But I could never give her up or walk away, so I nodded.

Without a word, she rolled to her side, and I went with her. Then she took my hand from her hip and brought it to her mouth, kissing my knuckles. "Do you want to touch me?"

"Yes."

"Where?"

I wanted to touch her everywhere, explore every inch of her body. My stare dropped to her throat, and she swallowed audibly as I pressed my hand there, my fingers brushing the vines marking her flesh. Her skin was smooth, warm, delicate. I glanced up as I moved down, her sweater catching on my roughened palm and the tips of my fingers. Rose watched me, her breathing fast. I looked back down to the gentle swell of her breasts. I could see the points of her nipples through the soft fabric.

Yes, I wanted to know how she felt there. I covered her and lightly squeezed. She moaned softly, and I liked the sound so much, I did it again. She squirmed, gasping when I did it a third time, then ran my fingers over her nipples. They were firm and I squeezed them gently between my thumb and finger.

Rose cried out, undulating in a way that was utterly mesmerizing.

"Where else d-do you want to touch me, Ronan?"

My gaze lowered to the place between her thighs. I wanted to explore there, badly. I looked back up at her. "Rose?"

She took my hand and placed it between her legs, pressing my fingers over the damp fabric of her jeans.

"You're so hot there." I cupped her more firmly, pressing my fingers deeper, seeking more of her heat.

She cried out softly but from pleasure, not pain. "You made me this way. I ache, Ronan."

"How do I ease your pain?" I asked, feeling helpless.

"It's not that kind of pain, it's a good feeling. Did you ache when you were on your own?"

"Yes."

"You liked it?"

A growl slipped out. "Yes. I was thinking about you."

"You were?"

"I thought I was losing my mind. The feeling so big, so all-consuming."

She nodded, biting her lips again, and this time one of her fangs grazed her flesh and blood bubbled to the surface. I couldn't stop myself. I leaned forward and lapped it up with my tongue. Her taste filled my senses, and I groaned. Then we were kissing, her tongue moving against mine, her blood and mine mingling in our mouths. I couldn't get enough.

Her hips moved restlessly, wanting more from me, and I wanted to howl in frustration that I didn't know what to do.

"Touch me," she gasped against my lips. "I need you to touch me, please, Ronan."

I'd been at the clubhouse a long time now. The hounds didn't always take the females they pleasured to their rooms. I'd seen the hounds with females on their laps, their hands moving under their clothing, between their thighs. Is that what she wanted? The thought increased my need even further. I wanted to touch her bare flesh there. I wanted it badly. "Should I slide my hand inside your underwear, Rose?"

"Y-yes," she said and sucked on my tongue.

I trembled, and with a shaky hand, tugged the button of her jeans open, slid down the zipper, then pushed my hand down the front of the soft cotton underwear she was wearing. My fingers grazed over incredibly smooth skin, then down to her delicate folds. I hissed at how perfect she felt.

She whimpered, breathing hard, fast. "Deeper. Press your fingers deeper."

I did as she said and groaned. She was so hot and slick there. I wasn't sure what I needed to do, but the hounds appeared to rub when they were touching females like this. I assumed using the slickness to ease the way. I pressed my fingers more firmly to her there and rubbed up and down. Rose gasped against my mouth and opened her legs wider.

"Yes, like that. Keep doing that."

She liked it. I was doing it right. Pleasure filled me even more. I concentrated on her reactions to my touch. I could feel her small opening, and my cock started leaking in my trousers, imagining pushing inside her. But when I rubbed over the tight little nub higher up, she'd gasp and squirm, and grew more out of control when I applied pressure there, then moved faster.

She wanted me to concentrate there, so I did. "Like that, sweets?" The endearment slipped from me. I'd never used one, but it felt right. Rose was lovely, inside and out.

"Yes. Yes, like that." She moved against my hand, her hips working, rubbing herself against my fingers faster. "Oh god, I'm... I'm going to..." She bowed and screamed, her wings exploding from her back, shredding her shirt. Pearlescent and glittering in the light, they weren't able to spread fully the way she was lying, so they were arched high above her shoulders.

I couldn't look away. She was ethereal, luminescent as her body moved from the pleasure she was feeling, her face somehow even more stunning while she was lost in it. Her pussy pulsed against my fingers, her juices covering them. The urge to taste, to lick it up, made my mouth water.

She slumped, breathing hard, and I stopped moving my hand but kept it there, reluctant to pull away. I wanted to do that again. I wanted to make Rose scream for me like that over and over again.

Finally, she blinked slowly, drowsily, up at me. "That was...that was incredible."

"I want to do that to you again," I rasped.

She smiled wide. "Oh, you will most definitely be doing that again. But it's my turn to make you feel good."

I swallowed, my mouth suddenly dry. "You don't need to do that."

"I want to." She looked down.

I followed her gaze. My erection strained against the front of my trousers, so hard every vein and ridge was outlined through the fabric. I'd never been so hard and long and thick.

My abs tightened as she popped the button, hissing as she dragged down the zipper. Azel's face slammed into my head. I jolted and tried to force it out.

"I've imagined touching you like this for so long," she said and reached for me.

Azel was still there. My erection softened, and my hand snapped out, catching her wrist, stopping her before I knew what I was doing.

She stilled suddenly, and her eyes changed, as if she were looking inward.

"Rose?"

Nothing.

"Rose?" I said louder.

She blinked several times, then she finally turned to me. "I'm being called to something or someone...something to do with my task. I need to let it lead me." She winced. "I'm so sorry."

I quickly yanked my pants together, thankful for the call to her task because she hadn't noticed my reaction. "You don't need to be sorry. We better go while we have a lead."

Rose quickly straightened her clothing, and I gave her one of my T-shirts to wear, then helped her into her jacket. I pulled on mine. Then I lifted my block again, to keep us hidden, because we didn't have time for questions, and I quickly led Rose back out to the car.

Chapter Twenty

Rose

"Turn here," I said.

I had no idea where we were going, but my instincts were leading me into the city. I glanced over at Ronan. His expression was strained. I couldn't believe we got interrupted when we did. I wanted to make him feel as good as he'd made me feel.

An image of him lying there, hard and straining, the look in his eyes, god, pleading with me to touch him, wouldn't leave my mind. I squirmed in my seat and made myself focus on why we were driving around the city instead of still in Ronan's bed.

He was quiet beside me, and I couldn't imagine what he was thinking. The feeling, the calling, inside me surged, guiding me. "Take the next left."

He did as I asked.

There were several restaurants along the street. The feeling grew stronger. "It has to be here somewhere, this is where I'm being called to." A small restaurant, the paint on the glass was worn and chipped, but the sign above it was freshly painted. Cafe Black Paw. "That's where we need to go."

We parked, and I reached for the door handle, but Ronan stopped me. I turned back to him and noted his eyes were a little lighter, making them look brighter and, right then, fierce.

"Are you all right?" He looked almost as wild as he had outside Agatheena's.

He shook his head. "I may not be a full-blooded vampire, but I'm more like them than I am any human, which means I am extremely territorial. I've felt this way about you, Rose, since I met you. I didn't recognize that's what I was feeling until those emotions returned, but I know that's what I was feeling. But after what we did, in my room at the clubhouse. Feeding you, making you...you..."

"Come," I said.

His gaze sharpened. "After making you come, I'm feeling that side of myself even more than before. So I need you to stick close to me. And if something happens again, like at that witch's cottage, where you might need to do something alone, we won't do it. We will find another way. I won't risk anything happening to you."

He was already so protective and now even more so? "I'll be okay—"

"No." He shook his head. "I need you to promise me, Rose, that you won't put yourself at risk like that again."

There was real fear in his eyes, but I didn't know if it was a promise I could keep. He needed this from me, though, right then, and if it would help him regain some control, I'd tell him whatever he needed to hear, and deal with the consequences later, if they arose. "I can do that," I said, purposely not actually promising. I sure as hell didn't want to go anywhere on my own and I didn't plan on it, but I had no idea what would come next, and I'd do whatever it took to protect my coven.

We got out of the car, and he took my hand as we headed to the restaurant. He pushed the door open, and we stepped inside. As soon as we entered, I knew this establishment wasn't owned by humans, and the way Ronan stiffened and scanned the room, so did he.

"Shifter," Ronan said, as if he could read my mind. "Cat."

I figured as much, but I doubted they were the domesticated house variety, like the five I'd counted lounging around the room. I Black Paws was one of those cat cafes I'd heard about.

There was no reason to think the shifters who owned the place would be any kind of threat, but I had no idea why I'd been drawn here so better to be alert. The place had several full tables and none of the beings sitting at them were human. I didn't know how I knew that, but I did. "Let's get a table."

A female strode over to us, her eyes were bright gold, and when she stopped in front of us they changed for a split second, her pupils elongating, definitely feline. "The Vault's only a few blocks away. I'm sure they'll have what you want there," she said and sniffed, giving us an up and down.

"Pardon?"

"We don't cater to blood drinkers in here, honey. You want to feed, take it to The Vault."

The Vault?

"We don't require blood," Ronan said. "But we would like a menu."

She narrowed her eyes, looked between us, then leaned in. "Fine, but any trouble and my boys will throw you out." She aimed her thumb over her shoulder.

Standing at the bar was a well-built male, and another sat on a stool opposite. Her *boys* were angled our way, watching the exchange closely, ready to jump up and throw us out if necessary and, judging by the scowls on their faces, hoping we'd give them reason to.

"We just want to eat," I said, feeling weird about the whole exchange.

"Fine, sit over there." She waved toward a booth against the wall.

Ronan was still looking at "the boys," and he didn't look happy. "Ignore them," I said and tugged on his arm.

He growled something under his breath. Then, ushering me into the booth first, he sat, blocking me in, so we were facing the big cat shifters across the room. He obviously didn't want his back toward them.

The female strode over and dumped a couple menus on the table. "Drink?"

I didn't want anything, honestly. Ronan's blood had given me everything I needed. But I was here for a reason, so I smiled up at her. "Soda, please."

"What kind of soda?"

I had no idea. I hadn't had a soda since I was young. I hadn't been able to tolerate it. "Um...Coke," I said and smiled at her.

She scowled harder. "You?" she said to Ronan.

"No drink for me."

She rolled her eyes. "I'll be back for your order in a few minutes." Then she walked off.

"Does that kind of thing happen often?" I asked him. "The blood drinkers comment? They don't want us here."

"Yes, I suppose it does." His thigh pressed against mine. "Blood drinkers make people uneasy. Understandable since to some of us, they would be considered food."

I leaned into him a little, not sure how I felt about that, about people being scared of me. "I guess that is understandable." Shaking that off, I scanned the room, looking for anything that stood out, any reason that could've brought me here. There was a big picture behind the bar. A photo, blown up, of the bar itself— our antagonistic waitress stood in the middle, and four large, burly males were on either side of her. One who looked older than her, her mate, I assumed, and three younger, their sons, I was also guessing. Two of which were our unhappy friends at the bar.

"That looks reasonably new," Ronan said, taking in the picture as well.

"They must've recently bought the place."

The female marched back to us and plonked down my drink, then stood there, pen poised, waiting for our order. I quickly flicked open the menu. I really wasn't hungry. "I'll have the chocolate cake, please."

She scowled. "That's it?"

"Yep, that's it."

"And you?" she said to Ronan.

"Nothing for me."

She shook her head in disgust and stomped off.

"She *really* doesn't like us."

"I don't like her either," Ronan said, a look of surprise on his face.

"You don't?" Ronan had spent the majority of his life feeling indifferent. Not liking someone because they were rude or there was just something about them that rubbed him the wrong way, and not because they were some kind of threat, was new to him.

"No," he said, brows low. "I don't."

"Why?" Watching Ronan, helping him figure this all out, was fascinating. It also made me want to wrap my arms around him and tell him it would all be okay.

His eyes lifted to mine. "I don't like the way she spoke to you or looked at you." He actually scowled, his face rearranging in a way it probably hadn't since he was a small boy. I had to bite my lips to keep from smiling. "I don't like those fuckers sitting at the bar, either, for the same reason. I'd really like to punch them both in the face."

"Fuckers? Those curse words are just rolling off the tongue now, huh?" I said, and my smile slipped free.

"The hounds curse a lot. I never understood why before, but the word fuck really does fit a lot of situations," he said, watching as I took a tentative sip of my soda. "For anger, especially. They also use it when they're talking about..." Those gorgeous eyes sliced to me, and his nostrils flared.

"About sex," I finished for him.

"Yes." It was one word, but his voice had dropped impossibly low, broadcasting a whole lot of things he was feeling.

I felt guilty for the way we'd left things at the clubhouse and also seriously cheated. "I'm sorry about before, having to leave before I got to..." I leaned forward. "Touch you."

His nostrils flared.

"Have you, ah...recovered?"

"The glaring males at the bar and their rude mother have helped get things back under control."

I grinned. "I'm glad—"

"Then we talked about fucking and the fact you were about to touch me, and now I'm in more pain than before." His eyes were dark and heated, and my belly curled.

"Perhaps we should change the subject?"

He shifted in his seat. "That would be wise."

The older female strode over to us and put my cake down in front of me, then stomped away. I took another sip of my drink. It was super sweet and fizzy, and it made my taste buds zing. Would food taste different for me now? I had to assume it would, since all my other senses had grown stronger. No, I didn't need to eat, but I'd always loved sweets.

I scooped up a forkful of cake and took a bite. "Oh...oh wow." I got another mouthful and moaned around my fork. "That's the best cake I've ever eaten," I said, licking my fork clean. "Do you want to try some?" I asked, scooping up more.

Ronan said nothing.

"Ronan?" I froze.

The heat wasn't just in his eyes, his entire face told me how much he wanted me. "I don't need to eat, but suddenly I'm ravenous," he said.

"What are you hungry for?"

His eyes widened a little, there was *so much* there, a little confusion, yes, but it was all mixed in with a whole lot of lust, and behind it all, the powerful predator he truly was. His gaze slid over my face, to my throat, lower, then back to my mouth before locking with mine again. "Everything, Rose. Everything."

Fire shot through my veins. I wanted that. I wanted it badly. "Will you...will you drink from me as well?"

He snarled low. "I don't think I'll be able to stop myself."

I squeezed my thighs together, the needy flesh between them growing slick and hot and achy. "I don't want you to stop yourself."

His stare moved over my throat again, and his nostrils flared.

Tension snapped and coiled between us. "How do you usually feed?" I said, something I'd been desperate to ask. "Do you go to one of those places where people go to be bitten?"

He nodded, his jaw getting tight in that way I was now used to. "Yes."

"Do you want that? To drink from someone else?" The very idea made me sick to my stomach.

He flashed his fangs. "No."

We'd made no declarations, or at least he hadn't, but there was no holding in my next words. "If you feed from anyone else, anyone but me, I'm not sure I'd ever forgive you."

His hand grabbed mine, resting on the table. His was shaking, strain lining his handsome face. He brought my fingers to his mouth and kissed them, his fangs peeking out from his upper lip, and he shook his head. "Hurting you, Rose, would destroy me."

God, the things he said to me. "When you need to feed next, you promise you'll come to me, and no one else?"

He gripped my hand tighter. "Yes."

We stared at each other for long moments. The tension was thick, pulsing between us. When it became too much, I scooped up more cake. "Will you try it?"

He glanced down at it on the fork.

"You can eat human food, can't you?"

He nodded, and his throat worked.

I had no idea what he was thinking. "Will you?"

He nodded again, and I held the fork to his lips. He opened his mouth, and I slipped it inside, then watched him eat for the first time ever.

"You like it?"

He swallowed and licked his lips. "It's very good." His gaze dropped to my mouth. "But now all I can think about is how it would taste on your lips."

I leaned forward. "Taste and see."

He stilled for a moment, then gently placing his fingers below my chin, he tilted it back and dipped his head. I held my breath, then his lips were on mine, and as soon as they touched, the world seemed to spin around me.

He slid his tongue over my lower lip, then sucked it gently. A rough groan escaped him, and I had to stop myself from climbing in his lap and straddling him.

"Good?" I murmured against his lips.

"Yes." He licked and sucked at my mouth some more. "I don't think I'll ever be able to stop."

"I don't want you to."

He deepened the kiss, and I felt one of his fangs scrape my lip. The taste of my blood hit my tongue, and Ronan's arm banded around me tighter before tugging me forward.

"Fuck," he grunted against my mouth.

His lean, muscled body, so strong and powerful, trembled against mine. His voice was full of wonder, of heat and need and hunger. It hurt my heart and filled it at the same time, that he'd been denied what he was feeling for so long.

"Take it outside," a deep voice said. "No one wants to watch you parasites suck face."

Ronan froze, swiped his tongue over the graze his fang had made, and lifted his head. He kept me tucked in tight to his side and turned to face the big cat shifter staring down at us. "What did you say?"

"You heard me." He smirked. "Parasite."

Ronan stood. They were about the same height, but the cat was definitely more heavily built. "I'm faster than you, stronger. I have powers that your small mind couldn't dream up. If I chose to, I could tear every throat out in this room before you realized that I was doing it." Ronan stepped closer. "I'd start with you, then your brother, then your very unpleasant mother."

The cat hissed and pulled back a meaty fist.

One moment Ronan was in front of him, and the next, he was behind the cat shifter, his head wrenched back by his hair. "So you chose to die today, cat?"

I stood frozen, stunned. The other male opened his mouth, then closed it, while his brother, who had shot to his feet and their mother, who stood with her hands over her mouth, watched on.

"I'm sorry," the guy said.

"Don't say sorry to me. Apologies to my female."

His female.

The cat's terrified eyes came to me. "I-I'm sorry."

Ronan shoved him aside. "Now we need to look around, then we'll leave. And if we have any questions, you will answer them, truthfully."

They all nodded.

"You can leave," Ronan said to the two tables with people still sitting at them. They rushed out, then Ronan glanced at me, silently telling me to start looking.

I jumped to it, checking out the place, the main restaurant, the storeroom, the office, and even the bathrooms. I made my way back to the bar. The big picture of the cat family seemed to call to me, so I took it in again.

Then I spotted it.

"The statue on the bar in this picture, where is it now?" It was only several inches high and looked to be made of carved wood.

"Answer her," Ronan said.

"It was stolen," the female said. "A couple days ago, during the dinner rush."

I turned from the image and to the older female. "What is it? Where did you get it?"

She shrugged. "It was here when we took over the place. The previous owners left it as a good luck charm."

I pulled out my phone and snapped a picture. Another demon effigy, it had to be. That was the third one stolen, including the one from the reptile guy's house and the museum. If that's what it was, of course, but I was positive that's what I was looking at. Why else would I have been called here?

I turned back to the cat family. "Thank you for your help."

"It wasn't exactly voluntary," she said, that scowl back on her face.

"If you had better manners, none of this would have been necessary," Ronan said. He took some money from his wallet and dropped it on the bar, then held his hand out to me.

I took it and we left.

"What do you make of that?" Ronan asked.

"Someone's getting desperate."

"Desperate enough to summon a demon and make some kind of twisted bargain," he said.

I looked up at him. "But why? What do they want?"

He shook his head, his gorgeous eyes locking with mine.

He didn't need to say it, I could see it in his eyes, and I was thinking the same thing.

Nothing good.

Chapter Twenty-One

Rose

I didn't want to go inside.

We stood at my door as low music drifted out from inside. Probably Else, she liked to listen to music while she worked.

I glanced up at Ronan again. I didn't want to say good night, I wanted to go with him, wherever he was going after this. But I didn't want to push. Maybe he needed space? This had to be a lot for him. He'd touched me, kissed me, and I wanted more of that, more of him. But I could only assume that everything Ronan was feeling and experiencing was confusing and no doubt exhausting. If he needed time to himself, I wasn't going to push for more.

"Thank you for today, for everything. There's no way I could do this without you," I said.

"I think you could, but I would hate it. I'd have to follow you, and I'd end up killing far too many people. This way is a lot more efficient."

I bit my lips together to stop my surprised laugh. "You talk about killing people on my behalf a lot."

His gaze moved over my face. "Because I feel the urge to do it multiple times a day. Every time a male looks at you, I want to tear their throat out."

I should probably be horrified by that. I wasn't. Maybe it made me twisted, but I didn't really care. "But you resist it, that's the important thing."

He licked his lips in a way that was completely unconscious, but he was looking at my mouth like he wanted a taste. "I wouldn't want you to think me a monster."

"That's the only reason you don't? For me?"

"That's the main reason, yes. Also, Relic told me I have to control my base instincts or no one will want to be around me for fear I'll kill them. I find I like your family. I wouldn't want them to be afraid of me."

Before he regained his emotions, he was indifferent. Now, these feelings were new to him. And even though Ronan once had a human mother, he was sired by a vampire. Vampires were cold, territorial, deadly. They were true predators. Born to kill. And for much of their existence had killed their victims when they fed.

Some still did, while others chose another way, like finding willing people to feed from. But those same instincts were part of Ronan, and something he'd had to learn to control—and that now included his instincts to protect me.

"They could never be afraid of you. They know you're a good male, Ronan," I said, then noticed his hands were trembling at his sides. "Are you okay?"

He nodded jerkily. "I—I need to leave now."

"Oh, okay." I forced myself not to ask him to stay, even though I really wanted to. I stepped closer to him.

And he did the same.

His hands shot out, and he gripped my hips awkwardly, his head dipping closer to mine. He wanted to kiss me. I tilted my head back and our noses bumped, then his arms banded around mine a little too roughly, and he jerked me against him.

As soon as our bodies made contact, I felt how hard he was.

Ronan hissed under his breath and jerked his hips back, then released me and stepped away. "I need to leave," he said again, desperation in his voice.

"Ronan—"

"I'll be here to collect you in the morning." Then he strode back to the car, fast, so fast I couldn't keep up.

"Ronan." I rushed after him, but he was already in his car and backing out. "Crap."

How did we get back to awkwardness? I reminded myself that he was still figuring it all out and that I had to be patient. Blowing out a breath, I headed inside.

Yep. The music was coming from Else's workroom, but the living room and kitchen were empty. Mom and Art would be working at the cemetery, no doubt. Several flowers only bloomed at night, and they were harvesting what they could before everything died off for the winter. There were already flowers and herbs hanging from every available space, drying for use later.

Voices came from the backyard, raised ones. I hustled to the kitchen window. Bram and Mags were standing out on the tree house balcony. Bram had his head dipped, and I could see his eyes blazing even from here. Mags's had her hands on her hips and a stubborn tilt to her chin, but I couldn't hear what she was saying. Bram lifted his hands and reached for her, then dropped them. He partially shifted, his wings exploding from his back, feathers glossy and black as he dove off the side of the balcony, catching the breeze, and with a couple of beats of his wings shot up into the sky.

Mags stared after him, then covered her face with her hands.

Shit. I darted around the kitchen table—

Someone knocked on the door. "Crap." I changed direction, rushed out to the hall, and pulled it open. An older gentleman stood there holding flowers.

He smiled. "Good evening."

"Um...hi."

"I'm here to collect Elsewyth," he said.

"Oh…okay. Let me see if she's free." I took a step back just as Else walked around the corner.

"Else," he said, his smile brightening. "You look lovely."

Else scowled. "What the hell are you holding, Conner Travis?"

"Flowers, for you," he said, the smile still in place. "You love hyacinths, so I don't want to hear any complaining."

This guy clearly knew Else well.

She took them from him and shoved them at me. "Do something with these, will you?"

I bit back my smile. "Will do."

My great-aunt turned back to Connor. "Come on, then. Let's get this over with."

The guy chuckled, completely unfazed by Else's attitude.

"And you can stop that as well, chuckles," she said and grabbed her coat.

He rushed forward, helping her into it. "You love it," he muttered under his breath.

Was Else blushing? "I won't be late," she said. "I'm being forced to attend the ridiculous CEA bimonthly gathering."

The CEA, the Coven Elders Assembly, had been trying to get Else to join for a long time, but she'd refused, until now apparently.

"You have fun, and there's no need to rush back."

She scoffed, then limped out the door. Conner smiled and waved, and then they were gone. I couldn't help but smile as well. Else had met her match there.

Then I remembered Mags and spun around, running through the kitchen and out the back door. She wasn't on the balcony anymore, so I climbed the ladder to the tree house, and knocked, calling out for her, but she didn't answer. I eased the door open and poked my head inside. "Mags?"

Nothing.

I went back to the house and searched for her inside, but she wasn't there either.

A car started. I rushed back to the front, but she was already driving off when I got there. *Dammit.*

I sent a group text to Iris and Willow, in case she was heading their way, then texted Mags, telling her to call when she could. I looked up from my phone, about to head back inside, and spotted a car parked across the street. There was an older, dark-haired male sitting behind the wheel—and he was staring at me.

He froze.

I lifted a hand and waved. Maybe he was a friend of Mom or Art? He lifted a hand, waving back. I took a step toward the car. He started it, and without looking back, sped off.

Weird.

The forest closed in around me, any light from the moon smothered by the thick tree canopy above. Wind whispered through the leaves. Howls and wails of despair filling the night.

I spun around, knowing who would be there. Terror quaked through me when he stepped from the shadows. I tried to take a step back, to run, but my feet were stuck fast to the forest floor.

The tall, broad figure draped in black moved closer, his twisted wooden staff gripped in his hand. "I waited and you never came," he said, voice so deep and terrible, I was positive it froze me to the marrow in my bones.

"I'm not sick anymore. You can't expect me to come to you now. I'm not ready."

He kept advancing. The hood of his cloak concealed his features, but as he drew closer, eyes, blue and frigid, glowed through the darkness, piercing my soul. "We had a deal, witch."

"I know, and I'll hold to our bargain, but not yet. When I'm old, when my time comes—"

"No," he roared, moving so close now, he stood over me. "I will not wait."

I still couldn't make out his shadowed features, but those eyes froze me to the core. "Please, I beg you."

"You have until the next full moon."

"But I'm not dead—"

"Come to the stone arch on the edge of Oldwood Forest. I'll be waiting. Your coven owes me, and if you don't come to me, witch, I will find a replacement, and you won't like who I choose."

I woke with a cry. Covering my mouth, I quickly smothered it.

My heart pounded so hard that I struggled to catch my breath. *Oh goddess.* What the hell was I going to do? Death wouldn't take no for an answer, and he wouldn't wait. I'd stupidly hoped that he'd forgotten me or changed his mind. But, of course, he hadn't. I couldn't see any way out of this. I didn't want to give up my life when I'd only started living it, but I couldn't let him take someone else, someone I loved, either. I wouldn't.

I snatched my phone from my bedside table and scrolled to my cousin Zinnia's name. If there was any help to be found, she would know where to find it.

It rang twice.

"Rose, are you okay?" Alarm filled her voice.

"Yes...no." I forced myself to take a calming breath. "I need your help, Zinny."

"Your task?"

It was forbidden to ask for help from your coven or family, we both knew that, but I was positive that this whole Death thing had nothing to do with my task or the mother. He started visiting me long before that.

But I could tell by the tone in Zinnia's voice she would defy the mother, she would break all the rules, if that was why I was calling. "No, it's something else."

"Everyone's okay?" she asked.

It was then I realized it was still dark outside. "Sorry, I didn't check the time before I called."

"I don't care about that, Roe. Whatever you need, I'm here, always."

Zinnia was the best. And she and her younger sister Jasmine were more like our sisters than cousins. "What I'm about to tell you needs to stay between us." She could also keep a secret.

"Of course."

No hesitation. Zinnia would do anything for the people she loved, a trait among all the members of this family. "So, when Iris completed her task and you guys sent those evil souls to Hell..."

There was a beat of silence. "Yes."

"Well, that night Death came to me in my sleep. He wants my soul as a replacement, as payment for what was taken from him. I agreed. I was dying anyway, and better me than one of you." I swallowed hard. "I'm not dying anymore, Zin, but Death doesn't care. He won't wait for me to grow old. And if I don't go to him during the next full moon, he'll take someone else. Someone from this family. You know about this stuff, is there any way out of this without anyone else getting hurt? Do you know someone who can help?" I was doing my best not to break down, not to freak out completely.

Silence again, this time longer.

"Zinny?"

"I'm here. Right, so the next full moon, which means we've got a week."

Fear gripped me. "Is there anything I can do?"

More silence, then she cleared her throat. "Yeah, I've kind of been expecting this."

"What?"

"Death spoke to Iris, Roe, right after we sent those bitches to Hell. He mentioned you, and she told me. I'd hoped...I don't know, that he was bluffing, or trying to scare her."

"Iris never said anything."

"She didn't want to freak you out, but it looks like we made a bad call, huh? But I've got this. Leave this with me, okay?"

I was too scared to hope. "Who else knows?"

"Just Iris and me."

"Let's keep this between you and me for now." Thank goddess for that. Mom had been through enough. "Do you really think you can help me?"

"I know I can," she said. "You worry about your task; I've got this, Roe. Everything's going to be okay, I promise."

It was impossible not to worry. This was Death we were talking about. He was older than time. The ruler of Limbo. The harbinger of darkness. No matter how much Zinnia was trying to make me believe this was no big deal, I knew it was the complete opposite.

Death would not go quietly.

Whatever Zinnia had planned, we needed to be ready.

Chapter Twenty-Two

Ronan

Leaving Rose last night had caused an ache in the center of my chest. It'd felt…wrong, which was why I was standing at her door now, so early in the morning.

I'd been tempted to follow her up to her room, to hide behind my powers and stay with her, but that was wrong. Even if I felt as if I was losing my mind when I was away from her, it still would have been wrong.

Rose wouldn't like that, being watched without her consent.

So I'd gone back to the clubhouse, stripped off, and stroked myself in the shower again, with my fingers pressed to my nose the entire time. Rose's scent had still been there from earlier that day when she'd fed from me and begged me to tough her slick flesh and make her feel good.

I wanted to do that again, badly.

At the thought, my cock hardened, and my hunger increased. I needed to feed, and soon. Now that I was feeding Rose, I'd need to feed more often as well, and I couldn't wait much longer.

I knocked and waited.

Rose said she wanted to feed me, but how could I do that? What if I hurt her? Despite what I promised, I couldn't bear to even think about my dirty, tainted fangs anywhere near her delicate veins. The very thought made me sick to my stomach. And she'd see me, the real me. I knew without a doubt I'd have no control if I fed from her. The way I looked when I was past hungry. I'd disgust her. Frighten her. No, I couldn't do it.

The door opened, and I straightened, every muscle in my body tensing. Rose stood there, so incredibly beautiful. I took her in, tracing her subtle curves, her thick, pale hair so glossy I itched to touch it. Her rosy cheeks and red lips made my mouth water. "Rose," I said.

"Hey," she smiled and stepped forward.

Was she going to kiss me? Last night, leaving without tasting her lips one more time had been torture. My arms opened and she stepped in. I dipped my head as she pressed hers to my chest. My mouth bumped her ear. She wanted a hug, not a kiss. Just because I wanted to kiss her all the time, just because she let me touch her yesterday, didn't mean she felt the same way or wanted that today.

It angered me how much I struggled to interpret these situations.

Rose lifted her head, her cheeks pink. She was embarrassed, that's what that meant. Frustration flashed through me. I felt like a fool, both feelings that I'd deciphered quickly since I'd felt them a lot lately.

"We should get going," I said, trying to keep what I was feeling out of my voice.

She called goodbye to her family and pulled the door shut. Then we got in the car, and I tried to gather my control, but if anything, it slipped more.

She glanced over at me, and I turned the key. "Hey, what's going on? You're angry."

I shoved my fingers through my hair. "Yes."

Her body twisted to face me. "With me?"

"No," I said quickly. "With me."

Her hand covered mine, and it was like my soul sighed in relief just from her touch. How could that be? I didn't even know if I had a soul. How could someone's touch affect a being so deeply? "Talk to me, Ronan. Please."

I couldn't take it, not knowing what she was feeling. This was torture. "I need to know what you're thinking, Rose. I can't work it out. I don't understand...any of this, what's happening between us. I don't know what the right thing to do is. I'm not a wolf, or a hound, or a witch. I don't understand females like they do. I'm afraid of making a mistake with you. That I could lose you if I keep...doing everything wrong."

Her fingers curled around mine, holding my hand tighter. "*Nothing* you do or want from me could ever be wrong, Ronan. I promise you, everything you want from me, I want from you."

I shook my head. "No, you don't understand the things I want, Rose. What I want from you, with you—"

"I promise you, I want those things from you as well. All of it."

My mouth went dry.

"I haven't said it again, the time hasn't been right, it's still not, but I need you to know that what I said to you that night, the night I thought I was going to die... Ronan, I meant every word. Those feelings, they haven't changed. So when you get the urge to kiss me or hug me or touch me, then you should do it."

My throat was so tight, there was no chance of speaking, so I let my instincts lead, and I reached for her, gripping the back of her neck and pulling her to me. I pressed my lips to hers. This wasn't the first time we'd kissed like this. But this time, it wasn't because of a dying wish or in the throes of blood lust, and I could acknowledge I felt completely out of my depth. But I wanted her so badly, there was no stopping.

I needed deeper, more. I growled in frustration, and Rose parted her lips. My tongue immediately slipped inside for a taste, and then instinct took over. I kissed her. I kissed my female like I'd been hungering to. Like I constantly hungered to.

Her hand touched the side of my throat, her fingers curling deep, holding me to her, kissing me back. She liked it, the way I kissed her, and she wanted me just as fiercely. Pleasure filled me. I never wanted to stop.

Finally, though, I forced myself to lift my head. Rose was panting, her lips darker and puffier than before. Her cheeks were darker as well, and her eyes were bright. I cupped the side of her face. "You're so beautiful," I rasped.

Her teeth sunk into that plump lower lip, and she looked up at me with soft eyes. "So are you."

I didn't know what to say. I'd never cared about my appearance. But it pleased me that she liked my features. "I want to keep kissing you." I pressed my lips to hers one more time. "But I think we need to leave."

She nodded. "You're right. We have to stop...for now."

I dragged my gaze from her mouth. "For now."

"You'll have to use your powers to get us in," Rose said when we pulled up in the museum's parking lot. We'd spent most of the day going over what we knew and chasing leads that didn't take us anywhere.

Now it was late afternoon, and we were outside the museum. It backed on to the witch's council building but was run separately. Rose had informed me it was more efficient like that, for warding purposes, and one of the reasons we'd left this place until last. It had been closed the last couple of days, more than likely due to the robbery and the missing guard who worked here, and had been well protected, making it harder to get into.

I took her hand and led her around the corner where no one would see us, then lifted my powers. We headed back to the front, completely concealed, and walked through the large double doors and into the main foyer. "There'll be cameras, and no doubt extra security. We'll need to stay under my block. The parking lot was relatively empty, but we don't want to be seen. There are at least twenty people here."

"Is that a rough guess, or something else?" she asked.

"I can hear their hearts beating."

"You can?" She tilted her head to the side. "Do you think I can do that?"

I stopped her in the middle of the wide marble floor. "I'm not a bat shifter, but it's a common skill among blood drinkers. Close your eyes."

She let her lids drift shut, and I immediately ate up the sight of her. She said nothing I did was wrong, that I could have whatever I wanted when it came to her, but if I kissed her now like I wanted to, would she like it? And would I be able to stop? I forced the image from my mind. "Block everything else out and slow down your breathing. Bats are nocturnal, they prefer the dark. With your eyes closed, your other senses should heighten."

The pulse at the base of her throat fluttered even as she worked at slowing down her breathing. I wanted to suck on her skin there, right over that pretty little vein—nibble, kiss, lick, bite—again, I resisted.

"I can hear them, Ronan." A smile curled her lips. "I can hear them." Her eyes opened. "I should feel weird about it, and I guess I do a bit, considering I have this skill to hunt people down to feed on their blood, but it's still pretty cool."

Her joy filled me somehow, her pleasure becoming mine.

"Next up, learning to fly," she said, beaming. "My wings are getting stronger every day."

The joy dissipated. "You could plummet to your death." I shook my head. "No. No, I won't allow you to do that."

Her lips pressed together. "No?"

I shook my head. "It's too dangerous."

"Hmm, not sure I love this bossy side of yours, Ronan." She headed across the foyer. "We'll revisit this topic of conversation at a later date."

A weird feeling gathered in my gut as I followed her. I didn't like it one bit. "Rose."

She rounded a corner and I followed. She stopped in the middle of a wide hall and pointed to one of the doors. There was a temporary barrier there and a sign with "restricted access" written on it. "I'd say that's where we need to go."

I strode over and tried the door. "Yes, it's locked. They obviously don't want anyone in there since it's still an active crime scene."

"Yeah, and thankfully, the council still thinks Willow's doing the investigating," Rose said. "I have to assume, whoever was behind this had someone helping them, someone who can use magic to block themselves or the council would've found them on their own."

A scent hit me, it was faint, but there was no mistaking it. "Blood."

Rose stilled, her nose crinkling as she sniffed the air. The sight made me want to kiss her again. "I can't smell anything."

"It's buried under bleach, but it's there."

She lifted her hand and pressed it to the door. "Blood magic. This door has been sealed tight. I'm not sure even your power can get us through."

I lifted my hand and it touched cool steel. "You're right." Not much could stop me, but there was no getting through this.

Rose glanced at me. "There might be a spell, one Iris told me about. She used it during her task. The ward is strong, but it's a couple of weeks old. It's weakened, and wards like this need to be maintained daily."

"What do you need?" I asked.

Rose slid her hand into her pocket and pulled out her small knife. "This."

My lips curled back.

"I have to do this, and you have to be okay with it," she said, reading me easily.

I wanted to snatch the blade from her hand when she lifted it to her palm but forced myself not to. There was no stopping my snarl, though, when she sliced a small *X* into her skin, trying to muffle her gasps of pain.

"I'm fine, Ronan," she said.

"Now what?" I asked, wanting this over with so I could heal her wound as soon as possible.

"You can't break a ward like this if you have evil intent. This spell can see right into the heart of the spell caster. The words have to come from light and goodness, and the spell itself acts as an impartial judge with the ability to grant entry or not. My blood is essentially giving the spell life, for a short time. That's how it works." She pressed her hand to the door handle, tilted her head back, and closed her eyes. She jolted, then began whispering, saying the spell over and over, faster and faster. She was breathing hard, her body trembling.

She gasped and was almost knocked back, barely keeping her hold on the door handle. I rushed in behind her, snarling as I held her up.

It came again, like a kind of surge that flowed through Rose, so strong it lifted goose bumps all over me.

Then the lock clicked, the ward breaking.

Rose released a breath and fell against me for a moment, then she tilted her head back and looked up at me. She was beaming. "I did it. I broke the ward."

The pride on her face and the happiness in her eyes was mesmerizing. "You did," I said, my voice rough as I lifted her hand and kissed the bloody *X* before swiping my tongue over it to start the healing process. Her taste instantly ignited my senses.

"I wasn't sure I could...but I did it." Her smile grew even more dazzling. "Right, let's see what they're hiding."

We walked in, shutting the door behind us.

"I smell it now…the blood." She spun around. "There was a lot of it."

"Yes." I moved across the room. "Here." Someone had tried to clean it up, but there was no disguising it from me or Rose, it seemed. She was far more powerful than she realized.

"Do you think it's the guard's? He's still missing."

"Possibly."

She rushed to one of the desks and turned on the computer. "They'll have a database listing their inventory. Hopefully, they've marked off what was taken." She tapped at the keys. "It's password protected."

"What about one of the other computers? Where someone's already logged in? Would they have access to the same database?"

Rose grinned. "You're not just a pretty face."

I paused. "You think I'm pretty?"

"I do. You have a problem with that?" Her grin grew wider.

Not if it made her smile like that, still. "I'm not sure."

She laughed, the sound musical, sweet. "Okay, handsome. Is that better?" She turned, scanning the room. "Before we go hunt down a computer, I want to try something."

"What do you have in mind?"

She spotted something across the room. "The visions I have, it's called scrying. I spoke to my sisters and did some research, and I think I know how to bring on a vision instead of waiting for them to randomly hit me." She strode across the room and picked up a silver tray from one of the shelves. She read the inscription on it. "Not a demon artifact, some award given to the department. It should be safe." She walked back. "Where do you think most of the blood was?"

I moved to the spot where the scent was strongest. "Here."

Rose placed the tray on the ground beside my feet, then pulled her blade from her pocket again.

"No," I bit out. "Not again."

Her head tilted back and her eyes widened, brows sliding high. "Excuse me?"

"You will not cut yourself again," I said, and even I recognized the fury in my voice.

Rose stood and planted her hands on her hips. "I'm a witch, Ronan. A witch who's been too weak to practice even the most basic of spells for a very long time. A witch who felt her magic dwindle and almost die right along with her. I've had to stand by while my sisters fight, while they use their magic, together, for a common cause and feel absolutely useless when I couldn't stand with them." She blew out a breath. "I love you, Ronan, more than you're capable of understanding right now, but this is my birthright, what I was born to do, what I've longed to do for my whole life. And I won't stop, not even for you."

Her words affected me deeply. Emotions swirled inside me. So many, I couldn't name them all, but I didn't like the way it felt. "Rose—"

She held up a finger, stopping me. "But I'm feeling forgiving, mainly because I'm looking forward to doing a whole lot of kissing with you later and we can't do that if we're fighting, so how about you try that sentence again? But this time, you think very carefully about what you're saying."

My female was angry with me. I didn't like that. I hated it. But she'd also just professed her love for me, for the second time, and I was positive the shriveled organ in my chest stirred. There was also the kissing. I didn't want to miss out on that. But most importantly, she longed to use her magic. How would I feel if I couldn't use my powers? I hadn't liked it when the mother rendered mine useless in that field. The feeling of powerlessness had been one of the worst things I'd ever experienced. "Apologies," I said. "I don't like seeing you hurt, Rose, that's all."

"I know, but you can kiss it better again afterward, and eventually I won't register the pain. I'll get used to it like my sisters." Then she lifted her blade and made a slice in her other palm.

I jolted, even as my fangs tingled. "Too deep, Rose."

"I'm okay," she said without looking up, then curled her fingers into a fist. She held it over the silver tray and walked around it. Her blood dripped from between her fingers, hitting the silver in fat, scarlet drops. Then she whispered words, a spell of some kind. She made another circle of the tray, then lowered herself to her knees and stared into it.

"Rose?"

She said nothing, lost in the tray's shiny surface. Seconds ticked by, and she began to slowly sway. Several minutes passed while I watched her closely.

Then finally, she gasped and fell back.

I rushed over, and she blinked up at me. "I saw something." Her voice trembled.

"What was it?"

"The guard. It's his blood...he was murdered. Right here. The night after the effigy was stolen."

"Did you see who did it?"

She shook her head. "The guard was standing here, then in a flash, he was on the floor, bleeding out. They were that quick."

I lifted her to her feet. She swayed to the right, and I pulled her into me to steady her. "You're not well."

"I was a little dizzy from the vision, but I'm fine now. See?" She pulled away from me, but I kept my arm around her waist.

"I don't like this."

"Well, the sooner we check the database, the sooner we can leave. Let's go find a computer."

I wanted to object. But I assumed she'd take that about as well as me telling her not to cut herself. "If you feel unwell, I want you to tell me, Rose."

She cupped my jaw. "I will, I promise."

Warmth flowed through me, and the urge to lean into her touch was almost overwhelming. Instead, I led her from the room. It didn't take long to find a desk manned by one of the museum staff. A female sat behind the reception desk just outside the office of the museum's general manager.

"Now what?" Rose asked.

There were seats nearby. "We sit and wait for her to use the lavatory or go to lunch."

"Well, that's annoying." Rose glanced around.

There were a couple of comfortable-looking armchairs, though one was occupied by a sleeping cat. The female behind the desk was a witch, so I assumed the cat was her familiar. "I'll move the cat."

She grabbed my arm, stopping me. "Don't do that. We only need one chair."

Then she led me to the available seat, pressed her hand to my chest, and tried to get me to sit in it. "No, Rose, you sit. I'll stand."

"No, Ronan. We will both sit," she said.

There was a glimmer in her eyes. "Rose—"

"You can be my seat," she said and pressed her hand to my chest once more.

I could be her seat? I liked the idea of that—a lot. I sat. Rose moved in between my spread thighs and sat on one of them, then wrapped an arm around my shoulders.

"There, now we're both sitting," she said.

The warmth of her body soaked into me immediately. Her bottom was soft, her weight slight, her scent intense. "I like this," I said to her.

"I thought you might." Her lips twitched.

Her legs dangled between mine, which couldn't be comfortable. We had no idea how long we'd have to wait. So I hooked her under the knees and draped them across my other leg. The change in position had her rear nestling against my groin. I realized my mistake when I hardened beneath her instantly. I quickly tried to move her.

She cupped my jaw with her free hand and shook her head. "I know you want me, Ronan, and I like that I can feel how much. You don't have to hide it. Can you scent the same from me?"

"Yes." My voice had grown gritty.

"We're seriously attracted to each other. We both know it, why pretend otherwise?"

I took her wrist, keeping her hand on me. "I would never pretend I didn't want you, Rose. But my control is already stretched thin, and having you on me like this…I find it difficult to keep my hands to myself."

She slid her thumb over my lower lip. "Do you want to touch me?"

"Badly."

"Then touch," she said. "Touch me anywhere you want to."

"Rose—"

"This body, my body, it's all new to me as well. It feels things I never could before. I want to experience everything it's capable of feeling, of doing…with you. Don't you want that too?"

My hand had moved to her waist without me even realizing, and I squeezed gently. "Yes, I want that. With me. Only with me."

"Then do it," she whispered.

Her need was right there in her expressive eyes. She wanted me to touch her. Her desire for me gave me more pleasure than anything else could. I was put on this Earth to give this female everything she wanted or needed. I was here to sustain her in every way. My gaze lowered to her chest, and my hunger increased. I slid my hand up under her sweater.

"I love the way your hands feel on my skin," she said and took a shaky breath.

"Your skin is soft and smooth and warm." I cupped her breast, and she took another shuddering breath. "Do you like that, Rose?"

"Yes."

"You're so soft here, I can't stop myself from…" I squeezed her and a groan slipped free.

Her hand lifted, covering mine, but over her sweater, as if she were afraid I'd stop. I couldn't, not now, not now that I had her tender flesh in my hands.

Her nipple tightened, pressing against my palm, and I swiped my thumb over it. Rose gasped. "That feels good as well?"

"So good." She lay back against me and pressed her mouth to my throat, sucking, kissing.

My erection throbbed harder. I swiped again, then pinched the tight peak between my fingers lightly, to see if she'd like that as well. She moaned and her fang grazed my skin, making me shiver. I did it again, alternating between massaging the soft flesh in my hand and toying with her nipple. Her scent grew heavier, her arousal filling my senses.

Her thighs tensed over mine, then she pressed them together.

"Your pussy is wet, isn't it, Rose?" I asked huskily.

"Yes."

She told me I could touch her wherever I wanted. "I want to touch you there, sweets. I want to make you come for me like you did in my room at the clubhouse." My voice was nothing but a growl now, and her scent was Heaven and Hell all in one. My cock was harder than before, and my mind kept throwing up images of me tearing her jeans off her body and sinking the iron-hard flesh trapped behind my zipper inside her.

But I wouldn't do that here. I'd never been with a female, and Rose was innocent. The thought of doing something wrong, of hurting her, eased some of the urgency I was feeling and made it possible to focus on my female, on pleasuring her.

"Yes, I want that. Please, Ronan."

My hands shook, but I managed to undo her jeans and slide down the zipper, then I slipped my hand inside her underwear. I tightened my arm around her and pressed my mouth to her ear, growling at the feel of her, so hot and slick. "The way you feel, Rose. It's for me, isn't it, sweets? This desire, it's all for me."

"Yes." She moaned and lifted her hips, silently asking for more. "It's all for you."

Another female walked in and began talking to the receptionist at her desk. They had no idea what was happening right in front of them. That I had the most perfect female on this Earth on my lap, desperate for me, lost to the pleasure I was giving her. I'd never felt like this in my life. This was joy, this feeling of immeasurable happiness. This sweet, precious female was squirming in my lap, because of me, because she wanted me.

I dragged my fingers through her wetness, and she spread her legs wider, inviting me to take more, wanting more. She was so incredibly wet. The more I touched her, the wetter she became, and the more she wriggled and moaned. "Ronan, please."

"Tell me what you want and I'll give it to you. Anything, it's yours."

Her hand dropped to my wrist, and she pushed it deeper. "Slide one of your fingers inside me."

She was panting hard, rocking her hips against my hand. Yes, I wanted to know how she felt inside so badly. I dipped my middle finger to that tight little opening and rubbed over it once, twice, before notching the tip against it on the third pass. I pressed my mouth to her ear. "Tell me to stop if you don't like it, or if I cause you pain."

She nodded and rolled her hips, forcing the tip inside her.

A growl ripped from me. "Okay?"

"Y-yes. More."

Her pleas burrowed into my chest, taking hold. I slid my finger inside, and goose bumps lifted all over me, a shiver moving through my body, my lower gut aching and tight, but that ache was nothing compared to my cock. She felt so incredibly good. I pulled out a little, then pushed back in, giving her more this time. She put more pressure on my wrist, silently asking me for more.

I gave her what she wanted, pushing in slowly, then sliding out, going deeper each time until I was inside her as far as I could go.

She gripped my shoulders, her nails digging into my skin, scoring my flesh. "Oh goddess," she cried and clung to me tighter.

I thrust faster, in and out of her wet heat. She was so tight, she gripped my finger. "I can feel your inner muscles clutching at my finger, Rose. Does that mean you're close to coming for me?"

"Y-yes." She rocked against my hand.

Her face was flushed a deep pink, and her lips were full and red. I couldn't stop myself from taking her jaw with my free hand and leaning in and kissing her. I wanted to taste her desire, her pleasure.

She squeezed down on my finger hard, released, then again, over and over as she cried out against my mouth.

Possessiveness roared through me, my fangs punching from my gums. I felt wild, like the predator I was. I would kill, destroy anyone who tried to hurt her, to take her from me. "Those cries are mine, Rose," I growled. "Only mine."

She slumped in my arms, trembling, and her hand went to my jaw once more. "Yes," she said huskily. "Only yours."

Chapter Twenty-Three

Rose

I shifted on Ronan's lap, reaching for the front of his pants—

He grabbed my wrist and tilted his head toward the desk behind us. Both females were gone. The desk unmanned. "We need to move, now."

He lifted me off his lap before I had a chance to protest, adjusted and did up my pants, then took my hand and led me to the desk. My legs were still shaky, but I managed to clear my head enough to round the desk.

I was fairly computer savvy. Not much else to do when you're bedridden most of the time, well, until I'd gotten too sick for even that.

This system had been designed specifically for the museum, but it seemed fairly basic. I hit the department's tab, then clicked demonology, searching until I found what I was looking for. "I think I've got it. There's an inventory register."

I narrowed it down to effigies. If this robbery was related to the others we knew about, then the missing items would be summoning effigies.

The screen filled with images. The pictures of each item were on the right, the details—what it was, where it came from, along with its purpose—on the left. Then below each were details of how the museum acquired it, how long they'd had it, etc. They'd also included other effigies, ones they didn't have but were of historical significance.

I quickly scrolled. "There's six pages." I hit print. "We don't have time to go through them all here."

Ronan tilted his head. "Someone's coming." He strode from the room.

Shit.

His voice echoed in the cavernous hall, lying about some appointment he had with the head of the antiquities department and asking for directions. A female voice followed, asking for identification, saying that he was in a restricted area.

Three more pages to go.

I couldn't hear what he was saying, but Ronan's voice was stern, authoritative.

The last page printed, and I snatched them up, closed down the screen I'd been on, and rushed to the door. I poked my head around the side, but Ronan was already walking away. He must've heard the printer finish. And judging by the light buzz I felt around me, I was still cloaked by his power. The female walked back in, picked up her phone, and asked for security.

I rushed out, ran down the hall, and rounded the corner. Ronan was there waiting.

"You have what you need?"

"Yes."

Ronan quickly led me from the building and out to his car. A moment later, we sped off.

"Where to now?" I asked him.

"I have some things I need to do...for the hounds. So I'll drop you off at your place, but I'll be back first thing in the morning."

I twisted in my seat. "You're taking me home?"

His eyes were focused on the road. "Yes."

"But I thought..." I stopped myself. I thought after what happened in that reception office, he'd take me back to the clubhouse, and we'd finish what we'd started. Turned out I was wrong. "Sure, you obviously have somewhere you need to be." I felt the urgency of this task, the ticking time bomb literally on my skin, but leads were few and far between.

Time was running out, and not just for my task. Death had laid down an ultimatum, and it was constantly on my mind. I still hadn't heard back from Zinnia. All I could do was wait for my cousin to call and go through what I'd printed out at the museum. We desperately needed a starting point for tomorrow.

Ronan pulled up outside the house. "I'll be here early tomorrow."

I searched his face. He seemed strange, distant, and his eyes were incredibly pale, lighter than I'd ever seen them. "I don't like saying goodbye to you," I said, because there was no reason to hold back how I felt.

His nostrils flared, and I knew he was scenting me. "I don't like it either."

I leaned toward him, and he did the same. I pressed my lips to his, and one of his fangs grazed my lower lip. I shivered.

He's hungry.

The knowledge hit me. Maybe it was the connection between us, or maybe it was because I'd drunk enough of his blood that I was starting to sense what he was feeling. I knew that could happen with mates and also blood drinkers. His eyes were glowing, lighter than normal. Was that a sign as well?

"Why don't you come inside and feed first," I said against his lips.

He froze, jolting slightly. "That's not...I can't—"

"Ronan, we talked about this. I can't bear the thought of you depriving yourself."

He shook his head woodenly. "I'm not." His voice was rough,

low. "I ah…I need to help out the hounds." He straightened. "I'll see you in the morning."

"Okay." It was stupid, but it felt like a rejection, even though he had a good reason to leave. "I'll see you tomorrow."

I got out of the car and walked to the front door. He didn't leave until I opened it. I waved as he drove off.

Well, that sucked.

I was about to shut the door when I spotted the same car across the street that I'd seen last night. It was too dark to see who was sitting in the driver's seat. I took a step toward the car and expected it to speed off again. It didn't.

The driver's door opened and a male got out. He stared over at me, his hands gripped tightly in front of him. He was tall, dark-haired, not human.

I stopped where I was, keeping space between us. "Can I help you?"

"Are you one of Daisy's girls?" the man asked.

"Yes."

"Were you born after Iris?"

I stilled. "Who are you?"

His dark gaze moved over me, something shifting in his eyes, something I couldn't read. Then they came back to me and there was surprise, maybe even alarm. "I think I'm your father."

I sucked in a sharp breath.

"The dhampir who found me, he didn't tell you about me?"

My father was standing right there. I'd always wondered about him, but I'd never tried to find him. Why would I? He'd run off. He'd left Mom and his unborn child. Wills and Iris had different fathers, but he'd been a dad to them as well, at least for a short time. When I'd gotten sicker, Mom had tried desperately to track him down in case there was something in his family history that could provide a clue about my illness. He'd remained elusive. But she'd always thought he was human.

He shifted nervously. "I thought you might try to find me...after..."

"There was no reason to," I said, and maybe that sounded cruel, and maybe I was trying to hurt him a little. But I didn't know this man. I didn't owe him anything, not even civility. The only questions I'd wanted answers to were about what I was, nothing more.

"I deserve that." He slid trembling hands into his pockets.

"Why didn't you tell Mom what you were?" I asked the only true question I'd had since we found out the truth about what I was.

He lifted a shoulder, then dropped it. "Blood drinkers aren't always welcome." He smiled sheepishly. "I had it bad for Daisy, and I stupidly thought she wouldn't want anything to do with me if she knew what I was."

"So you got her pregnant and took off instead?"

His smile dropped. "I was going through some things. Things that I didn't want touching my girls, so I left. I planned to come back, but things in my world were messy, and the longer I stayed away, the harder it was to come back. In the end, I thought you'd both be better off without me." He motioned to me. "I never dreamed you'd have anything of me in you... I thought you'd be all witch. Nothing like this has ever happened in our colony. You're unique..." He shook his head. "I don't even know your name. Christ, I don't even know my own daughter's name."

I crossed my arms. "Rose."

"Rose." He smiled. "Daisy always did have a thing for flowers." He fidgeted. "I know I don't have a right to be here, but I wanted to meet you. I've always regretted leaving the way I did."

He actually seemed genuine, but then I didn't know him. He could be full of crap. "I'm not sure what you want from me," I said, because he'd had my whole life to make introductions, yet he'd stayed away.

"I'm sure you have questions about what you are, where you

come from. I wasn't there when you needed me, but I'd like to be there for you now. You have family, a colony, they're your people as well. I'd like to share that with you, if you'd let me."

I suddenly realized I did have questions, a lot of them. I also had wings that I couldn't use, and maybe he'd be able to help me with that. As for a relationship of any kind or getting to know my bat shifter family, I wasn't so sure. "I'd like to know more about what I am, but as far as the rest, I'm not sure I'm interested. Maybe we could meet to talk sometime?"

He nodded. "I'd really like that, Rose. I'm not going to push for anything. It's up to you, all of it."

I didn't want him coming inside. This was enough of a shock for me, I wasn't going to spring a reunion on Mom as well.

He gave me his number and left, and I went inside. Today had been eventful, to say the least. My head spun, and I found my need for Ronan, to be with him, was so strong, it was a constant ache inside me.

He'd left only minutes ago, and already I missed him.

The sounds of the TV drifted from the living room. I didn't want to be alone with my thoughts, so I joined Mags and Iris on the couch.

"How's things?" Iris asked, throwing an arm around my shoulders.

"Okay, I think, or maybe completely terrible. Honestly, I'm not sure," I said and rested my head on her shoulder.

"Sounds about right," she said and gave me a squeeze. We were quiet for a few moments. "So, have you been studying up on your basic spells?" she said into the silence. She was worried about me.

"Yes, ma'am, and all I can say is thank the goddess I have Ronan to protect me or I'd be toast already. I'm so out of practice."

Iris's expression grew serious. "When you need it, your magic will be there for you. If you don't have a spell for what you need, follow your gut, the words will come. And if not, you can direct the energy you're feeling. A blast of magic disorientates an attacker and can give you the split second you need to get away. Practice, okay?"

"I will, I promise." All my sisters had been trying to hide their fear for me, but I saw it now in Iris's eyes. Time to change the subject. "Where's everyone?"

"Mom and Art had an early night. Else is out again with Connor." Iris's eyes went wide, and I laughed. Last year our gran predicted, from the spirit realm, that a male was going to come into Else's life. It looked as if her prediction was coming true. "And Wills is at the clubhouse. Ren was stopping by, he's been spending a lot of time there lately, the pull to be with her...he's finally giving into it again. He's also spending time with the hounds."

"Well, that's good." Willow had been trying to get him to leave his house more, and it looked like her efforts were working.

"Ren's been taking baby steps, but this seems like a big one to me," Iris said. "Though, I think the hounds have just given him another way to avoid dealing with what he went through."

"Oh?"

"Booze and females," Iris said.

I winced.

"Yeah." Iris chewed her lip. "But Wills is there, and Warrick. They won't let things get out of hand."

She didn't look overly confident. I wasn't either. Ren was still young, only twenty-two, and working through the trauma he'd suffered, something that none of us could ever understand. And no, getting drunk and sleeping around wasn't exactly a healthy way to deal with it, but if that was what he needed right now, I wasn't going to judge. I turned to Mags. "Where's Bram tonight?"

Magnolia shrugged. "Don't know. I don't freaking know anything anymore."

"He's still being weird?" Iris asked.

Mags twisted her fingers in her lap. "Yep. I feel...god, helpless, and I'm...I'm so fucking angry. Angry with Bram, angry at whatever's keeping him from me. Angry at everything." She clenched her fists. "I don't want to be angry anymore."

"Maybe I can help you with that," Asher said, walking into the living room, carrying a bowl of popcorn.

I hadn't even realized the wolf shifter was here.

Mags scowled at her. "You're not part of this."

Asher was Iris's bodyguard. Well, Draven assigned her to Iris whenever she left the keep. But they'd become besties, so Iris didn't complain about her mate's overprotectiveness. Mags, however, had no love for the other female, not since the wolf had kind of come onto Bram in front of my sister.

Ash held her hands up. "Yes, you hate me *yada yada yada*. FYI, I have no interest in your familiar. Is he hot? Yes. Would I go there for one dirty, sweaty night if he didn't have a feisty little witch ready to turn me into a toad if I so much as touched him? Again, yes."

Mags's face turned red with anger and she opened her mouth to say something, but Ash got in first.

"Whoa there, Nelly, you're gonna pop a blood vessel. First, your boy isn't interested in me. Second, you're angry with him, so keep a lid on all that pissed-off until he shows up and lay it on him. I'm just an innocent bystander. And third, I'm one of our pack's fiercest warriors, that's fact." Her golden eyes grew serious. "If you wanna learn how to direct all that rage into something more productive? Like kicking some ass? Come by the keep and I'll teach you."

Mags swallowed several times. I could see her trying to *put a lid on it*, even going as far as taking several deep breaths. "I'd rather not," she said scathingly but still holding back.

Asher plonked into a chair. "Suit yourself."

"It might not be a bad idea," I risked adding.

Iris gave me an encouraging nudge. Mags had changed so much these last two years. How long had it been since I'd heard her sweet musical laugh? I couldn't remember. We'd all been trying to work out how to help her, and redirecting all the anger she held inside couldn't hurt. Usually, she shut everyone down except me, but I wasn't sick anymore, so I wasn't sure how she'd take me butting in.

Mags looked at me, then back to the TV. "I'm done talking about this."

Well, I guess that answered that.

End of discussion.

Chapter Twenty-Four

Rose

I'd left my sisters downstairs to look through the pages I'd printed at the museum, which, to my surprise, had handily marked off which items had been stolen from their collection and confirmed that, yes, at least one of the statues stolen from the demonology department was a summoning effigy. Now I was working my way through the items that had historical significance. Some of the information had come from stories handed down through the generations or found in demon history books, which meant not all had actual real concrete proof of existence.

And on the bottom of the fifth page was a rough sketch that had been photocopied right out of one of those history books. I checked the photos on my phone. It was the statue we'd seen in the picture at the cat shifter restaurant. I quickly read the text beside it. *A summoning effigy carved in the likeness of the demon Xaeva. The demon has a fascination with shiny objects, and in exchange for the summoners request, prefers payment in gold and gems.*

I flipped back to the effigy stolen from the museum. This one belonged to the demon Creeg. *His preferred form of payment was severed limbs. The demon Creeg is sustained by pain and horror.* Holy hell. Well, that would do it.

There were more of these things floating around than I would have thought, and if the person who found themselves in possession of one of those items knew the power they held, they could be seriously dangerous in the wrong hands. People could be hurt.

Maybe there was a way we could get hold of the CCTV for the restaurant or the museum? I needed something to get to the next point. I felt stuck. I knew what our thief wanted, but that's all I knew. I stood, walked to the mirror, and pulled my left arm free of my shirt and sweater, checking the markings the mother had given me. Had they moved? I leaned closer to the mirror. Maybe a fraction? Panic welled inside me. I couldn't fail at this. How many times had I been forced to sit by, utterly helpless, useless, while my family worked to protect our coven? Too many to count.

They weren't showing it, but they had to be worried. My spelling skills were mostly untried. I was nowhere near as proficient as my sisters, yet somehow it was down to me to save our magic. I took a deep breath and squeezed my eyes closed. I'd tried not to let my fears get to me, but I was scared. Terrified that I'd be the one to let them down, that again, I'd be utterly helpless as everything came crashing down around me.

That this trial in my hands meant that failure, and our coven's loss of magic, was imminent.

Shoving my arm back in my sleeve, I strode to the bed and picked up my phone. Ronan said he was helping out the hounds tonight, but I needed to talk to him, to tell him what I'd found out. Maybe he'd have some insight I hadn't thought of. But mainly, I just needed to hear his voice.

I hit his number and waited.

No answer.

Ronan always answered.

A feeling I didn't like filled me, gnarly and thorny. Something wasn't right. I didn't know how I knew it, but I did. It sat like a cold rock in the pit of my stomach. I scrolled my contacts and hit Relic's number. I could call Willow or Warrick and ask if they'd seen Ronan, but I didn't want to risk involving my family if whatever I was feeling had something to do with my task.

"Roe, what's up?" Relic said in that voice that was so deep it could barely pass as human.

"Hey...um, is Ronan with you? I need to talk to him." I bit back the panic I was feeling. Why the hell was I panicky? It didn't make sense.

Relic was quiet a beat. "No, babe, he's not with me."

There was an odd note to his voice. "Has he been to the clubhouse tonight?"

"Yeah, then he left."

"What did he say? He said he was doing something for you."

Silence. "Rose, you don't need to worry—"

"He lied, didn't he?"

"It's not that simple."

"You know where he is, don't you?" The unease in my gut intensified when he didn't answer right away.

Finally, he said, "It's not my place to say."

"What did he talk to you about?"

"Look—"

"Relic," I bit out. The sense of urgency was building to extremes inside me, a cold sweat breaking out over my skin.

"Fuck." Relic blew out a long breath. "He needed to feed. We talked over his options. I thought I convinced him to go to you. He obviously changed his mind."

Dread gripped me in its sharp claws. "He's gone to The Vault, hasn't he?"

"Rose—"

"Hasn't he?"

"Yeah, I'd say that's where he is."

Pain seared me. "Why? Why would he do that to me?"

"He's not fucking anyone, babe, he's feeding. This isn't him cheating on you."

"That's what it feels like. That's exactly what it feels like." I was breathing hard, close to hyperventilating.

"Shit...Roe, he was past the point he usually allows himself to get. He was close to the edge. He was scared if he tried to feed from you, he'd lose control, that he'd hurt you. I told him he wouldn't, but that fear obviously got the better of him. He's still trying to work all of this out. He's confused. Give him a pass this one time, yeah?"

Like hell I would. I told him how I felt, and yeah, he was struggling to understand all he was feeling, but this was a betrayal. Honestly, it was the worst thing he could ever do. "I need to go. Thanks."

"Rose, hang on..."

I disconnected the call. I could sit here feeling sick to my stomach, or I could try to stop it. Maybe I was already too late. Nausea hit me hard at the thought.

But maybe I wasn't.

I had to try. Shoving on my shoes, I ran downstairs and grabbed Mag's keys. "Can I borrow your car?" I called to Mags, who was the only one there. Iris and Ash had obviously gone back to the keep.

She twisted to face me. "Yeah, where are you going? Will Ronan be with you?"

"It's fine. I'm meeting him," I said.

"You're lying." She stood. "Does this have to do with your task?"

"I need to go, Mags."

"Talk to me, Roe."

I forced myself to take a steadying breath, but my stupid lip started to quiver. "Ronan's at The Vault. He's gone there to feed."

Mags rounded the couch. "He's what?" Fury filled her amber eyes.

"He's scared he'll hurt me, but nothing could ever hurt more than him doing that with someone else."

"I'm coming with you." She snatched the keys from my hand.

I opened my mouth to argue.

"You can't even drive."

Damn. She was right.

Shoving on our coats, we ran to Mags's car and jumped in.

"Hold on," she said and tore out onto the street, speeding toward the city.

"If this all goes tits up and you want to make him pay for what is essentially cheating, I've got you," Mags said.

"It's not really cheating, though, is it?" My stomach was churning, and my heart was pounding.

"You tell me?" Mags said. "Have you fed from him? Like right from the source?"

The churning grew more intense. "Yeah, I have." And it was the most intimate thing I'd ever done. I mean, I was still a virgin, so I could only guess, but it had to be on par when it came to intimacy levels, right? Not only were you feeding, but there was this power imbalance when you fed from someone. They were sustaining you, giving you what you needed to survive, making you utterly vulnerable. You needed to trust the other person, especially with the whole sexual element that went along with it.

"Well?" she asked. "Would you do that? Would you be okay feeding from someone else and not telling him? Would Ronan be okay with you doing that?"

I swallowed painfully. "No." In my heart, it would feel like I'd betrayed him, and I knew for a fact Ronan would not be okay with it either.

"Exactly," Mags said and glanced at me. "I have a few elixirs I'm working on." Her eyes darkened, and for a split second, it was as if all the light left her. "If you want him to suffer, I'm your girl."

Yeah, that didn't sound good. And what the hell was Magnolia working on? "I don't want to hurt him, not like that." Mags had been working with Else, who was an expert with potions, elixirs, and tonics and also an extremely gifted healer. Mags showed an aptitude in Else's workroom at an early age, naturally skilled at making potions. She'd shown signs of healing powers as well, and we all knew it was only a matter of time before it grew more powerful, but this? I wasn't so sure. "Mags—"

"We're here." She pulled over and pointed through the windshield. "That's the Bank, The Vault's cover. Humans and others party in the main nightclub. The blood drinkers congregate in a second club below."

"How do you know all this?"

She glanced over at me. "Iris came here during her trial. The place is owned by a scary as hell vamp named Nero. And I've been here a couple times with friends. Though I stayed above ground. Unless you're there to feed others, fangs are a prerequisite for entrance to The Vault, and there's a hefty annual membership fee."

We got out and headed for the entrance. It was a Monday night, so the place wasn't packed. No line to get in at least. The bouncers gave us an up and down. We weren't exactly dressed for a night of clubbing, but we were let straight in.

The dance floor was still fairly crowded, and people sat at tables around the room and stood in groups drinking, but it wasn't full by any means.

"How do I get down there?" I yelled over the music.

Mags pointed to a door across the room. "That's the entrance, but you can't just walk on in."

I strode to the bar and shoved through the people waiting there. The man behind it raised a brow. I leaned in, and he automatically did the same. "The Vault," I said. "How do I get in?"

He moved to the side, away from the waiting crowd, then took me in, assessing my appearance. "You looking to get sucked, sexy?"

Sucked? Oh, I hated that. Anger spiked through me, and I willed my fangs to slide down. I flashed them at him. "No, I'm looking to do the sucking." As much as I hated how he put it, I assumed confidence and a little arrogance would work with a male like him.

He jolted. I'd surprised him. "Right, sorry."

Mags chuckled beside me. "Her mate's a regular, he's down there now. She needs to talk to him. It's an emergency."

"I'm not so sure about that—"

"You want money?" Mags said, pulling out a wad of cash and shoving several bills in his hand.

His brows shot up, then he looked up to a massive window high above the club. A viewing window of some kind? It was dark.

The bar guy leaned in. "Fine, but if someone asks how you got in, you tell them you snuck in. My name stays out of it."

Mags rolled her eyes. "Well, that'll be easy since we don't actually know your name."

He frowned, then scowled, then headed across the club.

"Where did you get all that money?" I asked Mags as we followed.

Her mouth twisted. "A loan from Bram. He has more than enough. Wads of the stuff, as a matter fact, stashed all over the tree house."

"Where did he get that kind of money?"

She shrugged. "How the hell would I know? He doesn't tell me a damned thing, remember?"

"Only you can go down," the barman said and pointed at me.

Mags planted her hands on her hips. "Now hang on a minute."

"One or none," the guy said.

Mags's eyes darkened. "I gave you a nice chunk of change, asshole…" Her eyes sliced to the side.

I followed her gaze. Bram was striding across the club, making a beeline for my baby sister. He was dressed all in black, his glossy black hair was longer on top and hanging forward, making it hard to see his black eyes, but there was no mistaking they were locked on Mags, and going by his clenched teeth, he wasn't happy.

Her back stiffened, and she crossed her arms, her attitude skyrocketing, but I sensed her relief at the same time. Wherever he'd been, he was back.

He strode up to us, took in the male next to us, and Bram was...well, terrifying. The barman took a step back, quickly looking down before Bram turned to me. "You have protection? This place is dangerous," Bram asked in his deep but quiet voice.

"Oh, um, yeah." I guess, I did. No matter what was about to happen, Ronan would protect me. "Ronan's here...downstairs."

Bram's hard stare immediately sliced to my sister.

He said nothing, but it was like Mags could read his mind and responded accordingly. "Really? You've been gone for two days, not a damned word—"

"I texted you," he said low.

"You texted me? You're my familiar. Where the hell have you been?"

His black eyes broadcast just how he felt about Mags calling him that. Of course, he was her familiar, but he was also her best friend, and he was family to us. He said nothing.

"Well?"

He lifted his gaze from Mags to me. "If you're covered, I'm taking Mags home."

I didn't dare tell him no, and if this place was dangerous, I didn't want Mags here anyway.

"I'm not going anywhere," Mags bit out. Bram reached for her, and she stepped back. "I said no."

The muscles in his forearms bunched. "Come here."

"No," Mags said again. "What the hell do you think you're doing?"

"Being a good familiar and keeping my witch safe."

Mags flinched.

Bram moved fast, hooking her around the waist, then he lifted my furious little sister off her feet, threw her over his shoulder, then strode out of the club.

I had no idea how they were going to sort out their differences, but I knew Magnolia was safe. No matter what, she was always safe with Bram.

I turned back to the male smirking beside me. "Let's go."

He punched a code into a keypad by the door. It opened and he led me down the stairs into the basement. There was another door down here, this one massive and round and made of steel. Like the door to a safe—or a vault.

He swung the thick steel rods sticking out of it, and the *clunk* of the door unlocking filled the small space, then he stepped back without opening the door. "You can let yourself in. Remember, I wasn't here," he said and turned, rushing back up the stairs and shutting me down here.

Grabbing the handle on the heavy steel door, I pulled. It swung open a lot easier than I thought it would. Dim light and music hit me first, slow, pulsing, sensual, so different than the frenetic beat in the club upstairs.

The room was large; the walls were red brick, and there was a lot of dark wood furniture and quite a few velvet couches in deep jewel tones scattered around as well.

I turned, searching for Ronan, and was confronted by a live sex show. Several male vampires, and it was hard to tell, but at least two females, were fucking and feeding. Most in the room were watching the show. And the smell of blood and sex filled the space.

Several people glanced my way, showing obvious interest. Some eyes were black, some different shades of purple, like Ronan's. They thought I was prey. Had they sensed my fear? Or could they hear my pounding heart? There was only one thing for it, I smiled, flashing my fangs, hoping they'd believe my reaction was from excitement not terror.

A male broke from the crowd and strode toward me. "You're new here," he said, his gaze dipping to my mouth, then up.

"Yes," I said, as I continued to scan the room.

"I'd like to offer myself to you. Let me feed you, pleasure you.

It would be my honor," he said, and I noted how his chest rose and fell rapidly. He was trying to play it cool, but he wanted it badly.

His words hit. *Pleasure me*, not just feed. That's when I took in all the couples dotted around the club. All were being sexual while they fed. Using hands, mouths, and some openly having sex.

I spun, frantic. Was Ronan doing that? Was he pleasuring someone else or letting them touch him? No. *No, no, no.* This couldn't be happening.

I strode through the room, searching every dark corner. The male who'd approached was still following me like a lost puppy.

Then I spotted Ronan.

My heart smacked hard behind my ribs.

He stood beside a couch, a female at his side. She watched him with wide eyes, so desperate, so excited for him to feed from her. She had her hand between her legs, under her skirt, and was obviously touching herself. He hadn't fed yet. Relief and fury roared through me at the same time. She was looking at my male. She wanted my mate.

I turned to the male behind me. "This way." He followed as I strode toward them. Ronan had his head dipped, not looking at the female at his side but at the floor, so deep in his own thoughts, or hunger, I wasn't sure. He didn't even sense me closing in. "Is this a private party, or can anyone join in?" I said.

His head lifted and his expression was blank. He'd heard my voice, but he still didn't expect it to be me. The look in his extremely pale eyes was desolate, quickly followed by surprise, then abject horror.

"Rose?" His voice sounded distorted, broken.

I closed the space between us. "You came here to feed."

His Adam's apple slid up and down his throat. "Yes, but you don't understand—"

"No, I don't. I don't understand this at all. You want me, but not for this? Not to feed, is that it?" I choked out. "Did you even drink the blood I gave your sister for you? Or did you toss it down the drain and come here."

His hands clenched and unclenched at his side. "No."

"Do you fuck them?"

"No."

He was shaking now, eyes wild, but I was too lost in my anger, my pain, to really take that in. "Do you let them touch you while you're feeding? Do you touch them?"

"No," he said, voice deep and impossibly low.

"She even looks like me. That's why you chose her, right? You choose females that look like me, but you won't actually drink from me, is that it?"

Ronan turned to the female, a look on his face that told me he hadn't consciously realized that's what he'd been doing, but I knew I was right.

"Well, go on, then. Feed from her, if that's what you want. But while you feed from her"—I grabbed the wrist of the male beside me—"you can watch me feed from my new friend here." It was a bluff, but I was just so goddamned hurt.

The air changed, becoming cold and deadly, saturating the space around us. Ronan's eyes were vibrant, glowing now, and rage lined his handsome features, twisting them until they were almost unrecognizable. His stare sliced from me to the guy beside me. "Lay one hand on her, get even a fraction closer, and I will tear out your fucking throat, then rip your twitching body to pieces while you're bleeding out."

The male pulled away, lifting his hands in surrender, and took a massive step back, then turned and ran. The female who had been beside Ronan was already gone. I hadn't even seen her leave.

I was breathing heavily, shaking. Angry, confused, hurt. But most of all, terrified that I might lose him. "I told you if you did this, if you fed from anyone else, I'd never forgive you, but you were going to do it anyway? I don't understand you, Ronan. You say you don't have sex with them, but everywhere I look, that's what's happening here. Tell me the truth."

His lips peeled back. "Do you think I want that? That I want that female? The idea fucking disgusts me. I don't want any of them." His chest heaved. "I don't fucking want them, Rose."

"Then who do you want?" I demanded.

His face contorted. "You."

I was having trouble breathing. "Then why?"

He moved, fast. Grabbing my upper arms, he pulled me in close, and those vibrant eyes, pale but still blazing, were filled with humiliation, with hatred, with horror, and fury. "Because my fangs have been in *him*. They've been in that monster, and I can't...I can't fucking bear to have him that close to you. I know he's gone. I know he's in Hell, but he's..." Ronan shook his head, like he was trying to shake the images out of it. "I still feel him there, in the middle of the night...his weight, his scent, his acid taste. My fangs in his veins, his poisonous blood burning my throat, choking me, making me sick to my stomach. I can't...won't taint you like that."

How could I have been so blind? The abuse of his past wasn't in the past, not anymore, not for Ronan. He was dealing with it now, like it'd just happened. Regaining his emotions meant he was living that nightmare all over again.

I took his face in my hands. "You're not tainted."

He clenched and unclenched his fists. Goddess, the expression on his face hurt to look at.

"You're not," I said again. He dipped his head, pale eyes closed tight, and I went up on my toes and pressed my mouth to his. His hands gripped me tighter, and he hissed low, his lean, muscled body vibrating under my hands. I kissed him again. "You're perfect and you're mine." There was nothing I could do to convince him that he was wrong. He had to work through this, through all he was feeling. I wanted to help him, though, but first, I needed him to get out of his head. "You're right, that monster isn't here, so don't let him ruin what's between us. I want you." I pressed more tightly to him. "You want me, too, I know you do."

"Yes." That one word was torn from him. "You're mine, Rose, and anyone who touches you will die."

My eyes stung. He was in so much pain, so conflicted. If only he'd trust me, trust himself. I let my fang sink into my lower lip, drawing blood, then slowly leaned in and pressed my mouth to his again. "Then claim me," I said against his lips.

His arms tightened around me, so tight I struggled to breathe, then his tongue darted out, swiping over the blood that bubbled to the surface of my lip.

His big hands took my face, and he looked into my eyes. They were feral and so full of hunger and fear. "What if I hurt you?"

That was an impossibility. He would never hurt me. Not on purpose, and not like that. "You won't." I pressed my face into his throat, trailing kisses to his ear. "I trust you, Ronan."

With a snarl, he yanked me off my feet and strode out of The Vault. "Not here," he said.

His voice was barely recognizable. It was the voice of a predator, of a ravenous monster, a creature from nightmares. It should terrify me.

Instead, it soothed me and comforted me. Made me feel safe. I recognized the monster in him and the call of his thirst—it was answered by something deep inside me.

I took him in, face twisted, fangs extended. He was utterly beautiful like this, lost in his violent hunger.

Wrapping my arms around his neck, I hung on.

Chapter Twenty-Five

Ronan

It took all my strength to release Rose so I could put her in my car. The monster in me wanted to lay her on the ground, strip her bare, and bury my fangs in her throat while I worked my way between her thighs. I shut her in the car and tried to force the images from my head.

I reminded myself that I was more than a starved predator ruled by hunger. I had to be, for Rose. I'd been without blood longer than this—many times.

When I was Azel's creature.

I got in the car and pulled out onto the street. Her scent already saturated the small space, and I had to bite back my snarl, because no matter how long Azel had let me starve, I'd never hungered like this. I'd craved Azel's blood, but only because it was all I knew, because I'd grown addicted to his poison. But even in the deepest, darkest depths of my addiction to that fucker's blood, I'd never wanted it like I wanted a taste of Rose right then.

Not even close.

"Ronan?" Rose said into the silence.

Her hand covered mine, and I hissed and pulled it away. "Don't. You can't...touch me. Not yet." Her hands on me were stimulus overload. One more touch and I'd break. I'd pull the car over and sink my fangs into her without restraint.

She pulled her hand back, curling her fingers on her lap, and I instantly wanted her touch back. The predator wanted an excuse, any excuse to have what it craved more than anything.

Since regaining my emotions, I'd felt that part of me more and more. The vampire part of my genetics had become my most dominant side in almost every way. "I'm sorry," I gritted out. "I'm...barely hanging on."

"It's okay," she said.

Her voice whispered across my flesh, lifting goose bumps, causing pleasure to fire through my synapses, igniting every nerve ending in my body. I was about to make the turn and head to the hellhound clubhouse, but at the last moment, I turned in the opposite direction.

Rose turned to me. "Where are we going?"

"My home." When I had her for the first time, it would be behind walls that I'd built, in my bedroom, in my bed. It wasn't completely finished, and I'd only been back there once since I'd regained my emotions. The quiet of the place had given me nothing to focus on but the thoughts and memories filling my head. But I didn't feel that way anymore, not when I had Rose with me.

"Your home? I thought you lived with the hounds?"

"I do most of the time, but I have somewhere else. Somewhere I plan to move into permanently soon." I made several more turns, the urgency inside me growing with every second. Rose's heartbeat raced, and it was all I could hear, the rush of her blood through her veins, the scent of her arousal.

I'd told her why I shouldn't do this, why I wasn't good enough to feed from her, and she wanted me anyway. My control, my willpower had shattered in that club, and there was no going back now.

We pulled up to a large steel gate, and I clicked the button on the remote to open it. The tall gates rolled open. As we drove in, Rose would see only an empty lot.

I felt her turn to me. "Ronan?"

I surrounded her with my powers, pulling her into my world. A place that no one could see or enter unless I permitted it. A place that had been only mine and now Rose's as well.

She gasped beside me.

The warehouse had been in good condition when I bought the property, but it was only a shell. I got the idea from the knight's compound. But instead of multiple levels, this was one large open space. I'd insulated it and built a mezzanine, turning it into a bedroom, and sectioned off another area for the garage. I hit another button so the doors would roll up as I approached.

There were several cars already parked in the space. Azel had occasionally needed human money, and it'd been my responsibility to get it. I found I enjoyed the stock market and had become extremely proficient. I'd taken it all when my sister ended Azel. She'd refused when I'd tried to give her half, so now I had more money than any one human could spend in their lifetime, and still, it grew.

"This is...it's incredible," Rose said as I shut the engine off.

An image of Rose living here with me—her things on the bathroom counter, her clothes in the closet, her scent on my sheets—filled my mind, and a snarl of possessiveness escaped me. She spun my way, and I tried to form the words to apologize or the strength to find an ounce of control—I couldn't do either.

I was in my domain. My female was here with me.

Right then, I was all monster.

All need.

All hunger.

I got out and rounded the car. Rose opened the door, and I tugged her out before she could and scooped her off her feet. Her legs locked around my waist instantly, her arms around my neck. I shoved my fingers in her long blond hair and took her mouth, kissing her hard and deep. My fangs were out and so were hers. The points nicked her lips and tongue, hers grazed mine. Our blood mingled in my mouth, and Rose moaned as I sucked on her tongue, wanting more.

Her arms tightened around my neck as I carried her through the garage. I shoved open the door to the main living area and kicked it shut behind me.

Striding across the polished concrete floor toward the stairs to the mezzanine, I took them two at a time and walked across the wide space to my bed. Lowering her to the mattress, I came down on top of her. Her legs wrapped around me again, and her hips lifted, rubbing the heat between her thighs against my erection.

I pulled away from her mouth with a hiss.

Her eyes were heavy-lidded but widened when they moved over my face. I knew what put that alarm there. My eyes would be glowing now, bright purple, like nothing from this world. My fangs, longer than she'd ever seen at the prospect of feeding, like an animal. And my face—it changed as well when I was starved like this, becoming all vampire, more angular, my chin and cheekbones sharper, my brow heavier. I could usually control it, but not with Rose, not with her.

My precious Rose was seeing the real me, the monster I transformed into when I fed, the male I truly was underneath it all. "Don't be afraid, sweets."

She jolted at the harshness in my voice, but then she shook her head, her hand lifting to the side of my face. "I'm not afraid of you, Ronan, I never could be...I've just, I've never seen you like this."

"I look like a monster—"

"No. You're beautiful," she whispered, lifting more of those goose bumps I'd grown to like so much. "I love you, Ronan, and I want you, in any form that you take."

At her words, I snapped, the barely there thread holding me back uncoiled. With a growl that echoed through the warehouse, I gripped her chin, turned her head to the side, and buried my fangs in her throat.

Her blood bloomed, filling my mouth, and at the first taste, I snarled. My cock surged, my nerve endings lighting up like fireworks. Rose cried out, shoving her fingers into my hair, holding me to her. She rocked her hips frantically, rubbing her pussy against my stiff cock. The scent of her arousal filled the space around us, then she orgasmed, crying out, and every pull on her vein seemed to send her higher.

I'd barely fed and already I felt nourished, more sated than I had been in my life. Rose was what I'd been missing, what I'd craved all this time. I never knew it was possible to feel this way. Luna was right, there was no chance of me hurting her because she was everything. I would die before I ever hurt her.

I lapped at the puncture wounds in her throat, and she jolted with each lick. "Rose," her name fell from my lips as I kissed my way to her mouth.

She whimpered as I sucked and licked her lips, sharing the taste of her blood. Trembling, she kissed me back just as hungrily, her tongue lapping into my mouth as desperate for me as I was for her.

"I want to take your clothes off, Rose. I need to taste all of you." I tried to sound more controlled, but the words came out as monstrous as the rest.

"Yes," she said. "Do it."

The words barely had a chance to leave her lips when I yanked at her clothes, tearing them from her body. I hadn't meant to, but my desperation for her was making me clumsy. I would have apologized, but Rose was now naked beside me and there were no words. I couldn't form them, except to say, "So beautiful," over and over again. Shaking, I covered one of her breasts and squeezed gently, rubbing my thumb over her nipple. She whimpered, and I leaned in and sunk my fangs into the soft mound, her blood filling my mouth once more.

"Oh god." She arched, her thighs squeezing tight, then falling wide.

I licked at her blood, smeared over her pale skin, sucking her nipple into my mouth and drinking more of her down at the same time. Then I reached down and covered her right over her hot, slick pussy. A growl was ripped from me. Mine. Every part of her was mine. I lapped at the fresh puncture wound I'd made, sealing it as well, and carried on down her body.

Her scent had been driving me crazy. Every time I smelled her arousal, my mouth watered. Her inner thighs were coated in her juices, and I parted her delicate folds. Her need for me was unmistakable, and the knowledge that it was me who made her this way filled me with possessiveness, with pride.

It wasn't just my bite that made her this way. Rose had wanted me, had grown wet and needy for me without my fangs in her flesh. I glanced up at her, and her beautiful blue eyes watched me, heavy-lidded with need. I wanted to make her feel good more than anything else on this Earth. I leaned in and lapped at her opening and groaned. *Yes. More.*

Holding her legs wide, I dragged my tongue through her center, and my world turned red. The predator wanted to mate, to fuck, to make his female scream. I licked and sucked, hoping I was doing this right, that she loved it as much as I did, but I couldn't stop to check.

When her fingers fisted my hair and she lifted her hips on a cry, a hunger deeper, more urgent, filled me. My cock was hot and impossibly hard, pulsing and aching. The urge to thrust, to rut, was a primal need inside me. Rose fisted my hair tighter and led my mouth higher. I sucked and licked the little nub there, giving her what she wanted.

Rose came again, crying out, her slight body trembling so hard

I wanted to soothe her and make her scream again at the same time.

I rose above her, and she looked up at me. "I want you. Please."

"I don't know what the fuck I'm doing, sweets, but I can't stop."

"I don't want you to stop." She yanked my shirt from the waistband of my trousers and frantically unbuttoned it.

She shoved my shirt off my shoulders, and my stomach tightened when her hands spread over my chest, then lower over my abdominal muscles. The need in her eyes increased. She liked the way my body looked. I'd never cared about it before, the way I looked. I kept fit because that was part of the way I was made. But vampires were designed to entice. They were predators, naturally in peak physical condition. I'd never thought about it much before, except the times I'd been required to fight.

But seeing the way Rose looked at me now, her fangs pressed into her lower lip as she explored my upper body with her hands, made me appreciate the way I was made. It filled me with pleasure that she enjoyed touching me and looking at me like this.

Her hands lowered, tugging on the button of my trousers—

I sucked in a startled breath, and my hand automatically dropped to hers, covering them, stopping her before I knew I was going to do it. The only other person to tug at the button of my pants like that slammed into my head and cold dread shot down my spine. My cock softened instantly and the ever-present feeling of nausea I'd felt when I was with Azel rushed back.

"Ronan?" Rose's voice was soft, god, timid.

I hated what I saw in her eyes. "I'm okay." But despite having Rose right there, so painfully beautiful and perfect, I wasn't. I wasn't okay. I'd let Azel in here, into this bed, and he'd destroyed something beautiful. I'd let him destroy it.

She shook her head. "You're not."

I looked away, shame filling me. "I'm sorry." There was a rustle of Rose covering herself.

"Come here," she whispered.

I forced myself to look at her, even as humiliation burned through me. She had her arms out, reaching for me, asking me to go to her.

"Rose, I don't think I can—"

She shook her head. "Just to hold you. I just want to hold you."

I eased down as a shudder rolled through my body, then continued to shake in her arms as she ran her hands over my back and into my hair. "I'm sorry," I said again, so fucking angry with myself I wanted to roar. I thought I had this under control. I thought I'd broken free from that fucking twisted male, but I hadn't. He still had his hands around my throat. I was still his pathetic creature. Azel was like dirt under my fingernails, the fallen angel, the trauma he'd caused clung to me like a layer of grime I couldn't wash off. No relief, no getting clean.

"You don't ever have to be sorry, not with me," she said into the silence.

I didn't know what to say, what to do.

So I lay there and let Rose soothe me. I let her take care of me when it should have been the other way around. What kind of male let his female take care of him? She deserved a male so much stronger than me.

I fell asleep in her arms, knowing I'd failed her and not sure how I would ever make it right.

How I'd ever rid myself of Azel.

Because until I did, he still owned a part of me, a part of me that had never been his to take.

And I didn't know how to get it back.

Chapter Twenty-Six

Rose

My phone chirped from somewhere on the mezzanine floor. Ronan was asleep with his arm locked around my waist, and his long, lean, muscled body pressed against the length of mine, his face buried against the side of my throat.

He was alarmingly still and utterly silent. It was strange not hearing him breathe. Other times I didn't really notice, but lying beside him, his skin cool, his body still, I'd never been more aware of the fact that his heart didn't beat.

Did that mean he was immortal? He didn't have a heartbeat, but he wasn't dead, his blood was still warm. Yes, his skin was cool, but it wasn't cold.

I needed to get up. I couldn't just lay here. Time was running out, and not just my task. In a matter of days, Death would be expecting me. But surprisingly, he hadn't come to me last night. No, instead, I'd had a nightmare of the same demon I'd dreamed of before. Everything had been dark, except for firelight, just like last time, while a twisted, hideous, horned demon stared at me with terrifying red eyes. Did he have something to do with Death? I didn't think so, but it had to mean something. I just wasn't sure what.

I also had yet to hear from Zinnia, but she promised she could help, and I trusted her. She wouldn't give me false hope unless she truly believed there was something she could do. All that was left for me to do was pray she was right. I'd learned a long time ago, while waiting for a cure, an answer to my illness, that hope was dangerous, but it was all I had.

The alternative—saying goodbye to Ronan, to everyone I loved—wasn't something I wanted to think about. But if that was my fate, there were things I needed to know. Like what it would mean for my coven.

My phone chirped again, and Ronan stirred, then lifted his head and blinked over at me. I sucked in a breath when those otherworldly eyes met mine. They were dark, the deepest violet because he'd finally fed. After last night, I wasn't sure how he'd react this morning. If he'd try to pull away or pretend it never happened.

He dropped his nose to my throat and breathed deeply. "You smell like Heaven," he said, his voice sleep roughened.

His hair was mussed and his face was relaxed. I'd never seen him like this before. "Did you sleep okay?"

"Yes." His gaze slid from mine, then back. "I'm sorry about last night..."

"Don't. Please don't apologize." I traced the line of his chiseled jaw. "You need time, and I'm not going anywhere."

He leaned in to kiss me—

This time, my phone rang. "I better get that," I said before our lips made contact. Ronan growled as I pulled away and leaned out of the bed, finding my phone poking out from under my shredded jeans. I didn't recognize the number. "Hello?"

"Rose?"

"Yes."

"Uh, sorry to call so early, honey. It's your dad."

Ronan stilled beside me.

I sat up. "I didn't expect to hear from you so soon."

"I know, but I...I'd love to meet up today if you're free?"

Ronan was watching me closely, and I knew he could hear every word we were saying. I had questions, and I needed answers. He knew more about what I was and what I could do than anyone else. Maybe that knowledge could be helpful during my task, and during my magical combat trial, that is, if Death didn't drag me into Limbo. But I was positive there was more to my bat shifter side. I just didn't know how to harness it. "Where?"

His sigh of relief reached me through the phone. "There's a cafe in the city, on Combes Street, Aunt Bel's, would that work?"

"That should be fine. I can meet you at eleven."

"I'll be there."

I disconnected the call and turned to Ronan. "He came to the house last night. Well, he stayed outside. He was waiting for me when you dropped me off. We spoke."

His expression darkened. "He was waiting for you?"

"Yes."

Ronan shook his head. "No. No way. You're not meeting with him."

My brows shot up. "Why not?"

"Because I don't trust him."

"Why?" This side of Ronan, this extreme protectiveness, was frustrating as hell, and I worked to keep my patience.

"I just don't."

I took in the look on his face. "Let me guess, you have the urge to disembowel him?"

His jaw tightened, and he didn't answer. Which could only be construed as yes. "Right, I'm going to meet him, and you're not coming."

"Like hell," he said and sat up, flashing his glorious, muscled chest.

As he turned more to me, the play of muscles almost had me

forgetting that I was highly irritated at his high-handedness. "I have questions for him that only he can answer. I'm not looking to build a father-daughter relationship or anything like that, but this is important to me. I don't want you standing over him making him nervous. I'll take Willow with me."

A stubborn look crossed his face. "I'm coming."

"No, and if you use your power and spy on me, I'll be pissed."

"You wouldn't know," he said, that stubbornness deepening.

"Don't give me another reason not to trust you, Ronan," I said, and though I tried not to, I let some of the hurt I still felt over finding him in that club slip through. "And trust me, I'd know."

The hard look on his face vanished, and he gripped the side of my throat, looking into my eyes. "I will never go there again, Rose. Never, you have my word."

"I do trust you. I know you'll keep that promise. But I need you to trust me as well. Do you truly think you could meet with my father and not intimidate or hurt him?"

His jaw worked. "No," he said finally.

"So it's settled. I'll take Willow."

"I don't like this."

I smiled up at him, trying to reassure him. His protectiveness was to the extreme, so much so, the male who had been ruled by logic for so much of his life forgot about it now completely. "I'll be in a public place. I'll be with my sister, who has a magic blade capable of telling her if he's even thinking about hurting me, a sister who could, and would, kill him in a split second if she thought that was his intent."

Despite my excellent argument, he still didn't look convinced.

"I'll text you when we get there and when we leave," I added.

He studied me for several seconds. "Fine," he said grudgingly.

"You know, this new Ronan is really bossy."

"Am I?"

"Yes. When something you don't like happens, your jaw gets

all tight and you get this stubborn look on your face right before the bossy comes out."

His gaze dipped to my lips. "Does it offend you?"

I licked my lips and his nostrils flared. "No, it's just new. A part of you that was suppressed. I guess we're both changing since... since that night."

A shudder moved through him. "Yes." He looked back up. "That night will forever torment me."

"If it wasn't for that night, we wouldn't be here together now," I said softly.

"Maybe." His lids lowered, concealing his eyes. "The thought of what could have happened, what I almost did—"

"You saved me, Ronan."

He looked up again, and his eyes were startling, so violet, so beautiful. "You know why, don't you, Rose?" he said, and there was a slight tremor in his voice. "Why I could never stay away from you? Why, despite the emotionless void I lived in, I was drawn back to you time and time again?"

"Yes."

"You feel it, too, don't you?" he rasped.

"Yes."

"You're mine, Rose Thornheart. You were born for me and I for you. You don't know it, but you saved me long before I saved you. You gave me a reason to carry on when I had nothing else. When nothing moved me. When all there was, all I felt...was nothing." His hand trembled as he lifted it and gripped the side of my throat again, brushing his thumb over my cheek. "My heart, you have no idea what you've brought into my life."

His heart. Word by word, he destroyed me. "Ronan—"

"I want you." He shook his head. "Don't ever doubt how much. Last night, I..." His throat worked. "I will make you my mate in all ways, Rose. I will get past this."

Lifting to my knees, I wrapped my arms around him. His banded around me instantly, so tight I could barely breathe. I squeezed him tighter. I didn't know how to help him, and I hated it, but this was something only he could work through. "I'm not going anywhere," I said again, choking back the tears clogging my throat. "No matter what, I'm yours, and I always will be."

Ronan

The clubhouse was mostly empty when I got there.

I'd just left Rose with her sisters to prepare for her visit with her father, and I felt restless. I clenched my fists. No, I was fucking pissed off. Rage boiled in my veins and blazed in my gut. Relic stood across the room with Warrick, and I changed direction, striding toward them.

Warrick turned my way and one of his brows lifted. "You look ready to fuck shit up, brother."

I was. I needed it. "Do you want to train?"

Warrick searched my expression, then nodded. "Sure. You need someone to kick your ass. I'm your hound."

I turned and headed belowground to the fighting pits, Warrick and Relic following.

Thirty minutes later, we were both bloody and bruised, and the fury inside me was still as raw and violent as it had been when we'd climbed into the pit.

"You want to tell me what crawled up your ass?" Warrick asked, then charged me, hooked me around the gut, and slammed me into the wall.

If I'd been human, my spine would have been crushed to dust. I shoved him back and slammed my fist into his side. He jerked when one of his ribs snapped, then laughed. The male was probably already healing. Half the bruises I'd given him were already gone.

"You're not just pissed, are you, brother?" Warrick said, looking into my snarling face.

"You having problems with Rose?" Relic asked from his spot sitting at the edge of the pit.

At the mention of her name, I roared and slammed my fist into the wall.

"I'll take that as a yes," Relic said and jumped down with us. "Talk to us, we can help. I'm smarter than all my brothers combined." He aimed his thumb at Warrick. "And he has a mate and can feel shit now. Lay it on us, we got you."

I may have emotions now, but I still struggled with what I should and shouldn't share. I felt close to these males. They'd taken me in and helped me when I was lost in every way a being could be. Planting my hands on my hips, I looked at my feet, unable to meet their eyes. "I couldn't...when Rose and I tried to...I couldn't..." I struggled to find the words.

"You couldn't get it up?" Relic asked.

My gaze shot up and locked on his surprised one. I nodded.

Relic smirked. "Dude, Rose is fine." His eyes grew heavy. "Yep, I'm thinking about her now and my dick just got hard." He shook his head. "You're obviously broken."

I ran at him and slammed him into the wall, then got in his face. "You ever think about her like that again, I will rip your dick off and feed it to you, then I'll tear your limbs off and shove them up your ass."

Warrick snorted. "Creative."

"I mean every word," I snarled into Relic's face.

"Brother, I'm messing with you," the male said and shook his head. "Shit, after our last talk, I know how much you want her. Your dick isn't the problem. It's nerves."

"That's not it."

"Then some kind of mental block?"

I shoved away from him. "It's Azel."

They both went silent, and Warrick's face turned to stone.

Luna and I weren't the only ones to suffer at Azel's hands. The twisted fallen angel had left Willow with scars of her own, both mental and physical.

We all thought he was gone for good, until he'd tried to escape Hell a couple of years ago to possess another body during Willow's task. They'd kept it from me at the time. But Warrick had almost lost his mate because of that fucker, and the hound hated that male almost as much as I did.

"Talk to us," War said.

They knew what had happened to me. I shared it with them in my emotionless fucking way when I first came here. At the time, I'd been confused by their reactions, their anger on my behalf. I understood now. "I want to make Rose mine, but he's there. He's always fucking there. In my head, crawling over my skin, talking in my fucking ear." I snarled and punched the pit's charred wall again. "I want to kill him, torture him, destroy him." I looked up at them. "How do I give all of myself to my mate when Azel still has a part of me that I can never take back?"

Warrick glanced at Relic, and the other male gave him a sharp chin lift.

The alpha of the Hellhounds strode forward and gripped my shoulder. "I think I can help you out with that."

I held his golden stare. "How?"

Warrick grinned, flashing sharp white teeth. "Feel like a little trip to Hell?"

Chapter Twenty-Seven

Rose

I turned to Mags sitting in the driver's seat beside me. "You promise not to hit him?"

Mags grinned. "I make no promises. But he's safe as long as he doesn't act like a dick."

I couldn't ask for more than that. "Fair enough. If he's a dick, I might just hit him myself."

Mags was with Willow at the clubhouse when we got there. I decided it best not to ask Wills to come with me since she'd been deep in conversation with Ren. He'd obviously stayed at the club-house last night and didn't look in great shape. So I'd asked Mags instead, something I wouldn't be telling Ronan until after the meeting. He wouldn't be okay with the change of plans, and I didn't have time to argue about it again.

"I'd like to know if there's anything I can tap into, power-wise. There's something more, I can feel it, something just out of reach. My magic is subpar—"

"Bullshit," Mags said.

"I haven't had occasion to use it, not like you guys. And I

don't have time to practice, not as much as I need. If there's something that could help me with my task, I need to know."

"Yeah, you're out of practice, but you're just as powerful as us. Don't underestimate basic spells and incantations. Sometimes the basics are all you need. It definitely throws the blowhards who always go for something flashier. Remember that. But yeah, if he can teach you some new tricks, I'm all for it."

Excellent points, all of them. Mags made a turn, searching for somewhere to park.

"I've seen the colony, you know," Mags said absently.

"You have?"

She nodded. "Bram's village is close-ish. We've flown by it."

Bram's family, his people, lived in tree houses deep in the forest. I didn't know much about them; Bram didn't talk about it much. He didn't talk much at all to anyone that wasn't Mags.

"What did it look like?"

"We didn't get that close. It looked like a cave in the side of a cliff. I wish I could tell you more."

For some reason, nerves filled my belly thinking about it. "How did it go with Bram after he carried you out of the club? He seemed pretty pissed." I hadn't had a chance to ask my baby sister what happened, and talking about something other than the fact I was about to sit down and have a proper chit-chat with my father for the first time was an excellent distraction.

"He got over it eventually," she said, giving me minimal information.

Mags parked. "Well, that's good, right? I've been worried about you, both of you."

My sister drew in a deep breath, then turned to me and smiled. It was totally forced. "We're fine. I guess things...people...change, especially as we get older, and we're just learning what that looks like for us." She didn't look convinced in the least. She looked sad.

She turned the engine off, and I covered her hand with mine. "I'm sorry you're going through this, but I know you two can sort things out." I didn't know specifics, but whatever was going on between Magnolia and Bram, they would work through it. They loved each other too much to let anything come between them.

"Yep," she said, pulling her hand out from under mine. "We'll be fine." She pushed her door open. "Right, let's go meet your sperm donor."

A nervous laugh burst from me. "Please don't call him that to his face."

She gave me another grin, this one genuine. "Again, that will depend on his dickishness."

Willow and Iris had been young when Vesa was with Mom, and they either didn't remember him or chose not to. But he'd left them as well. I shook my head and followed. This was more than likely a terrible idea, but we were here now. We headed down the block, and I spotted the sign for Aunt Bel's Cafe.

"You ready?" Mags asked as we got closer.

"No, but I'm doing it anyway." She grabbed my hand, and I pushed the door of the cafe open. We walked in and spotted him instantly. The table he'd chosen was farthest from the door, and he had his back to the wall. He stood as soon as he saw me.

I'd been too stunned to take him in properly when I first met him. But I did now. I couldn't tell how old he was, but I had to assume bat shifters were long-lived like most shifter breeds. He was tall, like me, and he looked fit. He was attractive, had dark hair and eyes, and deeply tanned skin. I didn't get my coloring from him. I wasn't sure where I got it from, because my mother wasn't fair-haired either. Darker hair and auburn shades were more prominent among the Thornhearts.

He smiled when we stopped at the table, the lines at the corners of his eyes fanning out. The only sign of age. "Rose, I'm so glad you could make it."

"Hi," I said and motioned to Mags. "This is Magnolia, my younger sister."

He inclined his head, his smile turning a little wary. "Nice to meet you, Magnolia."

"That remains to be seen," she said, then pulled out a chair and plonked down in it. "Depending on how this goes, will be the decider on how nice it was to meet me, yeah?"

"Of course," he said.

Oh great, she'd gone straight into peak Mags mode the second we walked in here. I cleared my throat, silently asking her to rein it back, at least until we knew what the guy had to say.

We sat as well, and his eyes stayed on me, taking me in the same way I had him, I guess. "You're beautiful," he finally said roughly.

"Thanks," I said, not sure what else to say.

He chuckled awkwardly. "You obviously get that from your mom. How is she—"

"She's happy." I sat forward. "The happiest she's ever been. And we'd prefer it if you stayed away from her."

His brows shot up. "I would never do anything to hurt Daisy. Rose—"

"Abandoning her while she was pregnant with your kid was a pretty hurtful thing to do, don't you think, Vesa?" Mags said, leaning forward.

His looked between Mags and me. "I never meant to hurt her... but I...I..."

"I'm not here to talk about Mom."

He sat back in his seat. "Of course. Look, I just, I want to get to know my daughter. I know it's probably too late, but if there's anything I can do, anything, all you have to do is ask."

A female came to take our order. Mags ordered us all a pot of tea.

"I have questions," I said when the female walked away.

"Anything." His expression was open, his arms uncrossed, hands on the table. His body language said that he was exactly that, open, that he was telling the truth, that he had nothing to hide.

"I lived my life not knowing what half of my DNA was made up of. I have this whole side I know nothing about."

"I'm sorry. I honestly didn't think that would happen. You're like a rare treasure, Rose. This is something that only happens every hundred years or so. Usually, when we breed outside the colony, the mother's genetics are dominant in our offspring."

"She almost starved to death after a life of sickness. Maybe you should have checked in just to be sure," Mags said acidly.

His gaze flew back to me. "God, Rose, I'm so sorry. I had no idea." He dragged his fingers through his hair. "I fucked up badly. I'd do anything to make that right."

He looked genuinely horrified, and maybe it was twisted, but I was glad he felt that way. Making him feel bad wasn't why I was here, though. "So what can bat shifters do? Do you have any special powers?"

He blinked at my sudden change of subject but rolled with it quickly. "Apart from shifting? And the way we feed? No, not really. We're stronger than humans, though, like most shifters, and longer lived."

"Do you shift fully into bats, or is it some other kind of transformation?"

"We don't shift into bats, not like our animal cousins. We do have wings, though, leathery in texture. Our ears elongate into points, as do our fingers."

"And you can control this? You can make the shift at will?"

"Yes. It can also happen during times of stress. Usually to adolescent bats while they're still learning to control it." He gave me a pointed look. "I'm not sure if you've shifted, or if you have the ability? But that's something you should watch out for."

"I haven't shifted like you've described, but I do have wings."

"You do?" He leaned forward. "And you can use them without physically shifting any other way?"

"Yes, so far. As for using them? I haven't actually flown yet."

"You will." He smiled kindly. "How many shirts have you destroyed?"

"A few."

"It's hard to get the tucking right when you're first learning. Our young often have half their wings tucked in and half out. Don't be embarrassed if that happens, it's all part of learning to control them."

"I haven't had that problem," I said and didn't miss the surprise on his face. "They don't fold into my back, they vanish completely."

"Jesus," he said and sat back. "You don't have wing slits in your back?"

Mags screwed up her face.

"No. I had a hump on my back while they grew, but once they broke through, my back returned to the way it was before."

He looked stunned. "Amazing. You really are a mix of your mother and I." He grinned. "Who knows what other differences there are."

"Are your wings translucent?" I asked.

His chin jerked back. "No."

"You said yours are black?"

"Yes."

"Mine are white."

He stilled completely, his dark eyes locked on my face for several moments, then he shook himself. "Your wings are white?"

"Yes, and shimmery."

He sipped his drink, and I could tell he was using it to gather himself.

"Is there something wrong?" I asked, watching him closely.

"No, nothing's wrong. But this is...it's a lot to take in, for both of us." He shook his head and put down his mug. "We have black wings, all of us. You're unique in so many ways, Rose." He was silent for several seconds, taking me in again, then his eyes lit up. "I'd love to introduce you to your family."

"She has a family," Mags said.

"Her other family. Rose has cousins, aunts and uncles, grandparents. I know they'd love to meet her. Some of our elders are extremely knowledgeable. They might be able to help you navigate this whole thing better than I can."

"Thanks, but I don't think that's necessary," I said and stood.

His hand darted out and wrapped around my wrist. I paused, looking down at it, and he quickly let me go.

"I'm sorry, I know you don't owe me anything, Rose. Not one thing. My only excuse for leaving was that I was young and stupid. I realized how impossible a relationship between me and your mother was. She didn't know what I was, and I really didn't think her coven would want me around once they knew. So I left before it became a problem. I was a coward, and you and Daisy suffered for it. But I would love to do this for you. For you to meet your family, your colony. Even if you don't want anything more from me, meet them. They're far better than I am. They could help you. Your wings work differently than ours, who knows what else might come up?"

Again, the sincerity was impossible to miss. He wanted this, badly. I still wasn't sure. "I need to think about it."

"Of course. If you decide you want to meet with me again, or you're up for meeting my side of the family, just call, whenever you want, okay?"

I nodded, and then Mags and I walked out.

"Okay?" Mags asked as we hit the street and headed back to the car.

"Yeah, I guess." I turned to her. "What did you think of him?"

She pursed her lips. "I'm not sure, honestly. I didn't have the urge to tear his arms off, well, not the whole time. He kind of seemed sincere."

"He did, right?" Maybe it would be a good idea to meet with his colony. It couldn't hurt, could it? He was right, maybe someone there would have more answers for me. My magic had morphed with that part of me, in a way my father had never seen. Maybe some of the elders in the colony had seen something like this before, or maybe it was just my curiosity getting to me.

We reached the car and got in, and I quickly pulled out my phone and sent a text to Ronan like I'd promised, then shoved my phone in my pocket.

"I'm supposed to be meeting Bram at home. You want to go there, or somewhere else?" Mags asked, glancing in the rearview mirror.

"Can we swing by the council? I want to borrow some books." I was hoping to find some information on the stolen effigies, or their uses, anything. I was getting desperate.

The world suddenly spun, and I grabbed the door handle as a vision rushed me out of nowhere.

The museum. I was in the museum. Dark. It was nighttime. Something moved in the shadows, almost gliding as they headed down the hall. I was with them, as if I were hovering behind, like a balloon attached by a string.

We turned the corner.

The guard was there. He was on his phone, arguing with someone.

The dark figure moved out into the middle of the hall, a male. The guard spun to the intruder, dropping his phone in surprise.

"Kick it to me," a deep voice said, echoey and strange.

The guard lifted his hands. "What are you doing here? I already told him—"

"Kick the phone to me. Now." I couldn't see the dark male's face, his back was to me, and he was wearing a hooded sweatshirt, the hood up, concealing his features, but whatever he did had the guard's eyes widening in terror.

He kicked over the phone, and the dark male stopped it with his foot, then smashed it with the sole of his boot.

"What the fuck do you want?" the guard said, stumbling back a step.

The dark figure said nothing.

The guard flinched. "I didn't do anything wrong. Mr. Kelley hired me. You got a problem, talk to him." He pulled a gun from somewhere at his back—

One moment, the male in black was across from him, and the next, he was behind the guard. There was a flash of steel, then a line appeared across the guard's throat. There was a second of nothing, of stillness, or surprise, then the guard opened his mouth, his hands flying to his throat. Blood spilled over his lips and down his chin, through his fingers, then he collapsed on the floor.

The male in black strode away, blending into the shadows once more.

"Rose?"

Mags's voice pulled me back from the scene playing out in my mind. I gasped, sucking down a sharp breath and then another.

"A vision?" she asked.

I nodded.

"Are you okay?"

No. I wasn't okay. I was so very far from okay. That might have only been a vision, but when you're in one, it felt *real*, and I'd just watched a man get his throat slit. I nodded and hoped I didn't look as freaked as I felt. Whoever the male in black was, the terrifying male who killed that guard, was a major part of my task. And I finally had another lead, a name. "I will be. It takes a bit to shake it after I get one."

She touched my arm, rubbing at the goose bumps that had lifted all over my skin. "What did you see?"

"I can't...I can't tell you." I worked at controlling my racing heart. "It was about my task."

Mags studied my face. "You can tell me, I just can't help you."

If Mags knew how much more dangerous this just got, she would want to help. Even though she knew she shouldn't, with her lack of impulse control lately, I'm not sure she'd be able to help herself. "I'm ah...still trying to sort it all out. It's a bit of a jumble," I lied.

She nodded, and there was no hiding her concern. "You're shaken. Let me get you home."

I nodded, and as she drove, I tried to work out what the vision meant. Who was the male in black? And why had he killed the guard? Mr. Kelley? Who was he, and what was his involvement? I checked my phone, but Ronan hadn't replied to my text. His replies usually came instantly. I shoved my phone back in my pocket and tried not to freak the hell out.

Chapter Twenty-Eight

Ronan

H*ell*

Warrick led us through another long cavern. Relic and several other hounds following.

"Here," Warrick said.

We'd reached a large wooden door, and Warrick strode up and pounded on it.

A few seconds later, it swung open. A female stood there, and when she saw Warrick and the other hounds, she beamed. "War! You're here early. I thought you weren't due back for a couple weeks?"

"Unplanned trip, Rox," War said. "Is he here?"

"You betcha. Come on in."

We all strode in, and I still had no idea what the hell was going on. We walked into a huge room, a kind of living room with several doors leading from it. Lots of black and silver and crimson. A large couch sat in the middle, and a male covered in tattoos, tall and lean and muscled, sat relaxed in a chair beside it. He had a glass of red wine in one hand and was stroking a black cat laying in his lap with the other.

Lucifer.

We were in Lucifer's quarters.

He took us all in. "Well, this is a surprise." he looked at me, then back to Warrick. "But not completely unexpected."

Warrick crossed his thick arms over his chest. "There's something we need your help with."

"Another favor, War? I'd say I've dished out enough of those where you and your mate's family are concerned." He stroked his cat slowly, his gaze sliding to me. "I think Ronan is capable of making his own bargain for this one. What is it you want, dhampir?"

I glanced at Warrick and back, confused.

"Think," Lucifer said. "You know exactly why you're here."

Rose filled my head, beautiful, bare, wanting. My mate. I wanted to be the male she needed, the male she deserved so badly. Rage filled my veins, and the reason I was here became crystal clear.

"I wasn't sure what fate had planned for your female." Lucifer said. "Turns out it was you." He took me in from head to toe. "Though, honestly, I don't give a fuck about any of that." He smiled, and it didn't reach his eyes. "Love is a load of old bollocks. Romance? Pass. Making googley eyes at each other and coming up with pet names. Gag. Fucking? Well, now, that's something I can get behind—"

"Ugh!" Roxy said and shoved the King of Hell's shoulder. "I hate it when you talk like that. One day you're going to fall head over heels for a female and you'll have to eat those words."

He smiled indulgently at who I now realized was one of his handmaids. "Rox, honey, that's the biggest load of horse shit you've ever spouted."

Roxy rolled her eyes. "We'll see."

Lucifer turned back to me. "So go on then, tell me what you want, dhampir, and we'll see if I'm in the mood to accommodate."

"I want access to Azel."

"You want to beat the fuck out of him? You think that will help you?"

"Yes," I said without hesitation.

Lucifer grinned, and it was pure evil. "Down here, neither of you will have use of your powers. You'll be as weak and breakable as any human. Only Azel can't die, because he's already dead. You can hurt him, though, make him bleed, break him. But if he shanks you, my man?" The King of Hell shrugged. "Well, War might be carrying you out of here minus your soul. You understand that, right?"

I had to do this. Not only for me but for Rose as well. I couldn't go back to her until I did this. Until I faced the monster who almost broke my sister and me, until I made him bleed. "Yes."

Lucifer chuckled. "Okay, cool. But you owe me, dhampir. If you don't die, just know that one day I might call on you for something, and it would be in your best interests to do as I ask." His gaze slid to Warrick. "Take him where he wants to go."

We left and headed back along the cavern. No one said anything as we made turn after turn down seemingly endless tunnels. I heard demons in the distance, their growls and twisted laughter, but I didn't see any until we rounded the next corner. There were doors at the very end, wide and made of charred wood and iron. Two demons stood on either side.

They weren't a breed I'd ever seen before, with their blunt features, hoofed feet, and short tusks protruding from either side of their nose. They looked more like animals or shifters of some kind, but the darkness that rolled from them was all demon.

"After Azel's attempt to escape, Lucifer's kept a closer eye on him," War said as we strode to the massive doors. He said something to the guards, and the demons moved aside.

I instantly felt him. Azel.

I'd fed from him enough that I sensed him even now. Icy spikes prickled my skin, and I broke out in a cold sweat.

Warrick waved one of the demons over and ordered him to unlock the door. He did as instructed, then stepped back again.

"Time moves slower down here. We might be here for only half an hour, but it'll be a full day on Earth. So you need to do this quickly. Azel will probably be confused when he sees you, about how much time has passed, about where he is," Warrick said. "They're all different, but the longer a soul is here, the more confused they can become. He might even believe he still has his powers, or that he's on Earth."

I dipped my chin.

"Ready?" Warrick asked.

"Yes."

He lifted the latch and opened the door.

I slid off my jacket, tossed it to Relic, and walked into the cell.

Azel stood on the other side of the room, his back to me. He turned at the sound of the door closing and locking behind me. "Ronan, where have you been? I've been calling for you."

He looked the same. As if no time had passed, and I guess for him, maybe it felt as if it hadn't.

The look in his eyes instantly turned calculating. He looked at me and saw someone he could manipulate. A plaything. Power, and a way to increase his own—if he still had any. He'd looked at me like that all my life, and I hadn't seen it, hadn't been capable of seeing it.

"You finally came for me," he said.

I didn't reply.

"I grow weary of this place, take me home." He took a step toward me.

I lifted a hand, warning him to stay back. "No."

He paused, his head tilting to the side, anger instantly lining his face. He hated being disobeyed. "Ronan, come to me. Now," he ordered.

"No."

"You refuse me?" The calculation turned sadistic. "You want to feed, don't you?" He began to circle me slowly, his gaze sliding over me, making me sick to my stomach. He still believed he was the mighty predator, that he was powerful, that he held power over me. "You must be weak, starved for my blood. Take off your clothes and come to Sir," he said huskily.

Yeah, he was definitely confused. Warrick was right, time was lost to him, and he didn't seem to understand the situation he was in or where he was.

"I'm not starved, Azel." He flinched at my using his real name.

"You dare call me that?" His face was a mask of rage. "When you address me, you call me Sir," he roared.

"No, I will not," I said, turning as well, following him as he circled me.

His face grew red, his body vibrating with fury. "You think I'll feed you now?"

I could see his hands flexing, the tendons in his throat sticking out. He was trying to use his power on me, even though he'd been stripped of it completely. "I don't need your blood, Azel. My mate sustains me, she gives me everything I need."

He froze, confusion filling his dark eyes. "What?" He laughed. "What are you talking about?"

"Look around you, where do you think you are?"

He glanced around the room and frowned. "I'm at the...I'm—"

"You're in Hell."

He spun back to me. "No, I'm not. I'm—"

"You're dead. Luna killed you."

The confusion grew, fear joining his rage now. I recognized it all, and I relished every moment of his growing horror. "No."

"Yes."

"No," he roared.

I took him in now. He was pathetic. Nothing. I didn't need to make him bleed, this was enough. Seeing him like this gave me all the peace I needed.

"You are mine!" he screamed. "Mine!"

"I am not. And I never was," I growled out.

He lifted his hands and roared, firing his nonexistent powers at me.

Laughter bubbled up inside me, born of true freedom. Freedom from this monster and the shackles he'd had on me for most of my life.

"I should have killed you like I killed your pathetic mother. I should have kept Luna at my side and removed your head as well," he said.

"It was you who lost your head, Azel. Luna relieved you of it."

Something flashed through his eyes, a memory perhaps, and the look on his face changed, becoming completely unhinged. He moved to block the door. "You're not leaving. If I'm in Hell, you're staying here with me."

He thought he could best me? He had nothing, not even his life.

I had everything. I had something to fight for, to live for.

I had Rose.

Azel's face twisted with hate, with rage, then he screamed and ran at me.

Chapter Twenty-Nine

Ronan

It was late. Dark outside.

We'd been in Hell for all of thirty-seven minutes, but an entire day had passed here on Earth.

No one tried to stop me when we returned, and I strode from the clubhouse. No one dared.

I was covered in blood, Azel's and my own. Adrenaline still throbbed through me. The monster in me roared and snarled when images of Azel's battered body, broken and twisted on the floor, filled my head again.

He was nothing.

No one.

He would never hurt Luna again. Would never touch either of us. He would spend the rest of eternity in that cell at the mercy of Lucifer and his demons, and he deserved nothing less.

I wasn't in my right mind. I should calm myself first and gather my control before I went to Rose, but that wasn't possible. No, there was only one place I wanted to be, and if anyone attempted to stop me, I couldn't be held responsible for my actions.

The drive to Rose was a haze. I had no recollection of it when I pulled up outside the house and turned the car off. I used my power to conceal it, to conceal myself. The predator in me wanted to hide, to stalk, to capture its prey. To take what was his, and as fucked up as that was, as out of control as I felt, I knew I wouldn't hurt Rose, not on purpose and not by accident.

So I let that part of me take over. I relished it. My blood was hot in my veins as I entered the house and took the stairs two at a time. Rose's door was shut, but she was in there—I could smell her.

The sound of the shower, of her humming softly from the bathroom, reached me.

I walked through the door and into her private space. Her scent was much stronger here, and I breathed deeply. My fangs extended, and my cock was pumped full of blood, growing harder than I'd ever been.

I walked through the only other barrier between us, my power cracking and sparking around me, feeding off my volatile emotions.

Rose.

My snarl escaped, ricocheting off the tile walls. My female didn't see me, didn't hear me. My hand dropped to the hardness behind my zipper, and I squeezed to relieve the ache. Images of what I wanted to do to her filled my head, and nothing else. There were no monsters in wait to pull me from her, no memories or nightmares to get between us. When I thought of Azel now, I saw him on that floor, bleeding and broken. Nothing.

My memory of him was of the sound of his bones snapping, of his cries of pain, and if anything, it only made me harder.

Rose ran her soapy hands over her beautiful body, and I growled with need. I didn't have a shirt, it'd been torn off during my fight. I stripped off what was left of my clothes and stepped into the hot spray behind her. She was breathing fast, her eyes filled with excitement, and as her hands made another pass over her hips and across her stomach, I covered them, following their path as I dropped my block.

She gasped, but she wasn't afraid. I pressed my lips to the side of her throat, dragging my fangs along the tendon there. "You knew I was here."

"Yes," she said. "I felt you. I felt your power." She turned, and a cry left her when she saw me. "Oh goddess. You're hurt."

Her hands moved over my chest frantically, as the blood was washed away, the water turning pink as it disappeared down the drain. I covered her hands, stopping her. "I'm not hurt."

"But you're injured," she said, taking in the bruises and cuts on my skin.

"They're already healing." My voice was all predator. The monster and my need for Rose made it sound even harsher.

She stared up at me. "Ronan, where were you all day? Whose blood is this?"

"I was in Hell."

"What?" Fear cracked through her voice.

"Most of this blood belongs to Azel," I said, my fangs fully extended now.

"I don't understand, what's going on—"

I pressed a finger to her perfect lips. "I'm going to fuck you now, my heart. First, to appease the monster inside me, to claim my mate, to make you mine. Then I'm going to carry you to your bed and make love to you. Are you okay with that?"

Heat filled her eyes, and her cheeks were slashed with a deep pink. "Yes, I'm okay with that."

With a growl, I hauled her off her feet and slammed my mouth down on hers. Her legs locked around my waist, and I pressed her to the wall, devouring her mouth. She kissed me back hungrily, nipping my lips, and sucking my tongue. I needed her now, but I needed her ready to take me. She was a virgin, and I'd never been with a female before. I wanted to make this good for her. I needed that more than anything.

So I dragged my mouth from hers and kissed a trail down her throat. Then, lowering her feet to the floor, I kissed a hot path across her chest to her breasts. Her nipples were tight, a darker shade of pink, and I groaned as I filled a hand with her soft flesh, then sucked one of the stiff little peaks into my mouth.

She shoved her fingers into my hair, holding me there with a needy moan that had my cock throbbing harder. Shoving a hand between her thighs, I sank my fangs into the flesh surrounding one of those perfect little nipples, and she cried out instantly, her legs almost giving out as she rocked against my hand, coming for me, from my bite, like I knew she would.

She was slick under my fingers, and I dragged them through her wetness, making her rock her hips faster.

"More. Please, Ronan," she cried.

I slid a finger inside her, and she gasped and clung to me.

"So tight," I growled out. "Need to get you off again, Rose. I don't want to hurt you when I take you."

"You won't...Please."

I slid in another finger, stretching her wider, and she groaned low. "One more time, my heart." I kissed my way down her body, dropping to my knees in front of her. Pulling one leg over my shoulder, I opened her wide for me and buried my mouth against her pussy, while I pumped my fingers in and out of her tight opening. She tasted like Rose, perfect, and I ate at her ravenously, sucking and licking every inch of her before I finally focused on her clit.

My bite had gotten her off the first time, but this one I wanted to be me alone. Her body trembled and her cries grew louder. I threw up my block again, around both of us, so no one in the house would hear her or walk in on us.

Her fingers shoved deeper into my hair, then she fisted and cried out, giving me what I wanted, coming for me again. Her pussy tightened around my fingers, and when the spasms eased, I slid my fingers free and stood. Mindless with hunger, I yanked her off her feet and her legs immediately locked around me once more.

I kissed and sucked her throat, kissing a path to her ear. "You ready for me, sweets?"

She whimpered. "Yes. God, Ronan, I need you."

I pressed her to the wall and, leaning back, looked down between our bodies. She was so impossibly beautiful, her pussy spread for me, puffy and pink and slick.

Taking myself in hand, I pressed the swollen head to her opening and looked up at her. "You are mine, Rose. Every part of you. I feel it. You feel it, too, don't you?"

"Yes," she said and rolled her hips, pressing down on the head of my cock. "And you're mine," she said, cupping the side of my face.

Teeth gritted from the strain of holding back, I dropped my forehead to hers. "Yes. I am yours. I've only ever been yours." Then I pushed the head of my cock inside her.

Rose's thighs shook, and she bit her lip, drawing blood.

I lapped it up. "More?"

"Yes, I want more."

The monster had wanted to fuck, but now, in the face of my precious mate, learning how I felt filling her while she struggled to take me, all I cared about was making this good for her. She wriggled her hips, working me in another inch with a little gasp that had me holding her tighter. I slid out, then back, giving her a little more.

"Oh god," she said, her head falling back.

I'd never felt anything like this, like Rose squeezing around me. This was as new to me as it was to her. "You feel perfect, Rose. I never dreamed it could be like this...I never knew."

"I want all of you," she said, panting. Her nails dug into my flesh, and she rocked her hips. "Give it to me."

I was powerless to do anything else. I slammed my hips forward, filling her completely.

A cry burst from her, and she wrapped her arms around my neck tight, holding still.

"Rose?"

"I just...I need a minute," she said breathlessly.

I locked every muscle in my body, forcing myself to hold still when what I wanted to do was slide out and slam back in. But I'd die before hurting her, so I gritted my teeth and waited.

The smell of blood hit me, and I froze. "I hurt you. You're bleeding."

She shook her head and drew a shaky breath. "It wasn't that bad. This can happen sometimes when a female loses her virginity."

"Are you still in pain?"

"It only aches a little. It'll pass."

I slid from her carefully. I couldn't bear that I hurt her.

"Ronan?"

And dropped to my knees. A watery trail of blood slid down her inner thigh, and the sight made my fangs tingle and my cock throb harder. I leaned in and lapped it up, all the way to the apex of her thighs. Then I lifted one of her legs over my shoulder like I had before, spreading her delicate folds again, and gently licked her entrance.

She gasped and thrust her fingers into my hair.

I licked her several more times, then pushed my tongue inside her pussy, gently swirling it, and hoped my saliva eased the ache taking her the first time had caused.

The tension slowly left her body, and she rolled her hips experimentally. I hissed out a breath, swirling again. She was so wet her juices coated my tongue. She did it again and my willpower frayed.

"I think..." She rocked her hips back, and I slid my tongue over her opening again.

I squeezed my eyes closed and tried to ignore the urgency of my need.

Her grip on my hair loosened. "I'm okay." She released a shuddery breath. "You can fuck me now."

I hissed. "Rose."

"Fuck me, Ronan. Please."

I stood and lifted her again, pressing her against the wall. I took myself in hand and brought the head to her tight opening and eased back inside her. A growl escaped, and I fought to go slow. "Rose?"

"I'm okay, Ronan. There's no pain. You feel...goddess, so good."

Somehow, I managed to contain my strength at her words. Rose was a shifter, she could take more than a human, but I needed to be careful with her. I slid out and back in, then again. Perfect, Rose was so perfect. I fought my need to take her harder, and my entire body shook from the strain.

She gripped my jaw and looked into my eyes. "You don't need to hold back. I can take it," she said as if she could read my mind.

I shook my head.

"I can take it," she said again and nipped my lip before swiping her tongue over it.

On a groan, I lost it completely, and I fucked my female like I'd been longing to.

Making her *mine*.

She clung to me, her nails digging into my flesh, her eyes hooded and bright. Her little fangs had slid down, and the sight only made me more feral and out of control.

"Every part of me is yours, Rose."

She moaned helplessly, tightening her thighs around my hips.

"You know that, don't you, sweets?" She nodded, those fangs puncturing her lip again. Blood dripped down her chin, and I lapped it up with a growl, my nerve endings sparking from her taste, my hips slamming forward with more force. "You are mine."

She whimpered. "Ronan..." Her back arched and she shook harder.

"Say it. I need you to say it."

Her desire-filled eyes locked on mine. "I'm yours. I've always been yours."

I snarled, her words filling me, settling deep. I gripped the back of her neck. "Bite me." I pressed her mouth to my throat.

She struck instantly, her delicate fangs sinking into my throat. The first deep pull had my balls drawing up sharply. The second had fluid pulsing from the head of my cock. She pulled away with a cry. I was going to come, and there was no stopping it.

I sank my fangs into her throat as she arched back and screamed, her inner muscles clamping around my cock so hard, all I could do was slam inside her and stay there, both of us rocking together as she trembled and cried out, coming for me.

Her blood filled my mouth, slid down my throat, and I dragged my tongue over her flesh, sealing my bite before I came, roaring and shaking in the small space, holding Rose so tight to me I was afraid I was hurting her but unable to let go.

Every muscle in my body spasmed in a way I'd never experienced before.

My limbs turned hot and loose as my thrusts slowed, as I slid inside her one final time and stayed there. My mind cleared then, and I became aware of Rose's hands moving over me, her soft lips against my throat, her tongue swiping over the bite she'd given me.

There was a low thudding sound in my head, echoing through my body. My blood felt hot in my veins. My head spun. I kept my arms wrapped around her tight, my face buried against her throat. "I love you," I rasped, the emotions inside me too big to contain. "I didn't know what love was for most of my life," I said against her skin, "but I do now, because of you."

"I love you too," she said, her hand sliding down my back.

I cupped the back of her head and held her to my chest—then drew in a breath, something I never usually needed to do, but for some reason, I did now. I released it, and my lungs compelled me to do it again.

"Ronan?"

"Yes?"

She moved her head against my chest, her arms tightening around me. "Ronan...your heart, its beating."

I froze as I dragged in another breath.

Rose pulled back, looking up at me. "Ronan?"

Was this really happening? Luna's heart started beating again when she mated with Gunner, but I assumed it had to do with her mating one of the knights. I never believed that would ever happen for me.

Rose smiled softly up at me, then taking my hand in hers, she pressed my palm to the center of my chest. I felt it. The low thudding behind my ribs.

She turned off the water. "Do you feel it?"

"Yes," I choked out and lifted her off her feet, holding her to me. I cupped the side of her face. "Because of you. My heart beats for you and only you, my precious female." I looked deep into her eyes. "My mate."

Chapter Thirty

Rose

Ronan carried me out of the shower, quickly dried us both, then carried me to bed. He lay me down and climbed in beside me, holding me close.

I listened to the steady thud of his heartbeat, and joy filled me. "We're mated," I said. "I can't believe it."

He tilted my head back and looked down at me. "Neither can I." His gaze moved over my face. "I can't believe you're mine. What did I do to deserve this much happiness? To deserve you?"

I ran my hand down his muscled chest. There were still several bruises and a couple of cuts, one deeper than the other. "I've loved you for so long. I fantasized about this. About being yours, but I never allowed myself to hope."

"I don't ever want to leave your side, sweets, not ever again," he said.

I ran my finger down the wound. It was raw and healing, but slower than the others. It had to be deep to still look that way. I leaned in and dragged my tongue along it, looking up at Ronan when he groaned and trembled against me. "Does it work the same way as my bite? If I lick your cut, will it heal faster?"

"Yes," he said huskily.

I licked it again, and he groaned deeper. It began to visibly heal. The redness subsided, and new, healthy skin slowly replaced what had been damaged. "You confronted him?"

"Yes."

"Are you okay?"

He slid his hand up and down my back. "I am." Ronan shook his head. "Yes, we fought, but in the end, only because Azel chose it. I don't think I needed it, because I'd already won. I'd won before I went down there; it just took me seeing him again to realize it." He brushed my hair back. "I have you and I have my sister back. Seeing him like that." A fierceness filled his eyes. "Without his powers, without me or Luna, I realized he's nothing. No one."

I pressed a kiss to his chest.

The fierceness remained in his eyes. "That doesn't take away all the things he did to me and Luna." He shook his head. "Nothing can do that. Beating or torturing him was never going to be a cure, but I won't say it didn't feel good to hurt him. And the knowledge he's burning in Hell, while I'm here with you, definitely helps."

"Will you tell Luna? What you did?" I asked.

"No. She'll never hear his name from me, not ever again. It'll only hurt her to think about him."

I entwined my fingers with his. "You're a good brother."

"I haven't been, but I want to be now."

He pulled me higher, draping me over his chest, and wrapped his arms around me. His body was smooth and hard. I rested my head on his chest so I could listen to his heart beating again. "So much has changed in such a short time," I said against his skin. "I just want to get past all the hard and scary things and focus on the good, on this. On me and you."

"We will, sweets. I promise."

I hugged him tightly and let his hands move over my body and lull me to sleep.

~

I woke with a start, a silent scream trapped in my throat. I spun toward Ronan. He was still asleep. I covered my face with shaking hands and tried to calm my breathing.

Death.

I had only days left, and he decided I needed a reminder. Zinnia hadn't called back with an answer, and I was starting to think that was because there wasn't one, that my cousin was scrambling to find something to help me that didn't exist. Ronan was finally my mate, and I might only get a few nights with him. I wanted to tell him, badly. But all that would do was spoil the time we did have left together.

I stared up at the ceiling, my mind racing. I knew we didn't have anything in our library about Death, but maybe we had something about the mother? Specifically, what would happen if a witch died in the middle of her task.

There was no way I was getting back to sleep now, so I eased out of bed, pulled on my robe, and quietly stepped out of the room. The house was dark and quiet, and I quickly headed downstairs to the library and shut myself in.

I turned on the lamp and made my way around the room, searching for anything I could find on the trials, anything we had on the mother, then sat down to wade through it all.

I don't know how long I was searching, a long time, when I shoved another book aside and dragged the next closer. Still nothing. I searched the shelves again. I was sure there was a book, a kind of rule book. We'd never had occasion to look at it until the role of Keeper had passed to Willow.

I scanned the shelves again, and with nothing to lose, I let my intuition guide me, like Willow told me to.

Running my finger along the spines, I stopped when it felt right. My finger was against a small red leather book on the shelf behind the desk. I slid it free.

This was it.

I couldn't believe it, it actually worked. Opening the cover, I ran my finger down the list of contents.

Keeper succession.

I knew what happened when one family lost the last Keeper in their family line because that's how we ended up in this situation, it shifted to another branch within a family. I also knew what happened if the Keeper died trying to complete their task or while they fought in their trial—they failed. Their coven lost the gifts the mother had given them.

But I didn't know what happened to a coven when a witch died before they finished their task but not due to the actual task itself. Like Death blackmailing you into giving up your life to live in his realm. Surely the mother wouldn't punish our coven for that? But then, the mother wasn't always fair.

I flipped to the correct page and quickly scanned it.

There it was. My stomach flipped.

If I died of causes not related to my task, the task would end, and a new one would be given to the next in line. Magnolia. Mags would be given a new task to complete. *Shit.* She wasn't ready for that. My baby sister was still working through her own trauma. She and Bram were shaky.

She was supposed to have another year to prepare. To mature. But if Zinnia couldn't help me, in a matter of days, I'd be gone, and Mags would not only be grieving for her sister but thrown into a task to save her coven.

I'd buried my head in the sand. All too ready to dump this on Zinnia's shoulders, to leave her to find the solution. I sat heavily and covered my face. I'd been a burden to the people I loved for my entire life, and not even my death would give them a reprieve.

Mags would suffer. They all would.

I cursed and squeezed my eyes closed.

A firm, warm hand squeezed my shoulder and I jumped, springing around. Ronan stood there, his hair rumpled and his eyes glittering in the darkness. His muscled chest was still bare, but he'd tugged on his trousers.

"I woke and you were gone," he said. "I didn't like it, sweets."

I stood and moved into his arms. He pulled me close immediately. "I'm sorry, it's this task. I'm worried," I said, omitting the rest of it.

"It's going to be okay. Everything will work out."

His voice was deep, soothing. I hoped he was right. I needed to tell him about my vision and what I'd learned, but I didn't want to right then. Everything was so messed up. Nothing was as it seemed. I was confused and scared and the happiest I'd ever been all at once. Ronan was finally mine.

And right then, that's all I wanted to think about. "Kiss me," I whispered.

The violet of his eyes deepened, heat firing inside them instantly. He leaned in, pressing his lips to mine. The kiss was gentle and tender, but right then, I wanted something else from him. I wanted an escape from all the fear and the worry. The thought that I could lose him was more than I could stand. I clung to him tighter and licked at his perfectly sculpted lips, and when my fangs slid down, I let one graze my own.

I knew the instant he tasted my blood. A growl rumbled through him, and he sucked and licked it off. His arms banded around me tighter. "You bring out the predator in me, Rose." His breathing was hard and fast. Something he hadn't done, hadn't needed to do before tonight. "I'm trying to be gentle, sweets, but your kiss, one taste of your blood, and the monster in me comes out."

I squeezed my thighs together. "I like the monster. And right now, I want to give him everything he craves."

His chest heaved. "Rose..." His words trailed off when I undid the button of his trousers and slid down the zipper, then lowered myself to my knees. He looked down at me, his throat working on a swallow. "What are you...sweets, what are you doing?"

I pushed his trousers lower and took his cock in my hands. He was hot and hard like steel, his skin like silk over the thick veins running its length. He was utterly magnificent. "You're beautiful," I said.

His Adam's apple slid up and down. The look in his eyes grew hungry, needy. "Rose, why are you..."

I leaned forward and dragged my tongue across the fat head of his cock. The sound of his hand slapping against the top of the desk beside me echoed through the room.

"Sweets," he gasped out. "You don't...I've never..."

I licked him again, and his groan was loud and low. "How does it feel?" I asked and did it again.

He shuddered and his chest and abs tightened. "You don't have to do that, you don't have to..."

I took the swollen head into my mouth and sucked. I'd never given a blow job before, but I wanted to make my mate feel good. I wanted him to know how desirable I thought he was. How much I wanted him. How much I cared about him. This wasn't about taking. Ronan had experienced enough of that in his life. This was all about giving, giving my male pleasure. Making him feel good.

I tilted my head back and looked into his wild stare as I sucked all the way to the tip and released him. "I want to. I've thought about doing this with you many times. Of worshiping you like you deserve."

His fangs punched down, long and sharp, and my core tightened, my own need shooting through the roof. "You humble me, my beautiful female," he said and cupped the side of my face.

"And you make me happier than I've ever been in my life," I said, then I sucked him deep into my mouth again, taking as much of him as I could.

He shoved his fingers into my hair and fisted on a helpless moan.

I sucked him deep, over and over. The desk groaned as he gripped it tighter, his hand shaking as he held my hair firmly in his grasp. I let his heavy length slip from my mouth and dragged the tip of my tongue along one of the thick veins, then back, rubbing it over the head, teasing the rim. I had no idea what I was doing, but everything I did seemed to make Ronan more restless, more out of control. His moans were unguarded, pure pleasure, and it filled my heart and turned me on all at the same time.

Tilting my head back, I locked eyes with him and sucked him deep. Stark need lined his handsome face as he stared down at me. I hollowed my cheeks and sucked him harder.

"Fuck," he barked out. "I've n-never..." He shook his head, his lips peeling back, baring his wicked-looking fangs. His thumb touched my lip stretched around his cock. "What you do to me."

My fangs were a lot smaller than his, and I mostly had control over them now, but the hotter I got, the more my gums tingled and the harder it was to keep them retracted. His cock pulsed hard in my mouth.

"I can't...I can't hold back."

My fangs slipped down a little, his words pulsing through me, and one of the pointed tips grazed the side of his shaft.

He snarled, and I tried to pull back, but Ronan's hold on my hair tightened and he held me there. I looked up at him, and his feral gaze hit mine. "Bite me, bite my cock while I come," he said through gritted teeth.

He was lost, to his need, to his desire for me, and I was lost with him. I did as he asked, and I took him deep into my mouth and bit down on his hard flesh, locking his cock deep in my mouth. He stilled, his body bowing, his growls filling the room. I withdrew my fangs, and blood and come filled my mouth.

His hips pumped, and I swallowed greedily, unable to do anything but follow his primal instincts.

He pulled from my mouth suddenly, hooked me under the arms, and hauled me to my feet. "The scent of your pussy dripping wet for me is more than I can take."

Planting my butt on the desk, he yanked my robe open, baring my nakedness. He gripped one of my breasts and dipped his head, sucking my nipple into his mouth as he rubbed the head of his blood-covered cock across my entrance. He sucked me deeply one more time, then lifted his head. He was still hard, as if he hadn't come moments ago, and his gaze holding mine, he slammed his cock inside me.

Straightening, he ran his hands down my sides, gripped my hips, then pulled out and slammed back in again. "You're the one that's beautiful, Rose. You're so perfect. Mine. All mine."

The scent of sex, of his blood, filled the room, and I lifted my hips restlessly, wanting more. I was still a little tender but nothing I couldn't take. I wanted all of him, everything he could give me. I tried to twist my hips against his hold, near out of my mind.

But he held me in place, his gaze utterly focused on me. I watched as it dipped to where we were joined. His eyes flared. "Look at you, sweets. The way your beautiful body accepts me." His gaze flew back to mine. "You want me as much as I want you, don't you, my heart, you can't get enough of me either?"

"No," I cried, arching against the desk. "I'll never get enough."

He dropped his hand between my legs, his thumb sliding over my clit. "You'll never leave me, will you, Rose? You'll never leave."

My body was burning up, his thumb a steady torment. I tightened around his length, even as my heart cracked down the middle, because I didn't know if I could make that promise. I didn't know what would happen when Death's deadline arrived. I couldn't tell him the truth, but I refused to lie either. "I will n-never willingly l-leave you. You're all I want, all I've ever wanted."

Ronan came down on top of me with a growl, covering my body with his. "I love you," he said, then took my mouth in a brutal kiss.

I clung to him as he kissed me, as he pounded into me over and over again. The pleasure so intense, I gasped for breath, clawing at him when I came screaming.

He kept his mouth against mine the whole time, holding my body tight beneath his as he thrust into me. Then he buried his face in the side of my throat and groaned, his cock pulsing strongly as he emptied himself inside me.

"I love you, Rose," he said again as his thrusts slowed, and his kiss went from brutal to tender. "I love you so much."

I wrapped my arms around him, running my hands along his sides, comforting him and myself. "I love you too."

Please don't take me from him, I silently pleaded.

But there was no one to hear me, and even if Death could?

He wouldn't care.

Chapter Thirty-One

Rose

Ronan looked sexy as hell in his black tux. But that square jaw was and had been clenched all day, ever since I told him about my vision. We'd done some more research and found out who the elusive Mr. Kelley was, the male the guard had mentioned in my vision, and the tension I saw in Ronan had only gotten worse.

The good news was we had a lead. The bad news was that Oliver Kelley was a criminal. A dealer of artifacts and priceless goods, a lot of them stolen. He was a bad dude who'd done a lot of bad things, and we had spent most of the day chasing our tails, trying to track him down and coming up empty, until now.

He was well known in parts of Roxburgh, the darker, seedier parts. Places your average Joe didn't often venture, until tonight.

I looked down at my outfit. It was like nothing I'd ever worn before. Nothing I'd ever had the chance to wear before. It was Mag's, and I felt as if I were playing dress-up in the slinky black number. When she wore it, it clung to her ample curves, but she always wore it under a jacket, with tights and her combat-style books.

I was taller than my sister, so instead of brushing just above the knee, it barely covered my ass. I didn't have her curves, so it hung lower in the front and back and gently skimmed my breasts and hips. And instead of tights and boots, I had on sheer stockings and sky-high black pumps that I'd found in Iris's closet —the only one of my sisters with the same sized feet as me— among the things she'd left behind when she moved in with Draven.

My hair was down and wavy, and Mags had done my makeup. Though it was light, the liquid eyeliner across my lids that ended with a flick and the bright red lipstick meant it was far from understated.

I looked like a vixen, and when I crossed my legs and Ronan's gaze slid down them and the muscle in his jaw jumped again, I felt like one too. "It's going to be fine," I said for the third time.

"The place will be full of monsters. Monsters and criminals."

"Okay, yes, there will be some…ah people like that there. But it's a bar. How bad can it be?" We'd checked the place out earlier and instantly felt the magic flowing from the building. It was heavily warded, or something like it, a type of magic that not even Ronan could get past, used to suppress magic users from turning on each other, and given the type of clientele, not surprising. But that meant we had to go in without the protection of Ronan's power.

His fingers clenched the wheel. "It's an exclusive club ' frequented by murderers and thieves."

"No one will pay us any attention. We'll slip in, watch, listen, maybe talk to a few people, then leave. I promise, it'll be fine," I said and tried to ignore the nerves going crazy inside me.

"You need to keep your coat on," he said in his bossy tone.

"That'll look weird." I curled my fingers around his forearm. It was hard as stone. "You know why I'm dressed like this. I have to fit in. Males like that treat their females as accessories. If I went in there covered from the neck down, they'd instantly be suspicious."

Ronan growled. "If anyone looks at you…touches you…" The steering wheel groaned. "I'll tear their arms off."

Well, crap. I should've guessed that was coming. "No one will be looking at me."

He scoffed. It was the first time I'd heard him do that. "You look so goddamn fuckable right now, sweets, I can barely think straight."

"Fuckable?"

"It means looking at you makes me want to fuck you," he said and glanced at me again before growling under his breath.

"I know what it means, but I didn't think you did."

"Until you, I've never had reason to use it, or think it."

I grinned. "I think you spend too much time with Relic."

"The hounds don't like to use a lot of useless words when one will do the job adequately."

He was so serious; I bit my lips to hold back my laugh. "This is true."

He glanced my way. "Are you laughing at me?"

"Possibly."

"Why?" he said, but I could tell he wasn't offended by the way his eyes sparkled.

"Because before you regained your emotions, you were prim and proper. Now you randomly come out with things like fuckable and shock the hell out of me."

"You don't like it?" he asked.

I smirked at him. "Actually, I kind of love it when you randomly say something dirty."

He glanced at me again. "You do?"

"I do."

"Like how I haven't been able to stop thinking about your lips wrapped around my cock, or the way it looked when it was covered in blood, filling your tight little pussy last night over that desk?"

I swallowed, my mouth getting dry as hell and my panties the complete opposite. I cleared my throat and wriggled in my seat. "Yes, like that."

He stared at me for a second, then he grinned, flashing me his white teeth and sharp fangs, and my heart nearly exploded in my chest. "I'll be sure to do that more often, then."

He turned back to the road while I reeled beside him at the sheer beauty of that smile. The first real smile he'd ever given me. "You do that," I finally managed.

"We're here," he said a couple of minutes later and parked the car.

"Right, let's do this."

He turned to me. "You stay plastered to my side at all times. We don't separate for any reason, understand?"

We were back to overprotective, bossy Ronan. "I sure do."

"Good." He got out and strode around the car, opening my door.

I got out and looked up at the old brick hotel in front of us. This place had been *the place* for rich and influential people back in the day. Now it was owned by the bad guys. None of them human, and all were the type of beings who preferred the shadows to the daylight.

The building was a little rundown now, but it still had its charm. Ronan took my hand as we headed up the stairs, walking in through the front door. We got in the elevator and he hit the button for the penthouse suite.

"Try not to make eye contact with anyone, okay? We're not dealing with humans. They're monsters. If you make eye contact and they decide they want you, they won't take no for an answer. It'll end in bloodshed," he said and gripped my hand tighter.

My nerves were insane now, my heart thundering in my chest.

"Rose," he said, taking my jaw and turning me to face him. "I can hear your heart racing, and they will as well. You need to calm down, sweets."

That was easier said than done. "I'm not sure I can."

"You have to," he said, his voice hard. "Breathe, Rose."

I dragged in a breath and slowly released it, then another. It wasn't working. The elevator dinged, and the doors slid open directly into the club. Several heads turned our way. My pulse jumped. *Shit.*

Ronan cursed under his breath, stepped through the doors, then spun me and kissed me hard and deep. I stiffened, then leaned into him, relaxing into the kiss. He pulled back, pressing his lips to mine, once, twice more, his lips moving to my ear. "Let them think your heart's beating like that for me."

When he looked down at me, I smiled up at him. "It is now."

His eyes darkened, but Ronan was in full-on protector mode. Something came over him, something dark and dangerous. The vibes coming off him lifted goose bumps all over me. He took in the room for a moment, then curled an arm around my shoulders, pulling me into his side, and led me farther into the room as if he belonged there. The vibration of the ward was a constant. These guys were serious about security.

The place was dimly lit, decorated in sapphire, silver, and black. It had an old-world feel, like stepping back in time. A piano player played in the corner. There were tables scattered throughout the room. People milled around in groups, talking and laughing, while others sat in the darker edges of the room, no doubt wheeling and dealing or whatever it was that the bad guys did. Ronan led me to a small table deeper into the room. He moved to the seat that would have his back facing the wall. I was about to sit beside him, but he stopped me, tugging me to him as he sat, and lifted me onto his lap.

He wasn't joking about keeping me plastered to his side. His arms came around me, one resting on my thigh, the other on my belly. A waitress came over for our order, and Ronan ordered bourbon for himself and a glass of wine for me. I glanced around the room. Several people glanced our way but most didn't pay us any mind.

The elevator doors opened and a tall male walked in. He was headed straight for the bar, and the intestine-eating, reptile shifter looked as if he belonged there. "Clay St. James."

"I see him," Ronan said, his body stiffening beneath me.

"Why do you think he's here? This seems a rather big coincidence."

"It does." Ronan's grip tightened on me.

Our drinks arrived, and I pretended to sip mine while I monster-watched discreetly.

Clay stood against the bar, tall and handsome. Several females were watching him or trying to catch his eye, but he didn't seem to notice. He appeared to be nursing his drink, trying to appear relaxed, but the stiffness of his shoulders said otherwise.

I leaned into Ronan. "Should we go and talk to him?"

"Not yet."

"Do you think he's waiting for someone?"

"Possibly. He seems on edge."

"I think so too."

Ronan's fingers slid higher, resting below the hem of my very short dress. "You seem to have calmed, sweets."

"You have that effect on me. I feel safe when I'm with you."

He pressed his mouth to my throat and sucked the skin there gently, making my breath catch. "You make me feel immeasurable things, all of them good."

Warmth filled me. "I'm glad to hear it."

His fingers slipped under my chin, and he turned my head to face him. "I don't ever want to be parted from you, Rose, not ever. Will you move in with me?"

I grinned, then Death's image filled my mind. I shoved him back out. There was still a chance I'd get out of this, a small one, but a chance, nonetheless. "Are you sure?"

"You're my mate. I want you with me always."

"And you love me," I said, still grinning.

"With everything in me," he said.

I kissed him and lay back, resting my head on his shoulder, somehow feeling completely safe in this room full of vipers. That's when I saw Clay turn to the elevator that had just opened and lock on to the male who was walking out.

He was older, fit, dressed in an expensive suit, and had shrewd, some would say cruel, icy blue eyes. If he'd been human, he'd pass for someone in their mid to late fifties.

He walked in as if he owned the place and paid Clay no mind at all, even while the male's gaze was laser-focused on the new arrival. Something strange came over me, like something pushing forward in the back of my mind. A vision. I needed something shiny. I needed blood. I bit into my palm, letting my fangs sink into my skin, and held up the wineglass in my hand.

"Rose?" Ronan lifted my fisted hand, instantly smelling my blood.

"A vision," I said as it crept in at the corners of my mind.

Ronan's arms tightened around me. "I've got you."

I was pulled under.

An image of the older male, the one who'd just walked in, filled my mind.

He was in his home, his den, sitting behind a massive desk.

Someone knocked on the door. "Mr. Kelley. They're here."

He leaned back, a calculating look in his eyes. "Show them in."

A shadow moved over his face, but I couldn't see who stood opposite him.

"Let me see it then," his new guest said, voice harsh, urgent. "This had better not be another dud, Kelley."

"I've been assured it's not." He smiled, opened the drawer of his desk, and pulled out a small carved effigy, setting it on the desk.

A hand snatched it up, and Kelley watched, not looking quite so confident anymore. "It's a fucking copy." The other male roared and threw the effigy across the room—

The vision dissipated, drifting from my mind, bringing me back to the here and now.

"Rose?" Ronan's voice was rough, concerned.

"I'm here," I said as he lifted my palm and sucked on the puncture wounds I'd made, sealing them closed. "It's him. The older male who walked in, he's definitely Oliver Kelly."

Clay was still watching him, then he pushed away from the bar and strode after him.

"I couldn't see his face, but there was another male in my vision, I heard his voice though."

"St. James?"

"No. I really don't think so."

I quickly explained to Ronan what I saw. "He's the one we need to find. Whoever Kelley's working for. Clay had his effigy stolen, and it looks as if he's worked out who was behind it as well."

"Kelley's the one sourcing and stealing the effigies, or at least paying people like the museum guard. He can tell us who the other male in my vision was. He's the one we need to find."

Ronan lifted me off his lap, and as soon as his hands left me and my feet hit the floor, someone grabbed my arm and hauled me into their side.

"My turn," a gritty voice said before he pressed his face against my hair and breathed deeply. I tried to shove him away, but he held me painfully tight, and because of the ward, I couldn't even use my magic. "Come on, legs, let's go get to know each other better."

I shoved at him again. "No…"

Ronan was a blur of movement. One moment he was by the table, the next in front of us, and his face had utterly transformed. It was as if he'd pulled on a mask, one that was as terrifying as it was beautiful. His fangs were long and deadly, his face more angled, his eyes those of a monster, and fury pulsed from him.

"Release my mate. Now," he snarled.

"I don't think so." The male smiled, flashing fangs of his own.

Ronan was stone, utterly cold as he moved around him slowly, primed, muscles bunched.

The male holding me smiled, then without warning, dipped his head and sank his fangs into my shoulder. Pain sliced through me instantly, and I cried out.

Ronan roared, his hand shooting out, his fist slamming into the side of the other male's head. His fangs were wrenched from me, tearing my flesh. The male grabbed his head, and Ronan pulled me away.

As soon as I was safely out of the way, Ronan attacked. He punched him in the throat, then grabbed his wrist and twisted, spinning it under, then wrenching his arm up.

There was a terrible pop and a tearing sound a moment before Ronan tore his arm completely off.

The male screamed, but Ronan wasn't done. He kicked his legs out from under him, planted his foot on the male's chest, grabbed his other arm, and twisted. The male screamed, but Ronan didn't flinch, tearing through skin and muscle. The other arm popped from its socket, and Ronan flung that one aside, then he dropped to the floor and used his fangs to rip out his throat.

Blood pumped from the male's convulsing body.

Ronan jumped to his feet, his eyes blazing, glowing, blood dripping down his chin. He turned to me, and I stared at him in shock. My hand was pressed to the wound at my shoulder, blood trickling through my fingers, and he closed the space between us.

"You're bleeding," he said, his voice unrecognizable.

People rushed to the torn-up male on the floor, and Ronan pulled me behind him, ready to do battle again. But a male stepped forward, tall and terrifying. Another vampire.

He took in Ronan, then his gaze slid to me and back. "Ronan?"

Ronan took a steadying breath and met the other male's eyes. "Nero, your soldier attacked my mate. You're lucky I didn't tear his head from his body."

The male's brow lifted. "Your mate?" His emotionless, icy stare slid from Ronan and moved over me again. "This is new."

Ronan stiffened.

"You would take on even me for this female?" he said, a chilly sort of amusement in his voice.

"Yes," Ronan said without missing a beat.

The vampire inclined his head, then he turned to the others with him and motioned to his soldier still twitching on the floor. "Get him out of here." He turned back to Ronan. "I hope to see you both at the club soon." Then he turned and went back the way he came, as if nothing of note had happened.

Ronan hooked me around the waist, lifting me off my feet and carrying me to the elevator. The doors opened.

"Wait, we can't go yet."

He ignored me and kept walking. Someone tried to get in as well, but Ronan growled and they stepped back out. As soon as the doors closed, he lifted my hand, covering the bite to my shoulder, and checked my injury. He cursed viciously.

"Ronan, we need to talk to Oliver Kelley—"

He said nothing, just took my jaw in his hand and angled my head to the side. Then his mouth was open over the wound, gently licking and sucking. It tingled, instantly starting to heal.

"I'm okay," I said, curling my fingers around the side of his throat. "Ronan, it's okay."

He lifted his head, eyes blazing. "He tried to take you against your will. He bit you. He fucking violated you. Nothing about that is okay, Rose. It's taking every bit of my control not to go back up there and finish him off."

I didn't know what to say. He was right, but we were there for a reason, and time was running out. "We can't leave."

He heaved several breaths. "I want to take you home."

I shook my head, curling my fingers around his forearm. "Kelley's the link. We need to wait and follow him. We have to question him, Ronan. Or at the very least, we need to search his place."

The elevator slid open, and he led me from the building. I got in the car and he rounded the hood and got in beside me. Then I felt the buzz of his power surround us, concealing us. He slipped off his jacket and covered me with it.

Clay St. James walked out.

Ronan was out of the car and in front of Clay before I knew he was going to move. He grabbed him by the front of the shirt and shoved him across the sidewalk, slamming him against the side of the car, trapping me inside. "You're following Kelley, are you working for him?"

Clay stared back, "No. I want my fucking effigy back."

"You said the collection was your grandfather's, you acted as if you weren't overly interested, and now you're here. Why?" Ronan growled out. "Were you following us? If you think you're getting anywhere near my female—"

"I'm not following you or your female." He shoved at Ronan.

Ronan gave him room but didn't release him completely. "Talk."

"The collection is mine. It's been mine for a very long time." He blew out a breath. "You know what I am?"

"Yes."

"Then you'll know that we're the cold-blooded outsiders. The truth of what I am can make a lot of beings uncomfortable. I'm used to lying about myself, concealing it. They resent our ability to regenerate, and we can be targets because of that. I was too weak after shedding to hide what I was from you when you came to my house, but I need the effigy to summon the type of demon I use to regenerate."

"You're still lying. We saw the demon in your basement. You managed just fine without it."

His eyes narrowed. "You broke into my house?"

"You're either in on this with Kelley, or you're trying to take my female, which is it?"

Clay hissed and the pair of them shoved each other several more times.

"Ronan," I yelled through the car window.

Clay, thankfully, did not look my way. I wasn't sure Ronan would attempt to control himself if he had. The male hissed out several more breaths, then straightened his tie. "I was following Kelley because I know he's behind the theft. I'm not in league with that fucker, and I'm not trying to take your female. You already made it clear she belongs to you. As for the demon in my basement, I hunted it and dragged it home. But as you can imagine, that is a lot more difficult, especially in my aged skin, and not something I'd like to repeat. Summoning a venious directly into my basement is far easier."

I believed him. Ronan studied him for several seconds, then stepped back.

"Are we done?"

"Yes," Ronan said.

"I want your word that if you find it, you'll return it to me," Clay said.

Ronan dipped his chin sharply. Clay strode off and Ronan got back in the car.

"Ronan?"

"We'll wait here for Kelley, but you need to sleep. It'll help you heal. I'll wake you when he comes down."

I shook my head. "I'm not tired." Honestly, I wasn't sure what he'd do to Kelley if I wasn't awake to stop him. He was as volatile as I'd ever seen him.

I wouldn't let my only lead slip through my fingers or possibly be torn to shreds by my overly protective mate.

Chapter Thirty-Two

Rose

I woke to the sound of Ronan's voice. He was cursing profusely.

I glanced over to see him scowling out the front window. I quickly sat up. "Where are we?"

"Outside Kelley's home." He turned to me, and his hard gaze softened. "How are you feeling?"

"I'm fine. Why didn't you wake me when he came out of the club?" The house was huge, and it was guarded to the eyeballs, and not just by fences and gates but by magic. I could feel it. "Kelley was obviously friends with a witch or two, the wards around this place are strong." I turned to Ronan. "Strong enough to cover up what Kelley and the guard were up to at the museum, I'd say."

Ronan growled under his breath. "I thought as much. I felt it when I got close earlier."

I spun to him. "You were going to go in without me?"

He didn't even have the decency to look guilty. "You lost blood." His voice vibrated with fury when he said that. "You need to rest. And I need to get you home and feed you so you can regain your strength. I was going to go in, get what we need, and get out."

While I slept like a baby under the protection of Ronan's power, he was going to do my task for me. "That's not how this works, Ronan. You need to include me in these decisions. I know you're feeling protective, but this is *my* task. You can help, but you can't do it for me."

He squeezed the steering wheel. "This was one thing. You've put yourself in danger for this task, repeatedly. You've bled and been attacked and..." He growled, his eyes growing brighter. "This was one thing," he said again.

"I know, but I still have to be the one to do it."

"Protecting you is literally what I was born to do, Rose. It's all I care about. Asking me to ignore that is impossible."

Ronan had seen another male bite me, violate me in that way, then literally tore him apart. He still vibrated with rage. It saturated the air around us. I remembered what Luna said about how hard this would be for him, to cut him some slack when he acted protective in the extreme. I released a frustrated breath. "I'm sorry. I know this is hard on you as well."

"You don't need to be sorry, sweets. You need to let me take care of you."

His voice was all rumbly, more predator than usual. There was no reasoning with him when he was like this, and the last thing I wanted was to fight with him. "Well, there's no getting in there tonight. There has to be a spell, something, that will get us through."

"Or we'll get here early and follow him. Corner him away from his fortress," Ronan said, starting the car.

"Good idea."

Ronan grunted and pulled out onto the road.

My phone beeped, and I looked down at it. A text from Mags.

Zinny and Jaz arrived. A surprise visit.

Then I saw I'd received one from Zinnia earlier while I'd slept, telling me she was here and we'd talk in the morning. Her visit was no surprise, not to me. She was here to help me.

Nerves filled me. No, not nerves, something a lot bigger. My blood turned cold in my veins, and it felt as if twenty spiders were crawling up my spine, one after the other.

Time had run out.

Tomorrow night, I had a date with Death.

Ronan

Rose lay naked on top of me, the heat of her body, her silky hair against my skin lifting goose bumps all over me. She whimpered as she suckled at my throat.

I dragged my hand down her spine and gripped her round ass. "Bite," I ordered, half-crazed, desperate for her to feed from me as an image of what happened in that club was on repeat in my head.

Rose groaned and rocked her hips, taking me deeper inside her as her little fangs finally bit down. My hips jerked up, forcing me deeper as pleasure spiked through me. Her tongue worked my vein, her lips sealing over the punctures she'd made and sucking deeply. I felt each pull in my gut, my balls, down the length of my shaft.

I gripped the back of her neck, holding her there. "That's it, sweets, take what you need from me. Take it all."

She moaned and rolled her hips faster, lost to the pleasure I gave her, the pleasure she chased. There was almost something different about her tonight, a desperation to her movements, the way she clung to me, the way she'd looked into my eyes, that had my head spinning. Subtleties I would have missed once, but not anymore.

I felt her flutter around my cock, then she dragged her tongue over my throat and her head lifted. Her eyes were black, her bat eyes front and center. Her pale blond hair was wild around her flushed face. My blood coated her lips and dripped down her chin.

So incredibly beautiful.

At the sight of her like that, my cock thickened even more, grew harder, throbbing. She squeezed down on me, then cried out, rocking on top of me. Gasping, she tightened around me over and over. There was no holding back my own release, and I took her mouth in a bloody kiss.

Rose shook and cried out again against my lips. My groan was deep, my hips thrusting up, slamming inside her, each pull on my cock pumping her full of my seed until we were both spent.

She collapsed on top of me, and I wrapped my arms around her, tucking her head under my chin and holding her tight.

Her hand slid up my side, over my ribs, and she pressed her mouth to my chest. "I love you, Ronan." She puffed out a soft breath. "Probably more than I think you can comprehend right now."

My heart felt funny in my chest. I shifted my fingers through her hair. "I understand it perfectly, because I feel that way for you, sweets."

She lifted her head and rested her chin on her hand, looking up at me. "I know, but I think the longer you have your new emotions, the deeper you'll feel them."

"You think my love for you is less? Underdeveloped?"

She shook her head, her black eyes slowly returning to blue. "No, I know you love me at whatever capacity you're capable of right now. It's fierce and wild, and the most beautiful thing I've ever experienced in my life."

I frowned at her. "What are you saying?"

"I don't know. Nothing." Her lips curled up in a small smile. "I guess, as big as this feels now, it's only going to get bigger. I feel it. And that's a little scary." She dipped her head, kissing my chest again before she looked back up. "If...anything happens to me..." She cleared her throat. "I just...I want to make sure you're going to be okay."

"Nothing's going to happen to you," I growled out. "I won't let it."

She leaned into me and pressed a kiss to my lips. "I know. It's just…"

I brushed my thumb over her chin, over my blood still there, wiping it away. "It's just, what?" My heart was beating erratically. I didn't like this conversation.

Her gaze dipped, and when it came back to me, her eyes were black again, every part pure onyx. "I want you to promise me that if anything happens to me, you won't hurt yourself. That you'll go to Luna or the hounds and let them take care of you, that you'll—"

"Stop saying that," I snarled. "I can't bear to think of it. I don't want to talk about it."

Her eyes grew wide, glossy. "I almost died, Ronan. I can't help but think about it. Please, promise me."

I took her face in my hands. "I cannot promise you that, my heart. If anything happened to you, I would lay waste to whoever hurt you, then I would follow you. Wherever you were, I would find a way to follow you. Understand?"

A tear slid down her cheek.

Alarm filled me. "Rose? What's going on?"

She shook her head and lay back against my chest. "Nothing. I got a fright tonight, that's all."

I rubbed her back and held her tighter. "Nothing like that will ever happen again, I promise you."

I held her tight, tighter than normal because she seemed to need it.

And after tonight, I realized I needed it too.

Chapter Thirty-Three

Rose

When all my family got together, things got loud. So when I walked into the house and heard all the voices and laughter, I knew we had a full house.

My heart filled with trepidation as I walked into the kitchen, Ronan right behind me. Mom and Art, Else and Connor, my sisters and Bram, while Nia danced around excitedly as everyone loved on her.

Warrick and Draven stood to the side talking, and Zinnia and Jasmine were at the center of it all.

Ronan gave my hand a squeeze and went to join my sisters' mates as Zinny and Jaz jumped up and ran to me, engulfing me in a huge hug. I held them both tight, and when we pulled back, Zinnia held my eyes, giving me a subtle nod.

She was here for me.

To help me.

I had no idea what that would entail, but whatever it was, I'd do it. To protect my family, to delay Death and get more time with Ronan, I'd do absolutely anything. And that subtle nod gave me more hope than I'd had since Death started visiting me in my dreams.

Hemlock, my cousin's elusive familiar, a sweet black rat, poked her head out of the hood of Zinnia's sweatshirt and greeted me as well. Jazzy's familiar situation was a little more complicated and something we were all still trying to get our heads around.

"Hey, Hemy," I said. She let me give her head a little scratch, then went back to her hiding place.

"Too many people," Zinnia said and pulled something from her pocket, a treat, and held it over her shoulder. Hemlock grabbed it and vanished again.

Wills joined us and put her arm around my shoulders. "How you holding up?"

"I'm good. I think we're close." I hoped so, anyway. I was sure Kelley held the answers. We just needed to get him alone. "Any trouble from Trotman?"

"Nope, and you don't need to worry about him," she said. "Just focus on your task, and make sure you stay connected to your magic and your instincts, and you'll stay on the right path."

Iris had joined us. "Even if that means standing up to an over-protective male." She grinned.

"What about a mate? Any tips there?" I said and laughed at my sisters' reactions.

"You've mated already?" Willow said, grabbing my hand.

I nodded, and my sister pulled me in for a hug before Iris had her turn. I felt her tremble against me. "Iris? What's going on?"

She lifted her head and shook it. "We'll tell you later, but it's a good thing, I promise. This is the best news."

"Maybe don't tell Aunt Daisy you're mated until your task is over," Zinny said. "Unless you have time for a mating ceremony?"

Willow snorted. "Yeah, after Warrick and I didn't have one, and all the drama around Iris's, she won't let you get away with it."

"Good point." I definitely didn't have time for that, not now. Not until we'd dealt with Death and I was sure my coven was safe.

Ronan joined us a while later, pulling me aside. "Hey." His gaze locked on mine, and my heart did a little flip. I was so gone for this male, it was ridiculous.

"I'm going to leave for a while...to hunt for Kelley." I opened my mouth to argue, but he kept on talking. "When I find him, I'll call you."

"Ronan—"

"There's no point in us both going when it'll be more sitting and waiting around." The look in his eyes was almost pleading.

He was trying to protect me again. It was a need in him that he was struggling to rein in. I was about to protest when Zinnia, who stood behind Ronan, gave me a look that was not difficult to interpret.

Whatever we needed to do, Ronan wouldn't like it. "I'm not so sure," I said, because if I gave in too easily, he'd get suspicious. I hated manipulating him, but if he thought I was about to do something dangerous, he wouldn't leave my side.

The line of his jaw hardened, his bossy side coming forward. "Do you trust me?"

My guilt grew. "Yes."

"Then I'll call you if I find him," he repeated.

"Okay, fine. But make sure you do."

He didn't answer. Instead, he took my hand and led me from the kitchen and out to the hall. "I don't like leaving you."

Pain sliced through me. I'd tried not to think about it, but I couldn't pretend this wasn't happening anymore. If things went wrong tonight...If whatever Zinnia had planned failed, I might not be coming back. This might be the last time I ever saw him. My eyes stung, but I ruthlessly held back my tears. I couldn't let him see what I was feeling. But I couldn't stop from cupping the side of his face and lifting to my toes. He immediately leaned in and pressed his lips to mine.

His chest heaved and his arms tightened around me. "Your heart's racing," he said against my mouth.

"My heart always races when I'm with you," I said, and that was the truth. Though, this time, it was racing for a very different reason.

"You have the same effect on me." He kissed me again, then lifted his head. "I'll call you when I locate Kelley."

The guilt grew so big it was unbearable. I nodded, then pulled him back down so I could press my lips to his one more time, then I stepped back. He studied my face, and I made myself smile. If this was the end, I wanted him to remember me with love and happiness in my eyes, not fear or sadness.

His chest expanded on a sharp breath, then he turned and walked to the door.

I called his name before he could walk out.

He turned. "Yes, sweets?"

"I love you."

His lips curled up in a grin that brightened his gorgeous eyes, and he flashed his white teeth and fangs. "Love you too."

My knees grew weak and my heart was still pounding in my chest when he walked out the door and closed it behind him.

My phone beeped. Ronan had been texting regularly, keeping me updated. He'd found Kelley, but the male had two witches in his entourage, and they were actively warding him, making it impossible for Ronan, or anyone, to get close. We obviously weren't the only ones who wanted a piece of the guy. Did all the security have something to do with the male he met with in my vision? The extremely angry male who had thrown an effigy across the room?

"Okay?" Zinnia asked as we walked through the wide iron gates of the cemetery.

We'd slipped out when everyone had finally gone to bed.

"Yeah, everything's fine." I wrapped my coat around me tighter. I could smell snow in the air.

Zinnia didn't look convinced but didn't press for more. "We need soil, lilies, and some nettle leaves," she said as we weaved through the headstones.

The thick slabs of marble and stone were all different shapes and sizes, some crumbling they were so old. I could feel magic all around me. It was comforting. I'd always loved this place. Gran's was the newest stone here, and it seemed to shine under the moonlight. The space beside hers was free, and when I thought I was going to die, I'd chosen it for myself. The only person I'd told was Iris, and I'd made her promise to keep it to herself until the time came. I thought I'd already be here, my bones adding to the magic of our most sacred place.

If it hadn't been for Ronan, I would be.

"You'll see him again soon," Zinnia said, reading my mind, a look crossing her face I couldn't decipher.

She'd been quiet, contemplative most of the night.

"What's going on, Zinny?" I stopped her. "What aren't you telling me?"

"Well, we're about to have some face time with Death." She chuckled. "I know it's rare, but I freely admit to being a tad nervous. But"—she held up a finger—"I have this all under control. Trust your awesome cousin."

"You know I trust you. I'll owe you forever for coming with me tonight. But Death doesn't seem like the kind of guy to change his mind, and you need to know, if it comes down to it and the only way out of this is to sacrifice me, I want you to do it. I won't let this hurt my family. The coven needs to be protected at all costs, even if that means I have to go with Death." The thought of never seeing Ronan again was killing me. If I thought about it, really thought about it, I started to shut down. It was too painful to comprehend.

Zinnia's green gaze held mine. "Rose—"

"And you need to make sure Ronan is okay. Don't let him hurt himself or anyone else."

"Roe, Jesus—"

"Promise me."

She nodded slowly. "Fine, I promise...if it's the only way."

"Thanks."

"No worries," she said sarcastically.

I quickly cut my hand, dripping blood onto the ground, an offering for what we were taking, and filled a mason jar with cemetery dirt while Zinnia harvested the lilies and nettle leaves from one of the small greenhouses Art had built last spring.

Certain things here required an offering, like the soil and stones, anything collected from the ancient trees surrounding the grounds, even the grass. However, the flowers, herbs, and shrubs, anything Mom and Art had planted, we could harvest freely.

We gathered everything we needed and headed back. We still had a little time but needed to get to the meeting spot early to prepare.

"Can you drive?" Zinnia asked when we got to her car.

"I haven't really needed to."

"Get in the driver's seat," she said.

"What?"

"I'm giving you a lesson. It'll take your mind off what we're about to do, plus I need to mentally prepare." She got in the passenger side.

Having a driving lesson was the last thing I wanted to do, but if Zinnia needed to prepare, then I'd do it.

"It's an automatic, so totally easy." She gave me a quick run-through and we were off. Granted, the takeoff was a bit jerky, and I drove a lot slower than Zinnia ever did, but I got the hang of it pretty fast.

"Where's Hemy tonight?" She was usually under Zinnia's sweater or in her hood or a backpack.

"I told her to stay with Jaz."

"Good idea." Who knew what would happen tonight.

We hit Oldwood Forest and drove as far as we could down the winding road before we were forced to park and get out.

"Take this," Zinnia said and handed me a knife. The blade was wicked looking, thin and pointed. Deadly.

I held it, not sure what to do with it. "I don't know how to use this." I had a small knife for spelling, but it was nothing like this.

She looked up at me, her eyes round, a little wild. She was nervous, of course, not something I saw in my cousin's eyes often. "If something gets too close, stab it," she said. "Over and over again, whatever you need to save yourself."

I stared down at the blade and imagined myself doing what Zinnia said. My stomach turned over. "Death said I'd have safe passage to the meeting spot. I won't need this," I said.

Zinnia didn't look up as she pulled a backpack from the back seat, full of everything we'd collected from the cemetery. "When this meeting is over, I don't know if that protection will still be in place." She glanced up then. "Can you use your wings yet?"

I shook my head, fear growing inside me.

"That would've definitely made it easier." She hitched the bag on her shoulder. "I can take care of myself. So when we're done, I want you to run as fast as you can. Don't stop, don't look behind you, don't worry about me, just run, okay, Roe?"

I gripped the knife tighter. "You're scaring me, Zinny."

She strode up to me and pulled me in for a hug. "I'm sorry." She lifted her head. "I don't want anything to happen to you, that's all. Against all odds, you're here, alive and well, and I want to keep you that way." Her eyes closed, and she drew in a shaky breath. When they opened again, they glistened with unshed tears. "I wish this could be done differently. I wish I didn't need to drag you into this fucking forest with me, that I could fix this on my own. But that won't work. You need to be there as well."

"I'm stronger than I look. Yes, I'm scared, but I'll do whatever I have to, whatever you need me to," I said, wanting to take some of the burden I saw in her eyes.

She smiled at me and tucked my hair behind my ear. "I know you are. You're the strongest person I know." She looked down at my feet. "Now double knot your shoelaces, tripping over your own feet while you're running the hell out of here would really suck."

She wasn't wrong. I quickly did what she said. "So, what's going to happen at this meeting?" I asked as we headed deeper into the forest.

"I'm not totally sure, but I'll explain what we need to do when we get there. Death said you had safe passage to the meeting spot, but that might not include me. So we need to stay quiet. We don't want to draw attention to ourselves. This place is crawling with demons."

I shivered. No, we most definitely didn't want that.

We moved quietly through the woods. Growls, cries, and other odd noises that weren't animal echoed through the trees. There were demons around us, but they hadn't approached, and I had to assume that was Death's doing.

Still, neither of us spoke as we made our way to the meeting spot.

We finally reached the small clearing that Death had told me how to find, and cold dread slithered down my spine. Yes, this was most definitely the place. "Here," I whispered.

Zinnia nodded and rubbed her arms. She felt it as well. Then she motioned to a tall pile of rocks, all fairly large, nothing smaller than a bowling ball. They formed a rough, misshapen mound that had to be the gate. "How much time do you think we have?" Zinny asked, taking off her pack and placing it on the ground in front of her.

I checked my phone. There was a message from Ronan, checking in again. I looked up at the night sky and the position of the moon. "About fifteen minutes." I quickly replied to him, telling him I was visiting a friend with Zinnia, lying through my teeth so he didn't worry, and shoved my phone back in my pocket.

Zinnia unpacked all the ingredients, along with a small mortar and pestle, then glanced up at me. "Strip."

"My clothes?"

"Yep, everything."

Awesome. I got to meet Death for the first time in person completely naked. "What kind of spell is this?" I hated that my knowledge was so limited. If I survived all of this, I was going back and filling in all the blanks of my magical education.

She poured oil into the mortar. "It's a variation of a ritual we use to protect ourselves from rogue spirit possession." She added the nettle leaves and a handful of cemetery dirt. "Only instead of locking a spirit out, we're locking yours in. So Death can't get his hands on it, or at least make it difficult for him to extract it."

I was scared before. Now I reached a whole new level. I quickly undressed. Zinnia added a few more ingredients, then motioned me forward. "Add a few drops of your blood, then cover yourself with the potion."

I pricked the tip of my finger and added the blood, then did as she said.

She stripped off as well and tossed her clothes aside.

I looked into the mortar. "Will there be enough?"

"That's just for you." Then she took her blade from her pack, sliced both her palms, and smeared blood over her face, chest, stomach, and thighs.

I'd never seen anything like that, never read anything like it either. "What will that do?"

Zinnia turned to me and flashed a grin. She'd been so serious, so unlike the Zinny I knew since she got here, that her grin, the confidence, took me off guard.

"Boost the hell out of my power...and make me look badass. I'm coming face-to-face with Death. I plan on making a memorable first impression."

I wanted to laugh, to cry, to scream and run like hell from this place. I stared at her in disbelief. "But your soul...you need the oil."

"My soul is going to be just fine. It's going to be okay, Roe, I promise," she said.

I quickly finished covering my body with the oily potion, and she reached out, taking my hand.

The stones rumbled and we spun to face them. The rumbling became a trembling shake, the earth rolling beneath our feet as if it were trying to force us apart. My hand was slipping from Zinnia's blood-covered one, but we linked fingers, refusing to let go.

The stones moved, reforming, and as they did, they revealed skulls, as if the bones had been fossilized in each one, empty eye sockets and jaws hanging wide.

A doorway to Limbo.

The shadowy forest behind it vanished and darkness, deep and cold, appeared. A distant thump echoed through the arch, rolling over us, slow and steady but growing in volume, until I felt it vibrate through my bones.

Death was coming.

I squeezed Zinnia's hand. "What should I say?"

Wind picked up speed around us, faster, more violent. I turned to Zinny. Her wild red hair was whipping around her face. She squeezed my hand in return. "Let me do the talking," she called through the storm now raging around us.

The cold and wind sucked the oxygen from my lungs, the wind somehow growing stronger, and the ground a constant rumble beneath our feet.

A dark figure moved into view, tall and draped in black. He lifted a twisted wood staff glowing with power, then thumped it a final time against the forest floor.

Everything stilled, the wind dying away to nothing.

Zinny and I gasped for breath, and I forced myself to remain where I was and not take a horrified step back. I'd seen Death in my dreams, but it hadn't prepared me for seeing him now. He was impossibly tall, close to seven feet, and broad shoulders filled out his cloak that concealed his form and face.

All I could see of his body were his hands, palms broad, fingers thick and long, curled around the staff he still gripped tight, and his frigid blue eyes glowing from beneath the hood of his cloak.

We waited as that arctic stare moved over us.

"I told you to come alone," he said to me.

His voice was the stuff of nightmares, resonating deep and cold, sparking a multitude of emotions—terror, despair, loneliness, heartbreak, grief. The urge to curl into a ball and sob filled me and had me shaking uncontrollably.

"I'm afraid you can't have her," Zinnia said beside me.

Her voice was strong, but there was no missing the slight waver. I moved closer to her; her hold on me so tight, it was painful.

Death studied her for several long seconds. "And you think you can stop me from taking what I'm owed?"

"If you take Rose's soul, you'll be interfering with a bargain between Lucifer and her sister's mate. Lucifer granted immortality to the Thornheart sisters if they mated. Rose is mated. She can't die."

I spun to Zinnia. What? We were immortal? I couldn't believe what I was hearing. Zinnia didn't look my way. She kept her gaze locked on Death.

His wide shoulders seemed to grow broader, his grip on his staff tightening and turning his knuckles white.

Zinnia continued, seemingly unfazed by the terror standing before us. "If you make an enemy of Lucifer, there'll be a war. You'll disturb the balance between the four realms."

Death made a sound that lifted the hair on the back of my neck, a sound not human, not of this world. "She doesn't need to die to enter my world, witch. I can take her as she is. Her soul will still be mine."

"Rose's brother-in-law is Lucifer's alpha hellhound, a male he considers a friend. Do you think Lucifer will let that stand?" Zinnia said, her voice growing stronger.

"The bargain grants her immortality, not where she'll live out eternity. Lucifer will have no grounds to start a war."

That dreadful voice rolled over us, and my knees almost gave out. Oh goddess, he was going to take me anyway.

"Come here, Rose," he said to me.

I turned to Zinnia, fear and horror making me shake so hard my teeth chattered. "It's okay," I forced out.

Death held out his hand.

My cousin didn't let go. "It's okay," I said again, and I took a step forward.

Zinnia pulled me back, refusing to release me.

I squeezed her fingers. "You did all you could, but you can't stop this. No one can."

Her jaw tightened, and she turned back to Death, staring him down. "It's not Rose you want, it's me."

"What?"

Death stilled.

"You've been searching for me for a long time, but I made sure you couldn't find me. I hid, using this." She held up her arm, showing him her forearm with a tattoo I'd seen many times over the years. "I'm the one you want, the one you've been waiting for." Zinnia released my hand and stepped forward. "You came to me in my dreams when I was fifteen years old. You told me who I was, what you wanted from me, and I ran. Do you remember?"

He said nothing, his massive form utterly still. I looked between Death and Zinnia. What the hell was going on?

"I woke up after that first visit from you, and I refused to go back to sleep until I found a way to keep you out of my head. It cost me, but I did it."

Death moved forward, not leaving his realm but so close to the edge that his robe brushed against the blades of grass on our side. "Who are you?"

Zinnia picked up the blade by her clothes, held it to her forearm, and with a cry, cut, slicing the small tattoo from her arm.

"Your birthright. I was born to be your consort, Mors," she said, using Death's true name.

Death rocked back, then jerked forward, his arm reaching for her, but she was still out of reach.

His consort.

No. What the hell was going on? My cousin was going to sacrifice herself for me. "Zinnia, no."

She turned to me, love and strength in her eyes as they met mine. "I've been running from this for a long time. He was drawn to your soul because of me. I need to make this right, to protect our family and our coven."

This couldn't be happening. "Don't do this."

"You were willing to sacrifice yourself for your coven, Roe. And so am I. It's the only way."

"Come to me, consort," Death said in that deep, bone-chilling voice.

Zinnia squared her shoulders. "Your consort must enter Limbo willingly, and I will go with you, but I have a condition."

"Name it," he said, his voice vibrating in a way that sent more shivers down my spine.

His focus was only on Zinnia now. It was like I had ceased to exist. He wanted my cousin, and he would do anything to have her.

"Zinnia, don't do this. There has to be another way."

She ignored me and kept her focus on the terrifying male watching her. "I have a sister who needs me, and I won't abandon her. I'll come with you, but only if I'm free to move between realms."

"No."

She squared her shoulders. "That's my condition."

He was silent for several long moments. "Each time you visit, you must remain with me for at least one lunar month before returning to your realm."

Zinnia's fingers curled into fists. "Then I want a lunar month here as well."

Death made a sound that punched you through the chest and grabbed on, violent and animalistic. "I will agree, but only until your sister's eighteenth birthday. After that, you will remain here with me."

"Her twenty-first birthday," Zinnia countered.

He shook his head, about to argue.

"If you agree, I'll leave with you now."

He was quiet again, then finally, he inclined his head. "But know this, consort, if you fail to return to me, the bargain is void. I will come for you, and when I have you back, I'll never let you leave."

"Understood," she said. "And if you refuse to let me leave, same deal, the bargain is void. And I promise you, I'll find a way to escape, and you'll never see me again."

"Don't do this," I sobbed.

She closed the space between us and pulled me into a tight hug. "I knew this day would come, Roe. I can't hide anymore. It's done." She lifted her head. "Take care of Jazzy for me, and Hemlock. It's only four weeks, then I'll be back."

I wanted to cling to her and drag her from this place, but that would only make this harder on her. "Thank you," I choked out.

She tucked my hair behind my ear. "I want a party when I get home, okay? Something to look forward to."

"You've got it," I whispered.

"Consort," Death said, and she jolted in my arms.

I swallowed down another sob as she stepped away, grabbed her clothes, shoved them in her pack, and turned to Death. He held out his hand, and she strode up to him and tilted her head up. "Pass on the hand holding. I'm not a fan of PDA." Then she turned back to me, blew me a kiss, and walked through the archway.

The gate closed immediately, the stones reforming, returning to how they were.

I stood there alone, naked, in shock.

I didn't have time to freak out, though. Forcing myself to snap out of it, I quickly pulled on my clothes.

I'd just shoved on my boots when I heard the whispers and movement through the trees.

Demons.

I was surrounded.

Chapter Thirty-Four

Rose

The hungry growls, creepy giggles, and hisses grew louder as the demons moved in for the attack.

I should have run as soon as the gateway closed, but I'd hesitated, and now it was too late. I was surrounded completely. I gripped the knife in my hand tighter. I would not die, not here, not now, not after the sacrifice Zinnia had made to keep me here.

She said I was immortal, but I knew for a fact that even immortals could be killed if someone or something tried hard enough, usually by removing their heads.

I backed up as the first demon approached from the trees lining the small clearing. Its eyes were glittering red and filled with hunger and rage. Its mouth was wide and definitely not humanoid in appearance, seeming to hinge just below its ears. Sharp teeth jutted up from its thrust-forward lower jaw, like a warthog. He wore only a pair of grime-stained jeans, and its upper body was muscled and dusted in dark hair.

"Look what we have here," he said, voice so rough and odd, it was like listening to nails being dragged down a rusted tin. "A gift from the gods."

Another moved in behind me. "A new toy."

A third. "Dinner."

They all took steps closer, as another group appeared a few yards from them, dark and misshapen, their forked tongues darting out. A different breed but just as ugly and angry. "No, she oursssssss," they hissed at the warthog-looking group. "She our giftssssssss," one of them said, its eyes darting to me and back as he took a step closer as well.

The four others with him nodded and hissed their agreement, shuffling closer.

I was in serious trouble here.

These two groups of demons weren't the only ones here, they were just the first trying to claim me. Trees moved, and I could hear the sounds of growls coming from all around the clearing. They were waiting to see what would happen, either waiting for a shot at me themselves or scavengers hoping for something to pick at afterward.

I needed an opening, a moment of distraction. "If you come any closer, I'll turn you all into slugs," I yelled.

The warthogs paused, the hissing group as well.

I bolted instantly, running for the opening nearer the warthogs, and sidestepped as one grabbed for me but missed, then I burst into the trees. They growled and hooted excitedly, making chase. The thunder of feet echoed behind me. They were coming after me, all of them, by the sound.

A demon jumped out of nowhere, swiping at me, its dirty claw slicing my upper arm. I spun with my blade, buried it in one of its eyes, pulled it free, and kept running, trying not to gag as I picked up the pace. The hoots and howls and hisses of the demons grew louder as they gained on me.

I was still a long way from the car. I wasn't going to make it.

A bone-shaking snarl came from behind, the thunder of a heavy gait growing louder as one of them closed in on me.

I pumped my arms, my thighs burning, but he kept getting closer.

Another snarl came a second before what felt like a boulder crashed into my back. I was slammed to the forest floor, then flipped. One of the warthog demons was looking down at me, drool sliding from each side of its wide maw. Then his companions were there as well, surrounding us, hooting and laughing.

I screamed and struggled, but he held me too tight.

"Can we keep her?" one of the others asked.

"Could be a good breeder," the one on top of me said and squeezed one of my breasts. "Her teats are small, but they'd grow when she was fat with my young."

No fucking way. This was not happening. I would not let this happen. "Get the fuck off me!" I screamed in his face.

He curled his hairy fingers around my throat. "Get used to it. I'll be spending a lot of time right here," he said, spraying spittle through the gaps in his sharp teeth.

"No." I shook my head as fear morphed into anger. "That's not happening."

They laughed, and I yanked a hand free from under him and struck, smacking him across the side of the face. Humor was replaced by rage, and pinning me with the hand around my throat, he slowly dragged one of the claws on his other hand down the side of my face. My flesh was torn open, and I screamed, but not in fear.

He was trying to scare me and paralyze me with fear and pain, and it only made the rage inside me grow bigger and hotter. Rage at these assholes, but mostly rage at what my family had gone through to save our magic, what Zinnia had sacrificed, all of it for no other reason that I could see other than to amuse the mother. I fucking hated her.

And I hated how goddamned defenseless I was. How weak.

If I was Willow or Iris, I'd know how to fight him off or use a spell or elixir to immobilize him. I couldn't do either proficiently, and at that moment, I couldn't even remember the most basic of spells. But the angrier I got, the more powerful I felt. I remembered what Iris said about my magic, and I felt it inside me, building, growing. My limbs felt tight and hot, the tips of my ears and fingers and my fangs tingled—and my back burned as hot as my fury.

The demon on top of me frowned, then jerked back.

"What is she?" one of the others said, head tilting to the side.

My muscles flexed. He'd taken some weight off me, and I shoved with a screech, with all the force of my magic behind it. The sound that left me was piercing and wild, a sound I'd never made before, and the demon flew back.

I jumped to my feet, and the other two with him stared in shock. Everything looked sharper, brighter. I could see into every shadowy corner, see at a distance I never could before. My hands felt weird, and I looked down and gasped. My fingers were longer, tipped with claws, red veins snaking along each one, visible through my now almost translucent skin.

I wobbled, almost unbalancing, as a breeze flowed around me.

My wings were out and strong and beating behind me. I don't know what I did or how this happened, but I knew if I concentrated really hard, I could make them beat faster, harder. My feet lifted off the ground.

The demons snapped out of it and pounced, grabbing at me, their claws slicing through flesh. I kicked out and let my wings lift me higher, until I was out of reach.

Blood poured from a cut to my thigh and from another across my stomach, making me dizzy, but somehow, I stayed in the air. It was precarious, and I dipped and weaved and almost collided with several of the taller trees, but from up here, I could see the edge of the forest. The car. Safety.

I weaved and dipped low, almost hitting the ground, but

managed to gain enough height again. I was nearly there. The demons' hoots and growls grew more distant, but they were still following, and I was making it easy for them, leaving a bloody trail.

So close.

Spots danced in front of my eyes. I'd lost too much blood, and I was close to losing consciousness.

I dipped and weaved again, and this time there was no stopping it. I hit the ground hard. There was another hoot and laughter as they got closer.

I scrambled to my feet and ran for the car, stumbling, but somehow managing to stay upright. Yanking the door open, I got in, pulled it shut, and slammed my hand down on the lock. I quickly found the keys in my pocket and started the car as demons burst from the trees.

I'd hit my head hard and darkness was trying to creep in at the edges of my vision.

Not now. Stay the hell awake.

I put it in drive and hit the gas, jerking forward. The darkness crowded in.

Not yet.

I just needed to get onto the main road. I just needed to stay conscious for a little longer. I bounced along the short dirt road, the highway just ahead. I glanced in the rearview mirror. They hadn't given up, still running after me.

Finally, I turned onto the highway—

Only making it a short distance before everything went black.

I was being jostled. I tried to open my eyes but couldn't.

"Stay with me, sweets. Stay with me."

Ronan.

He was here.

I stopped fighting.

Ronan

I lifted Rose from the car and carried her into my warehouse, running through the living room and taking two steps at a time to my bed. Thankfully, she hadn't hit the tree at too fast a speed or she'd be in a lot worse shape.

I needed to tend to her wounds. She needed to feed. The bleeding had slowed at least, but a couple of the slices were deep. And one look at them told me they weren't from the accident. The cuts were from demons, and they'd gotten close enough to use their claws on her.

Laying her on the bed, I tore off my shirt and lay beside her limp body. I was covered in her blood, and the sight sent my rage higher. Demons had followed her, and if I'd been a minute later, I could have lost her.

Biting my wrist, I pressed it to her mouth. Blood trickled past her lips and onto her tongue. Instinct immediately kicked in, and she sealed her lips around the wound, sucking greedily. When she hadn't answered her phone, I'd been worried and tracked her, right to fucking Oldwood forest.

"That's it, sweets. Feed." She moaned, her hands lifting to hold my wrist to her lips. I felt every pull behind my ribs. I brushed her hair back from her precious face, taking in the jagged slice down one of her cheeks, and fury filled me all over again. "Don't ever do that to me again," I rasped, my voice so rough and full of emotion that I sounded like someone else. It would never happen again. I wouldn't let it. Task or not, Rose was done. I didn't give a fuck about her coven. She was all that mattered.

Her eyes snapped open, completely black. She couldn't talk, but deep in those black-as-night eyes it was all there, her need, her hunger, her longing.

"I know, my heart. I'm here now." She whimpered, and the

scent of her arousal drifted over me. My body responded immediately. One of her hands left my wrist, and she took the other and pushed it between her restless thighs. "I've got you. I'll take the pain away."

Her legs fell wide, and I pressed my fingers to her hot, slick flesh. Her hips immediately rolled.

"Lie still, sweets. Let me take care of you." Doing this for her, giving her everything she needed, soothed the monster inside me. I kissed my way along her jaw while she drank from my wrist, and as I slid a finger inside her, I licked along the deep slice to her cheek, then made my way lower, kissing her blood-streaked skin to the gash across her stomach, to start the healing process.

She whimpered, groaned, and rocked her hips faster against my hand. Her grip on my wrist tightened, and she groaned against my skin as her pussy clamped down on my fingers repeatedly, coming for me instantly, her juices gushing out, making my mouth water.

Rose didn't release my wrist, she kept drinking, her hips still rocking. "Again?"

She nodded, and I slipped in another finger and took her faster this time, following the cues of her straining body, cues I already knew so well. She was desperate to come again, so as I took her with my fingers, I worked her stiff little clit with my thumb.

My beautiful mate bowed against the mattress and, unlatching from my wrist, cried out as she came a second time. Panting, she grabbed my wrist again and dragged her tongue over it to seal the bite. I rose over her, and she blinked up at me, whimpering, still hungry, still needy. "More," she said, sounding lost.

I brushed her hair away from her face. "Take from me, my heart. Whatever you want, it's yours."

Pushing at my shoulder, she moved over me as I fell to my back. Her fangs were extended, and I shivered as she nuzzled my throat. I tilted my head, and she struck, biting deep. My hips lifted off the bed when she sucked hard, and I cupped the back of her head, stroking her as she ground down on me, hot and slick against my blood-covered stomach.

After several more deep pulls, she licked me there as well, sealing her bite, and kissed her way down my chest, her hands moving restlessly over my abdominals, fumbling with the button of my trousers. Hands shaking, I helped her and lifted my hips as she pulled them down enough to free my erection.

I expected her to move back up, to take me inside her. Instead, she dragged her nails down my thighs and sucked the head of my cock into her mouth. With a shout, my hips lifted again. She suckled my cock like she'd suckled from my throat, and I couldn't stop my hips from twisting beneath her, fighting not to push deeper into her eager mouth.

"Oh god. Rose, you're killing me." I gathered her hair back so I could see her face, and she looked up at me with those beautiful black eyes as she sucked me deeper into her mouth. I knew what she wanted. "Do it, sweets. Take."

Her fangs flashed before she bit down on my shaft. I roared as she withdrew them from my rigid flesh and sucked greedily again, drinking from my pulsing cock so engorged with blood that it gushed into her mouth. My eyes glazed over, there was no holding back now. I came in hard spurts, my seed mixing with my blood as she drank me down.

I collapsed on the bed, and she lapped at me a final time, making me jolt, sealing her bite, then crawled up over me, curling into my side. She pressed her nose to my skin and held on as if I was the only thing stopping her from drifting away.

"Rose?"

Her body trembled, and she pressed her face against my chest.

"Why were you in that forest? Why did you keep it from me?"

A sob burst from her.

Panicked, I flipped her and stared down at her tear-streaked face in horror. Her eyes were no longer black but had returned to vibrant blue, and they were filled with pain. "What is it? Are you in pain? Did they hurt you more than I realized?" My heart gripped in my chest. "Did *I* hurt you?"

She shook her head. "No." She dragged her hands over her cheek, smearing her bloody tears. "It's...it's Zinnia. She's...oh god, Ronan, she's gone."

"Gone? What do you mean, gone?"

Her fingers moved restlessly against my biceps. "There's something...something I never told you."

Rose's emotions were rolling from her, being broadcast from her and through me as if they were my own. I'd never felt anything like it. I was feeling what my mate was—and it scared the fuck out of me. "Tell me."

"After Iris's task, when my family used magic to remove an evil soul from Limbo and send her to Hell, they made Death...angry. The spirit belonged in Hell. Death doesn't care about that, though, and he's been demanding a replacement..."

"Rose?"

Her lips trembled. "Me. He wanted me."

"What?" I spun, searching the room. Could he move between realms? I'd tear Death apart before I'd let him take her from me.

She took my chin in her hand and made me look at her again. "Death came to me in my sleep. He said it had to be me or he'd take someone else...someone I love. I was sick when I agreed to his terms. I thought I was going to die anyway."

There was more, and I waited, my heart pounding.

"That's why I was in the forest tonight. He gave me a deadline, and tonight, it ran out. Zinnia was here to help me. She said she could stop it. I didn't know what she was going to do, or if Death would agree..."

"You went there tonight thinking you might not return?" My voice was broken. I rubbed at the center of my chest. I thought I'd felt all there was to feel, but at her words, it was as if all the emotions I'd already regained heightened and became so much stronger. "Believing that you might die?"

Another tear streaked down her face. "Yes."

I wanted to roar, to tear everything down around me. I wanted to hunt down Death and destroy him, something that I knew was impossible. He was a being older than time. The ruler of Limbo. The harbinger of darkness. If he'd decided to take her, he could have, and there was nothing I could have done. "He wanted to possess you?"

"Yes," she whispered.

A growl was ripped from me, and Rose jumped.

Her hands flew to my face. "He...he took Zinnia instead. Oh goddess, he took her."

Chapter Thirty-Five

Rose

Ronan walked into the bathroom while I washed my hands and met my reflection in the mirror. He'd been quiet this morning, contemplative. I didn't blame him after what happened last night.

I was struggling to process it all myself, and now I had to go home and tell my family, tell Jazzy that her big sister was gone. That for the next month, if Death actually stuck to his bargain, Zinnia was trapped in Limbo, that she was Death's consort.

Whatever the hell that meant.

You know exactly what it means.

I shuddered, and Ronan moved in behind me and wrapped his arms around me. "Agatheena, she predicted this." The old witch had seen this nightmare coming. "She said there were two paths ahead of me, and no matter which one I chose, our coven would suffer. It was either me or Zinnia. One of us was always going to end up in Limbo. There was no escaping Death."

He pressed his mouth to the side of my throat, his eyes closing briefly before meeting mine again. He was relieved it wasn't me. I saw it on his face, and I was glad he didn't voice it. "It's okay, sweets, it's over now. You're safe."

"But it's not over." I lifted my hand to the side of my throat where his mouth had been, over the markings the mother had given me. The vines were closer this morning, a ticking time bomb on my skin, counting down to my coven's doom if I failed. "Until I pass this task, until I win my trial, the threat to our magic remains."

His gaze darkened, his jaw tightening, cheekbones sharpening. "It is over. I won't have you risk your life one more moment. I'll be the one to finish this, Rose, not you."

I bit back my frustration. He'd had a scare last night, but I had to make him understand. "That's not how this works. You know that. I know you're worried—"

"Worried? I arrived minutes before a pack of demons found you and tore you apart!"

"They were going to breed me, not kill me," I said and regretted it instantly.

His eyes went from violet to deep purple. "You will either stay here, or at your mother's home. I won't argue about this."

"No. I have to do this. If I don't, I fail, and my coven will pay for it."

He shook his head. "But I'll still have you, and that's all I care about."

I stared at him in shock. I couldn't believe what I was hearing. He was completely blinded by the fear of losing me, and he was willing to sacrifice my entire coven. "You can't mean that? You can't actually be serious—"

"I almost killed you, Rose. I would have drained your blood, you would have died in my arms, and I would have lost you. I dream about it, that I'm that cold, emotionless shell again. Nightmares where the mother doesn't call you in time, and I bite you. I sink my fangs into your vein and drink until you fall limp in my arms." He shoved his fingers through his hair. "I can't fucking bear it. Seeing you in that car, unconscious, bleeding, demons closing in, I felt it again. I was supposed to protect you, but I didn't. And I almost caused your death again, but this time I felt it. I fucking felt all the horror and fear, all of it."

"Ronan—"

"No. I'm your mate, and my decision is final." He gripped my arms. "You can't talk me out of this. Don't you see? The more time that passes, the more I understand these emotions I'm feeling, and the more I understand what I could have lost if I'd done what you asked. The threat of losing you, of living without you—that fucking nightmare feels so incredibly real. I won't let it become our reality, no matter the cost." He made a snarling sound, flashing his fangs. "I won't lose you, Rose."

I didn't know what to say. I stared up at him, utterly stunned. I understood where he was coming from, but he was being unreasonable, and struggling to come to grips with his new emotions was only making it worse. "Zinnia told me tonight that Warrick made some kind of deal with Lucifer, that my sisters, me, our mates are immortal. I can't die, Ronan."

He blinked down at me, but that stubborn line to his jaw didn't change. "You're immortal?"

"Yes, we both are."

"I already was." He took a deep, shuddering breath. His face was still set in stone. "But that changes nothing."

There was no biting back my anger now. "What do you mean, it changes nothing? We're immortal, Ronan. And if Warrick hadn't made his deal, you would have lost me eventually. Can't you be happy that now that won't happen?"

"Immortals can be killed, Rose. All it takes is a demon or someone else to remove your head." His voice rose. "So no, I won't change my mind. You're not doing this. You're not risking your life because the mother, that sadistic bitch, has decided to send you on a suicidal mission for her own personal entertainment."

"I'm not talking about this with you right now." I spun and

strode across the living room. "I need to go home and tell my family about Zinnia."

"Good, because I'm done talking about it as well. My decision is final."

I loved the male more than anything in existence, but I kind of wanted to punch him in the nuts right then.

The ride to my house was quiet. He was brooding, and I was silently fuming, at least until we pulled up outside the house.

"Shit," I whispered. How the hell was I going to do this? I reached for the door handle, but Ronan grabbed my hand. I turned back, and he pressed it to his lips, kissing my knuckles.

"I'm sorry I raised my voice at you. I've never...I'm trying to navigate these feelings. I just want to protect you. I don't want to fight, sweets."

God, the look on his face, so worried, so unsure, it made me want to lean over and kiss him, to reassure him, but he meant what he said back at the warehouse. Yes, he was sorry we fought, but he hadn't taken back what he'd said because he'd meant every word. "I know it's hard, and don't want to fight either, but I think if we continue to talk about it right now, we'll only fight more."

The door to the house opened and Mags strode to the car, then frowned at me through the window. "You coming in, or are you gonna sit out here all night?"

"I'm coming in." Mags headed back inside, and I turned to Ronan. "Are you coming?"

"No. I'm going after Kelley."

"Ronan—"

"If I manage to get close enough to him to question him, I'll let you know."

Unbelievable. "No, I need to be there when you question him. I need to be the one to ask the questions."

He stared at me with an expression that could only be described as panic, then he hooked me around the back of the neck, pulled me forward, and rested his forehead against mine. "Don't be angry with me, Rose. I can't fucking bear it."

I didn't want this between us, but I couldn't back down. As if his new emotions weren't enough, he was also a newly mated male, which on its own would have awakened an intensely protective side in him. I could only imagine all he was trying to come to grips with, but I couldn't allow him to let his fear control me, control us. There was too much at stake. "Are you going to let me question Kelley if you get close to him?"

His nostrils flared, chest pumping hard, then he shook his head. "I'm doing what I was born to do. I'm protecting you."

I pulled away from his tight hold and shoved the car door open. "Do what you think you have to, I guess," I said, holding his bright gaze.

And I'll do what's best for my coven. I had no other choice. I climbed out of the car.

"Rose?" he said roughly before I could shut the door.

I turned back.

"I'd thought about it, you dying before me. I'd planned to go with you...when you grew old and eventually passed...so I wouldn't have lost you."

I stared at him in shock. "Ronan,"

"Don't leave this house. Wait here for me until I get back. Promise me. Promise me you'll stay safe."

I couldn't promise any of those things. I didn't want to lie, but I didn't have any other choice. I nodded, and he blew out a relieved breath before I walked away.

I left the kitchen with Jasmine's sobs ringing in my ears. Mom was hysterical, and Else was carrying around a big bottle of calming elixir and shoving a spoonful of it into everyone's mouths.

Willow grabbed my hand, stopping me. "Roe, wait."

"I need air." I tried to pull away, but she wouldn't let me go. She tugged me around the corner.

"You know this wasn't your fault, right?" She tucked her wild red hair, so like Zinny's, behind her ear. "From what you said, Zinnia knew this was coming."

"She's in Limbo, Wills, with Death. You didn't see him when he realized who she was. She said he'd been waiting for her, and he wanted her with him right or wrong. I'm afraid he won't stick to his end of the bargain. I don't think he'll let her go easily."

Willow's lip quivered, but she smiled gently. "Zinnia's tough, smart, resourceful, and resilient. If anyone can get through this, it's her. She'll walk through that gateway in a month's time, I believe that."

I nodded, but another tear streaked down my face before I could stop it. "What if he hurts her, Wills? What if he—"

"You can't think like that."

"Iris's been to Limbo, do you think there's any way she could get us in? We could rescue her." Panic filled me. "We have to do something, anything."

Willow shook her head. "Iris didn't go there willingly, she was sent there with the help of some really dark magic. It's forbidden, you know that. We're trying to save our magic. Going down that road would be the quickest way of us blowing our coven all to hell." She took my hand and held it tight. "Zinny wouldn't want that, and you know it. There's nothing we can do to help her now. Thinking about what might or might not be happening won't help her, and it'll distract you from what you need to do. You can't lose focus, not now."

She was right, but I still fucking hated it. I had to pass my task and my trial. For Zinnia, for all the people I loved.

"You coming back in?" Willow asked.

I didn't want to go back in there, into that room filled with my family's pain and horror. I couldn't do it. "I need a minute."

Wills nodded. "Take your time."

She went back into the kitchen, and I headed upstairs. My phone vibrated in my pocket, and I checked the screen. It was Vesa.

I rushed to my room and shut the door before I answered. "Hello?"

"Rose, hey."

"I'm sorry, this isn't a good time."

"Is everything okay?"

There was a lot of noise in the background, music, talking, and laughing. He was at a bar or a party. "Is there a reason you're calling?"

He chuckled. "Straight to the point then...definitely my kid."

I didn't reply, just waited for him to tell me what he wanted.

"Okay, I won't hold you up. The reason I'm calling is we're having a kind of gathering at the colony today, and I thought it might be a good way to introduce you to everyone, to your family."

I had a family, and I wasn't looking to extend it further, but I did want to know more about myself, about what happened in the forest last night. I'd transformed, I'd felt...different. Ronan hadn't mentioned it, so I had to assume I'd returned to normal when he found me. But I'd definitely transformed, and I needed to know what I was capable of.

Now wasn't the time, though. I had other things to deal with. I opened my mouth to turn him down when I felt it, a pull, an extremely strong one, my magic flaring inside me, telling me to say yes.

Fuck.

Was my father somehow involved with my task? How?

"Rose? You still there?"

"Ah...yeah. I'm here. Sure, okay. I'll come, but I'll be bringing someone with me. A friend."

"Of course. The more the merrier."

He gave me a time and where to meet him and hung up.

Ronan had made it impossible for me to tell him about this,

but I wasn't an idiot. If this had something to do with my task, there was no way I was going alone. I scrolled through my contacts and hit Relic's number.

He answered on the second ring. "What's up, Roe?"

"I need your help."

"Does your mate know you're calling me?"

"No, and he can't know, not yet."

Silence.

"I wouldn't ask if there was any other way. I need your help, Relic."

There was another beat of silence. "When and where?"

I released a relieved breath. I'd deal with Ronan later.

Chapter Thirty-Six

Rose

The Roxburgh State Forest was incredibly vast, beyond anything I'd imagined.

"Watch your step," Relic said beside me.

"Have you been through the entire forest?"

"Most of it. Though, we try to avoid the fae territories, since they're just beyond the border, and we have no fucking desire to get in between them and the vamps."

The vampires and fae had been warring for centuries. Everyone else tried to stay out of it.

"What about the bat colony? Have you been there?" I asked him.

"Nah, but we've scouted it. Different shifters have their own territories. Some stay close to home, some venture into the city. When we came to Roxburgh, we made a point of learning where they were, made introductions, that kind of thing. We didn't want to fuck off the locals, but we needed them to know that we were here and not to be messed with. We didn't go to the colony, but we met with Kefir, the Bat King."

"What did you think of him?"

Relic shrugged. "He mainly spoke with War. The rest of us were below his notice."

"So you're saying he's a douche bag?" Great.

"Most leaders are a bit douchy, Roe. It's a prerequisite of the job."

I smirked at him. "Are you saying you think Warrick's a douche?"

"Nope. War's the exception." Relic was hyper-vigilant, searching the forest as we walked. "Your male's gonna be seriously fucked off when he finds out about this, you know that, yeah?"

"Yep," I said. "But right now, he's in the middle of a full-blown mated male meltdown, and if he knew about this, he would have stopped me from coming. The way he was acting, I don't think he's above locking me in a room or tying me to a table leg to stop me from doing anything that he considers dangerous."

Relic nodded. "Our boy's been through it. Going from not giving that first fuck to where he is now must be a serious mind fuck."

Guilt filled me again. "I know, and I want to help him through it, but I have to do this. I can't sacrifice my coven for his peace of mind."

"He'll get over it eventually. Warrick struggled when his emotions kicked in, but he's got a handle on it now. And Ronan and I will sort it all out in the pit."

"What is it with you males and fighting? And Warrick's as protective of Willow now as he's ever been."

Relic grinned. "Can't see that changing. The way I see it, mating for a male is like having a fucking lobotomy, but he might be a little more reasonable in time." He cracked his neck. "And fighting is a fast and effective way of getting over shit and blowing off steam."

I rolled my eyes. "So what about you? Do you want to find your mate?" Relic was hard to read. He'd adjusted to the human world, and I got the feeling what he put out there and what he was thinking were two different things completely.

"Was hoping to get myself a hot witch, like War did, but all but one of you are spoken for, and Mags is too young. Though I like the female's feisty attitude. Maybe I'll give her a couple years then swoop in," he said.

I snorted. "Well, that isn't going to happen. Bram would remove your spleen with his bare hands if you so much as looked at her sideways."

Relic grinned. "The boy needs to make a move or move over."

I shook my head at him. He was joking, or at least I hoped he was. "God, you're cocky."

He threw me one of his flirty grins. "Got good reason to be."

"If you say so."

The grin slipped from his face, and he tilted his head back, scenting the air. "I smell bat, babe. Your old man's close."

Nerves fluttered to life in my belly. I searched the trees around us. "I don't know if he's got something to do with my task, or it's someone at the colony, but my instincts are telling me I need to go there. Things could get dangerous."

"I got you, Roe."

I knew he did. Relic would keep me safe no matter the cost. "Thank you for agreeing to this. I know it's asking a lot."

"It's all good, babe. I'm fucking hard to kill. Want you safe, same as Ronan does." Relic grabbed my arm and tilted his head ahead.

I followed. Vesa was there waiting. He smiled when he saw me and strode over. "I was worried you were lost."

I aimed my thumb at Relic. "My friend here is a hellhound, there was no chance of that happening."

My father held out his hand. "Vesa, nice to meet you."

Relic took it and shook but didn't share his name or the sentiments. Instead, he scanned the area.

"Are you Rose's mate?" Vesa asked.

"No," Relic said.

Vesa turned back to me and smiled. "We should get going. We have to walk a bit farther yet." He glanced at Relic. "Flying would be faster, though."

"I'm still learning," I said.

"Right, of course."

"So what can I expect when we get to the colony? Do they know I'm coming?" I asked.

"I've told them about you," Vesa said. "They're excited to meet you."

Relic stopped suddenly, his head tilting back. He growled. "Here, Rose. Now."

I spun, took one step toward him—

There was a thud, and Vesa hit the ground, unconscious.

Relic went down next, something flying through the air out of nowhere and cracking him in the back of his skull. He went down hard on the forest floor. Arms banded around my waist and I was yanked off the ground.

I grabbed at the thick, tattooed arms holding me in a ruthless grip, tearing at them, trying to get free. Relic tried and failed to get up, while Vesa lay motionless on the ground beside him.

"Let me go!" I screamed, fighting harder.

One of the arms left my waist and hot fingers pressed to the side of my throat. There was pressure, and darkness crept in at the corners of my eyes.

Then everything went dark.

Ronan

Relic's words were on repeat in my head as I ran through the forest. The trees were nothing but a green haze as I pumped my arms, my breath exploding from my lungs.

My Rose was missing.

Someone took her.

I would lay waste to this entire forest if she was harmed in any way. Whoever did this? Their suffering would know no end.

Relic howled in the distance, letting me know where he was, and I picked up on the hound's scent.

A few minutes later, I spotted him. He stood in the middle of a small clearing, pacing, head tilted back, scenting the air. Blood dampened a patch of his hair and smeared his shirt, and fury burned in his eyes. I growled and ran straight for him. He turned, and I collided with him, taking him to the ground.

I snarled in his face. "I'm going to fucking kill you."

Relic's long fangs flashed, but he didn't try to fight me. He shoved me back. "Kill me after we find your female."

I dragged in a breath, then another, then shoved away and paced the clearing. I smelled blood, one I'd scented before. Vesa. "What the fuck happened?"

"Vesa called and Roe felt the call to go to the colony. She knew she had to go for her task and didn't think you'd be okay with that."

"No. I fucking would not," I snarled.

Relic planted his hands on his hips. "I was knocked out. I didn't see who took her, and their scent is all fucked up. I don't know what they were, but they definitely have wings. Because I can't get her scent, and the only way for that to happen, is if she's in the air."

"Where's Vesa?"

"There were more on the ground. They moved in after Rose was snatched and took him before I could get to my feet. I couldn't follow 'cause I lost their scent as well." He bared his teeth again and scented the air once more. "They have to stop at some point. They'll land and I'll have them."

I shoved my fingers through my hair and squeezed my eyes closed, trying to get a grip on my control. I reached out for my mate through the connection we had through feeding. I could track her via her blood, but not when she was in the air and still in motion. She was still alive, though, I was positive of that.

"Are you sure they weren't bats?" None of this made sense.

"I know what a bat shifter smells like. I've never smelled anything like that before."

We paced the forest for the next hour, waiting. "Where the fuck are they taking her?"

Relic shook his head, focusing inward, using his tracking abilities as well, and on constant alert. He spun to me right as I finally felt her. Relic shifted, exploding into his hellhound form, and followed me as I sprinted deeper into the forest.

She's alive, I said over and over again.

I'm coming, sweets.

I'm coming for you.

Chapter Thirty-Seven

Rose

I blinked, then blinked again.

Complete and utter darkness surrounded me. Rough wood was at my back, the air musty, smelling like timber and dirt. I was lying down. I lifted my arm, more wood, on all sides.

A coffin.

I shoved at the wood above me. It didn't budge. Someone had buried me alive. Oh goddess. Breathing hard, I pushed at the lid, screaming out, scratching, trying to tear at the wood above me. My head spun, and I struggled for breath, each inhale shallower than the last. I was hyperventilating.

I couldn't stop, couldn't breathe. I was going to suffocate.

~

My eyes snapped open. It was colder. I'd passed out. I had no idea how long for. I was still underground. I tried to stay calm. It wasn't easy.

I froze when a scratching sound came from above, followed by a low growl. Voices. There was something up there. The voices were muffled and strange, but with all my sight gone, my hearing heightened. I realized the sounds had been going on for a while, while I'd been regaining consciousness. I opened my mouth to scream, then slammed it shut, as my other senses increased. I could smell them. Demons. There were demons above me. They'd found my scent and were looking for me.

If Zinnia was right, being buried alive couldn't kill me. The demons above me couldn't either, unless they managed to remove my head. I could pass out, though, and my oxygen had to be low. There was a possibility of me never waking back up. This was my only chance.

My mind spun. This grave, whatever it was, had to be pretty shallow, but there was too much dirt on top for me to open the lid. There was only one way out of here that I could see.

Taking a deep breath of precious air, I called out. "Hey! I'm down here!"

There was a burst of activity, the growls growing in volume. They'd heard me. I called again, banging my fist against the lid. The muffled sounds increased. They were digging.

I only had a matter of minutes before they uncovered me, before they pulled off this lid. I didn't think I was injured, I couldn't smell blood, but even still, I wasn't some great fighter. I'd only have seconds to run for it, and even then, I might fail. I thought back to all the spells Mom and Else and Gran had taught me before I became too sick to join my sisters in their lessons.

Mags said never to underestimate basic spells and incantations, and I just had to survive long enough for Ronan to reach me. Relic would have called him, and they'd be searching for me.

The fear grew when the sounds of the demons above got louder. I called on my magic. They were almost at the lid. Goddess, help me get through this—

Something scratched directly on the outside of the lid. Then another, and another. There was a hoot of victory, the growls becoming frenzied. They were about to pull off the lid.

My body felt hot and my head spun as adrenaline pumped through me. My magic swirled wildly. My ears and fingers tingled, along with my fangs, as they slid down. Something in me, my subconscious, tapping into my base animal instincts. My body knew there was danger and was readying for it.

I pressed my hands against the lid, ready to shove, preparing for whatever came next.

Ronan

Demons. The echo of their excited frenzy traveled to us through the forest.

Rose.

Relic snarled beside me, and we ran full speed toward them.

I spotted them a moment later, at least six, far in the distance. They were digging, scraping at the dirt.

Rose was there, somewhere. I felt her, sensed her, but I couldn't see her. *Fuck.* "She's underground," I roared.

Someone had buried her alive.

The demons didn't see us, too intent on uncovering her. We were almost there. Almost. *Hold on, sweets. Hold on.*

The demons reached down—

Planks of wood flew up, splintering, and Rose exploded out of the ground.

The demons stumbled back, and I stared in shock. She hovered above the ground, her white, glittering wings sprouting from her back, beating heavily, holding her in the air. She was completely transformed, her fangs had extended past her lower lip, and red veins were visible through her now almost translucent skin. Her ears were pointed, fingers elongated and tipped with deadly claws, and her eyes were glossy obsidian and filled with fury.

One of the demons collected himself and ran at her. Rose swiped a clawed hand, cutting open the demon's face and throat, and he fell to the ground. She beat her wings harder, trying to get higher as another went for her. She shrieked, but not in fear, in rage. The sound wasn't human and echoed like a warning through the forest. The demon paused, and she lashed out with those deadly claws a second time, slicing the demon's chest wide open.

We were almost to her when another demon ran at her—

Bats burst through the trees, so many they were a moving black cloud. They flew around Rose, swooping and diving at the demon, covering it in thousands of tiny cuts from their sharp claws and fangs.

One of the demons dropped to the ground, rolling away from the bats, then jumped up and ran at her again. Rose lifted a hand and shrieked a second time. The demon didn't make it to her, hitting an invisible barrier and flying backward.

He got back up, but instead of running back at her, the last demon spun and ran into the forest.

Then we were finally there.

Rose hovered above, surrounded by her army of vampire bats as power radiated from her.

I looked up at her, breathing hard, as she lowered herself to the ground. Her wings folded in, disappearing completely. Her ears, fingers, and claws doing the same, but her eyes were still black as night when she ran to me.

I caught her in my arms.

"I knew you'd come," she said against my throat.

I lifted her, her legs coming around my waist, and she clung to me tighter. "I've got you, sweets." Though I'd done nothing, my female had saved herself.

Relic shifted back to his human form and cursed as he looked up at the bats still flying above.

Rose lifted her head, and tears filled her eyes. "I called and they came," she said. "I didn't know what I was doing until they were there. But now I do." She smiled up at them. "I didn't think I'd ever have a familiar, but that's what they are, Ronan, all of them. I can feel them." She made a strange sound, tiny, high-pitched noises and little shrieks. The bats responded, swooped in a wide circle above her, then flew back to wherever they came from.

"What did you say to them?"

She frowned.

I cupped her dirt-streaked face. "You made sounds, not words."

"Fucking hell, the female speaks bat," Relic said.

She had.

I knew she was strong and brave, but what I'd just seen—my female was fucking powerful. But then, that was something I'd already known, even without having witnessed what I had.

She released me, and I reluctantly lowered her to her feet. She swiped away her tears. "What happened to Vesa?" she asked Relic.

"He was injured, and taken."

I searched her for injuries. "Who did this? Who brought you here?"

"I don't know. I didn't see his face. His scent was weird. I couldn't place it. Then he knocked me out, and I woke up in that box in the ground. If they wanted me dead, why not just kill me?"

Relic planted his hands on his hips. "It makes no sense."

Rose looked into the hole in the ground. "It doesn't, but I'd rather not repeat the experience if I can help it."

I moved up beside her and looked into the coffin-sized box someone had buried my female in, and fear spiked through me.

Whoever did this would pay with their life.

Chapter Thirty-Eight

Ronan

Rose lay against me, sleeping.

We were at her mother's house. Someone had buried Rose, and we didn't know why. Vesa had been hurt and was still missing, and after what happened, I wanted to make sure Rose's family stayed safe behind their wards, because whoever was behind this could try to use one of Rose's family members to get to her.

I'd also called Draven and Warrick to let them know and to stay on high alert.

Rose made a breathy sound, and I studied my mate in the moonlight. Her skin glowed, her hair impossibly glossy. She was an angel, my angel, and I'd do whatever it took to keep her safe, but I also realized tonight that Rose wasn't only strong, she was immensely powerful.

She'd transformed before my eyes, taken down three demons while her glittery wings kept her above the ground. I looked at her shoulder, to the markings there, markings made by the mother's venom. The vines twisted around her upper arm, and one of the vines had traveled higher, curling over her shoulder, reaching out for the vines on her shoulder, crawling up her neck, so close to touching now.

She was almost out of time. Her family, her coven, were on the verge of losing their magic—magic Rose was only now getting the chance to use.

I released a harsh breath. I couldn't let her suffer that loss. She'd never recover from it, and she'd blame herself, convince herself that she'd let down the people she loved.

A knot formed in my gut. As terrified as I was, I had to relinquish some of the control I was clinging to. I realized that now. I would protect her at all costs, yes, but I had to trust her.

And I had to stop smothering her, because that's what I was doing. If I didn't, one day, I'd lose her.

This was all so new and fucking hard.

Shoving off the sheet, I got out of bed. Then, tucking the covers around Rose, I pulled on my trousers and slipped out of the room.

Sleep wasn't going to happen tonight, and, yes, I was going to try to stop smothering my female, but that didn't mean the urge to protect her went away. Far from it. I headed downstairs and checked windows and doors. No one was getting through the wards surrounding this house. I knew that for a fact. Especially not some twisted fucking shifter assholes.

I wanted this over with. An uneasy feeling settled in my gut. Rose wanted to do this, all of it, and I understood that now more than ever. But I couldn't just stand around and wait. Until we knew who targeted her and what they wanted, they were a threat.

Rose said the bats, possibly Vesa, had something to do with her task, but there was a missing piece, and I believed that missing piece was Oliver Kelley.

I'd keep my promise. I'd make sure she was there to question him. She was right, this was her task, and she needed to be there, but first, we had to find the male. And so far, getting to him, getting past his security, had been impossible. I knew her phone was on silent, so I quickly sent her a text, telling her what I was doing so she'd find it when she woke.

Then I walked out.

I was getting to Kelley tonight, whatever it took. I was ending this.

Rose

I checked my phone again.

Nothing.

No more texts from Ronan.

He said he'd call when he got to Kelley, and I trusted him. We'd made progress. His need to protect me was still at insane levels, but he wasn't being as rigid about it. I just wish he hadn't left me here and gone on his own.

It was early, still dark outside, but I was dressed and ready to go at a moment's notice. I paced my room again, then headed downstairs. What I wanted to do was call Ronan, but I resisted. He'd call when he could.

I headed to the living room, where I paced some more, then moved to the window and looked outside.

The first rays of morning sun had changed the color of the sky. No sign of Ronan or his car. Sighing, I stepped back—

Something moved outside. I got close to the glass again.

Vesa.

Oh goddess.

He stood swaying at the end of the driveway, unable to get through our ward. His shirt was covered in blood, his face a mess. I dashed from the living room, quickly unlocked the door, and rushed out to help him. He stumbled back several steps, almost falling down. I quickly grabbed his bloody shirt, stopping him.

"Quick, we need to get you inside," I said. There was a deep gash on the side of his head.

He shook his head. "Wanted to m-make sure you were okay."

"But you're not. What happened? Who were those guys?"

He took another step back. "I need to g-go. Needed to see you weren't hurt."

"Did you lead me into that ambush, Vesa?" Despite the way he looked now, I had to ask.

"N-no, I swear. That wasn't supposed to happen. There's been unrest at the colony..." He shook his head. "I never thought...I have to go." He strode toward his car.

My instincts were all over the place. Something pulled me to follow the male who fathered me, while alarm bells wailed in my head at the same time. I'd seen how close the vines on my arm were this morning. Something needed to happen, and now, or we were going to lose everything. And I was positive Vesa knew something, more than he was letting on. "Wait."

He kept walking. "I need to go."

He rounded the car. I followed. "You're injured. Come inside, let me help you."

"No, I'm fine—"

"I know you're keeping something from me."

The doors in the back of the car opened, and two massive males got out. I hadn't even seen them, too focused on Vesa. I instantly knew what a huge mistake I'd made leaving the safety of the ward.

I threw up my hand instinctively, trying to do what I had in the forest, to block them, but it didn't work because I'd overshot my magic yesterday, almost draining myself completely, and because I was still building my magical stamina, hadn't fully bounced back. I spun to run, but the male closest grabbed my hair and wrenched me back, throwing me down.

"Gag her, quickly. And be careful not to draw blood, it only strengthens her magic." I tried to will myself to shift, but I didn't have that kind of control over it, especially not when I was freaking the hell out. Vesa opened the trunk and pulled out a rope, no longer as unsteady as he'd led me to believe, and passed it to the male kneeling on my back.

"Quick, let's get out of here before someone notices she's gone," Vesa said.

One of the males jerked me off the ground, tossed me into the back seat, and got in beside me. Vesa and the other male got in the front.

The engine roared to life, and we sped away.

Vesa pulled out his phone and glanced back at me as he held it to his ear. He looked different, I realized. The fake concern was gone. This was the real Vesa, the calculating look in his eyes as he stared at me, the triumph. "Got her," he said to someone.

The bat who'd buried me alive, no doubt.

"Yes," he said, eyes blazing. "I gave you my word. Something you seem to have trouble with. I'll stick to my end of the bargain as long as you do. If I see any of your warriors before I get to the colony, she's dead." Then he disconnected.

I fought against my binds, and all it accomplished was making the ropes tighter.

Vesa smiled. It was smug and evil, and I wanted to slap it off his face. "Can you believe I all but forgot you existed?" He shook his head. "Thanks to your dhampir friend reminding me I had a kid, you're about to make me rich and powerful beyond my wildest dreams."

I stared him down. It was all I could do, showing how much I hated him and that if given the chance, I was going to tear him to shreds.

We drove to the edge of the city. Then all three males got out and stripped off their shirts. Their wings, leathery and black, unfolded from slits in their backs, and then I was pulled from the car, still bound, hoisted into one of the male's arms, and we shot into the air.

Neither of the males with Vesa was the one who'd buried me. This guy didn't have any tattoos, and the other goon Vesa had brought with him only had a couple on his chest. We flew above the forest, going deeper and deeper. I shivered as the freezing air seeped through my clothes. Finally, we reached a tall cliff, and I stiffened when we flew straight for it.

A massive shadow appeared on the cliff face, not an opening. We flew into it, into a cave, and the male holding me landed on his feet smoothly and, not breaking stride, strode ahead. Vesa and his friend followed. Light flickered in the distance. We turned the corner, and the cave opened up, becoming much wider and lit up with torches. There were doors all the way along. People, bat shifters, stopped and stared in shock as I was carried by, but no one tried to stop them or help me. We carried on, turning several corners until we walked into a large, cavernous hall. Long dinner tables and chairs filled most of the room, and along the top of the wall were openings in the stone, covered with glass, that had obviously been dug right through to outside, like windows letting in natural light.

As we walked in, an older male turned, his black eyes coming straight to me. The male carrying me dropped me to my feet and held me still as the older bat shifter strode our way.

As soon as he reached us, he lifted a hand to remove the gag.

Vesa grabbed his wrist. "No, she's part witch, remember? You remove that in here and she'll use her magic to escape."

The other male pulled back his hand, his eyes narrowing. "That won't be happening. My great granddaughter is far too valuable." His black gaze slid to Vesa. "If I find out you were purposely keeping her from me—"

This male was my great-grandfather?

"Think about it, Kefir? If I knew she existed, I would've brought her to you when you first exiled me. I could've used her then." He gave his grandfather an oily smile. "My daughter could have made me even more powerful than you." He took in the large room. "But I don't want what you have, not anymore. I only want what was promised to me."

"What's stopping me from taking her and killing you?" Kefir said.

And judging by the look in the older bat's eyes, that's exactly what he was contemplating.

The males with Vesa moved quickly, one grabbing me around the chest and pressing a blade to my throat, the other jumping into a combat pose, knife drawn.

"Like I said earlier, if you attempt to take her from me again without giving me my dues, or try to harm me, they'll slit her throat." He shrugged. "I want our bargain in blood, and until we've both signed, she'll remain with me."

The older male's eyes narrowed. "Take her from you again?"

Vesa motioned to his wounded head. "Don't feed me your bullshit. We were ambushed earlier. I was knocked out and woke up in the middle of fucking nowhere. Thankfully, she had a hellhound with her, and he got her away from your men. If he hadn't, I wouldn't be here to make a deal, I'd be here to slit your wrinkly fucking throat."

He had no idea I'd been snatched from the ground, carried to a secluded place, and buried alive, and neither, by the looks, did Kefir. What the hell was going on?

"I assure you, you'd know if it'd been me," Kefir said.

Someone stood on the other side of the room and strode toward us. A male, tall and bare-chested, covered in tattoos. His hair was black and slicked back, and his eyes were as dark as night, glittering as they locked on me.

It was him, the male who snatched me from the forest, who threw me in a box in the ground and left me there to die—I knew it instantly. I recognized the tattoos on his arms. Somehow, he'd disguised what he was. Because he was a bat, I could sense it clearly now. And the way he held himself, the way he walked, I realized he was also the same male I'd seen in my vision, the one who'd killed the guard at the museum.

He strode toward us, the thud of his heavy boots on the stone floor echoing around the room, his hard stare not leaving me once. I tried to step back but couldn't move with the hold Vesa's guard had on me. Something shifted in the male's dark eyes, something I couldn't read, but it vanished when he stopped beside Kefir.

"I see you found a way to slither back, Ves," the tall male said.

Vesa looked at the male with pure hatred. "This is where I belong. And you should be thanking me. If I hadn't found her, this colony would soon be without its king."

The tall male's shoulders stiffened, but then he inclined his head. "You're right. I am grateful, even if it means we must endure your presence once again."

Vesa's hand shot out to strike him, but the younger male snatched his wrist out of midair and held it in a grip that caused Vesa to wince. "I'm not a pup anymore, Vesa. Best you remember that."

The knife was pressed more firmly to my throat instantly.

"Daire," Kefir barked.

The younger male, Daire, stared down the guard with the knife, chest heaving, but he finally let Vesa go, shoving him away.

"You heard what Vesa said?" Kefir said to him.

Daire jerked his chin.

"Find out who was behind that ambush and bring them to me. I don't want anything getting in my way. No matter what, we start when the moon is at its highest," Kefir said.

Daire nodded and strode out. What he didn't do was acknowledge that he knew who I was or what he'd done.

Chapter Thirty-Nine

Ronan

I tried Rose's number again but got no reply.

I'd been gone all day on a wild-goose chase. Oliver Kelley seemed to be forever on the move, meeting after meeting, never in one location long—except for now. I'd given Rose my word, but I wasn't going to get this chance again and I needed to take it.

The restaurant was full, and Kelley's minders stood outside the bathroom, guarding the door. This was the only shot I'd get, so hidden by my powers, I walked through the guards and into the bathroom. Kelley stood at the urinal, zipping up his pants.

I moved up behind him and covered his mouth as I dropped my block. He exploded into action, yelling for help under my hand. I easily subdued him, forced him into a stall, and pressed him against the wall.

Judging by his wild eyes and how much he was sweating, Oliver Kelley believed he was about to die. If he hadn't already urinated, he would have soiled himself. Fear rolled off the male.

"I'm going to remove my hand from your mouth, and you're

358

not going to make a sound. If you make a sound, I'll hurt you. Nod if you understand?"

He nodded.

I eased my hand away from his mouth.

"Tell Kefir I didn't know. I thought it was legit." He shook his head. "That was the last one, I can't find anymore. I've tried."

"Last what?"

"Effigy," he sputtered, then his eyes narrowed. "Who are you?"

"Kefir? That's his name? That's who hired you to source the effigies?"

"Who the fuck are you?" he asked again.

"Someone who will kill you if you don't give me what I want, understand?"

He nodded, swallowing hard. "Y-yes, it was Kefir who hired me to find the effigies."

"Do you know why?"

"There's only one reason someone wants one of those things. To make a bargain with a demon."

"Why does he want to kill you?"

A breath shuddered out of him. "Because the three effigies I did find that were the real deal summoned the wrong kind of demons, and couldn't give him what he wanted. And the last one was only a replica. He wasn't happy. I barely made it out of our last meeting alive."

"What kind of bargain does he want to make?"

"I don't know, he refused to tell me."

I studied his expression. I believed him. "Where do I find this Kefir?"

"At the colony," he said.

"Colony?"

"He's king of the bats."

Ice filled my chest.

The bats were behind Rose's attack. They'd disguised what

they were, but it was them. I was sure of it. For some reason, the king of the bats had ordered his people to bury her alive.

Why? What the fuck was going on here? And what did Vesa have to do with all of this?

It was obvious Kelley had nothing more for me. So I threw up my block and walked out of the room, out of the restaurant, and tried to call Rose again. Still nothing.

I called Mags while I got into my car.

"Is Rose with you?"

There was a pause. "I assumed she was with you."

"No. She was asleep when I left." I could hear Mags running through the house, the sound of doors banging open, of her calling for Rose.

"She's not fucking here, Ronan. Oh goddess, she's not here."

I sped out of the parking lot.

They'd gotten to her.

Somehow, they'd gotten to her.

Rose

An hour had passed, and I had no idea what was going to happen when the "moon was at its highest," but considering my welcome to the colony, I knew without a doubt I wasn't going to like it.

I wanted to ask the male standing outside my cell what he got out of this. But I was still bound and gagged. They definitely over-estimated my magical skills. I had a few tricks up my sleeve but nothing that would get me out of this cell.

The males Vesa had brought with him had dumped me here, and one had stayed to guard me while the other had left with Vesa. These guys appeared to be loyal to him for some reason. He had to have offered them something substantial. I'd only spent a handful of hours with my father and already knew he wasn't the type of male to instill loyalty in others. No, he was the kind of male who would use his own flesh and blood to increase his power and standing.

I'd finally calmed enough to think somewhat clearly and to gain control over my own body. What I needed was to bring on a vision. Any hint of what was to come would be immensely helpful about now or possibly utterly horrifying. Either way, forewarned is forearmed, right?

But, until now, I hadn't been able to get my fangs to slide down, which wasn't surprising considering how vulnerable a blood drinker was when they fed. I wasn't safe, and with my magic still depleted but rebuilding slowly, my subconscious knew it, causing my body to rebel at the idea. It helped that my fear had shifted to anger. It wasn't easy with the gag, but I managed to sink one of my sharp, pointed fangs into my lower lip, and as soon as I tasted blood, I focused on the polished steel blade tucked in my guard's belt, the only shiny thing in the room.

I looked deep into the blade, and my pulse throbbed through my head, my hands growing clammy. I didn't know if it would work, but I tried to guide the vision, repeating in my head what I wanted to see.

The blade vanished as the vision hit me.

Flames. They surrounded me, flicking up high, licking at my skin, burning my flesh. Kefir stood to the side, head tilted back, lips moving rapidly. An effigy stood on an altar. It looked familiar. I'd seen something like it before, hadn't I?

Yes, I'd dreamed of this room, the darkness, the flames.

Something moved in the flames, something big.

It roared and came for me.

A cry yanked me from the vision.

Was that my scream? Panting, I blinked several times to clear my sight. The tall male, Daire, crouched over my guard, and the male wasn't moving. I tried to reconcile what I was looking at, my mind still fuzzy from the vision.

"Where are the fucking keys?" Daire growled out as he searched the dead guard's clothing. He looked up at me. "Did he have them?"

What the hell was going on?

He moved to the bars and motioned me forward. "Let me take off the gag."

This was the male who had plucked me from the forest floor and buried me alive. I didn't want to go anywhere near him. He'd just killed my guard, for reasons unknown. Not that I gave a shit about the guard, but I wasn't excited to hang out with this guy either. Things were already shitty, but they could also get much worse. My vision had shown me that and answered the question of who Oliver Kelley was stealing and selling effigies to.

The male growled. "We don't have fucking time for this. You want to keep the gag on, keep it on."

I did not. *Shit*. I moved up to the bars. He couldn't exactly do much to me while I was locked in here.

He reached through and dragged the fabric down over my chin, and I quickly stepped back. "You're the one who hired Kelley to steal effigies? Why? What are you planning to do with them?"

"Question time will come later. First, I need to get you the fuck away from here before it's too late," he said, flipping over the dead male on the floor and searching his back pockets.

I took several more steps back. "I know you killed that guard at the museum, and you buried me alive. You disguised what you are, but I know it was you. You're a goddamned monster. I'm not going anywhere with you."

His black eyes sliced to me. "The museum guard was a piece of shit, a thief, and a lot worse. He was on Kelley's payroll and stole several effigies for him, and I needed that to stop. I disguised what I am because Vesa couldn't know it was me. And if you'd stayed aboveground, either Vesa and his lackeys or Kefir's warriors would've found you and you'd already be dead."

"You're telling me you were protecting me?"

"Obviously," he said as he shoved his hand in the dead male's jeans pocket.

"And if you'd stayed in your damned house, behind your wards, we wouldn't be in this mess now."

I moved back to the bars. "There's nothing obvious about it. You literally buried me alive. And what do you know about my house? Have you been watching me?"

"Not all the time. You had protection. I did track you after you were aboveground, though. You were safe, then you fucking showed up here with Vesa." He scowled at me. "And you act as if you've never been underground before."

"Why the hell would I have been?"

He glanced up. "Because you're a bat shifter."

"So?"

He frowned. "Vesa never taught you?"

"He taught me nothing. I've only just met him. He was absent my whole life. And considering the way things are going, I'd say that was a good thing."

Daire muttered a curse. "No wonder you freaked after I knocked out Vesa. I tried to explain when my people moved in to take him, but you screamed and clawed so much it was easier to knock you out as well. I assumed once you woke, you'd know what was going on and wait for me to come back and dig you out."

"No, I woke up convinced I'd been buried alive and left to asphyxiate. So I'm gonna need a bit more information, thanks," I said.

He yanked up the legs of the male's jeans. There was a leather pouch strapped to his ankle. Daire pulled out a knife, sliced the pouch off, and opened it, producing the key. He looked up at me. "Vesa was bringing you to Kefir, your great grandfather. He needs you as a sacrifice to appease the demon he made a bargain with a very long time ago."

He quickly unlocked the door. "What kind of bargain?"

"Eternal life. When he found the demon Nomas' effigy, he

summoned him, and bartered his queen to that monster not long after they mated, agreeing to do the same every hundred years with the next queen that came of age."

I couldn't believe what I was hearing.

"There's a reason you look different, Rose, and it's not just because you're half witch. The white wings gave it away. You were born to rule the colony. As the time to renew his bargain with Nomas approached and none of our female's wings turned white when they reached maturity, Kefir knew he was in trouble." Daire grabbed my arm and led me out of the cell. "He's been desperately trying to find another effigy. He didn't have an offering for Nomas, so he needed to make a new bargain with a different demon. Then Vesa showed up and told him about you."

"So he had an effigy all along, he was just missing the sacrifice he'd promised to its demon?"

"Yes."

I jogged to keep up. "And you don't want this?"

Daire scowled. "No, very few want Kefir as ruler. The elders are afraid of him, the rest of us want him dead and the new queen to take her rightful place."

"And I'm...the new queen?"

His dark gaze slid back to me. "Yes."

This was insane. "And who are you?"

"Your cousin, and if I'd killed Vesa instead of knocking the fucker out, you wouldn't be here now, but if I get my way, he and our piece of shit great grandfather will be dead by the end of the night."

We rushed down a long hall, my mind spinning. We rounded another corner.

Shit.

Several males, warriors, stepped out, blocking our way.

"Fuck," Daire muttered and spun around, dragging me back the way we came. More warriors approached, blocking our escape.

Daire backed me into a wall, standing in front of me, trying to protect me as they moved in. He pulled a knife free, and his fangs punched down as he exploded into action. He took down one warrior after the next, but there were too many. They overpowered him, and he snarled and bucked as they dragged him away.

Two of them closed in on me then, and as the fear in me exploded into rage, I felt myself transform.

I lashed out, clawing at them. My magic swirled inside me, coming alive, but then they had hold of me, gagging me again and bound me tight.

I screamed, but there was no one here to help me.

Ronan

I climbed higher, nearly at the cave opening, over a hundred yards from the ground. I gripped the small ledge and pulled myself higher. Far in the distance, too far for human eyes to see, there was another settlement. Not a cave though, tree houses by the looks of it. Which meant it probably wasn't more bats. Thank fuck.

Hours had passed since I spoke to Mags. I'd run through Oldwood Forest, then deeper, into places I'd never been to before. The demons who lived here were different, and there weren't just demons. Creatures I'd never in my life laid eyes on crept and slithered through this part of the woods. It had been untouched; the creatures left to take over.

It was a good strategy. Protection for the colony. The first defense against anyone who didn't have wings from getting close to them.

But nothing would keep me from Rose, and if anything had happened to her—if they'd hurt her—

I shook the thought from my mind. She was alive. I knew that much. I felt her heart beating right along with mine.

With a snarl, I heaved myself over the edge and got to my feet.

A large cave yawned ahead of me. Strengthening my powers and concealing myself, I ran into the cavern. Light flickered ahead, and I turned a corner, running by doors until I reached the end.

Several more caves branched off this one. I closed my eyes and called on Rose's blood—something was blocking her from me, something dark and volatile.

Something violent and pure evil.

I opened my eyes and took in the three tunnels ahead. All I could do was guess.

With a growl, I made my choice.

Chapter Forty

Rose

They stripped me down and made me change into a sheer white dress that covered nothing.

I stood in a large cavern with no natural light and only a few lit wall sconces. The flames danced against the stone walls, and even though it was still too dark to see much of anything, I recognized the room immediately. It was the room from my vision.

Evil saturated it, a dark magic that felt like a physical weight pressing down on me, suppressing my own completely. I was helpless, a feeling I was all too familiar with.

The two males holding me dragged me around the edge of the room, then out to the middle. Rough hands shoved me forward. My chest slammed against a cold slab of stone, and they quickly chained me to it with iron cuffs around my wrists and ankles.

They vanished into the shadows, and all I could do was wait helplessly for whatever was about to happen.

A shuffling sound came next, someone moving in the shadows of the vast room. I shivered from the bone-aching chill and the terror rising inside me. Something moved toward me, shrouded in black. I bit back my cry as it came closer.

A torch flared to life.

Kefir held the torch aloft. He wore a deep-red cloak, and his coal-black eyes didn't waver from me as he closed the distance between us.

"What have you done with Daire?" I asked.

"Nothing, yet. He's my great grandson, and as much as it'll pain me to kill him, I won't have anyone threatening my rule." He lifted his other hand, showing me the effigy I'd seen in my vision. "The time has finally come," he said.

"What are you going to do?" I struggled against my restraints.

He tilted his head to the side. "You haven't figured it out yet? I assumed your father had filled you in."

Vesa hadn't, but Daire had, and if I could delay this by keeping him talking, I would.

"I'm going to sacrifice you to the demon Nomas, like the four queens who came before you." He placed the effigy on a stone altar. "You will die so I can live," he said, then tossed the torch he held down beside me. It fell, then kept on falling, revealing a hole in the stone floor several yards wide. I was on a walkway suspended over the opening, and it was so deep I couldn't see the bottom. The light from the torch grew faint, then disappeared completely.

Everything went dark and utterly silent. Several seconds ticked by.

Then a low rumbling sound rose up from below me, deep in the massive pit, a faint light growing with it. The sound increased, and so did the flickering light—

Boom.

I cried out as the sound rolled through the room and flames shot up all around us.

"I've had that effigy for five hundred years, maintaining my bargain with Nomas," Kefir said. "And it was almost voided because of you. I searched for another like it, but my search was futile. I thought all hope was lost." He smiled. "But then Vesa found you, Nomas' next bride." He gripped my jaw. I jerked out of his hold. "Unfurl your wings, Rose."

I stared up at him in horror, afraid, confused. Then I saw them —four sets of white, shimmery bat wings hung on the walls in large shadow boxes, wings stretched out and pinned in place like some twisted butterfly collection. Nausea gripped me. "No."

"Unfurl your wings," he said, his grip bruising.

I shook my head.

A cry echoed around the room, and one of the guards dragged a young girl forward. Another male stood behind her, holding her black wings wide. "Either you give me your wings or I take hers. And if you still refuse, I'll do it again and again until there are severed wings piled up at your feet."

Oh goddess. My limbs shook so hard, it was only my shackles holding me up. What choice did I have? I couldn't let him hurt anyone else. I nodded and unfurled my wings, feeling their weight as they appeared.

Kefir's eyes lit with glee. "Vesa said they were magical. The same as those who came before you, but also different, unique. They'll look beautiful on my wall, Rose. I promise I'll think of you whenever I look at them, of your sacrifice." The unmistakable sound of a blade ringing as it was pulled from its sheath came next. He walked around behind me and gripped the base of one of my wings. "It'll only sting for a moment."

"Please...no. Don't, don't..." He sliced, and I screamed, the sound raw and animal, morphing into a shriek like I'd made in the woods. He hacked and hacked until the weight gave, followed by the thud of my wing hitting the ground. I sobbed and collapsed against the stone wall.

"Almost done," Kefir said.

The pain was so excruciating, the act so horrifying, I vomited on the stone walkway by his feet. He gripped the second wing, and the shriek that came from me as he sliced the second time was deafening, reverberating around the cavern. Warm blood trickled down my back and pooled at my feet. My legs gave out completely, and I hung there from the shackles at my wrists.

The loss of blood should weaken me, and eventually it would, but skilled in witchcraft or not, I was still a blood witch, and as blood poured from my wounds, the magic inside me stirred. It pressed against the darkness in this room that was stifling it, trying to expand and grow.

Kefir moved to the altar, placed his hand on the effigy, and tilted his head back as he chanted, repeating the words that would call Nomas, over and over again, like I'd seen him do in my vision. I searched the flames, knowing what came next.

There was a terrible sound, then something moved in the flames, something huge.

Oh god, he was coming.

Nomas was coming.

The demon from my nightmares rose up, his upper body looming above the flames, a twisted, hideous, horned demon. His piercing, cruel red eyes came straight to me.

"Bride," he said, his voice distorted and strange.

I shook my head, my soul screaming as I opened my mouth and did the same. I screamed loudly, the deafening sound filling the space again. Nomas paused, then his face twisted with rage and confusion.

The females that came before, who had stood where I was now, betrayed, bleeding, their wings sliced from their backs, terrified of the twisted demon coming for them—I felt them now, I felt their pain and horror, and rage exploded through me, the kind I never knew I was capable of. The dark weight lifted from the room and my magic burst to the surface. It no longer stirred, it was a violent storm inside me, its strength growing with my fury.

An indescribable sound echoed in the distance, growing louder and louder until it was deafening. Then I felt them—bats, thousands of them, exploded into the cavern. I understood their little chirps and clicks and called to them, telling them Kefir was a bad man, that he wanted to hurt me, and half of them swarmed him.

Kefir screamed, flailing, the knife in his hand clattering to the ground as the bats clawed and bit at him. More bats came to me, forming a moving, breathing, flapping wall between him and me, trying to protect me.

I focused on the savage roar of my magic and looked up at my shackles. "Release me!" I screamed, barely recognizing my own voice. The iron around my wrists flashed with heat, burning my skin—then shattered. And as soon as they did, I felt myself shift, the bleeding stumps where my wings had been moving awkwardly in my back.

"Bride," Nomas roared in that distorted voice and grabbed my wrist.

I threw up my other hand with a cry and my magic shot from me, crashing against the demon.

He roared again, releasing me, his massive body seeming to freeze in place. I felt Ronan's blood inside me, his power twisting and blending with my magic. I'd felt the same thing in the forest when I'd stopped a demon, blocking him from getting to me.

I couldn't hold Nomas like this indefinitely. I had to stop him, stop this from ever happening again—I needed to free the females that he'd taken before me. They didn't belong in hell. They'd suffered long enough.

Swiping up the knife Kefir had dropped, I ran at the demon, leaping from the edge of the pit and onto him, digging my claws and the knife into his thick skin. I scrambled up his arm and grabbed him around the throat, then wrenching back the massive demon's head, stabbed repeatedly at his throat, hacking and slicing, trying to cut through his thick skin to remove his head.

The loss of blood was making it hard to maintain the hold I had on the powerful demon, and he roared again, but this time it came out a wet gurgling sound. I gritted my teeth and kept stabbing and slicing.

My magic, my hold on him, weakened, and he flailed his powerful arms. I slipped, almost falling, but dug my claws deeper into his skin and hacked one last time with a scream of rage.

The demon's head fell to the side, tumbling into the flames.

His body lurched to the side, and I dove to the edge of the pit, grabbing on to the lip as the demon toppled and disappeared back into the flames.

I clawed at the stone edge, somehow managing to pull myself up.

Kefir still flailed at the end of the platform, calling for his warriors to help, but none came. They were already fighting.

Then I saw him.

Ronan.

His face was lined with fury, trying to fight his way to me. Daire was with him; others in the colony were now fighting as well.

Kefir exploded through the wall of bats, his face a gruesome mask, clawed and bitten and bloody. He held a flaming torch, using it to drive my little familiars back.

I stumbled to my feet as Kefir grabbed my arm.

"Hurry," he said, trying to drag me along the walkway.

"It's too late. Your demon is nothing but ash," I said.

"He'll be back, and we'll be ready and waiting," Kefir said, fury and desperation in his voice.

He looked down and his grasping hands fell from me, then he roared, but not in rage this time. The sound was one of pure terror. He stared at his own hands, watching as they wrinkled and aged before his eyes, the rest of his body following. Nomas was dead; the bargain had been broken; that was the only explanation for what I was seeing.

In a matter of minutes, Kefir shrunk and grew hunched over, his hair graying and falling out as he aged five hundred years. Bats were long-lived, but Kefir had already defied nature, and he quickly declined until his breath wheezed from him, then stopped completely. He disintegrated in front of me, turning to dust.

I stumbled away, along the platform, and used the wall to hold myself up, trying to get to Ronan, but then Vesa broke from the fight and ran for me.

I was his pawn, and he wasn't ready to lose me yet. Calling on the last of my strength, I threw up my hands.

I aimed it all at Vesa, throwing up a wall of magic in front of him before wrapping it around him tight. He jarred to a stop, then I lifted him off his feet and sent him flying into the stone wall. Hands still aimed at him, I poured out the power, holding him there as I walked toward him.

He struggled, teeth gritted, and his body half shifted. His fingers clawed, his wings spread wide, and his fangs extended.

"No!" I screamed in his face when I reached him. "I am not yours to use, to barter, to bargain with. You betrayed your people, your family, and you betrayed mine. You won't win. I won't let you."

Ronan was suddenly there at my side. He wrapped his arms around me, pulled me back, and pressed his mouth to my hair. "We need to tend to you, sweets, you've lost a lot of blood." He trembled against me, his fear and rage pouring from him.

I sucked in a breath and staggered back a step as Daire closed in from the other side, only then feeling the weakness set back in as my adrenaline subsided.

As soon as my power dipped, Vesa slashed at me with his knife. Ronan moved fast, grabbing his wrist, wrenching it back, and shoving Vesa's own knife deep into his heart. Then he twisted it, pulled it from Vesa's chest, and slashed the blade across his throat.

The flames in the pit receded, then extinguished, and the cavern went silent around us.

Gasps filled the space as four distinct shapes of light, carried on ghostly white wings, rose from the pit, hovered for several seconds, then vanished through the stone ceiling.

The four females sacrificed before me. They were freed, able to fly once again, and headed to their rightful place, to finally rest in peace.

It was over.

Tingles danced along my shoulder and upper arm, burning along the markings the mother had given me. I covered it with my hand as pain arrowed down my spine, and I dropped to the floor.

A silent scream tried to burst from me as power crashed through my body, once, twice, surging higher and higher. The gifts the mother had given our coven strengthening and solidifying.

I'd passed my task. Oh goddess, I'd passed.

Ronan crouched over me, holding my face in his hands. "Rose? Talk to me."

I opened my mouth, but I couldn't speak, arching against the stone floor as another great surge cascaded over me, through me. The pain grew higher, higher still. Oh goddess. I couldn't take anymore—

It crashed, the waves of power ebbing, washing away the pain with it.

"Sweets, please—"

"I passed," I choked out. "I passed my task."

Ronan scooped me into his arms. "Thank fuck," he said, pressing his lips to the top of my head. "I've got you. You're going to be okay."

I'd passed my task. Somehow, I'd done it.

Chapter Forty-One

Ronan

Rose sat up and winced.

"Careful." It'd been two days since her wings had been sliced from her back. Since I watched my reason for being throw herself at a demon four times her size, surrounded by flames, and defeat him. It would haunt my dreams for the rest of my existence.

She was still pale and bandaged. She'd lost so much blood. I'd been feeding her several times a day, but her slow healing was using all her energy. The wounds from her wings still looked as fresh as the day it happened. I was worried but trying to keep that to myself.

Her shirt hung over her shoulder, revealing the markings there, no longer black but colorful against her pale skin, and it now covered her entire upper arm and joined the one higher on her shoulder.

If only the danger were over, but it wasn't. She still had to pass her combat trial to ensure her coven's magical gifts remained theirs. I had no idea when the mother would call her for it, but she was in no condition to fight, and she wouldn't be for a while.

She shoved back the covers.

"What are you doing? You need to rest."

Rose scowled. "I've been resting my whole life. I'm not staying in this bed a moment longer." She planted her feet on the ground and swayed. Her balance was still off with the weight of her wings gone.

Mags knocked on the door. "Daire's back, and he wants to talk to you."

He'd come by several times to speak to Rose—her cousin was persistent. I'd found my way to the cells while I'd searched for Rose, and he'd been locked inside one. Somehow, he'd convinced me to trust him. I hadn't had much choice. But he'd proven himself to be a man of his word.

Rose pulled on her robe. "Send him up."

"Are you sure you're well enough for visitors?"

She moved into me and wrapped her arms around my waist. "I'm okay, Ronan. A little sore and tired, but I'm fine."

We both knew that wasn't the truth. Her wings had been sliced from her body. She hadn't had them long, but they'd become a part of her. The trauma and the brutality of the act would take a long time to recover from. "We'll get through this," I said, looking into her beautiful eyes.

She looked up at me, her own eyes glossy, a sadness in them that had been there since she woke up at the colony bandaged and weak. She tightened her arms around me. "As long as I have you, I can get through anything."

I could tell she was trying to convince herself as much as me.

There was a light tap on the door and we turned.

"Rose, Ronan," Daire said, inclining his head.

Rose smiled. "Hey, Daire."

The male walked into the room. "You're looking much better today."

"I feel better," she said.

I stopped myself from telling him to make it quick, that she was tired and needed her rest. Rose had endured more than enough of her life feeling weak in front of others, and I wasn't going to do that to her now. So when she leaned into me, I slid my arm around her, holding her up, giving her the support she needed, and ignored the urge to scoop her up and put her back into bed.

"I have something I need to discuss with you."

"I guessed as much," Rose said.

"You're the rightful queen of our colony, Rose, and I was hoping we could talk about when you'll be ready to come home."

Rose stilled and so did I. "You want me, a bat shifter without wings, to live at the colony? Rule over your people, people who don't know me and have no reason to trust me?"

"They'll learn to trust you," he said. "You'll regain your wings, so I see no reason—"

"What?"

"They'll learn to trust you."

"No. The part...about my wings."

"They'll grow back?" Daire asked.

"What?" she said again.

Daire frowned. "I thought you knew."

She trembled against me, her relief raw and palpable. "How would I know that? I know nothing about the colony or your people."

"I assume your wounds aren't healing?"

"No, they're not."

"That's because your new wings are regenerating. You're a queen, Rose. You're powerful, special, chosen by a higher power to lead us, which is why you have that ability. We need our queen. We've been without one too fucking long."

Rose was quiet for several seconds. "What will happen if I don't? If I refuse?"

He frowned. "Without Kefir and his bargain, and the absence of a queen, a new one will eventually be created. But that could be years."

"Can the current one appoint someone else to lead until that happens?"

His eyes narrowed. "Yes."

"Then I appoint you."

"No." He shook his head. "It needs to be you."

"Your people don't know me, Daire. I'd have to be extremely arrogant to insert myself in their colony and presume to order them about. That's not me. They'll hate me, and I'd hate myself. You know them, they know you. You helped liberate them from Kefir—"

"It should be a female," he said low. "They've already had one arrogant asshole leading them."

"Are you saying you're an arrogant asshole?"

He shrugged his wide shoulders. "I can be."

Rose moved to him and patted his arm. "Well, you'll probably need to do something about that."

"Rose," Daire gritted out.

"You've got this, cousin. If you're that uncomfortable about it, tell them you're their interim leader and appoint one of the females as an advisor. Keep the colony safe until a new queen is created. And when she is, she'll have you both to help her navigate her new role."

Daire scowled. "You have it all figured out. Is this an order, my queen?"

Rose grinned up at him, far more relaxed than when her cousin had walked in here. "Yes, my one and only order as your liege." She lifted her hands to her head, removed an invisible crown, and placed it on her cousin's head. "It suits you."

He scowled harder and shook his head, but the male knew when he was beaten.

Three days later

. . .

"We better not be late, Else has been cooking all day," Rose said as we headed for the warehouse door.

"She does realize we don't need to eat, yes?"

"That won't stop her," Rose said with a laugh.

She'd moved into the warehouse with me the day before. I loved seeing her things scattered around the place. I loved having her here with me, in our home, and I loved lying down with her at night and waking up with her in the morning.

Rose froze, looking down at something.

Someone had slid an envelope under the door.

"What is it?"

She picked it up and carefully opened it. "My trial. A date's been chosen." She scanned it quickly, then looked up at me. "It's in two days."

"That soon? You're still healing." I took the letter from her and read it as well.

Fuck.

Chapter Forty-Two

Rose

Blood Hill Grove had been used for our magical combat trials for as far back as the covens' written histories went.

I stood outside the massive clearing, light snow softly falling around us, and felt the vibration of power. This place was concealed by the mother's magic and only visible when there was a trial. I felt her here with us now.

This entire area was protected during the trial. The only place a witch could use her magic at Blood Hill Grove was inside the clearing, which meant right now, my coven, and all the others gathered around it, were powerless.

I took a deep breath and shook out my hands. I'd only had two days to work on a game plan. I'd learned a lot since this whole thing started, but I was still studying. The witch I was up against would be far more advanced than me.

My coven had come to support me. Rowena had hugged me tight and told me no matter what happened today, she loved me, that they all loved me. I knew that, but the thought of letting them down was more than I could bear.

I never thought in a million years I'd be here, in this position, but against all odds, I was. The fates had obviously had other plans for me, and I was going to give it my all. No, I wasn't magically skilled, but I was stubborn and determined. When I left this clearing, either on my own two feet or being carried off these sacred grounds, I'd know, and everyone here would know, that I'd fought with everything I had.

We were still waiting for my opponent, and when a commotion came from behind us, I knew they'd finally arrived. Ronan took my hand, holding it firmly in his, and I looked up at him.

"You've got this, sweets. You hear me?"

"Are you trying to boss me into winning?"

He held my chin between his thumb and finger. "I don't give a fuck about winning or losing. All I care about is you, back beside me at the end of this, your hand in mine."

I smiled and tried not to let him see how hard I was shaking. "You got it."

"Good."

My opponent and her coven had moved to the opposite side of the trial grounds. It was Marianne Winter. She'd lost her trial two years ago, when all the covens and their Keepers had officially taken part. She'd been vocal about her loss at the time and her belief that her opponent had somehow cheated. Now, thanks to the uniqueness of our coven's situation, she'd been given a second chance.

For tonight only, the mother had returned the gifts Marianne and her coven had lost. She looked at me now and smirked. I could imagine how it felt, having a large portion of her powers stripped away, because I'd felt my own magic slowly dying inside me for years. So no, Marianne wasn't going to waste one second of the chance she'd been given today.

My sisters moved in, blocking her view of me. "Marianne has something to prove," Wills said. "She's desperate, which means she'll make mistakes. As long as you remain calm, you can best her."

"She's confident," I said. "She knows I've been sick, that my magic is largely untried, and my spelling skills..." *Sucked*. "Are subpar."

"Stop it," Iris said. "No negative self-talk. Yeah, she knows you've been sick, which means she's going into this fight greatly underestimating you."

Magnolia smiled, and it wasn't a nice smile. "Marianne Winter is an arrogant bitch. She's not just going into this battle underestimating you, in her mind she's already won, and that immediately puts her on the back foot. Yeah, she has something to prove, she wants all the covens here to see her as powerful, to believe her bullshit story about being cheated last time. The female also loves an audience, which means she'll be going for flashy and dramatic." Mags rested her hand on my shoulder, and her dark smile turned into a grin. "Bitch is gonna burn herself out before she knows what you're doing. Stick to the game plan, no matter what she throws at you, and you can't lose. Okay?"

I drew in a steadying breath and nodded. *You can do this.* I let the words repeat over and over in my mind.

"You ready, Rose?" Marianne called across the clearing. "Or do you need help onto the battlefield?"

My sisters all stiffened.

"Bitch," Wills muttered.

Mags balled her fist, and I knew she was on the verge of losing her cool. I grabbed her hand and shook my head. "They're just words. She'll show everyone here who she truly is," I said.

Magnolia nodded, but her anger didn't diminish, and Wills and Iris were right there with our baby sister. I glanced at Mom, and she and Else looked ready to tear Marianne a new one as well.

I handed Wills my knife—no weapons were allowed during the fight. Smaller things that could be used for spelling were okay, but our main weapon had to be our magic, which made it difficult for witches like the ones in my coven, who, more often than not, used blood to spell. Thankfully, we didn't fight to the death anymore, but "accidents" had happened in the past. Certain spells were also frowned upon, others, the covens had agreed never to use, but you never knew what would happen once you were out there and witches got desperate.

I slid off my shoes and socks; the snow freezing against my bare feet, and took a step toward the clearing. Ronan stopped me, pulled me back, and planted a hot and heavy kiss on me. My nerves instantly melted away.

"Hurry back," he said and released me.

I walked out onto the field and the edge of the clearing shimmered, the mother's magical barrier shooting higher, locking us in.

Marianne kept her smirk front and center as she strutted over to stand opposite me. Her coven excelled in pyro-magic. Producing and spelling with fire came easy to them, and they loved to show off their skills. Wills had faced something similar during her trial. Images of the pit at the colony filled my head, the flames licking at my skin. Everything was still so fresh from that day—the pain, the fear—and panic tried to rise up inside me.

Marianne flung her hands in the air and spun in a circle with a little dance and a giggle. Fire exploded from her fingers, the flames growing, taking shape.

My fangs punched down from my gum, and I sunk them into my lower lip, drawing blood, preparing for her attack. My magic sang, pulsing to life inside me. I let it grow and feed and intertwine with the power that had become a part of me from drinking Ronan's blood.

Blood dripped down my chin and onto the snow, and I stepped on it, pressing my frozen bare toes through the snow, forcing my blood to touch the ground below, connecting myself to the earth, feeling it flow through me, strengthening me.

"You think blood will help you?" Marianne's grin was nasty as she worked her flames higher. "You're unskilled and weak. Coven Thornheart is supposed to be a big deal, but look at you." Her expression filled with delicious glee. "I promise this will be over fast, then you can go back to bed."

Oh yes, she was a bitch, all right. She was trying to distract me, throw me off, so I'd be unprepared when she attacked. This was always going to be a defensive fight for me, and she knew it as well.

She hissed, her eyes flashing with rage, and she threw her arms toward me. The flames reshaped into a dragon, and it stormed toward me, breathing fire. I ran, diving to the ground and tumbling out of the way. Fire licked at my hand, burning my skin before the dragon of fire flamed out.

Marianne laughed again. "You're pathetic."

I was almost ready. I could feel the magic growing steadily inside me. Like a lot of the members of her coven, she was a one-trick pony. They relied too heavily on their fire magic, the fear it induced, and the destruction it caused.

She was building up again, fire dancing in her eyes now. She smiled wide and did another of her little dances for the crowd. Several members of her coven laughed as they cheered her on.

My anger rose. I wanted to go on the offensive, badly. There were spells I could use to throw her off her game, but only momentarily, and I didn't have the knowledge to back them up. I also didn't want to expend an ounce of my magic, not yet. So when she spun and fired her next creation at me, I rolled again, crying out when the claws of a big cat made of fire swiped at my ankle and burned through my tights.

Marianne laughed again as I crawled away, and so did several members of her coven. I didn't look over at Ronan or my sisters surrounded by members of our coven. I didn't need to. I felt their quiet support, their love for me, win or lose. And I felt their strength. I also didn't need to look to know Bram was probably holding Mags back from those laughing in Marianne's coven.

My own anger shot higher as well, but I kept it under control. I had to stay calm for this to work. My hand and ankle burned, and as Marianne stood over me with that smirk on her face, the urge to retaliate caused a spike of adrenaline that had me gritting my teeth. I flexed my fingers, calling my magic forward, because I knew what was coming, and I was going to be ready.

"That's right, crawl away, Rose," Marianne taunted, fire dancing between her fingers. "Crawl back to your coven before I burn up that pretty face."

I didn't bother responding. Instead, I bit down on my lip again and smiled up at her when more blood slid down my chin.

She scowled. "Are you stupid? What the hell are you smiling about?" The fire grew between her fingers. "Run, or I'm going to burn you."

I let go of the anger I was holding back—and I had a lot. Not just at Marianne or at the mother, but for the years I spent in that bed slowly starving to death and the pain my family had gone through because of it. The shift came instantly. My fingers elongated, claws growing from the tips, red veins now visible through my skin. When her eyes widened, I knew mine had changed and were now totally black, that she could see my fangs and pointed ears.

"What are you doing?" Marianne's face screwed up in disgust. "What the hell are you? You're hideous."

In two days, the stubs of my wings had started to grow. Small, perfectly formed bat wings had sprouted, white and shimmery, and were currently not much bigger than one of my little bat familiars. I quietly said the spell I'd created, unique to me, repeating it over and over again.

"I'm going to burn those disgusting things right off your back," Marianne said down at me and lifted her hands, muttering her own spell. No little dance this time, no messing around, she fired a stream of fire right at my face.

I threw my hands up as well and fired my magic back at her, calling out my spell louder. Her flames collided with the barrier I'd created, causing the fire to flow to the right, singeing the ground.

She shrieked and fired more flames as I got to my feet,

repeating my spell without pause. And again, her flames didn't touch me. Flames danced in her furious gaze. I wanted her angry. It was her anger that would cause her to lose.

She screamed, again telling me I was disgusting, that I deserved to die, while she tried repeatedly to burn me alive, throwing more and more power at me in her rage, until her flames became weaker. I wrapped my magic around her, pulling it in tight, and she screamed louder, struggling, and when she tried to throw fire at me again, nothing happened. Using my magic, I tossed her to the other side of the clearing and released her. She quickly staggered to her feet, and with a cry of alarm, tried again and again to burn me. Nothing.

In her rage, she'd drained herself of power completely.

The barrier that surrounded us dropped, the mother's way of declaring a winner.

I'd won.

"No!" Marianne screamed. "No. You cheated. You're not even a proper witch. This isn't right. It's not fair."

I turned away from her and strode to my cheering coven. Ronan grinned down at me, so incredibly handsome, he stole my breath. He caught me up in his arms. "You were magnificent," he said against my ear, before he put me back on my feet, something I knew he didn't want to do, judging by the look in his eyes.

If my mate had his way, he'd carry me everywhere and never let me out of his sight. "Thanks," I said.

He took my hand, and surrounded by my coven and my family, we headed back down the road and away from Blood Hill Grove. Ronan glanced down at me. "So that's it for you, right? You're done?"

"Yep," I said, still riding my high. Hopefully, we'd be done with the mother for a while, at least for another year, until she called on Magnolia.

His expression was serious as he nodded. "Good. Now say goodbye to your family, sweets."

I frowned. "What? Why?"

"Because I'm taking you home, and I don't plan on letting you leave our home, or our bed, for at least a month, maybe longer."

I laughed.

Ronan did not.

Epilogue

Three months later

Art tucked my hand tighter against him as we walked through the cemetery. "I couldn't be prouder if you were my own flesh and blood."

I leaned into him. "Flesh and blood isn't everything."

"No, it's not."

Art was the dad of my heart. He was all I'd ever needed. He'd been there for me my whole life, and he was here for me again now. "How do I look?"

"Stunning," he said roughly and swallowed.

"Don't you dare cry. If you cry, I'll cry," I said.

"I think that ship has sailed," he said as a tear streaked down his face.

I leaned in and kissed his freshly shaved cheek. "Love you, Art."

"Love you, too, Roe." He glanced ahead, then back down at me. "We better get going, he's probably getting restless."

I laughed and dabbed my own tears away. I had no doubt he was. Ronan hated being parted from me for any length of time. My sisters had insisted he and I spend the night separately. We'd had a girls' night, facials and manicures and bubbly, prepping for today. Then I'd gone upstairs to my old room, and a short time later, so had Ronan. I hadn't been surprised when I'd felt the buzz of his power and he'd literally walked through my bedroom door.

Art and I walked through the smaller gate on the other side of the cemetery that led to the field behind it. The warm spring sun shone down on the wildflowers that had sprung up over the last couple of weeks. And Mom had commandeered Daire to string up colorful bunting in the trees. Yesterday, the coven had made a blessing arch of woven willow branches and covered it in foliage and flowers.

Ronan stood on the other side of it, the hounds who had claimed him as family, Luna and her mate, and the other knights were there as well. My family, my coven, stood on the other side waiting for me.

As I walked up, Ronan's gaze burned into me. He took a step forward, and Relic put his hand on his shoulder and muttered something, reminding him he had to wait, no doubt.

Because I had to walk through the arch to him.

I had to offer myself to him, give myself to him as a symbol of strength and a new beginning.

Rowena moved to my side and handed me a small terra-cotta pot. I clutched it, holding the wilted vervain plant close to my heart. The herb protected against evil spells and negative energy and could be used to purify sacred places and private dwellings. It was also used for medicinal purposes. Every bride was given one to take into her new home, and it was the first herb to be planted in her own herb garden.

My heart filled as she started the chant. Else and Mom stepped forward, joining in next, then Willow, Iris, and Magnolia. The voices of my remaining coven joined. They were one voice as they called to the mother for her blessings.

Else stepped back and Mom and Art took my hands, leading me to the arch. I stopped in front of it, and they both kissed my cheek and stepped back.

My gaze locked on Ronan's.

He drew in a sharp breath, his wide shoulders shifting under his dark suit. He was so incredibly handsome, and as I looked deep into his intense and utterly gorgeous violet eyes, I saw my future, an eternity of joy, of happiness, and love. Everything I'd ever wanted and never dared hope for.

He held out his hand, longing in his eyes. My mate was always impatient when it came to being close to me.

I stepped through the arch and took his hand in mine.

He clutched it tight. "You are breathtaking, sweets."

"So are you," I whispered.

Hooking an arm around my waist, he pulled me close and kissed me hard and deep in front of all our family and friends. "And for the rest of eternity, you are mine," he said when he lifted his head.

I smiled up at him. "I love you so much."

"You hold my entire heart in your hands, my precious mate."

"I promise to keep it safe, always."

I looked down at the small pot in my hands, and Ronan did as well. We watched as the wilted little herb transformed, becoming green and lush as the little dry purple flowers unfurled, revived, so many of them that they overflowed the edges.

The mother had given us her blessing.

The entire coven cheered, and the hounds joined in, tilting their heads back and howling.

Mom rushed up and hugged us both. My sisters moved in and joined the huddle.

I was so happy I couldn't contain it.

Music started and people ran out to dance.

A short time later, the smell of the open fire crackled, while the hounds worked on constructing a spit for the meat.

I spotted Ren, who stood among them. I waved, but he didn't see me, he was staring out at the forest beyond, where he'd lived, escaped from everything, even himself in his animal form for so long. Wills walked over and bumped his elbow, and he turned to her, some of the sadness leaving his eyes.

"I'm gonna go see if Jazzy wants to dance," Mags said, drawing my attention away. I scanned the field. Bram was late. He'd promised to be here but had yet to arrive.

I glanced over at Jasmine. She was sitting by herself, several butterflies fluttering around her, more than one sitting on her shoulder. Whenever she was outside, they were there. I followed her gaze. Ren. I'd caught her looking his way more than once. Ren was the kind of handsome that drew attention, so it didn't surprise me, but there was something else in her eyes when she looked at him, something that broke my heart a little.

Jazzy looked up when Mags reached her and shook her head. My shy cousin was turning Magnolia down.

She missed her sister—we all did—when Zinnia was gone.

Ronan tugged on my hand and pulled me close. "Dance? They're playing our song."

The first strains of "Yellow Ledbetter" started, the song we'd danced to a year ago in my room when I was still sick and he didn't understand what love was. He did now. I'd made sure of it.

I wrapped my arms around him, and we swayed to the music, surrounded by the people we loved most.

Ronan kissed me. "I can't believe I get to dance with you like this forever," he said, his voice low and rumbly.

"Me either." I rested my head on his chest, listening to the steady beat of his heart.

Magnolia was dancing with Rowena and several other members of our coven. Relic moved in, grabbed her hand, and spun her around, and Mags rolled her eyes. When he did it again, she busted out laughing. It was her turn next. Something was coming for my baby sister and none of us knew what the mother would put her through.

Wills, Iris, and I, we all had an eternity ahead of us, and we wanted Mags by our side. She needed to find her mate, but I was afraid she'd never drop her guard long enough to let him in, whoever he was.

Movement. Something dark caught my eye—a massive black crow landing in the trees high above.

It shifted forms.

Bram.

His black jean-clad legs hung over the branch, and his black eyes were locked on Mags dancing with Relic. He sat there for several moments, then his bare tattooed chest expanded, and he shifted back to his crow form and exploded from the trees and into the sky, flying away.

I looked back at Magnolia. She'd stopped dancing, watching after Bram as he flew away, and the look on her face cracked my heart down the middle.

"Okay?" Ronan asked.

I smiled up at my mate and nodded.

"I love you, sweets."

"I love you too." He pulled me back in close and I hung on tight.

I just hoped that when the mother did call for Magnolia, she and Bram had sorted out whatever was going on between them, because she was going to need him then—more than ever.

About the Author

Sherilee Gray is a kiwi girl and lives in beautiful New Zealand with her husband and their two children. When she isn't writing sexy contemporary or paranormal romance, searching for her next alpha hero on Pinterest, or fueling her voracious book addiction, she can be found dreaming of far off places with a mug of tea in one hand and a bar of chocolate in the other. Visit her at: www.sherileegray.com

Also by Sherilee Gray

Blood Moon Brides:

Blood Moon Bound

The Thornheart Trials:

A Curse in Darkness

A Vow of Ruin

A Trial by Blood

An Oath at Midnight

A Promise of Ashes

Knights of Hell:

Knight's Seduction

Knight's Redemption

Knight's Salvation

Demon's Temptation

Knight's Dominion

Knight's Absolution

Knight's Retribution

Rocktown Ink:

Beg For You

Sin For You

Meant For you

Bad For You

All For You

Just for You

The Smith Brothers:

Mountain Man

Wild Man

Solitary Man

Lawless Kings:

Shattered King

Broken Rebel

Beautiful Killer

Ruthless Protector

Glorious Sinner

Merciless King

Boosted Hearts:

Swerve

Spin

Slide

Spark

Axle Alley Vipers:

Crashed

Revved

Wrecked

Black Hills Pack:

Lone Wolf's Captive

A Wolf's Deception

Stand Alone Novels:

Breaking Him